Muckle

It's no ordinary existence on the rugged isle of Muckle Flugga. The elements run riot, and the very rocks that shape the place begin to shift under their influence. The only human inhabitants are the lighthouse keeper, known as The Father, and his otherworldly son, Ouse. Them, and the occasional lodger to keep the wolf from the door.

When one of those lodgers – Firth, a chaotic writer – arrives from Edinburgh, the limits of the world the keeper and his son cling to begin to crumble. A tug of war ensues between Firth and the lighthouse keeper for Ouse's affections – and his future. As old and new ways collide, and life-changing decisions loom, what will the tides leave standing in their wake?

HB | 9780571387724 | £16.99
Export Trade Paperback | 9780571387731
Ebook | 9780571387762

Michael Pedersen is a prize-winning poet and author of *Boy Friends*, which was a *Sunday Times* Critics' Choice and shortlisted for the Saltire Scottish National Book Awards. He was awarded a Robert Louis Stevenson Fellowship and is the current Writer in Residence at the University of Edinburgh, and Edinburgh's Makar.

Muckle Flugga

Michael Pedersen

faber

First published in 2025
by Faber & Faber Limited
The Bindery, 51 Hatton Garden
London EC1N 8HN

Typeset by Faber & Faber
Printed and bound by CPI Group (UK) Ltd, Croydon, CR0 4YY

*This is a work of fiction. All of the characters, organisations and
events portrayed in this novel are either products of the author's
imagination or are used fictitiously*

A CIP record for this book
is available from the British Library

ISBN 978-0-571-38772-4

2 4 6 8 10 9 7 5 3 1

to be what we are, and to become what we are capable of becoming, is the only end of life

Robert Louis Stevenson

PROLOGUE

On the island of Muckle Flugga sits one of the most formidable lighthouses on this, or any, planet. Its wild pearl of light is capable of guiding boats – and their humans – to safety, in spite of all manner of storms, gales and hails; not to mention whirlpools, pirates, straying submarines and a litany of other hunters of the aquatic deep. As for the more malevolent presences the light keeps at bay, the less said the better.

On account of being charged by starlight, the beam of Muckle Flugga Lighthouse is rumoured to be infinite in its luminosity. The great light, which starts the size of a modest meteor, if mishandled has been known to dwindle to little more than the circumference of a gold coin. That might sound useless, but to a poor soul lost in a thick haar or pernicious squall, even a glisk of light can prove enough to rope the way home.

The island itself is a dramatic uprising of rocks, precipitous cliffs and treacherous walkways – rocky enough to be deemed born of volcano; sequestered enough to have been described by some as the one true space station of the sea. Like many lands deemed unwieldy to the human foot, it has been branded a shape-shifter by those that lose their way.

The plump lighthouse nests smugly on the highest summit of Muckle Flugga – the most northernly inhabited island of the United Kingdom. As a result, it's no ordinary living up there. When storming, the unbroken waves can rise a hundred feet high, their spray coming thick and heavy enough to make the whole lighthouse

1

disappear: a sapling lost in the billow of an oceanic bushfire. Its rain-for-days is the most fragrant in the hemisphere – depending on the season, it comes peppery, fruity, mossy or floral. If the odour turns rancid, that's a tell-tale sign something's gone awry and it's prudent to run for cover.

Formerly co-captained by three keepers (prolific lovers with subsequently large families), the lighthouse (plus auxiliary properties and environs) is currently manned by just one – The Father, with a little help from his progeny, the laddie, Ouse. Though just beyond the schooling years, Ouse might be described as manoeuvring adulthood with the stabilisers still on.

Despite the extremity of their home life, Ouse can't stand it when bombastic mainlanders call Muckle Flugga 'inhospitable' or 'infernal'. He finds the remote island to be a glorious and gracious host, albeit it chippy and capricious. It simply depends who it's dealing with – after all, Muckle Flugga, like all the best ancients, has excellent taste.

Quite in defiance of nature, Muckle Flugga is not without its fecundity of flora and fauna. At the north of the island, a copse of fir trees huddles together against the lashing winds; a thicket of feathery ferns maps the way in. To the south of the island is a modest orchard of trees: spruces, willows and hazels, crowned by a single bony crab apple; an eruption of flowering yellow gorse shrouds around it like a bodyguard. Barely worth mentioning is a fastidiously kept, yet relatively unsuccessful, vegetable patch; and a quite ludicrous man-made pond inhabited by waterlilies, fish, a squiggle of frogs and a toad or two.

Muckle Flugga is, in fact, shockingly virile – a tree trunk felled in the night might be blanketed in flowers by the morning. The fact stands, if not for the lighthouse and assorted living quarters book-ending the island, the weather would beat the life out of everything that grows here. These structures aren't just homes and ship-savers but bulwarks and buffers – both castle and its protective walls. The sea up here, despite accusations to the contrary, is never grandstanding; more accurately it's casually underplaying its epic strength.

Muckle Flugga is also frequented by a menagerie of curious creatures that range from daily to seasonal visitants: otters, seals, walruses, dolphins, seabirds, jellyfish, crabs, turtles etc. The rumour mill churns for a range of mythical beasts that might appear once in a lifetime and leave the mind carouselling ever after: the likes of krakens, selkies, vampire geese, black-arrow sharks, bear eagles, dragon-whales and swimming wolves. It's this ilk of lore-mongering that earns Muckle Flugga, together with its sibling island Out Stack, the moniker of Scotland's Galapagos Islands.

Despite teeming with natural life, Muckle Flugga can be supremely peaceful, but never quiet – no, not that. There is no real silence living on such a vociferous wing of the world. Aloneness, too, can be an issue for those seeking it. Most parts of the island are visible from the rest of it – though there are nooks and crannies, fissures and gullies, chimerical spaces out of sight, if you know where to find them. Ouse has his favourite hideaways, whilst spending more time than The Father would like in the theatre of his own mind.

On the human front, sociality on the island is scant. However, Ouse, unlike The Father, has a friend or two of value. There's lovely Figgie, the mainland storekeeper, who makes deliveries and serves as an unofficial postie. Figgie keeps a watchful eye on Ouse; always has, always will. Ouse is also blessed enough to keep company with one of the greatest thinkers in literary history, and his favourite of all the writers stocked in Muckle Flugga's flourishing library

– Robert Louis Stevenson. Or rather, the ghost of his human form, who serves as a life coach, confidante and sparring partner in what can be challenging place to be young and lost. Coincidentally, the writerly dandy started appearing to Ouse the very same day The Mother died.

To keep the wolf from the door, metaphorically speaking, Ouse and The Father are joined by the occasional lodger. Muckle Flugga is ornithologically orgasmic on account of the island's unique position as a stopping station for several species of rare migrating birdlife.

Lodgers are always ornithologists due to an 'ornithologists-only' policy put in place by The Father – a policy based on his disdain for garrulous know-it-alls, snoopers and queer bohemians. From The Father's experience, birdwatchers tend to be none of these things; instead they are timid and introspective, taking the majority of meals in their room and paying upfront with little quibble. Although observers by nature, they keep their eyes sunk into binoculars and their fingers busy scribbling annals of their sightings.

It is both a simple and a complicated life for The Father and Ouse on Muckle Flugga; mercurial as the moon might make it. Night after night, the lighthouse tears its silhouette into the horizon, taking the gloaming to task for the sins it's covering over. The same stars that reflect dreamily in Muckle Flugga's windowpanes are those that send ships spinning in circles until the sea's ready to claim them – them and all life on board.

ONE

Muckle Flugga – that is, the main massing of the original stone living quarters – could be said to display a gothic splendour, were it possible to ignore the wounds thrashed upon it by the tyrannical ocean swarming around its outer rocks.

Despite being its most devoted, and only, inhabitants, Ouse and The Father, in their grief, have taken to regarding these buildings as the place relatives once lived in, rather than their very own home. The Father's name is not on any deeds, nor Ouse's either. Yet there's more of The Father's blood seasoning the soil than some who died here, and the memory of The Mother is kilted into the sky.

Even the slowest days on Muckle Flugga are brimful, the elements constantly finding new ways to make a mockery of humankind's need for consistency. The lighthouse is both voracious and incessant in its demands; The Father is forever chasing after it. The island's myriad other needs fall upon young Ouse. There is foraging and fishing and errands on the mainland, housework and groundwork and the investigation – and subsequent auditing – of all strange things that wash ashore here. There are several fires that need constant feeding – they must sizzle like fried eggs or hissing snakes; must always smoulder, never choking out. On this matter The Father has been resoundingly clear, some say superstitiously so.

It's a rare one that sees The Father in a conversational mood, stalking Ouse's shadow as he narrates the day away – then remonstrating at the lack of work done on account of their blabber pussyfooting. More commonly, at least post-The Mother, barely a word wiggles free from his gob that isn't glued to its labour-intensive purpose. The prospect of a conversation unspooling into casualness is now practically unheard of; The Father prone to forget the mouth can do such things.

On a rarer day still, The Father might be caught napping off the night's exhaustion amongst the long grasses, stark bollock naked. Upon encountering this sleeping giant, Ouse begins the games he's forbidden from playing under The Father's waking watch. The library is kitted out with all sorts of bookish contraband for just such opportunities. Reading bare-chested up a treetop, straddling the branch, remains amongst his most-cherished acts.

Back on his feet, The Father has the frame of a man built to be busy, stiff as a sundial. It is a mien that served him well on getting here to Muckle Flugga in the first place; on being the type of crusader lazier men will make a stake on; on answering the clarion call of a needy lighthouse. Yet bodies rarely come just the way we want them, and so the physical prowess of The Father has equally done him a disservice: exempting him from being the type of man other men share secrets with, lend books to, invite out walking, or dancing. Ouse, however, is made of softer shapes, more creaturely, plump-hearted and wispy when he needs to be.

The stewardship of a lighthouse, and its island, is a life of servitude over sentiment – wonder-filled yet often painful. And the days of other keepers, other kids, other othernesses, have shown their first signs of rusting in the memory banks of Ouse, which is a terrifying prospect, and so he does mental acrobatics to prevent any further fading of the past. The Father, on the other hand, only too frequently sees faces from the past appear in the oceanic night, or leaping out from behind a troublesome fog. He would not admit so to Ouse, but he does occasionally take comfort in these eerie sightings.

No matter how challenging the daily tasks, how elsewhere they find themselves, food will bring The Father and Ouse back together; it is the second most unifying force here. Ouse comes first to the kitchen, for of the two he is the cook, though The Father will soon appear, following the belly's compass. Ouse is as talented as The Father is mighty, when dealing in flavours.

Though The Father's not for stomaching spiritualism, after dinner he will observe the moon as it shifts in shape from (in Ouse's words) a gong to a broken plate, a question mark to a needle. Wordlessly, yet agog, the two will observe this milky saucer in the sky: though its wreck is too far off to salvage, neither would deny their admiration for this celestial bounty.

When Muckle Flugga had its full staffing of keepers and their families, lodgers were not 'a thing' – a distinguished guest or family member, sure, but never a foreign lodger. That, however, like much around here, has changed. Since it's been just the two of them, financial pressure has fired its lightning into The Father's chest, and lodgers seemed like the best solution (best of a baleful bunch).

As they come only when the coffers dictate, days when lodgers are beetling around Muckle Flugga are not typical days. Ouse counts in their coming like yuletide – visitors are both highly anticipated and much missed on their leaving. He continues their stories in his head, narrating their lives like characters in his beloved books. And without fail, lodgers depart Muckle Flugga speaking of its timeless qualities, its quality of infinity. Many hearts have healed after a sojourn on Muckle Flugga.

Currently, the calendar has just one name on it, scratched into the guest listings in The Father's own hand: Firth. Not an entirely uncommon name, not the first Firth The Father has known either. But something salient is already rumbling in Muckle Flugga's youngest resident's fervent mind. The Father too feels it. He experienced a prickle down his arm as he etched the letters across the paper. A sense of, if not foreboding, uncertainty. It occurred to him to call the booker back and say they couldn't take a lodger this time around, finding an irrefutable excuse. But money is tight, and needs must, so he wrenches the thought from his head and stamps it silent on the ground.

The future visitor is himself no stranger to Muckle Flugga, at least not in his imagination; not in his dreams. Inspired by the stories of his grandfather, Firth has quested to Muckle Flugga umpteen times over – in the kingdom of his subconscious he is in kin with these salt-ravaged lands.

TWO

He won't miss being alive, Firth concedes. It would be an audacity to mourn something he never made the most of. Particularly as he's thrashing out these thoughts hanging off the side of a metal monster – Fort Eidyn Rail Bridge. Having trudged along the tracks, full of gin, wet with woe, he barely even notices the tears now, streaming though they are.

He's never doubted his conviction to jump: to keep something as unrelenting at bay as the will to die is a conquest beyond his resolve. That clawing, grating part of him too stubborn to give up its grip would eventually relent.

It's not *not* terrifying. It's everything he knew it would be, everything it was before, the last time he tried: foul winds, snarling ocean, massive boats tossed around like toys beneath him. The drop is bone-chilling, the sea petrifying, the tiny North Star Light Tower below offers little reassurance of safety. He takes solace in knowing that, for a second, its fickle beam will light his weightless body in a moment of unstoppable descent.

The lights of Edinburgh tremble pitifully in the distance. The entire city of Auld Reekie is clinging on for dear life, hanging off hills, cliffs and old volcanoes; even the bravest are buckling. Everything starts at the top and slopes downwards. It's no wonder so many of its denizens end up mulching in the gutters: the city was designed this way.

Being born beneath a fish-wives' gutting table on Leith Docks had two strident effects on Firth: he'll always be as terrified of water as he is enthralled by it and he'll never shake the reek of fish guts (in truth, he never wanted to). Though he left Leith while still a laddie and had since beguiled many of the New Town glitterati into thinking he could afford his seat at their table, the sham had always rested on a shoogly peg. What else could he do – dream wee, drink drams and stay low? Naw. Absolutely not, there is nothing worse than settling for a meagre lot. That was his dad's mentality, not his, and look where it got the old man, poor wretch. Then again, look where this hullabaloo has got him.

For the briefest of moments, life had been as spectacular as blue sunsets over Mars. Now, on a good day, it resembles cheap hotel art, hung squint, above the bacon tray of the breakfast buffet. His was a life spent waiting for the next thing, plundering from the present any chance of happiness. He was not a real writer, not mordant, not cryptic, not even clever, not really – all bile and blather; damn emotion thief, cheating the reader: reader-cheater-cheap-trickster-fool. Faking the unfakeable, that's all he'd worked out how to do: fudge it, smoke and mirror it; flog the old horse far as it would go then sell it for meat. Damn dilettante – didn't even know what that meant until he was called it; took it as flattery at first.

It's clear now, the future is a vision of a pussing wound. What a waste of a brain. Drugs: too many. Booze: too much. Compassion: not nearly enough. His best had been a leaky tap that eventually filled the glass whilst nobody was looking, so he offered it up to the thirsty like the gift of first water. Better fish feed, better compost, better make room for more worms. Good, gorgeous, wiggly worms whose value to this planet is ten times his own.

Who's going to miss him, *really*? After the obligatory platitudes, who wouldn't be better off for his absence? It's his mediocre achievements that make him tolerable, and those are hyper-inflated or outright frauds. Besides, there might be something more, something numinous, a kingdom in the clouds. Unlikely, very fucking unlikely they'd let this uncommitted atheist sidle in, but not impossible, someone might forget to shut the door. Story of his life, sneaking in late and then pretending he was first to arrive.

Firth spits viciously off the bridge, globular and dense, following the fall with his eyes – a bit of him once warm inside is now faraway drowning. It's not the actual dying Firth wills in – not pain, penance or comeuppance, not the process of extinguishing life, certainly not the damage it'll cause those caught in the crossfire. It's the stopping, everything stopping, and the silence that follows. No battles to fight, anxieties to ebb, or pretences to maintain: it all just stops.

And it's not that he doesn't believe in wonder, champion kindness, or give, receive and foment love. He does, he wants that more than anything. He just makes such a mess of chasing it – every success is embellished, every good thing cheapened, each moment hijacked by the auspices of something bigger, gaudier. A few times now, he's worked hard enough to make his lies become reality. *Become the bullshit*: what a macabre and twisted mantra. What a sad, sad, sad man, Firth calls himself, adding repetitions until the words feel like home. He hates being so obliteratingly jealous of the version of himself he thinks he should be.

If only he could pause time just before the hubris kicks in, before the self-sabotage; where life is rejoiced for what it is, not bemoaned for what it's missing. Because he has to admit, the last few years have not been without their boons and beacons. Even this moment of despair, gripping on to the cold shoulder of a giant that will see him to his end, is not without its inconvenience of beauty. Yes, the damn stars, still irritatingly lovely, flaring up in all their gloriosity.

11

So clichéd to be rethinking life's dominion at the mantel of their silly astral light – one more hexed hellboy smitten by the celestial.

He knew the risk of attempting to make his death dream a reality: he'd bungled this flimsy ceremony before. Firth recalls another crapulous crusade he made onto a bridge, when the rain was apocalyptic and the soaking went so deep that his brain clamped with cold and the notion of ever drying out seemed farcical. He had hoped his body would begin to let the water in and wash the muck out of him – a colonic irrigation of the soul. There's a certain amount of booze addling that keeps his mind convicted; it's an exact discipline to ensure pain and shame remain at the reins – in clever cahoots, protecting each other from any intruding hopefulness. There's nothing more lethal than hope to someone lost and losing – damn Christmas carol of the subconscious, damn do-gooder stowed away in the synapses.

Firth feels himself failing, softening to the idea of living a little longer, searching for any teeny cosmic spark of significance to sanction his refusal to fly from this bridge. And it comes – the distant cry of the big old lie.

It's not a shooting star, a good Samaritan or a sexual uprising that calls out to him, but a gobshite of a gannet. A blasted seabird, in full flight, cruising past, all chutzpah and vibrato, as if it was their big finish and not his. A presence so close Firth hears a swoosh in the air. So close he could have touched its svelte feathered carriage.

The trouble is, to Firth, the gannet is not just a creature that's appeared from nowhere, but a winged sigil. It couldn't be more sickeningly redolent of the best bits of his boyhood; its yellows turned ultraviolet having once filled him with the grit of life. Even in the stubborn dark, the gannet glows. This googly-eyed lantern of the sky is the only creature capable of revivifying a forgotten promise he's held in storage all these hard, long years. From deep within, a promise made before his decency curdled comes back to haunt him.

In his youth, Firth had been enthralled by his grandfather's tales of life in the navy – a world of open waters, comradery and sleeping under starlight. He especially revelled in his grandfather's vivid descriptions of all the fantastical beasts he encountered – those that lurked below or soared above the high seas; some without names, without body or form. Yet beyond any doubt, the old man's favourite of all these wild and motley creatures was the yellow-capped, brown-booted brute: the northern gannet. The very same bird that had just dived past Firth, inches from his perch, shrieking and shocking him out of his latest attempt at a premature ending. Back then, with brass and conviction, he had vowed to seek out his grandfather's favourite bird and paint it. The best place to find them, so the old man waxed on about, was Muckle Flugga and Out Stack – those magical islands. And thus it became a quest Firth vowed to fulfil one day on both their behalves. A quest that his own selfish ambitions had sidelined until it fell entirely from his memory – that is, until this raucous reminder.

Such a common bird may be direful inspiration to some, but for this particular aching heart, it's just the tonic. A treaty between a grandfather and grandson to paint some daft-looking bird has come forth to save his life.

Firth is no artist, not since his teenage years, and his grandfather is long dead, but he has money enough to buy a decent case of paints and time enough to travel north to Shetland to settle something once made with purpose – something honest, imbued with purity. After steadying himself, he barks it out: *Muckle Flugga*. It falls off his lips predictably flat, so he tries again, this time with gusto: *Muckle Flugga. One last, one last and then we go.*

It had not been a very merry ride for Firth's kind – his own father had died young, killed, having been one of the droves who worked beyond darkness and drunk past their emptiness. His type had always been the trodden on, but at least they were fighters. He would not be their next great failure. At least, not today.

Screaming with the same urgency as the bird, the night train riots into sight, shaking the bridge until Firth is struggling to keep balance. On this occasion, the caterwauling wind plays to his favour and pins Firth's pish-thin vessel to the metalwork. Carriage after carriage comes galumphing by as the bridge rings like a cluster of church bells. The vibrations shake every morsel of his body. Eventually, he becomes brave enough to re-open his raindrop eyes – the horizon, sharpened by the fear in it.

Firth's alien hands are cold and cut and barely capable of gripping on, yet they do. His protean reversal of mindset is barely believable, even to himself, yet here he stands, intent to live whilst the train's tail-lamps disappear into the smudge of a city up past its bedtime.

Imagine falling now, Firth gasps, dying after deciding not to. A goblin-green hue sloshed across the firmament, for what must be astral miles, confirms he doesn't die tonight. With a gulp of icy air, he begins his descent, paggered and doleful yet pumping blood. By the time he trundles home to Candlemaker Row, Firth is fixed on the notion that the bird is a portent – his grandfather as winged messenger; a summons.

The matter is settled – to Muckle Flugga: to paint, and then to die.

THREE

Once again, Ouse is attempting to count the innumerable miles of North Sea stretched out in front of him; the vast expanse that sprawls beyond Out Stack and eventually becomes the Arctic Ocean, where the deep icy water is as queer and unconquerable as the surface of a distant planet.

He is perched atop a boulder, a throne-like seat chiselled into the rockface. A gaggle of puffins makes mischief around him. One has shat on his lap, delighted with the result. Another nestles up to his ribcage; either itching or snuggling, it's difficult to decipher the body language of birds – not to mention puffins are masters of deception.

To his left flank, a fishing rod is wedged between two rocks, the line thrashing about several feet above the ocean's froth as the wind makes a theatre of the surf. Ouse is more enamoured by the fat hook's gymnastics than the prospect of catching any sea-dweller. Besides, with a sketchbook on his lap, his hands are busy working a piece of charcoal into soft spirals – dark strokes thrust across the paper's snowy white.

To his right, a slender figure in a velveteen jacket, riding boots and a lilac, felt fedora: his companion, the ethereal, and invisible to all but Ouse, Robert Louis Stevenson; RLS to friends.

Ouse stops sketching, crunches closed his eyes, and begins chewing on his questions like a twist of tough jerky.

Do you miss being alive? he finally spits out, after some wrangling.

I don't miss being alive, RLS responds without hesitation, *by which I mean I don't miss being within the prison of a body, but I do* miss being among the living. And I was alive a lot, Ouse, especially for one of such a sickly disposition, bowling from convalescence to convalescence.

What a legacy.

To blazes with legacy, I judge my life on the people I loved and the worlds I conjured for them.

Ouse, sated by this response, and only too aware of the extended version of the answer coming his way, begins sketching again.

And I died fatuously contented, RLS roars, *in a favourite far-flung corner of this exquisite world, cogitating my next epistle to a friend I adored completely. My body waned young and given a few more years it would have taken my jollity captive too. Today, in this spectral shape, at least I'm pain-free, although less mettlesome of mind. Aye, the novelling has stopped and that's a quandary, but these old bones have worked hard enough to ensure the name Robert Louis Stevenson stakes literary claim to the initials RLS for a few years yet – have they not?!*

There's plenty of beastly hedge-creepers out there who say I courted praise, RLS flails, *which isn't entirely untrue, but never just for me. Praise for all, I'd say. Och, take my musings with a pinch of salt, young Ouse, for they come from the son of a family of lighthouse engineers who, despite their wicked wishes, resolved to be anything but a man of the family trade. This very lighthouse you live within has the Stevenson stamp smacked upon it. My ancestors heaved up Muckle Flugga brick by brick just a few years after I was born.*

So it's your fault I'm here? Ouse teases.

RLS sighs and softens. *In a way, this lighthouse was Dad's* ars poetica, *more important to him than all the books ever written. Over the course of building Muckle Flugga – known ever after as The Impossible Lighthouse – the sea stripped the bricks bare and sent workmen cowering into their cabins, fearing for their lives. That great oceanic*

16

juggernaut protested every iota of the Stevenson family's presence here . . . yet they prevailed. My life's work, inking up empty pages, seems a little poxy in comparison, don't you think?

Ouse's face rallies against this notion, having spent so many hours with the life's work in question.

You know I don't! All those imaginations you enlivened, they'll save just as many lives.

Having quenched his thirst for compliments, RLS switches into the more avuncular role he's prone to play. *To travel hopefully is a better thing than to arrive. What a sad map it would be not to go wading in the world's gullies and grooves.*

This remark lands more cuttingly than RLS intends, or Ouse cares to admit. Ouse's mind goes kerplunk reflecting on what now feels like his lean orbit of living. *I'm such a coward. I've never left these islands, except in books and dreams, and I doubt that counts.*

Truly, Ouse's map could be etched out searingly fast in comparison to the average islander: Muckle Flugga, Out Stack, Unst, Yell, and Shetland's mainland – plus the wild waters surging between them, but no-one seems to count that which they can't put their boot on. To Ouse, Lerwick feels as bustling and imperial as Constantinople, at least the version of it he's read about. Even during his schooling years on the mainland, he always had one foot back on Muckle Flugga. Both The Mother and The Father regularly found excuses for him to stay at home, and the gonzo weather and arduous journey prevented him attending – nearly half the time anyway.

And what do you intend to do about it? RLS demands. *Youth is the time to go flashing from one end of the world to the other.*

But I'm ignored and spoken over even here, population of two, what would happen if I went somewhere bigger? In fact, don't answer that! Ouse snaps, needy and uncertain.

Patience, my dear buccaneer, there's exploration aplenty ahead of you, RLS utters reassuringly. *But don't be too patient, time's not one for treading water.*

This seems to do the trick as Ouse's next words come gooey as fresh dough. *There would have been very little joy in my life this past wee while if not for your friendship, RLS.* Ouse lets his eyes marble, then tosses a great grin at RLS, as if handed a win at the tables just when he needed it the most.

Ouse's peculiarities made him a wayward sort of friend-maker growing up. His trenchant tender could be magnetic – pulling other humans towards him too quickly, or pushing them away without meaning to. Those that wanted to need him either became frustrated with his allusiveness or threatened by his contentment without them. It was a guttery rut, as RLS would say. The Mother's absence has been gargantuan and the hurt catastrophic, and The Father's grief has made the distance between the two of them – and the rest of the world – inexorably bigger. What a godsend RLS is proving to be in this void.

Although Out Stack is the most isolated of all Ouse's many haunts, it is also where he feels most luminous. There is nothing as far off as the next human being north of Out Stack. However, behind the rocky deposit that forms this island broods its bigger, more histrionic, be-lighthoused sibling, Muckle Flugga. Ouse and his spectral companion might be cunningly in the blind spot of the lighthouse at the moment, but one hop to the left or jump to the right and its keeper, The Father, can fix his beady eye on all that's going on.

A fierce flash of the great bulb beckoning Ouse homewards comes as no surprise. The Father, farouche as the sea itself, is hungry and impatient for the evening's cooking to begin. Having been summoned home by the light, Ouse gets to his feet and stretches his limbs, ready to make the journey between the two outcrops.

Readying his trusty wee boat, Ouse shoots RLS one last question that has been somersaulting around his mind. And though his voice is throttled by the wind, the savant scribe hears the question just fine: *What was the best day of your entire life?*

Without missing a beat, his eyes trailing coruscations in the sky, RLS delivers his answer like a parliamentary decree.

A split decision, stalemate, the most admiral of draws.

Exhibit A: finds your RLS idling, lolling on the sandy banks of his Samoan paradise when the post comes in – by boat, of course. In amongst the parcels of trite proofs from budding writers is the next, highly anticipated, correspondence from a cherished friend in Scotland. Hopelessly and pathetically, RLS is in love with a man he's never met, and relishes every fragment of that feeling. Sometimes the anticipation outweighs the actualising. Then again, when it comes to my Softy Softy – J. M. Barrie, sire of Peter Pan, as you may know him – I was never that lucky.

Exhibit B: canters in a couple of decades prior, a summer's night under the wide-eyed stars of Grez in France, the very day your RLS fell for the Weird Woman – a brilliant bizzom unlike any he'd ever dared to love: handsome waxen face like Napoleon's, insane black eyes, boy's hands, tiny bare feet . . . and hellish energy.

Now I think about it, a third day comes to mind with my club in the wine cellar of Advocate's Close. How about we make it a holy trinity of favourite days? Actually, that's a crooked idea, some things are best kept under wraps, heaven knows who's listening – a jilted paramour or, worse still, the family biographer!

Never gives me a straight answer, the old toad. What a gift, Ouse smiles and shakes his head.

Now sensing The Father's impatience, even from this distance, he scrambles down the craggy cliff face and unmoors the boat.

Remember, RLS bellows, *don't trust a joker that doesn't make you teary, nor a tragic ending that doesn't come with a side of snigger!* In a spirited send-off, RLS howls into the wind, loud as his ghost throat can holler.

As Ouse's boat finds pace in the gathering tide, he swears solemnly and silently to live his life by RLS's instruction. The sea, feeling tempestuous, sees Ouse's boat clomp, not glide, across the waves. His vessel is allowed to pass by the good graces of greater forces. This stretch of ocean between Muckle Flugga and Out Stack, although serious in its bloodlust, is a giddy bairn compared to the feral behemoth just a few miles up. Though he's made this voyage hundreds of times, he never takes a safe landing for granted.

Awaiting Ouse to drop his anchor, The Father, lurking below the mammoth lighthouse, rides his heel into the coarse sand, teeth gritted. *Any fish?* he grunts, knowing damn well there's none, for he has a fine pair of peepers that have been tracking Ouse to shore.

Ouse may be fishless upon his return but he feels miles more marvellous from an afternoon basking in the company of RLS. And so, in an act of derring-do that he hopes will coax a smile out the old warrior, Ouse shrugs his arms and puckers his lips comedically, as if to say: blame the fish, not me.

The Father puffs out in irritation. *Did ye feed the beast?* he slings back, taking no notice of Ouse's funfulness.

Aye. I gave her food, Ouse confirms, a little chastened, but holding on to the glory of the day – the sky turning technicolour in the gloaming.

The Father, steeled as someone entering a graveyard for the first time knowing the person they love's now in it, points to the kitchen and rasps: *We've wasted enough time already. God's watching you squander the life he's gifted.*

As their shadows seesaw off towards whisky and cooking pots, a noisy gannet corkscrews overhead, signalling to the pack that change is coming, and coming fast. A sudden garish green in the night's cloth confirms it to be true.

FOUR

To those who never knew him before, The Father is notorious for his temper: a rage labelled a danger to other bodies. He has been called bitter, hostile and violent; an aggressor, fuelled by flame, by smoke.

To those who have glimpsed his tenderness, who did know him before, thriving and in love, he is an incorrigible curmudgeon; all caught up in knots. A fighter plane with its engine out, the pilot embracing the fall.

The Father is known to have pushed the other keepers away, after she passed, The Mother. The snide side of the camp say it was his fault, that he is to blame for the dying, the horribleness, its unending ache. They say The Father propagates pain, that he has made a loyal pet of it – trained it by firm-handed scoldings to do exactly as he says. All discipline, no cuddles. They say The Father is a traitor to his kin – the harvesters, the lost wanderers, who shirk any form of heraldry. He has brothers and sisters who have learned to forget his name.

Some believe the Keepers & Lighthouse Association of Majestic Scotland (the KLAMS, who are draped in heraldry) have chosen to forget about the island of Muckle Flugga, because The Father poses such a dilemma to them that they'd prefer to remain in ignorance. In his prime, The Father was a keeper of the most extraordinary stock – decorated with medals for gallantry and cups for exemplary service.

In order to enter the service of the KLAMS, The Father had chanced fate, fled a loveless clan and riddled the past invisible.

Those that were once close to him firmly believe that it bothers The Father insuperably to have fallen from their grace. Those that distrust or fear The Father, who feed on the fruits of his demise, swear the KLAMS are coming for him. These self-proclaimed enemies would gladly see the KLAMS plunge a stake into The Father's heart and boil his bones for broth.

The Father rarely leaves Muckle Flugga, except when he has to, like to fetch dark drinks or as a show of strength to his detractors. He leaves the island to prove he will not be held hostage by the condemnations they cast.

Sometimes the drink enters The Father like a sonic boom like a blazing bolide like love letters torn to shreds – the spark in him, a savage blaze. It is rumoured that the sadness locked in the chest of The Father is heavy enough to bring a building down. Other times, the drink enters The Father like snow – quashing snarling flames, smooring the embers.

The Father takes refuge in his off-limits area, his lair, his shrine, his dirty den, his torture chamber, his purgatory, his hidey-hole, his cave, his club for one, his cage. A cage. Inside this liminal space, The Father melts his skin away, with booze and ire, poring over old photographs, pickling the few treasured memories he can still taste.

He burns sentimental things in the fire to make memories disappear, forgetting he's done so in the morning then weeping uncontrollably. Head thumping and organs throbbing, he will admit he, too, is vulnerable – denying this as soon as mended. He will feel ashamed of each outpouring, of his *boo-hoo-hoo*, and will suffocate the bits of himself that permitted such fancy. He will make Ouse watch. For The Father is of the old school of thinking that if-it-was-done-to-him-but-harder-and-he-survived-it then anyone under his care should be grateful (lucky stars thankful) for any less.

The piffling punishments he doles out to Ouse are small potatoes in life's great mash.

The Father has a glass eye; his own father is responsible for the eye's absence.

The Father washes in cold, cold water and thinks of The Mother as the needles strike.

The Father does not sleep much, despite a madcap tiredness.

The Father does not eat well, despite a constant hunger.

The Father once had a knife fight with an American soldier that got handsy with another keeper's wife, and won. He has never bragged about it.

The Father once met a pretty man who said, *Years from now we are nothing more than the echoes of the kindnesses we cast,* and it moved him deeply. He's since denied being stirred by such slop.

The Father used to be an excellent horseback rider and hoped healing animals would be his primary usefulness to this world. The Father now forbids such foolish fancies. There are no horses on the rocky sprawls of Muckle Flugga and Out Stack. It is hard for him to remember there are any horses at all.

The Father is a cruel brave man: he has struck braver men; embraced crueller.

The Father is strong, yet unwell, and unfortunately handsome.

The Father would rather see sickness prevail than pander to doctors.

The Father finds peace in the tempest's ninth symphony – when battling storms he is reminded of his value. He doesn't name the storms that gush through here, for it is easier to slay, hate and forget unspeakable things. The Father has seen such darkness that a little blood upon the feet of saints is a mere trifle.

The Father has been many men – many, many men. He once tried to write a poem: although pleased with the outcome he chewed it to pulp when a friend mocked its sweet sentiments. It was about a gosling playing in the shallows; also, ostensibly, The Mother.

The Father insists the best protectors are wounded beasts that season the meat inside them out of courtesy to what hunts them. The Father despises emotional multitudes, in men, believing they would hinder his ability to work the lighthouse as if he were three keepers rather than just one tough old son of a gun. This work requires of The Father: heaving, digging, pulling, wrenching, yanking, howling, blasting, chasing, pranging, thumping, crying, hunting, battling, sacrifice. He deems these the (bare minimal) ingredients for survival when manning The Impossible Lighthouse.

The Father charges himself a sentinel: twisted, flawed, dreadful, but not faithless, never faithless. It's faith that keeps him fighting. He has sacrificed everything to be here, to serve the light. His family: gone, betrayed, lost. The Mother: gone, betrayed, lost. The dead: invisible but far from silent.

Ouse, his son, will learn by his teaching. He cannot fail him. He cannot.

FIVE

An oyster-scavenger wolf-whistles into the wind, alerting his coterie to a fine old find. The pack of men come darting over and are soon slopping oysters from the weedy shallows. They make fast work of the molluscs, quaffing back the first run and filling their sacks with the rest. Like soil onto a coffin, they toss their shells into the tide and slink off hoarse-throated, sacks clacking.

When spotted watching, Firth averts his eyes, pretending he's distracted by the watery distance. The men stare back menacingly, assessing the threat of him. Fortunately, Firth is summoned forwards to pay the fare for the foot ferry, dropping a couple of coins into the ticket issuer's metal pot, which looks suspiciously like a bedpan. Metal upon metal tolls in the air funereally. Appropriately, perhaps, the jetty to the boat feels like a gangplank, but he'll be damned if he's not going to make the most of this final trip.

The ferry from Aberdeen to Shetland is an infamously tumultuous, mammoth of a journey. Whereas some passengers dread it, for Firth, the opportunity to be at the mercy of the ocean, miles from the wreckage his life, is as sweet a proposition as returning to the womb.

Firth's carrying a satchel full of his finest clothes, rolled up tight to maximise space, and a hefty cloth-cut suitcase; which is, in fact, the carry case for an old sewing machine his mum picked up in a charity shop. The case is full of paints, brushes, sketchpads, a little whisky, some bric-à-brac and books. It's heavier than it looks, although he tries to disguise any sign of strain so as these north folk might reckon he packs a punch, in spite of his tailored sheepskin coat and colourful cravat. Both he and the case are as tatterde-malion as each other, but in that prim, affected way that attracts compliments from the bohemian crust of society.

He sits down on the lower deck, indoors, in the cheap seats, as if to label himself humble and non-intrusive, a take-one-for-the-team type of guy. It's gloomy out, there's a sticky wetness to the air and the sky droops as it might on the eve of a blizzard. Scottish sum-mers are other folk's winters.

The ferry's disappointingly deserted; the main trade is a clique of women hoofing bags of wool on board. Once the heavy lifting is done, they sit and begin talking in a tongue that's barely deciphera-ble to Firth. On the far side of the boat, a gaunt-looking man with an aged sheepdog stands, staring unflinchingly into the sea as if readying himself to scatter the ashes of a child. To his far left, a spry goat is rope-tied to a life-ring, wrangling with its constraints. It appears un-chaperoned, its mouth frothy and tumescent pink lipstick garishly on display; a look of unquenchable thirst in its mad goat eyes.

Firth checks his own eyes in the reflection of a penny, then loses himself in the hypnotic stare of the crazed beast until a klaxon goes off to indicate the ferry's moving out. The boat has what feels like a seizure, rattling all its parts out of their joints to the point of collapse. Once reset, the ferry thrusts forwards with a jolt that launches Firth off his seat and onto the floor. The wool women chortle without taking their eyes off each other. Firth laughs with an exaggerated brio to give the impression of someone gay and unabashed.

As he wipes grime off his corduroys, he hopes they don't see the tears in his eyes and his face radishing. His knees are cut but he's too craven to check them. He hopes he doesn't bleed so much that it seeps through the fabric and subjects him to ridicule.

Eyes closed as the boat swings in the swell, Firth begins to hear beyond the engine of his embarrassment. He hears the waves lash against the vessel's lean curvature, and the mellifluous rhythm of the knitting cabal's chatter. He hears the old sheepdog snoring in a timbre that confirms it's deep within the throes of an arousing dream. He hears words ring out from the last time someone told him they loved him and truly meant it – it was by the sea in Portobello; a joy supreme until mauled by his ego. He lets his mind nestle into the memory and drifts off into slumber.

Opening his eyes, he knows hours have passed, as there's renewed vigour in his tired bones and the sun is now rushing across the ferry floor. A patch of light on his lap warms his crotch as if a cat had been sat there this last while. From within this delicious slice of summer, it occurs to Firth that this will be the last ferry he takes and he repeats again what he vowed upon the bridge – to Muckle Flugga: to paint, and then to die. A journeyman's grand finale, and here he is sitting downstairs like a wanker, like he's in a dentist's lobby waiting to be called in for a drilling. Above him is the open air, a deck from which to gaze upon a hunk of world utterly unfamiliar to him. He'll be damned if he squanders it.

Firth re-dons the sheepskin coat and cravat and loads himself up with satchel and suitcase, ready for lift-off. That's before clapping eyes upon the tiny metal ladder he'll have to scale to get up to the top deck. The first rung of the spindly contraption is a ridiculous three feet off the floor – an Olympic-sized leap even for a lanky one. Uncharacteristically vehement, he leaves his luggage to fend for itself, declares to hell with it, and makes his break. After all, who's going to pilfer such dishevelled-looking wares on a near-abandoned ferry whilst they're out at sea?

With that settled, Firth careers up the ladder with a litheness that surprises even himself, emerging onto the top deck a younger-looking specimen of a man. The viewing platform is slippy, pint-sized and rust-riddled. The handrail is cold as ice and uncomfortable to grip. The waves come slapping over the flank of the ferry, sloshing everything with spume. That aside, Firth couldn't be more content with his choice to ascend.

Utilising the full grip of his boots, he is astonished to find his muscles preventing him from being pulled overboard – customarily he'd be battling the instinct to plunge himself into the deep. He's closer in spirit to a stone than a great many living things: born to sink. After a moment thinking on it, Firth attributes this sudden peacefulness to having hatched a plan; a mission, a task, a solid conclusion. As the mizzle makes a mockery of his misery, so too does the sun offer succour to those parts of him starved of joy.

Trust him to nearly miss this belter of an experience on account of a lacklustre sense of adventure. In truth, he's missed out on more for less, but not today. Today, he steadies his feet with flair. Until now, the pastel blue cowboy boots that he's wearing have been outshone by the coat-and-cravat combo, but as they transform his feet into anchors they come into their own. After one last look for dolphins leaping, he closes his eyes, releases one hand from the rail and leans his body into the wind, which has just enough propulsion in it to keep him upright. He's the human equivalent of the Leaning Tower of Pisa, wavering in this off-kilter position for a short eternity. He begins to float from his skin, channelling a kite tied to a bench on a very long string – chuffed to be flying yet relieved to be tethered – until a sound that's neither bird, beast nor ocean's echo, breaks the spell.

Yil no last long playing games like that wi da wind, laddie! Rake o'thing like you, be carried oot into the middle o'the sea afore it puts you doon again.

Opening his eyes, and returning to his physical form, finds Firth in close contact with one of the knitting women from below deck. All four feet tall and a hundred years old of her, he can't fathom how she managed to scale the ladder with such stealth.

Here! Aren't du that writer? she horns out.

Firth is stunned by the recognition – the pitiful number of reviews he's received outside of the Scottish central belt (where at least he can coerce journalists into giving him the column inches) means this very rarely happens, and that's likely for the best.

I am 'a writer' . . . mibees even 'that writer', but that all depends who exactly you're looking for?

Och aye, it's you alright! the woman toots, churlish yet tickled.

Still mystified, Firth probes at how she knows him well enough to recognise, and tries to mask his gladness.

The knitting woman talks at Firth with both a pace and intensity beyond her years. She explains they had no choice but to rummage through his belongings and check his papers – questioning what sort of 'weirdo' abandons all their worldly possessions when travelling alone on a ferry to the north's north. She explains, too, that she has a 'queer sort of laddie' for a son that read one of his books and raves about it – noting him to be the type that heads off into the hinterlands singing songs about creatures from other realms. When Firth enquires whether she likes his stuff, sensing it's not for her, she replies curtly, somewhat affronted: *Och aye, I like aw his stuff. Even when it's shite, I like it. I'm his ma, um I no?*

This strikes Firth as one of the most beautiful things he's ever heard, and serves as a stark reminder to never stop being grateful to his own encouraging mum, who passed before her time.

The woman then goes on to ask an onslaught of impertinent questions about how much money Firth makes, what famous faces he's hobnobbed with in the capital, and what's really going on in those wine cellars after dark.

To every question Firth answers he's aware that the words coming out his mouth are only part-truths, embellished to inflate his grandeur. For every answer he spews out, unable to control himself, there's a more honest, humbler response hiding behind it. The main thing he keeps hush is that although he does write books for a living it's only made possible by his mum leaving him her wee flat on Edinburgh's Candlemaker Row; Firth's old dear having become the sole veritable candlemaker on Candlemaker Row, after her spell on the gutting tables down Leith's dock. The latter fact is something Firth's boastful of when around the working classes and keeps entirely schtum about when surrounded by snobs.

As if that wasn't enough, most of the money he actually makes comes from his side hustle as a scout for his old university: Edinburgh's Academy of Art & Thinking – the crux of which involves convincing wealthy trust fund kids they've got what it takes to change things with their art. He does this with such vehemence they feel compelled to blackmail their parents into paying exorbitant fees to enable them to doss around drinking foreign beer and smoking rolls-ups for a few years – covering their fine clothes in just enough paint to create the sartorial façade of an impassioned artist on the brink of brilliance. Wannabe poets, painters, philosophers, playwrights, sculptors: he's conned them all into thinking the world needs their paper-thin, grandiloquent insights, knowing fine well nobody cares. And, of course, when it all comes tumbling down, when the critics vent their spleen and the publishers mock their triteness, cheerleader Firth – like all the best charlatans who've sold an impossible dream to the ignorant or vulnerable – is nowhere to be seen. Yet even with this monetary crutch, he lives much more hand-to-mouth than he'd care to admit, slinking out of soirées by insulting the guestlist, rather than admitting he's clean up broke. He's had to sell two pieces of his mum's prized jewellery just to keep up the charade. All sold cheap for crap nights that cost him something soft inside that's never coming back.

In response, the knitting woman, taking no prisoners, blasts out a gristly and fast-paced vent, completely obliterating the capital and those drawn to it, marking them all carpetbaggers, without the usual wry nicety of marking present company excluded.

As she rants, Firth's mind drifts deeper still, into the ulcerated parts of himself responsible for spewing out all manner of shite to hyperinflate his status. Is it so unfeasible he might give an honest response? Firth begs of himself scoldingly. If not in Shetland's distant waters, then where might he be free from such crippling vainglory? But then, triumphantly, land appears on the horizon, curtailing his melancholic thoughts. Not just land but land with sunbathing seals on it, including several pups. And beyond that, a huge, isolated rock formation that looks like a giant pushing a wheelbarrow, but on closer inspection is just the way the sea carved up the coast – the ocean still being the world's greatest sculptor, despite what Michelangelo might say to that. This reminds him of another element of the story his grandfather told him about the islands of Muckle Flugga and Out Stack – that they had been formed by two warring giants lobbing boulders at each other in a battle to win the affections of an enchanted mermaid. Yes, it wasn't just the birdlife but the folklore that saw a young Firth fall in love with these mythical islands that his grandfather never tired of lionising.

Not until his late teens did Firth realise that his grandfather had only been stationed here as a cadet and so these memories allowed the old soul to tap into a version of himself that hadn't seen the savagery of death, destruction and war; someone plucky who was able to dream the whole night through without waking from a ghoulish nightmare. Rather than sully the romance of the place for Firth, it added to it, insurmountably.

Abruptly, the woman's tirade comes to sharp end, concluding with the commentary, *But that's Edinburgh fur ye, is it no?* Firth, caught completely off guard and elsewhere, tries to think of something witty to say but lost track of the thread completely some time back.

In light of this series of distractions, Firth replies, not with insight, but with a grandiose remark that immediately makes his teeth hurt – *Quintessential Edinburgh and don't we know it.* A remark cast with zero understanding of exactly what he's sentencing the great city to. This has Firth regurgitating the painful memory of the time he tried to assume the *nom de plume* Melodious Green, a title he presumed would make him more enamouring to the upper classes. *Quintessential Edinburgh* was something Melodious Green would have uttered unironically, spraying spittle and sherry over the cheese fondue.

Firth moves matters onwards with alacrity; he doesn't want to talk about money he doesn't have or be tarred with the pomposity of the capital, nor does he like the way his own voice just sounded. Besides, he's keen to divulge his plans for the weeks ahead before they hit the harbour. Hoping to earn some local kudos, he explains he's rented the bothy on the island of Muckle Flugga from its lighthouse keeper.

The knitting woman gawks at him, gesturing to say something but stopping herself and then instead wishing him luck with the look a farmer's wife might give the goose they're fattening up for Christmas dinner – so not the executioner's glint, but the gaze of someone who has cleaned blood from the blade in years gone by.

Before she tunnels back down the portal like a mystic mole, Firth begs her to disclose a little more about the place he's heading, desperation in his tone.

She stops stock still, then after a moment's hesitation begins her response with the sentiment, *Have ye heard the expression: a wise man doesnae stand next to a falling wall?* She then goes on to describe an irascible keeper, ruined by grief, with a viper in his throat and a broken soldier's thirst for whisky. She talks of a darkness in him death delivered, yet lauds the way he channels it – his hauntedness – into manning the light. How unyielding he remains in his battles with the abyss. She stresses, however, that his bairn is a queer sort, chuckling, having tarred Firth with the same brush; her son too, she adds again as a softener. She details how the bairn's voice sounds as if he's been sooking helium out of party balloons, and bemoans the way he's always staring off into the distance for so long folk reckon his mechanisms have busted. The final point she makes reluctantly – that despite the laddie's kindnesses, in fact on account of them, he is totally unfit for taking over the keeper's vile duties, something The Father is stubborn set on.

Sensing Firth recoil at this harshness, she qualifies the statement, expressing her love and admiration for the boy, who happens to be the best knitter on the island and one of them '*artistes*' when it comes to design and needlework. Not only that, they sell his wares at all the craft fayres they travel to and, after taking their rightful commission, pay him good coin. She says there's fancy city tailors with laurels to their names that would take the laddie on as an apprentice in a heartbeat, but The Father wouldnae hear of it, hissing like a cat with a snake for a tail at the mere suggestion. She then, to Firth's astonishment, defends this odious-sounding figure, The Father, claiming:

It's not that he's blind tae hiz ain flaws, it's mare hiz mind's made up and too mangled to ken any better. She concludes this divulgence by remarking: *Ack, it's just as weel they'll be automating Muckle Flugga Lighthoose afore long. Demanning the lights. Or so they're saying. But fur love and mercy, didnae mention that to The Faither or he'll have yer heid fir a keychain. In fact, dinnae mention ony o'this,* the woman pleads, suddenly panicked. *Gibbering will be the death o'me.*

I won't. That's a promise, Firth rejoinders. *You have the word of someone who'll not be around long enough to break it!*

Here – if you write aboot me, the woman yells as she begins her exodus. *Make me younger! And taller! I wiz once.*

Oh, I'm actually here to paint, not write . . . but before Firth can finish the sentence, she's down the ladder, again with a haste and dexterity that doesn't marry up to her wizened face and mature vintage.

Left alone, Firth does a 360-degree spin, taking in the panorama, again, then again, then again. Dizzied enough that the horizon and the ocean and the boat's exterior keep spinning once he's stilled. He takes the ladder back down, hoping to fall but trying not to. No such luck. He lands on the floor of the ferry to find it emptied and the other passengers spilling onto the boat's drawbridge and up the seaweed-soupy incline of the harbour onto Unst land. The sole remaining creature is the lascivious-looking goat, which has gnawed through its rope and appears to be sharpening its teeth on the metalwork. Firth gathers his belongings in a tizzy, even more convinced that the goat's a bad omen.

One more thing, the woman calls from up on the precipice. *Whatever you do, don't go wandering aroond after dark, batten doon the hatches and wait until the birds are singing. Promise me that, won't you?*

I will, Firth utters as if swearing an oath to a prophet he knows to be false.

35

SIX

A greedy gull moves in on a handsome crab – fireworks in the bird's eyes as the clawed crustacean looks set to become the next short-term solution to its unshrinkable hunger. Just in the nick of time, Ouse lashes a tail of seaweed like a whip, seeing off the feathered bruiser. The gull, dissuaded, huffs away, unimpressed but far from afraid. Squatting over the traumatised crab, Ouse whispers a reassuring mantra that seems to put it at ease.

The Father scowls and ruminates the wider implications of all the times he's chosen not to interfere with nature in the face of the barbarity about to unfold. Despite being torn as to the better route, he masks any whiff of indecision with the arrogance of certainty. *Save 'em today, scoffed tomorrow – don't think yer doing any mare than delaying the inevitable!*

Ouse by this point is lost in song, lullabying to his crustacean queen, who has her claws in the air and her legs mad jinking. Irritated, the Father heaves up a clump of all sorts from the pebbly beach and hurtles it skywards, sand and shells raining down upon Ouse and the crab like a miniature missile assault. Once again, the oneiric bubble Ouse immersed himself in is burst by The Father.

Abruptly, as if to justify his peevishness, The Father begins briefing Ouse on the new guest coming to stay in the bothy. The Father keeps his distance from lodgers, so the briefing mainly consists of relaying the increased chore load that a lodger's presence demands of Ouse. There's the checking-in, without being over-friendly; the induction tour that should remain perfunctory – where to go, where not to go – so as not to encourage aberrant explorations. There's answering irksome questions with curt responses; and cooking meals, some of which are included in the board so as they can charge the highest rate the booker offers. Any washing the lodger might want done should be discouraged and comes at an additional cost. Any trips to the mainland for supplies, sightseeing or letter-sending should also be discouraged and comes at an even greater additional cost.

If the lodger's an insistent spendthrift, the journey should coincide with Ouse picking up his takings from the market. This can be managed by fibbing to them about weather forecasts and swell levels (the threat of an incoming storm that can later be said to have changed its mind is an easy yarn to spin).

A bit of covert reporting is required to make sure lodgers aren't meddling or prying. There's the spying The Father instructs Ouse to do, and the spying The Father does himself; because this element of the job can't be entrusted solely to Ouse, who is, in The Father's opinion, far too trusting. The Father, on the other hand, trusts no-one, and doesn't put it beyond the KLAMS to engage in espionage themselves – sending spies under the guise of birdwatchers to snoop on him: gathering evidence for when they choose to make their move.

When the KLAMS deem a situation necessary of being 'dealt with' there's no measure they won't take. A bunch of despots, The Father often barks – even he's heard about those secret societies in Edinburgh, all their venal ways and relentless jiggery-pokery. The Father's only too aware he's ruffled the feathers of this new political breed – academy gimps, he calls them, lapdogs of diplomats, aw soppy-bawed and sherbet-bellied.

With a razoring flick of the eyes, The Father gestures to the approaching vessel on the horizon. His subtle gestures are palpable to

Ouse, who comes out in flamed cheeks when summoned.

As part of the lighthouse keeper's remuneration, food, fuel and other supplies are regularly delivered to Muckle Flugga from the mainland. The Father's thankful Ouse is too young to recall the times of pucker and plenty, compared to the paltry shipments that come their way now – the load ever lightening. He's doubly thankful Ouse's mind is too wonder-lusty to fear each delivery being their last – The Father stomachs that stone alone.

When the water's too choppy to get a goods boat into their cove, the vessel tarries just off-coast and connects to the island by a rope-and-pulley mechanism. Food is bundled into a hefty basket and pulled up the cliff face by The Father, with Ouse behind him – the rope belted around his willowy waist. Ouse has a fond memory from when he was little of The Mother bundling him into the basket and The Father pulling it up whilst dosing the air with his laughter. He's not sure whether it's a real remembering or a figment of his imagination, but won't dare ask The Father for fear of losing something cherished; something he perhaps never had in the first place.

When the currents are tranquil, the delivery boat can drift into the sandy bay where The Father will exchange brief pleasantries with the goods-givers before heaving the provisions into a wheelbarrow and having Ouse lug them off to the pantry. This latter form of delivery only happens if Figgie is shepherding the load – no-one else – for Figgie alone possesses the patience and fortitude to engage with The Father on a close and personal level.

Today the sea is languorous, and Figgie is deftly working the oars, reversing the boat into a paramount landing position. She is slight yet skilled, poised yet purposeful. Her eyes are gentle whilst fiercely alert. Ouse is first to greet her, splashing into the shallows.

He always welcomes Figgie first, makes a point of it, with kind words and a resplendent smile – the calibre of address she deserves. He's also terrified she'll stop coming. Since his schooling on the mainland came to an abrupt end, Figgie and RLS are the only two humans, other than The Father, Ouse regularly confers with – Figgie being the only one with a heartbeat. There's also Carron and Shannon from the knitting club, who sell his creations at the mainland's market, but that's irregular contact and he always leaves conflicted by their encouragements – knowing false hope to be more dangerous than tiger sharks around these parts. With Figgie it's different: she comes to them, though she shouldn't. They've a sense for each other, mystic maybe. Ouse resonates with the way she fractures, being equal parts in love with living on these remote islands whilst remaining entranced by the promise of leaving (again).

Figgie, too, always looks first to Ouse, even when The Father is nearer. *My sweet sugar-snap darling of the divine, ma wee oodle of joy, my Ousling, you welcome me as if family, and it thrills me to the core,* she sings. Except, of course, she never actually utters any such sanguine sentiments aloud. Instead, she smiles coyly, as is her way, and says, *Hello, Ouse, that's another lovely jumper. You really are so talented.* And it really is a lovely jumper – a huge sun exploding from the chest rippling into rings of amber, gold, butterscotch and Tuscan sun. The neck-and-cuff work features intricate waves of detail worthy of their own tapestries. Plus, they sparkle: Ouse adds glitter.

The Father, keen to shut that conversation down, issues Figgie a nod and some form of vocal salutation, which is friendly in tone yet indecipherable as language. There's a sentence underneath the gravel of it, but it's hard to say which words are buried there; likely not even The Father knows. This is a stoic greeting compared to the way other men address Figgie – for she is undoubtably beautiful and caring and is treated as such – yet animated and congenial in comparison to The Father's conventional social interactions.

You're doing fine? Figgie mouses out, chastising her meekness whilst hiding behind a smile.

Fine. Aye. The Father confirms as if agreeing to an unsatisfactory deal for a box of shrimp. Nearly knocking Ouse over, he lunges forwards to take hold of a beefy sack of tatties. The Father's face changes not a jot with the immense bulk.

As Figgie dishes out some meat and fish, The Father makes his usual dry comments about the rations waning as the budget pinches in, about the top dogs taking a bite out of each cut until the keepers are left with the type of gristle, guts and offal that hoity-toity types leave on the side of their plates. He jokes about Ouse eating like a rabbit these days, or a cat – though no-one is too sure what he means by the latter, the mocking herbivore metaphor being completely off when it comes to felines; then again, The Father has never kept a cat.

Just a few weeks back, Figgie nearly revealed to Ouse that she regularly tops up their shop of her own charitable volition – sometimes with excess goods, other times buying from the shop's purse. It was a moment of needy desperation that almost got the better of her. What she'd never even think of mentioning to anyone is that a few times now she's paid for the full load out of her wages when The Father's allowance has been late coming in from the KLAMS. In fact, it's been both late and inconsistent recently. Coal, candles and clothing are supposed to come their way alongside all edibles; slim pickings in every category is making it harder and harder for Figgie to conceal her philanthropy.

To his shame, without fail, as soon as the groceries have been unloaded, The Father hastily disappears up the shore path – commonly crashing off midway through a conversation. He is a tidy executioner when it comes to exterminating small talk, which has a most unfortunate effect on the uncommonly kind.

On this occasion, however, as has only happened once or twice in these recent years of making deliveries, Figgie calls The Father back. Because sitting patiently at the rear of the boat – behind a fish bucket, a flare gun and her yappy poodle Clyde, who accompanies Figgie everywhere – is Muckle Flugga's newest visitant. With a satchel looped around his chest and his suitcase grappled tight, Firth delays standing up, only doing so when beckoned.

At the sight of Firth The Father's eyes boil. He's not one to tolerate early arrivals, and is unprepared for a stranger to set foot upon Muckle Flugga, their eyes scanning its everything and anything. A raged panic at what they might discover seeps into The Father's bones.

I'm sorry I'm early, Firth says, clearing his throat anxiously. *It's just when Figgie said she was heading your way, and hearing the crossing isn't always the easiest, I was eager to get here. And, well, if it's a problem I can always come back tomorrow.* While he phrased it as a question, Firth doesn't wait for an answer, leaping off the boat and plunging into the water below – not expecting it to come knee-high, nor be quite so bracing. In a clumsy attempt to traverse the seaweed-greased rocks, he stumbles and his suitcase falls open, spilling paint into the shallows. *Damn goat must have been at it, the freak-faced shitesniffer!* Firth yells, forgetting himself.

Figgie lets out a half-gasp half-chuckle, as Firth tries to stop his cheeks flushing beetroot and the tide commences its own purpling – the paint mixing with the frothy ocean. Without thinking, Ouse lunges forwards to assist, but The Father extends his arm to prevent his son helping the newcomer, creating a barricade

41

against which Ouse's chest collides. Ouse, feeling courageous, proceeds to limbo underneath the obstructing arm and dives into the shallows.

To The Father's dismay, Ouse emerges clutching the art supplies. The Father, vexed, issues his words like a sentence: *Lodgings are for birdwatchers only. Nae artists. Nae nothing but birdwatchers! Couldnae huv been clearer on that. Couldnae — huv — been — CLEARER. You'll need tae go.*

The Father is at once the magnet of the group's attention – his ire palpable. After a few seconds of tense silence, Firth begins haphazardly attempting to rebrand himself as an ornithologist, noting the sketching and subsequent painting comes only after hours and hours of careful watching, and in fact may not come at all if the watching doesn't go according to plan. A cavalier statement about true artists being the great watchers of the world comes closest to altering the countenance of The Father, who stares so penetratingly into Firth his gaze all but bores below the skin.

Feeling like he's nothing to lose, Firth lunges towards The Father, attempting to be winsome, whilst coming off cocky – ironic given he's terrified, his teeth beginning to chatter from the cold plunge. The Father steps forwards and Firth springs back, as if a frightened rabbit evading the jaws of a hound. Ouse and Figgie, who've been watching bemused, finally break their silence fearing for the safety of the young bumbler – who was, in truth, only seconds away from what would have been a catastrophic attempt to physically embrace The Father. Meaning Firth was perhaps only seconds away from being meat upon the rack.

Before The Father has a chance to retort, Figgie intervenes on Firth's behalf, noting him to have been a very courteous passenger in her boat, helping unload previous deliveries and being patient with the stories of those that tend to talk in circles. Not only that, Clyde found Firth likeable – lickable on first sniff, in fact, which nearly never happens.

Ouse considers backing Figgie up, but abstains from doing so, noticing The Father wavering and fearing that his support might tip the scale back in the opposite direction. Ouse is also reticent to splurge any words because an electric charge has begun levelling up inside him, a current in the body surging. He immediately finds Firth both utterly compelling and intensely unsettling.

Firth begins his deep-breathing exercises, teasing out the silence to cajole another into speaking. He lets his eyes pass from the daunting face of The Father to the softer shapes of the son. He notices Ouse's elongated eyelashes, his quirky handsomeness, his gaze either on the floor or off in the distance. He appears, at once, both entirely elsewhere and resolutely in the moment – still nervous, but seemingly accepting of what any nervosity might bring forth. Firth finds this totally enviable and wants it for himself.

Neither Ouse nor The Father are anything like how Firth imagined them from the knitting woman's descriptions. Though there's nothing in the way she described them he could fault – each write-up entirely apt – he didn't expect either to have such earthy presence. He breathes in again, follows Ouse's gaze out into the ocean, and leaves himself hanging in the air like a fog.

The Father, pacified by Figgie's interference, lets his eyes leave Firth for the first time, as if having finished assessing the danger. Seizing the opportunity, Figgie, the clever fox, offers the reassurance that most painters she's met tend to do a lot more watching than painting. And then she more subtly reminds The Father that the boy's paid upfront, and no doubt arrangements have already been made for the weeks ahead.

43

In truth, Figgie feels she's overcommitted in her championing of Firth, having become consumed by the notion of selling The Father something he didn't want. She convinces herself the impetus to do so is borne from a desire for Ouse to have fresh company, knowing too well the loneliness brought on by loving those resistant to love. Though mainly she was propelled to act by an insuperable desire to prove The Father capable of bending his dogged will. Figgie is ever trying to make a new man of him, a kinder man, or egging him on to rediscover parts of himself he's kept locked away for so long he's likely forgotten they exist.

The Father relents with a grunt of acceptance, ashamed of the weakness in him that stems from their lowly financial standing. Where once there were three keepers tending to the miscellaneous expenses of the island with their surplus coffers, now there is but one – one who does his best to barely exist on paper and takes a foul view of charity.

Indicating the negotiation is over, for now, The Father begins to retreat, but not without casting a disdainful eye over Firth's appearance. Soaked, Firth's colourful cravat now appears to flop from his neck like a tinsel noose, his cowboy boots squelch out seawater and his cords stick to his scrawny frame. *You'll no get very far here in that costume. The parrots'll mistake you fir a pirate*, The Father sneers, then without so much as a glance in his direction, he signals for Ouse to begin the induction.

Figgie, continuing with her uncharacteristic bravery, calls after The Father to not be a stranger next time he's on Unst. He raises his right hand just a smidge, which could well be as warm a gesture as Figgie wants it to be, though more likely is just a body moving involuntarily as bodies are known to do when summoned, no greater portent to it than daffodils bopping in a breeze.

SEVEN

Ouse hoicks up Firth's bags and begins walking militantly, climbing the hill towards the island's cluster of buildings. Firth, still flustered, exhales deeply and follows suit, diligent as a dog in this moment. The sky is already darkening around its edges, which seems perplexing to Firth because it felt like morning when he boarded Figgie's boat – although he is exhausted from all the travelling and lost track of the clock some time ago.

You're going to love the bothy, Ouse assures Firth on the way over, *everyone does*. The sound of Ouse's voice takes him by surprise. Although he overheard Ouse greet Figgie, this is the first time he's addressed Firth directly. There's a warmth to his brogue that brings to mind roasted chestnuts and mulled wine. Being spoken to whilst not being looked at will take some getting used to, Firth thinks, but given the gravity of what's brought him here that's not a priority. All the same, Firth can't shift the niggling feeling that perhaps it should be.

In the past, Ouse has been more thorough, and garrulous, on this first stage of the lodger's check-in. Prone to informing visitors that the bothy was constructed by the disgruntled spouses of previous keepers who couldn't get a decent night's kip due to a virulent strand of snoring flu that was running rife around these islands. Of course, the majority of the year any level of human snoring is drowned out by storminess, but on the rare occasion the temper of the ocean and skies are, well, tempered the opportunity for a solid eight hours' shut-eye is not to be missed. The Father has since

45

instructed Ouse that local history lessons are too much information and courts nosiness, so he now tries to keep such extemporaneous detail to a minimum; given to talking as if The Father is listening in. Besides, the day's weather has become suddenly inclement – rain enough to snatch the birdsong away – not conducive to al fresco storytelling. Ouse, however, is able to hear a few barking seals down by the shallows and points these out to Firth, who is suitably impressed.

The pair arrive at the path to the bothy, soaked to the bones below, the door beating off its hinges. Ouse leaps forwards to catch it. *There's no locks here*, he boasts, *but we won't come in unless invited.*

Appalled by this notion, Firth begins mentally listing all the unwelcome visitors that would waltz right in if such a policy were adopted back in his wee Edinburgh flat. Not to mention the ransacking of everything of value. He cringes about that time he did forget to latch the door and was caught wanking with his chest caked in garlic oil – terrible at the time, though it means nothing now. Likely he'd have not been so mortified if it had been handsome Ouse chancing upon him, as opposed to an old aunty come to talk about his absence at church.

Ouse stops beneath the bothy and gazes up at it like a chick that's chewed free from its shell and emerged beneath a supermoon. The bothy has a silvery seaweed thatched roof, driftwood covered in eel grass that resembles a huge, flapped trapper hat drowning a pea-sized head. *Unburnable*, Ouse announces, showy with it, *gifts from the sea, and it lasts two hundred years.*

Enthralled as Firth is by these facts, he's also cold and drenched, so scurries past Ouse and into the bothy – shivering in the doorway, he drips like a kid who's fallen in a gully. The fire in the bothy is already thronging and Firth's immediately chasing its heat. The splendour of the place warms him in umpteen different ways. It's almost unbelievably capacious on the inside. Firth's gobsmacked expression attests to this revelation.

Ouse notes his confusion: *Bigger on the inside? Some think it's cursed because of it.*

It's the stuff of dreams! Firth fawns, his pretences down. *Outside it looks like a toy, but inside it's momentous. Twice the size of Robert Burns's Ayrshire cottage. I was invited there once.* In saying this he sinks in shame, realising it's just another showy reference to the pampered scholarly stock of which he's not even part.

Ouse doesn't take the bait, and instead begins the tour. The bothy is kitted out with its own wee guest library; a four-poster bed with black velvet drapes; a little stove and cooking pots; and an enormous free-standing copper bathtub, sat like a compass in the middle of the room. Above the bathtub is a hammock and above the hammock is a skylight – the hammock strewn at such an angle that should one topple out of it they would land, plop, into the tub. Firth makes a mental note to always leave the bath full of water if sleeping in the hammock to avoid a harsh landing.

There is a huge beast of a schoolmaster's desk with all sorts of clever drawers and compartments thrust up against the only wall with windows in it. The bothy's two front windows look off to the cliffs, down a terrifying drop to a cove that's currently being punished by an onslaught of breakers. On the way in on Figgie's boat, Firth had openly admired the sea arches guarding this particular cove, but being up above them feels more ominous, like they're drowned dragons willing on his fall.

One of the windows is much bigger and more striking – its stained-glass circular portal depicts a ship in trouble out on the waves. Before Firth gets the chance to ask about it, Ouse intuits the question.

The only surviving relic of a church that burned down on Unst. It's Noah's Ark taking float as the flood comes.

Now noticing what must be fire damage on the paint, the black crispy bits begin to give Firth eerie feels. *Isn't that a tad ominous? Spooky even? Given you're living on an island susceptible to flooding in the middle of nowhere. And for the love of God what started the fire? I mean, did people die?*

Ouse makes a move towards the door, avoiding the question. *I'll leave you to settle in. Remember, this bothy is as much a lighthouse as the lighthouse, don't let anyone tell you any different.*

Firth gets a sudden panic as Ouse begins to leave: panic about being alone, panic about what comes next, panic about trying to be productive before settling things. *Wait,* he grabs Ouse's arm and gets an almighty electric shock in return. Firth jumps back, yelping like a creature that's just had its tail trod on, then examining his hand as if there might be a baby bolt of electricity circling his palm.

It'll be the jumper, Ouse softly proclaims. *Get some sleep. There's food in the cupboards and we'll do the full induction tomorrow afternoon. The morning's your own.*

Wait, Firth mouths, seconds after Ouse has disappeared from sight.

EIGHT

After the wind blows out the candles for the third time, Firth relents and climbs into the bothy's salubrious four-poster bed, thinking this must be the earliest, and most sober, he's hit the hay in months. Little does Firth know the island of Muckle Flugga has a habit of telling its residents when it's time to rest and time to wake. Though Firth remains unaware of how meddlesome the island can be, he does drift off with an inkling of something significant at play, a notion that stalks him into a suspiciously blissful night of nod. Whereas slumber for Firth often involves waking in hot flushes and fevered panics, coughing up blood and dreams of snakebites, he sleeps the whole night through, waking early to a rustle in the trees outside – birds loading up on berries and attempting to out-sing the sun.

Firth, tousled and floppy-eyed, rolls from the bed onto the floor, then crawls on all fours to the window. He's hungry to cast his eyes over the landscape he's quested to after years of worship from afar, keen to get to work and do his grandfather proud. Ill-fated though this mission is, he's determined to ensure there's some enrichment to his time here; if not enrichment then accomplishment.

He arrives at the window squash-kneed and smelling of pine. He's not sure where the spicy fragrance is coming from, but it's on him, all over him, and he's grateful for the fresh aroma; in the city, if he's not smelling of wax and wine, it's smoke and beer. The small window is the only one worth gazing through. Less spooky for not being the orphan of a church fire and bearing the crispy edges of something scorched of all its goodness. He loads himself onto a conveniently located pouffe, smears a peek-hole through the condensation with the sleeve of his nightshirt, and smooshes his face to the glass.

What's outside hits him like a flying hug from a fond face in a faraway place. For all its isolation and alienation, its geographical extremity, the land outside appears rich and full and close to him. It's as if he's looking out the window from a seaside cottage in North Berwick, just thirty miles from home – rather than somewhere that identifies more as Viking or Nordic. A certain vista of greens and reds and stony walkways could be mistaken for the rolling slopes of London's Hampstead Heath. A turn in the other direction and it's ravishing gorse and gradients galore, strikingly similar to those that stud the way up Edina's Arthur's Seat. Over the horizon is a more dramatic parade of cliffs and thrashing ocean than he's ever seen from any city lookout, a sight that feels like it should be viewed through the portal of a ship.

Of course, he's gazing through the rose-tinted glasses of someone who's feasted on stories of these lands since he was a wee boy; someone who needs to find something beautiful here to justify the arduous voyage, and make his subsequent big finish as meaningful as it should be. But it's true, Muckle Flugga is spectacular and he doesn't have to force his awe. The ancientness is immediate and palpable. It causes Firth's belly to gurgle in ardour, and even has him humming. He feels that perhaps Jesus walked here, at least the Scottish Jesus. Firth may be an atheist but he'd not deny that someone called Jesus once walked this earth doing good deeds and saying clever things. A Samaritan, an entertainer, a storyteller, a human worthy of some followers.

At this exact moment Ouse breezes past with a watering can to hand. The sight of the boy captivates Firth. The cadence of his movement, the softness of his steps. Though he thinks of Ouse as a boy, he's aware he's likely only a few years younger than himself. Years of machinations, of social manoeuvrings under the shadow of the capital's endless tenements, has made it mark upon Firth's eyes. His colours have shifted from the strain of a life lived holding on by a thread. The city has aged Firth, has him haggard, he's Haggerston Castle after a siege. There's an easiness to Ouse's face, a suppleness to his skin that speaks of a life lived in open air with fresh fish and home-grown vegetables.

Ouse empties the watering can with precision over a few carefully selected saplings, tickling the leaves and softening the soil by running it through his fingers, removing any stones. Then, as if a deer stilled by fright, he freezes. The Father comes flying into view and the whole energy changes. Firth watches Ouse watch The Father traverse a hillock at pace. Firth watching Ouse, Ouse watching The Father, The Father racing like a locomotive to the door of the lighthouse, where he thrusts the keys into the lock as if a sword into a stone. Before Firth can think of what to make of it all, the lighthouse door thumps closed and a hefty vibration echoes out.

With The Father out of sight, Ouse eases back into his body, discarding the watering can into the soil and dashing off in the opposite direction. As if pulled by magnets, Firth is into his dressing gown and out the bothy's door. He follows Ouse, barefooted, over gravelled then marshy ground, over a series of stepping stones across a pond, and then through a rich tangle of reeds. Slowing down to keep his distance, he stumbles upon the perfect-sized tree for climbing up and surveying the scene. A strategically placed whale vertebra offers him the ideal leg-up into the tree's bottom branches.

Ouse is about twenty metres ahead of him, hovering on the tip of the island's most abrupt headland. By the curl of his arms, and

51

flick of his wrist, it's apparent to Firth that Ouse is pretending to be an orchestra conductor conducting the wind with his invisible baton. It is very odd behaviour and has Firth both slack-jawed and entirely rapt, as if suddenly finding himself in the front row of an absurdist performance he'd expected to be dull as dishwater. Initially it's a gentle melody and then Ouse is thrashing more erratically, the tempo rising as the symphony reaches its first clattering crescendo. This carries on for a good few minutes, Firth thrilled to be eavesdropping on the theatrics and then increasingly wracked by guilt for stealing pleasure from such a joyful indulgence.

So captivated by what's in front of him, Firth fails to notice The Father leaving the lighthouse and heading down towards the shallows. Ouse, however, does not. He about-turns with urgency and dashes back towards their living quarters. Firth quickly realises this route will take Ouse straight past the tree he's huddled up, which has some leafiness to it but not enough to camouflage a brightly bed-dressed, lanky human slung around its bottom branches.

In a moment of stupidity, Firth reaches the conclusion the only way is up, and frog-leaps into the air to try and catch the branch above. Although he manages this, the branch is thicker than his hands are able to clutch around, and its bark is silky smooth, too smooth to grip. Firth falls from the tree into the shrubs below, clouting his chin on a branch in the process. Firth's body whacks upon the ground like an old rolled-up carpet tossed upon a skip. Dust shoots up as his head throbs from the impact. A searing pain rips through his mouth, and he feels blood gush from his tongue where he's inadvertently bitten it. He lies there with the world spinning, with his face leaking, pretending to be a perfect pond of pure glass.

By the time Firth steadies himself enough to cautiously sit up, Ouse is well past and off towards the buildings with watering can

52

to hand. Firth has no inkling as to whether he saw him, or whether he heard the fall, but takes it as an encouraging sign that The Father's now nowhere to be seen.

Firth crawls most of the way back to the bothy, out of dizziness and fear and by the time he's back inside can think of nothing better to do than plunge himself into a warm bath, then start the day again. He'll slick his skin clean of mud and blood, unpack his art supplies, and make no mention of any of this when Ouse comes knocking to induct him to these lands of his final days.

The water is rejuvenating and his art supplies are in far better shape than anticipated given their dip in the sea. Eventually, he convinces himself that his abysmal attempt at espionage must have gone unnoticed; a sudden burst of birdsong beyond the bothy confirms it to be so.

NINE

Later that afternoon, Ouse will come for Firth, but first he must make The Father lunch and give an initial report on his brief interactions with the new lodger. He tells The Father that Firth seems focussed on making the most of his time here, that he's travelled light with inappropriate clothing for expeditions of any sort, that he's wimpy with the weather, suggesting he'll spend the majority of his time indoors. Ouse knows fine well this is the type of report The Father is eager to hear. The Father, though realising it's a tweaked measure of the man for his gratification, is satisfied all the same.

What Ouse doesn't tell The Father is that he spotted the lodger spying on him. What he definitely doesn't tell The Father is that he hammed up his performance for both of their amusement. He also doesn't tell The Father that there was something immediately familiar about Firth, something that caused him to take avid glances at Firth's profile when the coast was clear. He definitely didn't tell The Father that the electric charges that build up inside of him went berserk when they touched, and that he'd fathomed Firth's unease with himself is at least part responsible for the vicissitudes in the atmosphere.

Post-lunch, The Father busies himself with radio dispatches to vessels passing both north and south of Muckle Flugga – cargo trawlers, military ships, fishing boats, tourist cruisers, and those that keep their business strictly to themselves. He has a sneaking suspicion the KLAMS are listening in today: when an untoward clicking sound distorts a couple of his broadcasts it's as good as confirmed in his mind. No matter. The Father doesn't discriminate when it comes to offering navigational steers to the needy. However brusque, his oceanic illuminations are unrivalled in this quadrant of Scotland, a fact well kent by regular sea sailors, corsairs and the shyster authorities.

Firth, having scrubbed himself clean, unpacks his belongings as if moving into a new home – shirts on hangers, jammies under the pillow, art supplies scattered over the desk in an organised chaos. He's already got paint on his sleeves and has begun getting mawkish about the work ahead. His mind calls out to all his clothes on the line back home – all the silked-sleeved puffy shirts, tweed waistcoats and cabled cardigans he'll never see again. He wonders who'll wear them next. As he shaves his barely stubbled face in the mirror, he has to steady his hand so as not to cut his cheek. In the one sense he is heartbroken at his dire circumstances, yet in another sense he is relieved and staunchly pragmatic about making this final Muckle Flugga chapter a success story.

All of the past, that speaks through the flesh, stares back at Firth into clean-shaven cheeks; sometimes it whispers, though mostly it screams. He unscrews the mirror from the wall with a coin and turns it into a palette for his paints. As he does so, he finds himself thinking not of his friends back in Edinburgh but of the keeper's son – Ouse's image itches under his skin like a family of mice making home in a hay bale. Using the same coin Firth scrapes a stick-man into the stone wall of the bothy where the mirror had hung, a hieroglyph to immortalise his time here. He considers scoring dashes alongside the lined figure for each day that passes, then baulks at the thought of how few he might cast.

The island itself feels both on guard and tickled by the new visitor's arrival; the unrest already at play in Ouse and The Father is extreme, even for lodger season. Further out at sea, there's a restlessness in the deep that's not yet decided how it's going to manifest – only time will tell.

TEN

Firth is out the door of the bothy before Ouse gets the chance to knock. *I think you're way more like a cat than a rabbit!* Firth spouts as soon as in earshot. A pre-planned remark to break the ice and make Ouse think twice about bringing up anything he may or may not have seen fall from a tree.

Ouse ponders the comment a minute, playfully perplexed, until Firth jogs his memory by recounting the clumsy jibe The Father made about his rabbit-and-cat-like diet (Firth listening in from the rear of Figgie's boat at that stage). Ouse finds it strangely pleasing to know Firth has been mulling him over, more pleasing still is the idea of being part of the feline brigade; in his memory there's never been any cats on Muckle Flugga and he should like to be the first. He has often considered himself akin to cats and is commonly caught loafing in crates and boxes. He also adored his old teacher's cat, Mersey, who, defying moggy nature, had a propensity for swimming, catching fish in her fangs as a bear might.

Trying to be patient, for he knows he's one to talk into other people's silence, Firth buckles and probes. *Sorry, that sounds odd. I mean, I really don't know you at all. Maybe the cat thing's weird. I mean they deliver mouse heads to doorsteps, and mutilate for fun. Is it weird? What I mean is . . . I'm here for the fresh air as much as anything,* Firth fumbles, unable to stop talking until he provokes a response from the seemingly kind-natured man-boy, whose face appears unenamoured if not a touch forlorn.

Firth's voice brings Ouse back to the present, realising he has

57

yet to say anything out loud. Ouse is only too aware that he has the type of face that seems vexed when resting. He's been told it has a gothic architecture. The sort of face impertinent strangers yell *cheer up* at, or worse. Mostly worse.

Picking up on Firth's last few words, Ouse finally breaks his silence. *What's truly weird is that all these city dwellers, their lungs full of soot, don't just move out of the cities, rather than taking expensive trips away during which they mither on about pollution in the cities.*

I'm here to paint birds, Firth rushes to tell him.

We once had a lodger fill a hundred bottles with our clean air just to take them back to a factory they managed in London, Ouse recounts ponderously. *A bit like eating strawberries sat on a pile of manure, don't you think?*

At this comparison Firth guffaws so manically it feels as if skin strips from his gums: he absolutely doesn't agree, but won't dare say so.

Ouse gestures the direction for them to head off in and they march together in silence up the hoof of the steep incline. Firth notices a buoyancy to Ouse's gait: he walks like there are springs in his shins, like he's constantly on the cusp of leaping up to catch a frisbee. Wouldn't get away with that loopyness in Edinburgh, Firth thinks, not without being recruited for the circus.

Light flares punctuate the walkways, birdsong rises up in tuneful climaxes, and wind sweeps through the garden and slaps the top of the rocks; everything outdone by the gurgling, groaning ocean. Firth tries to look like someone taking it all in with a scholarly appreciation of nature, just as Ouse appears to. Ouse is at an apparent ease with walking to a soundtrack of nature's making. Firth, on the other hand, is not. He makes a commentary on virtually everything they pass, talking near feverishly when Ouse gestures to bring something to his attention.

You must be sick of me already, Firth winces after one of his lengthier and more inane remarks.

It's your turn to talk actually, Ouse rejoinders. *I said something a moment ago, you just missed it. But that's okay, everyone talks over me. I'm soft spoken, but I get braver as the day grows.*

Relieved, Firth queries, *What did you say that I missed?*

Not wanting to look to the past, Ouse points to a rocky outcrop in the distance, informing Firth where its best rock pools are to be found, and how not to drown trying to board it.

That's Out Stack, isn't it? Firth marvels as if witnessing a shooting star spell his name out in the sky.

The voices in the wind are loudest on Out Stack, Ouse confirms plainly. *Some say it's the songs of lovers lost at sea. A love that never sleeps. It is part that.*

Well that sounds freaky as fuck, Firth blurts, forgetting his manners and letting the Leith seep out of him. He then immediately revisits the sentiment with his New Town brass. *Stupefyingly, tantalisingly spooky.*

Remembering the reason for his companion's stay on Muckle Flugga, Ouse changes tack: *We see a lot of otters here, sometimes dolphins, even orcas, but I suppose it's only the winged variety you're after?*

Firth, somewhat affronted by this comment, explains to Ouse he appreciates all animal life democratically, that his penchant for birds, in this instance, is due to an artistic ambition rather than favouritism. It could be said that Firth uses an over-abundance of adjectives in delivering these sentiments; then again it could be said that Ouse is ungenerously short (with shades of whimsy) in his replies. Either way, Ouse draws Firth's attention to the triumphance of animal life that dwells on Muckle Flugga, cage-free and crusading. He hints at beasts beyond the pale of what might be seen in zoos or guidebooks, but is nebulous enough to avoid saying anything that could be relied upon as fact. He takes Firth on an eccentric ramble around Muckle Flugga, walking them in figures of eight and star shapes in order to keep the geometry of the island as much a mystery as when they began.

I've been thinking on what you said, Ouse admits. *I think I'd like to be a cat. But it would be cruel to have a cat as a companion here. The frost can be skin-needling and the haar comes in like wet ghosts. A cat needs weather that's more dependable, better for lolling in.*

I'm allergic, Firth concedes. *To cats, but not to dogs . . . or rabbits.*

Good, then you be the Rabbit and I'll be Cat, Ouse settles.

And though Firth has a plethora of sarcastic responses to this notion, especially given he's just noted a cat allergy, he instead nods with affection and makes daft bunny ears with his fingers. Ouse leads them further forwards as Firth banks his witty routine for a later date when they're more familiar.

And so Cat continues to lead Rabbit around the island of Muckle Flugga, pointing out all the structures and outhouses, paying homage to creatures great and small, to the taste of the air and the colours of the pansies, to the distance between them and everything else in the world, and to the sea – gargantuan, giddy, intransigent.

Firth attempts to amaze Ouse by recounting the story his grandfather told him of how these islands (Muckle Flugga and Out Stack) were formed by two rock-lobbing giants, sworn enemies, warring for the heart of a mermaid.

It's the way that story ends I find most romantic, Ouse notes. Firth, of course, probes for more, and Ouse, in his own good time, delivers.

The mermaid grew so bored of their fighting and machoism that she challenged them to follow her on a swim to the North Pole. The first one to meet her there would win her heart.

Ouse then stares off to the horizon as if replaying the swim in his mind.

And then what happens? Firth blurts, rattled by how Ouse could kibosh such a story halfway through.

Herman and Saxa, Ouse announces.

What?

Their names. Herman and Saxa. Herman . . . and Saxa. Ouse says it this final time with a slow and deliberate prosody, gaining pleasure from the process, as if blowing bubbles with the words.

Yes, great, so what happens to Herman and Saxa? Firth snaps, flush with anticipation.

They follow her. They charge into the sea, but in their bravado forget they can't swim. So both of them drown and leave the lovely mermaid in peace.

That's not romantic in the slightest, Firth protests.

Oh really, I always thought it was, Ouse responds, genuinely confused.

You're a one-off! I can tell that already.

Well, isn't everyone? Ouse refutes tersely. And with that he's hurrying off to the next stop on the tour, which is seemingly causing him much excitement, marked by an acceleration in pace and some canorous whistling.

As they pass a small orchard of trees, Ouse notes to Firth which is the eldest and which is his favourite, referring to the latter as Grandfather Crab and paying it appropriate reverence. It's now Firth fully notices the lilt in Ouse's voice – a sing-song rhythm he associates with country and western songs.

Firth is on the cusp of asking a few of his rehearsed questions about Muckle Flugga, but Ouse intuits what's coming. He always was obvious in his intentions when seeking answers.

61

The name Muckle Flugga's Old Norse. Yes, that's right, Norse of Old. Mikla Fluggey means large steep-sided island. Ouse beams at this unearthing, having always previously muddled this part up.

Attempting to suck up, Firth suggests the translation somewhat anodyne for just how blisteringly beautiful the island actually is. To hammer the point home, he begins listing other names he finds underwhelming in nomenclature for what they actually represent – foremost of which is sunset, which sounds so mechanical to Firth, clinical, and not at all like the light explosions of burst cherries that slink down the sky's bib as the darkness spirals in and starlight be- jewels everything.

Ouse, offering nothing in response, chooses to keep his feelings on the matter to himself. He often finds it sufficient to feel the words hatch at the back of his throat without the need to send them flying out of his nest of a mouth. It's quite enough to have them lie down on his tongue, unfurl and make a mystery of themselves.

There is a brief, almost begrudging, pause in the tour, to feed the fish, during which Firth talks incessantly about a huge fishpond in Edinburgh's National Museum of Scotland where the bottom of the tank is entirely covered in coins from people making wishes. Ouse gets distracted sympathising with the poor fish, considering how coin collisions must be at least five times as painful for them as a hailstorm is for him. And the hail on Muckle Flugga is known to fall the size of chestnuts and leave bruises mottling the skin. He explains that this is why there's no greenhouses anywhere to be seen in Muckle Flugga – this causes Firth confusion, not having been privy to Ouse's side of the conversation, which occurred entirely in his head.

Having shown Firth around the perimeter of the island, it is time for Ouse to penetrate the main living spaces, which bulge out the side of the lighthouse like the pregnant belly of a giraffe.

This is my joint favourite room in the whole world, Ouse declares, unfastening a heavy bar on the door and watching it swing open by bulk alone. Firth nods Ouse's way in praise of the surprising strength he displays in tackling the door's iron fastening, to which Ouse instinctively replies, *I'm at least twice as strong as I look*. Muscles like knots on wire, The Father would often deride – though Ouse does not care to share this slight.

Inside the building is a great rolling catwalk of a rug: purple-trimmed with a tapestry of arabesque details the like of which Firth has never seen. Amongst its busyness the rug displays the full gamut of lighthouse life, with keeper after keeper, and their families, attending to the dailies. Alongside these are scenes of a more leisurely or domestic nature: a snogging couple, a child pissing off the cliffs, a dog chasing its tail as fish leap from the pond into the fryer. The work is intricate enough to identify changes in attire and hairstyles on the tiny little thread people. Down in the cove, Firth spots the depiction of sailors with the faces of seals unzipping their skin. The evolution of the lighthouse building is captured with bravura.

The sea appears to be more of a beast than a body of water, the waves crashing in like huge paws shoving at the rockface, thinning out as they spill to shore and taking the form of serpents. The night sky is stitched with such extravagance it makes Van Gogh's *The Starry Night* seem bland and balding in comparison. What Firth feels from that rug puts all the astrological drawings he'd leafed through in the University library to shame – more enthralling even than the time he'd seen the actual moon through a professor's telescope. The experience of viewing it leaves Firth in a state of dazzlement.

The enormous rug is too grand in scale to take in within a single gulp, so sprawling it appears to be in constant motion. Kaleidoscopic, hypnotic, carouselling art – it acts as a galvanic thrust into Firth's ribs, a reminder of how much he truly does love art, attesting to the fact that he has at least learned how to look at something beautiful and appreciate it, deeply. Attesting to the fact he's not dead inside, not yet.

Ouse, having removed his shoes, is tiptoeing across the rug as if passing over stones that cross a stream. His ballerina-esque elegance marks a movement beyond walking but not quite dancing.

You look like a reader, Ouse proffers warmly. *I imagine it's commonplace in the city, but not here.*

Guilty as charged, Firth confirms, making himself nauseous from just how smarmy that sounds.

With this, Ouse ushers Firth towards his bookcases with excitable urgency. Firth had not yet clapped eyes on the books, too beguiled by the rug. It's only then it occurs to him that the inhabitants of Muckle Flugga are in complete ignorance of his own writing credentials and in fact presume him a low-level painter. Although punishing to his pride, he decides maintaining this disguise would be the most prudent thing he's done in a while. And so, he reiterates his love of reading and leaves it at that.

The bookshelves climb as high as the roof, narrowing in width as they rise. Each shelf appears to be composed of a different wood, suggesting they've been fashioned over a period of time by carpenters of different generations and skillsets. The books are stacked haphazardly into the gaps, no wiggle room, packed in with such vigour it'd be a strain to yank one out. A rickety ladder wobbles on its run, for those wanting to risk reaching any top-shelf tomes. On the only book-free wall is a massive mirror, which has the power to multiply the scale of the room tenfold. It's the only mirror in the house Ouse can tolerate, because it amplifies people's accomplishments rather than their insecurities.

Ouse presents Firth to Muckle Flugga's huge array of books, introducing him with a cordial bow. Firth, a visitant painter, kneels before the vast gallery of words and recites a few lines of dreich verse (secretly his own, for in truth it's all he kens off by heart despite knowing that any writer of merit should be able to recite at least five classic poems at the drop of hat).

Ouse goes on to explain that the number of books fluctuates as he picks up new ones from lodgers or second-hand at the market. Firth, understanding fine well how the books grow in number, is curious about how the collection might shrink in size. Ouse unriddles that particular conundrum by divulging how some of the books end up in the fire or at the bottom of the sea if he leaves them lying around. It becomes apparent that The Father is not only a reluctant reader but sees reading as a form of intellectual bragging, something he has a proclivity for putting a stop to. Though the notion of burning books strikes Firth as fascistic, he'd fathom The Father's destructive wrath comes more from a hostile self-doubt. Firth, being a people person, or a people player, is already deliberating how to work this to his advantage.

He barbequed my Byron when I went skinny-dipping, Ouse laments. *I think he knew.*

Knew what? Firth probes.

About the decadence, how it spoke to me. Ouse confesses this with a sad sincerity that makes Firth conscious of the shame in Ouse that The Father draws out.

I've been to city libraries with fewer books than this, Firth remarks, celebratory in tone, by way of an upbeat offering. *Then again, you're a bit more in need of entertainment, I hope you don't mind me saying?*

Say what you like. It doesn't mean I'll agree, Ouse snaps back.

Canny. You'd make a good journalist.

Ouse's memory is triggered by this, and he breaks some bad news. *The newspapers come weeks late here on Muckle Flugga, and the letters don't come at all . . . not unless I fetch 'em. So if you do happen to need mail then . . .*

No mail, Firth interjects with a chilling certainty, then changes the subject. *I wouldn't have thought a few families of keepers could have accumulated this many books?*

Oh they didn't. These are mostly from when they decommissioned the library on Unst. It's all the cast-offs from when the big library on the mainland swallowed up our little library. Doomed books.

So these are your wee rescuees? Firth suggests.

Ouse beams in delight, having thought the books more hostages than rescuees, now warmed by this more kindly notion. *Most are damaged or have pages missing, but the majority of any good story is enough for me. Then there's the poor sparrows no-one took out. Lots of odd topics and local authors keen to see their work in print. I saved them from cremation.*

Perhaps you shouldn't have, Firth mumbles mockingly before changing tack. *But why did The Father let you take in such a ginormous cache of books if he hates all literature?*

Ouse likes the way Firth brands his books as 'literature' and so finds himself more forthcoming than he intended in reply. *He didn't. It was The Mother, and the other keepers. The Father was easier to persuade back then. The Mother even had books of her own before these all arrived. The most special ones I keep . . . somewhere else.*

Sounds secretive?

Not secret, just safe, Ouse reports, clasping himself for comfort.

What would you say the most special one is? Firth prompts, a little begging.

66

The Mother didn't care for the books about family life and cookery the KLAMS issued all the keepers' wives. She loved stories, Ouse declares proudly, ignoring the question at hand. He goes on to explain how The Mother would often give hilarious recitals to everyone's delight, especially The Father, who laughed the most although he now has a tendency to deny this. Ouse suggests The Father would rather forget the sound of laughter altogether, which causes such upset in Firth he, too, offers up personal information he'd promised himself to always hold back. That being that his own mother's laughter is the thing he misses most about her, and was his favourite sound in all the world.

Ouse, appeased, steers them back to the library, avoiding eye contact with Firth at all costs, as he believes this better for the books. Ouse wishes people's eyes were fastened on with pins and could be removed for all important conversations. No decoration, just mind's melding together, preening each other. People think it's the other way round, that intense connection in the eyes hones concentration, but that's poppycock in Ouse's opinion. The iris, that pigmented rapscallion, with all its lights and darks, is a glassy globe designed to bewitch. Eyes colliding whisk up all manner of distractions. What do people expect when reaching so deeply inside of each other? When forced to stare someone in the eyes while talking Ouse will always lose his way. In fact, he makes a point of it.

As Ouse tells the full story of how he saved this crop of orphaned tomes – which involves a rusty wheelbarrow, a cherry Bakewell tart and a bellicose crow – he sees his plan working. Firth begins nimbly reaching high and low, exploring the range of literature on offer – reference journals, encyclopaedias, academic and religious texts, treatises, fairy-tales, magazines, out-of-date maps, volumes of poetry, cookbooks, instruction manuals, fantasy, thrillers, dramas,

67

aphorisms and about every which other type of read a scribe had rite to write.

As Firth parses the shelves, Ouse notices his painted nails, his shiny rings and the thin pearls bedecking his neckline. They don't seem to fit with his body, these accoutrements – they hang off him like theatre props, and the brightness of the paint and stones carry something vulgar. For that, Ouse admirers him greatly – the perseverance it must have taken to continue to don them despite the gawky nature of the way he wears them.

I've buried the Walter Scott under the shed in a turnip sack, Ouse whispers, hoping Firth won't hear it. *The Mother made a joke about doing that the day before she died. I took it to oath.*

Ouse turns around to see Firth instead engrossed by the murder mystery section, his least favourite genre. Content that the books are being rightly admired though, he takes a first full gawp at Firth's face – jaggy and angular, a skull skilfully skinned, no excess. He's entranced by how peaceful it feels to glance over him compared to strangers in the street. The stressfulness of Firth's frantic energy has lifted since they entered this room, as Ouse had suspected it might.

Firth, too, has been admiring Ouse as he narrates the lore of the library – his careful movements, the deliberateness in his action. So forensic, so superior to his own flailing and flossing. Whilst he aims to be taken as quicksilver in his demeanour, what he undoubtably delivers is the galloping flappery of an upstart crow. He wishes he could move like Ouse does, gliding, buoyant yet adorably aloof.

Firth revels in the sound of Ouse's name, repeating it in his mind whilst letting his fingers play the top of the books like piano keys. It occurs to Firth that Ouse exudes more purpose dusting down a bookshelf than he summoned pleading with himself for his own life. He will have to hide from Ouse that he's spent the majority of the last few years surrounded by facetious men that take great pride in pointing out other people's weaknesses. All these thoughts spiralling around his head, Firth can't help but break the silence once again, embarking on a philosophical conversation about how humbling it is to be surrounded by more words than any one person is capable of consuming in their lifetime. Some people panic when met with their limits; Firth feels safe.

Ouse eagerly reminds him that if he does borrow books not to flaunt them in front of The Father. Ouse can't help but vaunt about how much time he spends in the library, and brags that he'd rather be locked in this library than any other room on earth; though admits he's light on stamps in his passport.

What Ouse doesn't admit is that he still loses whole afternoons examining these books: admiring their bindings; stroking the cloth covers; fingering the embossed lettering; running the silk ribbon page-placers across his skin; testing the sheen of the reflective lettering and searching for glisten. He has sniffed every page whilst contemplating what words were like when there were fewer letters in the alphabet. In here, he feels boundless, he touches the void and kisses favourite passages in moments of elation. He reveals to Firth that he suspects an old Norse god has taken lodgings in this library, assuming the mantle of Muckle Flugga's librarian. Someone has been moving books around in the depth of night, and Ouse deems this the only rational explanation. This is something he's only ever discussed with Figgie or RLS – he feels careless for having given it to Firth so quickly, but not in any way remorseful.

To showboat his knowledge, Firth cumbersomely recounts a tale he's heard about the great librarian of Alexandria – a scroll keeper who took his own life when his eyesight went, failing to comprehend the point of living without the ability to read. Ouse, finding himself susceptible to Firth's obvious grandstanding, unpacks a fact and then a question – a classic left-right combo honed on the playground to escape many a thumping. In this case it's a tactic deployed to prevent himself divulging any further secrets.

There's more fairies in a peat bog than any other type of bog, Ouse bugles. To avoid a response, and keen to get on, he follows up, *What do you think happens when you die?*

Firth, still thrown by the comment about fairies, is stunned by the forwardness of the ensuing question. He reroutes his cerebral network to address this query, one which he's better equipped to handle. *I'm agnostic, and a cynic, so the wrong person to ask if you're looking for puffiness or religious drivel.*

I'm looking for neither, Ouse responds sharply, offering Firth the conversational in he's already taking.

Likely life just leaves us, abandons our fleshy matter, we rot, and we spoil. We're maggot food in the making –recycled into the soil finally doing some earthly good. Other than that, it simply stops. Nothing more than a big old end of the line STOP. You can stick your judgement day scare tactics up yer arse, your life of pious servitude, daily offerings and bogus confessions, screw 'em! Get them tae flying fuck! Firth halts himself here feeling loutish, though his mind steamrollers on.

That does sound peaceful. So you're a romantic?

Flabbergasted by this response, Firth grins like a big dippy dodo; this is the second time Ouse has used the word romantic in an askew manner. Little does Firth know, Ouse considers himself a student of romance who's learning to find many typically odd things romantic, including: pigeons, inappropriate laughter, class revolt, and list-making. Firth points to Ouse and implores his answer to the very same question.

70

I think readers turn into characters from the stories they loved and listeners become sheet music for songs. The sea, naturally, takes payment from all of us.

Just like that! How did you manage such an incredibly neat answer? Firth queries, still dumbstruck from the life-stopping-sounding-peaceful comment.

I've been thinking about death, hoping someone would ask. My main worry is who would take care of the books and the animals.

Firth appears as bamboozled as Ouse hoped and he gestures (by putting on his shoes again) that it's time to leave the library and head to Firth's digs in the bothy.

But what about that little door at the other end of the room? Firth enquires, now more than a little bashful because he didn't take off his boots and has clomped dirty footprints over the rug he was only just adoring.

Ouse had closed the door to this space as soon as he noticed it left open. Unbeknown to him, Firth had already caught a clandestine glance inside where he spotted what appeared to be wool, reams of paper, tools, trinkets, and plenty of other trumpery. It looked a bit of a mess to Firth and made him feel at home. Ouse ignores the comment about the little door and ushers Firth out with a lessened lilt to his voice, so Firth knows he's serious.

Upon leaving the library, Firth is immediately both jealous and pitying of Ouse's view of things, how he sees Muckle Flugga as the centre of the world. He wants to teach him about life on a bigger scale yet feels supremely smug for feeling that way. As they plod across the lawn, both boys can't shake the notion that they gave a little too much to each other in those hot moments. At the same time, it suddenly occurs to Firth that this island-noodle might have read more books than he has. He doesn't talk the talk, hasn't

71

intellectually jousted with city flâneurs, quaffed free book-launch champagne served in scandalously shaped flutes, or convinced everyone he's worthy of the fuss, but he has devoured the vast majority of that hefty library. Firth doesn't know how to feel about all that so just keeps trudging on.

A tad regretful now, Ouse announces the raspberries they pass as he plucks one up from the undergrowth and gobbles it without offering any to their visitor; something he'd never normally do.

Wild raspberries grow here? Firth cries, already imagining how the juice might delight a parched mouth but not tarrying to take one on account of the sudden cold. Firth is, once again, bewildered by the swiftness of the change in the weather here. The rain is porridging the soil as shapes like spider's webs emerge in the puddles from the wind gusting over them. When they went into the library it was spring-like; now the whole island appears lost within a soggy gauze. Firth attempts to express his disbelief at the sudden shift in the weather but the sentence fails to form on his cold-crippled tongue.

Ouse pulls in close to Firth's ear to ensure his words aren't lost to the sky's rancour: *Wild? I suppose we all are up here.* Firth smells the aroma of raspberry on Ouse's breath and feels the warmth of the words tingle down his neck. He watches Ouse march ahead and ponders where he gets it from, such sweet and curious surety. Catching himself falling behind, Firth canters off again, warming his fingers on his belly as he goes.

Ouse, suddenly conscious of time passing, stops abruptly and announces the induction tour over.

Wait, Firth squeals, his hands in the air as if facing down the barrel of a gun. *I know we've only just met, but I feel like there's something that connects us.*

Perhaps it's the way we die? Ouse responds coolly, before running

72

off at great pace. As he does, he drifts into a premonition that soon they're going to have the type of night that is at once both too much and not nearly enough.

Firth, genuinely boosted by the encounter, is more than aware his emotional extremities are, at this point, only half-truths he's willing into existence. At best hyper-inflated, at worst cruelly manipulative. Though he re-enters the bothy spryly, a feeling of foreboding soon follows when the door thumps closed, as if the weight of all the anchors lost at sea were descending down upon him.

Ouse has taken too long with Firth, he's played up when challenged and divulged deep truths he never meant to. Worst of all, he's late. The Father is calling with rage in his voice; eyes like flags on fire.

ELEVEN

The Father has never known Ouse to take so long on an induction. He's known Ouse to take too long, but never this long. Ouse will have to be punished. What's more, The Father will need to keep a closer eye on his interactions with that shagsack of a lodger. He can think of at least five shitty things Ouse should have been doing before dinner instead of daisying around with that gadding wankstain.

• • •

Firth plunges into another bath; he loves a bath. The bath is serene; it soothes the climate of his ungirt mind. This threshold of a space invokes cleansing thoughts in him. Coevally, Firth knows fine well its tranquillity is not to be trusted. He is not the unencumbered great thinker he canonises himself for being in the hot water throne. The bath's tonics don't last beyond the soak; they masquerade as a permanent fix but are, in fact, ephemeral as the soapy bubbles. He mustn't forget he is a fire ravaging the leafy gardens of everyone he loves.

• • •

Ouse knows The Father treats his heart like the sacrificial pawn in a game of chess, where the loss of one piece is of little consequence in a greater battle. Anyone who has no joy in the game shouldn't be playing when the consequences are so grave; then again, that steel is what makes for a skilled player. Ouse thinks on rules and risks until the questions in his mind become so all-consuming he's up on his feet and thermalling the room.

• • •

The Father has taken a belt buckle to Ouse a fair few times, and once a hot kettle – but not for a while, and never at full wallop, because it hurts him more than it hurts Ouse. He's sure of that, even if Ouse doubts it. So he stopped and made a joke of it, allowed Ouse to sear his seeping wounds with pride in the belly. *You never wallow in it*, he assured Ouse one night after a beating, *you wailed like a jessie but never griped on about it after. That's good*, he said to him, *that's brave*. The Father could be warm like that. It's hard for him and he does wish he could do more of it, but there's only so much; there's only ever so much. He's obliterated less books than Ouse thinks, there's a few stowed away he might well gie him back. He is, after all, his father.

• • •

Firth has no option but atheism. He is unworthy of the affections of the rascals of humanity, never mind the do-gooder godly types. Funny how there's so few people in his life capable of understanding his case for unhappiness – to some poor fuckers he's a man of enviable talents; Edinburgh's primo drunken peacock. It would seem to most a rash decision, wasteful even. *But he's so charming* some would say as if a defence for villainy, as if a defence for anything. None of them would love him if they knew the extent of it, just how far he had been willing to go to win. There is a small bubble of air inside of him, growing and growing, vindictively consuming all his precious emptiness. It's pernicious, and he's determined to stop it before it bursts from his chest and injures those around him; a brave soldier falling on a live grenade.

• • •

Ouse is very rarely angry or jealous, those feelings just don't fit him, and yet he tries to understand The Father's ire, why he's hoarding all that soot and grime. What a privilege to be able to just get on with living after each skirmish. He should be thankful, he is thankful – thankful to make a nonsense of the business of self-sabotage. The Father to him is a wild dog biting out at every friendly hand come to pet him. Ouse is aware The Father hasn't had loving in an aeon but will never broach this topic, because just as The Mother is the thing that binds them, so too does her absence raze them.

• • •

The Father is terrible to Ouse in front of company, he can't help it, it's too easy. He shouldn't goad but he does and he goads good. He wants Ouse to stand up for himself, he'll need that pluck in the years to come. He's fast and getting stronger, he'll give him that, but not as clever as he thinks he is, and prone to blubbering. It's not his place to cry, crying's done. Crying's no good for facing down terror. That's The Mother in him. That's her gentleness.

• • •

76

Firth will get on with living for the here and now, for a few weeks, for this slice of summer. Study, sketch, paint the birds. Enjoy the same nature they bask in. Take what joy he can from the land-scape and the weather. No matter how many times he puts this task through the wringer, it always comes out kosher. He'll stop thinking beyond this trip, make this finite existence as enriching as possible: fulfil his promise, then leave this world humbly on his own terms.

• • •

Ouse has hope for The Father, who always says sorry and really does mean it. He could never hate him as much The Father hates himself. The Father is pained by his missing of The Mother, he is vandalised by grief. It's ugly as mould spreading over good wood, yet Ouse can't help but find some solace in it, knowing his pain is born from a love for The Mother, a violent longing for her. And The Father could be darling, at times. In the mornings when there's jam on the table and crumbs on his beard and they laugh together as The Father mimics a rare birdsong and Ouse learns where he first heard it and for how long he's carried the tune.

• • •

The Father can't stand it when Ouse apologises without a fight, denying him the right to set the matter straight. It's weak and the people round here will see it as an invitation to walk all over him.

• • •

Firth hears The Father shouting at Ouse, not the exact words but a furore nonetheless. Trust the one sound that seems capable of penetrating the storm's storminess to be mean and rabid. He hopes it's not his fault. Ouse's upset pierces him, fishbones in the gums, powdered glass underfoot. The bath water is freezing now, his body goose-pimpled. How long has he been in here? Popping the plug, he vows to try and make Ouse's life a little better. Just a scintilla, just a speck. The Father is not to be provoked, menacing at best, malicious at worst.

• • •

Ouse has learned to feel nothing for being on the receiving end of The Father's bile; like when his leg's gone dead and he bites it to check. He's unsure why today is different; he thinks of Firth. The weeping is common, it's Ouse's loudest sound – a terrifyingly true release. It's in these moments dear RLS comes forth. How grateful he is for RLS watching over him – stroking his hair as they lie face down on a rug of Ouse's making.

• • •

Fists of The Father keep banging on the cupboards and counter-tops. His violence echoes through the walls and into the stone floors. The Father would have normally simmered down by now, becoming contrite, but there's a bigger flame behind his eyelids than usual; an inferno.

• • •

Firth watches a spider's web on the skylight quivering – vile vibrations get everywhere. Firth crutches down into a silent arc vowing not to speak again until spoken to.

• • •

What a mess, Ouse apologises over and over, releasing his upset in repetition until it's gone.

• • •

Ungrateful shitehawk!
This is all for you.
Solid job. Proper purpose.
Served up on a silver platter.
Too fucking good for it are ye!
You! YOU! I don't think so.

I'm sorry.
I'm sorry.
I'm so so sorry.

You better man up.
Better get yer arse in gear.
You think that's what The Mother would have wanted?
Nae chance. Nut.
Are you listening through there?

* thump * thump * thump *

Oh RLS.
I'm sorry. I'm so SO sorry.

* thump * thump * thump *

SAW-WAY! SAAAAW-WAY!
Why are you always fucking apologising?
Fucking baby!
I was going to take you to the mainland tomorrow,
I hud a treat in mind.
But no anymore. Hear that. You've fucking lost it.

Now fetch that fucker for dinner!

TWELVE

The short walk from the bothy to the kitchen is illuminated by water. A colossal moon dominates the sky, bouncing light around like a brute – the cove, the pond, puddles, raindrops, anything reflective amplifies its glow. A peat pit is burning on the cliff edge; the smoke comes thick and billowing until hitting the wind and thinning out, fleeing like spirits from an open grave.

If he's frugal, Firth has enough provisions in the bothy's cupboards to see him through the first week of meals, but the 'welcome supper' is part of the package, a compulsory activity, the weight of which bullies his brow. Although being cooked for is a luxury, he'd happily duck out of it, especially given The Father's screaming is still hissing in his ears.

The row sent The Father up to the lighthouse's gallery deck for several hours to continue blowing off steam. And for the first time Firth witnessed the great light prowling over the surface of the ocean, briefly mistaking it for an alien invasion. Soon after, he heard The Father yelling trash talk into the abyss, all sorts of obscenities. Whereas this would have been gold dust for Firth the writer, it serves little purpose to a doomed man at this late juncture.

Before entering the kitchen, Firth gulps back a few bulbs of breath, feels it gloop inside him and become the custard of courage. Ouse is alone in the room, cooking by the stove, humming, stirring pots, appearing blissful. Firth's relieved by the sight and wonders whether he mistook the severity of what he overheard. He expected Ouse to be a red-eyed ball of nerves. It strikes Firth that it's perfectly possible such fierce fights are by the by to these island dwellers.

Although the table is long enough to host a feast for twenty, there are just four solitary seats laid out. The room is lit by a couple of ornate multi-armed candleholders. He's brought a bottle of wine, with the stopper in it, one glass down – a big swig of something to steady the nerves was simply unavoidable. Having added a touch of water to it, he's hoping it still appears full, if handled right.

For the artist: bread to break! Ouse turns to Firth and thrusts a wooden board into his hands with three fat steaming boules on it – salt flaked, pretty and fragrant as a French cake.

You made these?

Oh yes, there's no bakeries here. Besides, The Father reckons my bread's the best. It's The Mother's old recipe, so a bit like spending time together, he adds softly. *The secret's in using seawater sieved to the right weight, but you didn't hear that from me.*

Mum's the word! Firth smiles, then sinks with the notion that they're just a couple of motherless bairns. The dolorous thought doesn't last long as the aroma of Ouse's cooking enters his nostrils. Ouse, perceptive as ever, senses his brio.

That'll be the Cullen Skink – the creaminess of it calls out to kindred spirits. It's a mainland dish but we add our own twist – a Muckle Flugga mix.

Firth scans the room for signs of The Father, conscious of how his presence might tailor their chat going forth. Approaching Ouse with some degree of suaveness, Firth decides to seek assurances. *Is The Father joining?* he enquires, chancing now that The Father might well be suppering in his room after running his throat raw.

I'm no sure about 'joining', but I'll be eating ma fill if that's alright by you?! The Father barks, taking everyone by surprise. Firth, attempting

82

to cover his shock, lunges at The Father, pushing the wine bottle into his hand at an advantageous tilt. He then, with a cough, remarks steadily as he can, *Didn't see you come in. This is for you.*

Aw, so you're secretly a woman? The Father chides, shoving the wine aside dismissively then pouring himself a hefty glass of whisky. *It'll take a measure and a half tae get through this stramash right enough*, he mumbles to himself.

To defuse the tension, Firth sits down and begins sucking up to The Father – pandering is, after all, one of his most adroitly employed social skills.

The isolation of this place is so inspiring. It's a remarkable thing to live at such extremity. Firth's own stomach jolts at the insipidness of this remark.

You like isolation, di yi? The Father extends his arms out wide like a muscle-ripped Christ, then laughs all crooked. *Ha! After a sunless winter o'drenching upon drenching this hunk o'earth will make a mockery of yer inn-spur-ation.*

Firth changes tack, deciding The Father is more than likely looking for him to give as good as he gets. He's met many terrible fathers in his time, thrice as sharp as this one, though perhaps not as strong or as ruggedly good-looking.

I'll have you know I spent a two-month stint in a haunted tower in Northern Ireland. In the dead of winter. A hot brick and my dressing gown for company, Firth brags.

Did ye aye!? This tower on an island marooned in by world's most vicious sea, wiz it? Staring off into a void so dark aw the candles in the Caledonia couldnae carve a tunnel through it?

Well, no. But it was coastal. And it did have a dungeon! Firth's aware how desperate that sounds but there's no way back.

Coastal, he says. Coastal. If only the thoosands who died oot there could have seen the coast again. By the end of this statement The Father is on his feet and appears to have grown taller, cobwebs trembling in his shock of hair.

Well, I think it sounds magical! Dungeon dwelling, Ouse interjects, moving one of the circular boules onto each of their plates. With everyone plated up, Ouse then splats a fresh candle into the first of the bunch to have become a slosh-pile. Wax blobs on the rim of the candelabra and drips down its stem, which is near disappearing under the bulk of the candles that came before.

The Father makes a dismissive noise and slurps his whisky as delicately as a royal sips tea –cacophonous yet tidy, and ridiculous enough that Firth has to suppress his laughter. With everyone seated at the table – Firth resenting not having been offered whisky or wine or both – The Father gestures for him to begin.

Eat! he growls.

Yes, please, eat, Ouse repeats.

The Father stabs irritably at a plate of sharing veg in the middle of the table. Firth snaps up two carrots and a whole ginger root, making murmurs of contentment at their firmness on his fork. Ouse could be accused of many things, but not waterlogging the veg, no not that.

In front of Firth sits a whole boule, about sizes with a turnip, but nothing else – no butter, no cutlery, no fishy soup anywhere on the table. Flummoxed as he is, he feels the anticipation of kicking off the eating. The Father, braced like a martyr about to have his fingernails vindictively removed, soon looks like he's going to take a bite out of Firth if he doesn't get going.

Firth wonders whether he's expected to fire into the loaf with his bare hands – Ouse did, after all, mention breaking bread. Perhaps it's a ritual, Firth quizzes to himself; break the bread before the meal then the skink comes out, an island bread-breaking ceremony.

Cementing that premise, he decides that, yes, this must be some skewed biblically inspired ceremonial. And so he lifts up the great boule like a baby lamb and bites into its belly. As soon as his teeth sink in, he realises the grave error of his actions. Scorching hot soup comes gushing out the rupture, slopping across the table and over his lap. Panicked, he grabs the butter bowl and lets the remainder of the creamy soup stream into it, the liquid quickly encircling the golden knob then taking it captive.

Firth bites his tongue trying not to scream from the searing pain of the scolding liquid, which has found its way to his crotch. The Father howls in laughter, squirting whisky out his nostril and down his woolly jumper.

Firth now sees that the boule, having had the soft bready centre pulled out of it, has been filled with soup and turned into a bowl. An edible bowl! The top fastened back on concealing the whole sly transformation. He debates if this is some sort of prank or initiation – serving up soup as subterfuge.

Ouse relents and comes to Firth's aid, repairing the puncture in his boule with a clump of doughy middle and wiping what spill he can from the table. Firth fumbles frantically, trying to neaten up the chaos with his bare hands. Ouse stops him with a clutch and another jolt of electricity – more minnow-sized this time – courses up Firth's wrist as he continues to apologise.

Don't worry about the mess, Ouse whispers reassuringly, gesturing to get Firth another ladle full of soup. Firth protests and continues to eat his Cullen Skink from the overflowing butter bowl – the hot liquid having dissolved a sizeable slab of butter into its already rich base. The Father, clearly irritated by Ouse's attentiveness to their lodger, sets about eating his own meal at an increasingly disruptive volume.

At least your kind of clumsy has panache, Ouse offers. This irks The Father further and spurs him into action.

Don't imagine you had many rules growing up? The Father jibes haughtily in a caustic conversational shift. *Lighthouse keepers, we follow rules. A code. To man a lighthouse takes military precision. Dawn rises, slogs through sleepless nights, walking the tightrope, burning for it. There's nae room for weakness, for laziness, when death awaits any opening.*

Firth begins readying a genuine, encouraging remark, but holds it back so as not to be so crawling when clearly he's being roasted. The Father, not happy with the failure of his words to make an impact, swigs back more whisky, which is already taking effect, and decides to play up to the role of host in order to give the boy a good, stiff schooling. Alongside that, The Father takes a certain pride in regaling guests with the braveries and vagaries of lighthouse keeping, even if he has to shove it down their prissy little throats.

They thought it was hopeless to try and build a lighthouse aw the way up here, then that shambolic Crimean War came crunching in and the navy's ships needed to take this passage. And that wiz that, The Impossible Lighthouse made possible – born fur war, it huznae stopped battling since.

Have you heard it said that lighthouses are the signposts of the sea? Ouse remarks, trying to support The Father in his sermonising. *Lampposts of the whale road. You know it was streetlight designers that came up with the idea for our modern Scottish lighthouse.*

Naw, naw, that's no strictly true! The Father petulantly squabbles. *If you're going to tell it, tell it right. The Lighthouse Stevensons were mare than the cronies of lamp designers turning their honds to lighthooses. They were pioneers, naw, they were saviours!*

From what Firth can garner – realising how little he knows about this stuff – a lighthouse can either illuminate rocks to be avoided, on which it's likely sitting, or guide a ship to safety.

Given his soapbox, The Father is relaxing, and they all feel easier for it. *Ouse, a little whisky over here*, The Father calls, pointing to Firth's deliberately empty glass. Ouse fills Firth's tumbler full of whisky, having now received the nod, and he beams in appreciation.

Get yer laughing gear roond that! The Father spits at Firth, who takes the mucklest of gulps to prove his grit. In the talk that follows, Firth begins to taste what it feels like to have The Father enamoured by your presence. He likes it, savours the triumph of it. When chipper, The Father's intoxicating company, a rare storyteller. Although Firth hazards a guess that some of his best lines are well-rehearsed, landing on Ouse's ears for the hundredth (perhaps the thousandth) time. This old battle-worn crusader has charisma, Firth can't dispute that. And come to think of it, Firth fathoms, he's likely not that old either – he's looking ever better from behind the amber blinkers. He'd face-swap with him if offered, at his age, perhaps even now.

The Father flings too much salt on his supper, even though he's already full of it, caked in flakes of the sea. Ouse thinks that his body needs it now, craves it like a big tuna fish – it keeps him quick-witted, despite his best efforts to flood his brain with grog. Once, when younger, Ouse snuck into The Father's bedroom at night and sprinkled salt on his feet and watched it dissolve into his skin. The Mother woke, smiled, then returned to her dream, muttering as she drifted: *Save a little for me, honeyheart.*

Although the soup is delicious, a flume of flavour, Firth doesn't dare praise it. To praise the soup would only draw attention to him

87

having melted their butter ration whilst making a goofball mess of dinner. What he does observe is that The Father doesn't savour, he snaffles and scoffs. And Ouse, despite his more delicate deportment, is exactly the same.

Firth has an ostentatious manner of eating he's copied off the city's New Town snobs – specimens he's resentfully kowtowed to in order to gain social standing. People around whom he'd learned never to talk about money worries, definitely not the splitting of a bill – those with heaps of cutter consider such matters trivial at best and vulgar near always. *If you have to check who's picking up the tab you shouldn't be wielding the silverware*, a more sympathetic friend had told him. Around a glut of Edinburgh's oak dining tables Firth had learned to clean the muck out his accent, soften the sharpness of his vowels and reinhabit missing consonants. As far as he could tell, top-tier dinner party tactics involve: never turning up hungry; drowning each mouthful in booze; and always leaving enough food on the plate to call into question the integrity of the meal. Adding to that, social climbers like himself were tasked with being the most outlandishly entertaining; after all, they were the most disposable pieces on account of their inability to host.

Firth quickly realises the subtleties of his fine-dining credo are best left at the door on Muckle Flugga, and what a bloody relief. He is even more relieved to get a good slurp of whisky down him, noticing Ouse takes none for himself. The sweet fires of the whisky fizz upon his lips then blast from his tongue like a treacle rocket. He batters straight in for another glug, The Father seeming to sanction his thirst with a top-up. Firth, like The Father, is much more at home in the company of booze – it worries him immensely, but only the following morning. He's labelled his penchant for the sauce just one more indicator of the slow puncture inside.

The dining table of Muckle Flugga has rarely seen The Father and Ouse so invested in the outcome of a meal with a lodger. Each of them feels something of great import at stake, each of them suppressing a fear or vulnerability, a frustration or anger, in their own unique way. Firth is turning his charms to The Father, putting his kitbag of people-pleasing skills into full effect in order to implore the keeper towards him. Ouse is mediating with every word and every movement, nuanced and slight so as no-one detects his manoeuvres. A small tickle on his chin from an owl feather he carries, whilst taking dishes up to the sink, calms his nerves. The Father, now feeling in charge of the situation, is desperately trying to maintain his dominance over the room whilst not appearing fussed for doing so.

See Ouse here earns a little pocket money knitting jumpers, scarves, tablecloths, all yer girly bits, but he'll be taking over Muckle Flugga when the sea claims me, or ma body buckles. He's like The Mother was, soft enough to be hooked and used for fish bait. But dinnae fash, a couple more coats of grease and I'll gie them a laddie to be reckoned with.

Firth notices Ouse grow distant as The Father takes off on this particular rant. His quiet, attentive, admiring mien fractures.

Wee sleeve puller, eh! The Father ridicules, mimicking the act. *Whit's it that lad at school called ye? Och, I cannae mind. Point is, we made a fair enough keeper of The Mother, despite aw that – her being a gown-wearing city rat I mean. Trained her maeself, first female keeper in Scotland. Hud to be done, hud ti be.*

Course, she and the other keepers did half the work, at half the welly ah did, The Father roosters on. *But that was always the plan. Get the KLAMS off oor backs. Get 'em tae fuck. Now I've got Ouse as my trainee, for my sins. For my sins, is it no!?* The Father laughing at this point because the boy in him, then trucking sternly into the story that follows.

Jesus joke, thinks Firth, the ogre did nowt but growl and grumble this afternoon, a few whiskies in and he's a bloody raconteur.

The KLAMS huvnae inspected since The Mother died, The Father brags hauntingly, *they might be snooping, but they're no coming up here in a hurry. Their ships leave Leith but never get as far as Lerwick. We've a good thing now, a twisted truce. That's the silver lining that comes with reeking o'death, folk avoid you, their sensitive snouts cannae handle grief's punchiness.*

They ken fine well we're no gonnae let any starched-collared welt tell us what's what up here. The new breed, the poll-it-ical breed, they don't know their elbows from their arseholes when it comes to manning a lighthouse. But they'll tell us how to 'operate more efficiently'. They'll tell us! Will they fuck. Tailcoat goons! We're just barry by ourselves, and that's what she would huv wanted, The Mother. I can handle this beast solo – youngest Principal Keeper in the service, and the best. Ouse'll huv to marry right enough, and I'll train 'em up together, eh laddie, keep this ship on course. We'll see to that, aye, we'll see to that.

And with the KLAMS taken care of, The Father shoves the remainder of the skink-soggy bread boule into his mouth, squeezing its fat edges to hoist it all in at once.

Firth, feeling brazen and gooey from the whisky, finds himself talking tauntingly. *Seems like you've got it all figured out, but what I'm curious about is what Ouse wants for his own future?*

The Father stops chewing – wasps throng into his eyes, stingers at the ready. A sharp, ringing sound invades Firth's ear. He has relaxed too much into the room; the generous measures of whisky have caused him to forget his surrounds, who he's dealing with. After a couple of hopeful seconds, Firth thinks he might just have got away with it – that they're going to collectively move past his remark for the common good. Alack no, it appears The Father was simply too enraged to speak.

You're a bit of a dandy, aren't you? Likely straight fae the nanny's tit and into a big boarding school before pansying off to yer fancy college, where you and a squad of fuckwits covered your cocks in clay and called it art. Well, you'll need to keep that shite in check up here if you're not wanting swept away in the night.

As the violence in The Father becomes palpable, Firth scrambles to retain his cool – questioning whether that was a genuine death threat. Playing to the advantage of his own death wish, Firth lets the booze do the talking.

I actually come from working-class stock, though I've drifted up a bit with the . . .

And what of God? The Father booms. *WHAT OF GOD?*

Well, I'm an atheist, or maybe it's better to say I'm agnostic, but that's doesn't mean I don't value the religious texts as stellar stories. I've read them all, and . . .

FAITHLESS. Faithless. And too smug to admit it! The Father bellows back, snatching the whisky away from Firth and pouring what's left into his own glass.

Had the local congregation been present, they might well have claimed this to be hypocritical of The Father, for he commonly misquotes the bible and has made no effort to attend church in many months. Attempting to defend his non-attendance to a local busybody, The Father claimed he values religion immeasurably but has no time for those who mistreat and monetise it – referring in this case to their minister, rumoured to be both a lech and a swindler.

In the moment before Firth responds to The Father's uproarious reaction to his remarks, the candles all flicker in sync. This causes first a bolt of darkness then a shot of light. Ouse is nervously

91

preparing a plan for if the situation escalates, crestfallen at feeling unable to come to Firth's aid more immediately. The Father is entirely consumed by controlling his rage, whilst Firth is desperately searching inside himself in the hope his notable 'silver tongue' might be able to deliver a way out of this debacle.

I believe in what you do here, Firth begins with a stilling sincerity. *I believe that providing light for the lost is a noble calling. Of more value than anything I've ever done, or ever will do.*

A former fishwife, my mum became a candlemaker – the only veritable candlemaker on Candlemaker Row. She also made light to rally the darkness, to let people know there are safe havens waiting for them. Every night she lit a wick for someone's safe return. All over the city, her candles in windows helped guide the way home.

She never let the flame in our own front room go out, day or night, summer or winter, it was there taking vigil, keeping watch. She too was a purveyor of light, by which I mean hope.

The Father takes a breathy moment, clenches his fist into the shape of a child's skull, then opens it up – tipping some whisky back into Firth's glass without looking at him. He beckons Ouse closer and pours him another thimbleful. Without a word spoken the glasses are raised and The Father speaks. *Sounds a good woman, yer mother. I'll wet my lips to that.*

Ouse smiles contentedly, pulling his chair from the server's side into the middle mix, a sort of lit manner in his eyes that Firth can't quite read. Though he does think it's funny how the most interesting people in the room are commonly forced into being the quietest.

The Father gestures out the window with his still-raised glass as if assembling the troops. *That's one of the most brutal shipping lanes in the world. Busy by day, busier by night. Food, wood, animals, humans, medicine, guns, they're moving it aw through there. The cargo they're keeping a check on, the creatures that move it they couldn't give a flying fuck about. That's up to us.*

Though Firth has something to add to this, a cousin who perished needlessly in a shipwreck, he thinks better of it and fills his face with whisky to dam the words climbing out of him. The Father is talking slower and fuller now, his timbre has changed, so that each sentence feels totemic and true. Firth can't help but be enthralled, though he hates himself for it.

The Father picks up the candelabra and shoves it out in front of him like a burning club from yesteryear. *There's serrated rocks all around this coast. If it's night and a ship sidles into that passing, or is shoved in by the tide, me and this light are its only chance of survival. If my light fails, or I lose them,* The Father suddenly blows all the candles out with a great puff that sprays wax over both Firth and Ouse, *they wreck themselves and everybody dies. More bairns whose daddies dinnae come back.*

Rocks as sharp as werewolf fangs, Ouse seasons in, making fangs with his hands.

Whirlpools that could suck doon a fleet in the time it takes you to shit yer pants, The Father furthers.

The beast is always feeding, Ouse laments.

By this point Firth resembles the only audience member sitting in the front row of a father-and-son stage show. When it comes time for The Father to take back over the leading role, Ouse returns to the top of the table, seated in what would be the side stalls.

Whoooooosh! The Father gusts. *Seven thousand pounds of pressure per square foot.*

The boat cracks in two down the bottom of a swell it's not climbing out of.

The sea muddies over its tracks the moment it lays them. It's always shape-shifting, be certain of that.

Every day, every night, I'm looking for danger with my light, stalking it, hunting it. It's no about winning, that's impossible, it's about bettering the odds.

Soon as they're in peril and my light's come to their aid, well, from that point on I'm co-captaining that ship. And ye better believe I take that seriously. If it sinks, a bit of me goes doon with it. Some people 'hink Muckle Flugga is manned by the spirit of a deid keeper who fed himself to the flame after the storm of a century. Starved and spooked he fed himself to the flame. Can you imagine holding that much fear in a chest?

That's back when right enough, when it wiznae so much a lighthouse but a bonfire in a basket. It's us they're stuck with noo. And I'm immune to bullshit, you ask Ouse, we dinnae believe in hocus-pocus. Nut, just God and destiny, those things we know to be true. Anyone fated to be a keeper learns to sync up wi the sky, God gifts us that. A keeper feels a storm in the body before it lashes oot – the same way a man feels pish careering up his cock before it begins spurting.

The Father, having finished the sermon, is pained to see Ouse staring out the window, rather than revelling in his tale. Firth, noticing this, edges to jump in and tell him that just seconds ago, when The Father's eyes were shut from passion, Ouse was locked on him, him alone, swooning for the story. He wants to clarify this but doesn't find the courage in time.

Enough of that! The Father razors, shoving at Ouse. *It's an early yin the morrow. Ohhhh, I've work in mind for you, laddie – since you fannied aboot most of the day.*

The Father, rising to his feet, brushes a clot of soggy crumbs off his chest in amongst the wax oozing across the table. *This place*

94

is a shite stack, nae keeper of any mettle lets it go to the pigs. Get it scrubbed before bed, The Father snarls cruelly, pounding out the room with the whisky bottle tucked into the waistband of his trousers and the weeping candelabra in his hand.

Firth, too, gets to his feet and exits promptly, pondering the repercussions that might result from a skirmish with The Father, the ferocity of the retribution. He would choose his battles wisely and with great reluctance, verging on cowardice. He regrets not tarrying to talk more intimately to Ouse, but he is drunk, embarrassed and exhausted, and suspects The Father would be listening in.

Left alone, Ouse knows just how to shift that wax, and so begins the healing.

THIRTEEN

Daily dawns deliver their squashed-strawberry morning sun and purple gloamings end each day. The birdlife outdoes itself in both song-singing and feather-fluttering. The flora gets in some growing. The dreams are easy. It is Muckle Flugga at its acme.

And each day, before the sun rises, The Father is up dealing with a glut of passing tourist boats chasing feeding whales and a pod of dolphins. He curses the stupidity of these new wildlife cruisers, rogue rangers making a quick buck off tourists determined to catch the silhouetted tail of a colossus of the deep. Just last month a full boat's worth of tourists perished when a whale, a male bull, surfaced directly underneath the bow of their vessel and tipped the lot of them in and under the waves. No survivors, except the ranger. The Father puts aside his frustrations; keeping folk safe as he can from his trusty station is his only priority. That said, if he gets his hands on the ranger, off-duty, in one of the mainland bars, it'll be a different story altogether.

Ouse, taking some time to reflect on all the dramatic goings-on since Firth's arrival, has been keeping to himself and working with verve. Although he might catch glimpses of their curious new lodger, he leaves Firth to his own devices for a couple of days and busies himself fulfilling the duties of both a trainee keeper and an overworked housemaid. Having done so to an exemplary level, Ouse permits himself certain extra-curricular activities in his library-adjacent workshop. The Father, having not offered any opposition to his son's intention to do so, as good as sanctions this so-called 'creative time'.

. . .

By the window of the workshop, RLS is practising hat tricks with a straw safari helmet. Twirling it, throwing it up in the air and catching it behind his back, seemingly causing it to levitate between his hands as if reading the future through a crystal ball.

What do you think of him? Ouse asks unassumingly, staring down the sea – whilst his quick hands waltz a threaded needle in and out of cloth with apparent ease. Beyond the reach of his eyes, gannets streak the sky – today they are princely fisherman, part spear, putting the Norman kings with their wobbling lances to shame. On the workbench there's a sketchbook laid open, pullulating with designs and drawings. The pages reveal: octopi morphing into seaweed wreaths; a collared walrus holding communion with a regiment of starfish; a craterous moon with moon-milk trickling from its nippling peaks.

Your new designs are wildflowers, RLS raves. *I think these will be my favourites yet. It's fascinating not knowing what'll they become – jumpers, scarves, socks, tablecloths or talismans – the exquisite destinies that await them.*

It's cardigans I really want to master, Ouse replies humbly, *they're trickier. It's a jumper you need to split open. I just don't have the heart.*

You know, I sometimes joined the artists at the easel, and passed the afternoon away, RLS announces with pride. With this he flings his hat onto Ouse's head and begins looping a shawl around him and the tailor's mannequin – yoking them together like an elaborately wrapped gift. RLS attempts to kicks off his boots, but has some trouble, having gotten into a crazy tangle, and knocks them all flat to the floor.

He could be rabbit to my cat, Ouse suggests needily from within the knot of bodies, *but there's an unrest in him – it's deep, deep and*

97

dark, and I'm not sure what he wants from here. And The Father, he's uneasy about everything to do with him.

Perhaps he's right to be, RLS responds kindly. Having untangled themselves from the shawl's grasp they sit side by side and brood – appearing as thoughtful as two old friends watching the world rush by from the same Parisian café they've been coming to all their lives.

So, what do you think of him? Ouse repeats.

I've watched him some, RLS reveals, *now and then, and though I know he's troubled, impetuous too, I'd say . . . he carries mostly good in him.*

But is there wonder in him? Ouse blurts beggingly.

Oh yes, RLS remarks breathily, drawing it out, *I've seen him up high in North Queensferry, making mischief with the ocean . . . rallying, then settling. There's characters we care not a doit for, whether they win or lose, sink or swim, these are antiheroes, plot pushers, red herrings for our affection – my point is, Firth isn't one of those. He's, well, something more.*

So he's safe? Ouse ventures.

In each of us, two natures are at war – the good and the evil. All our lives the fight goes on between them, and one of them must conquer. But in our own hands lies the power to choose – what we want most to be we are.

That's really not an answer . . .

I think young Firth takes a dash of winter with his summers. There's fracture in him, a sliver of Jekyll but far more Hyde. I'm not sure he's found the right serum to suppress his particular darkness, but that doesn't mean he won't.

Still not an answer, Ouse snaps. *Not at all in fact.*

Maybe not the answer you were after, RLS retorts. *I can't call these things with exactitude – I'm the afterlife, not* all *life.*

So hold back, is that what you think? Ouse queries, trying to sell himself on the path of caution.

Having been lost in thought, RLS comes back full throttle, though just out of Ouse's earshot now on account of his perambulations.

It's amazing he's not yet splayed all his published works in front of you. Maybe there's more of that Softy Softy decency in him than first I thought. The kid's got chutzpah, as they say in New York, or at least that's where it's said best. Quiddity, yes, he's not short of that either, which is in high demand and low in supply, but there's ego too.

Do you think he's a sulker? Ouse shouts, reflecting on all the sulking he's had around him, more specifically all the times he's been robbed of an opportunity to experience joy.

Absolutely, but I've sulked with the best of them – fat lot of good it did me. If you took the totality of my time wallowing in the mire it might make for a full year of my short life. And from within that wallow not one jot of sapience ever came.

Ouse has begun writing down the things RLS is saying, underlining words, and drawing arrows out of them. RLS, upon noticing, snatches the pad from his hand.

Why trust me, when you're younger, faster and more alive? RLS cries, up on the table now, his safari hat whizzing around the room like a panicked bird. *Ouse, it might be said you're getting skinny-hipped from a lack of adventure. Get out there. Take it from someone who spent far too many days stricken in bed, time is not so easily wasted when you're dead.*

An adventure? Ouse propels these words from his body as if already marching out the door.

I suggest a trip to one of your favourite places, RLS clarifies. *It's the litmus test of true companionship, the unveiling of a scared place to a fresh set of eyes – seeing if they spoil it or enhance its splendour.*

For me it's thinking of a person pooing, Ouse admits sheepishly, *then checking if you still find them worthy of a dance.*

Genius, Ouse – pure genius. Remember that time when the band stopped playing though the music kept on in your head? RLS whispers.

I never stopped burling though everyone was laughing! Ouse yells, with a fought-for pride RLS has instilled in him.

Salve upon the chapped lips of the puckered mouth of hell! RLS booms back.

Ouse holds a finished work up to the light and lets a gladness shimmer from his skin.

I told you it'd be my favourite yet! RLS cheers. *Remember, if the bastards tell you a surfeit of imagination is a failing, you tell them what in response?*

I love you, RLS.

FOURTEEN

Firth is gangly, but with hidden sinews – a friend once remarked that he has a wiry determination to his scaffold. The hip bones of an overworked camel, sharp and sturdy as machine parts, his spine poking through like a walkway of rocks across a loch. So whilst appearing ill-equipped for scaling mountains, he has proven himself to be more capable than most – burning his body to embers when called upon. Firth rules he will work doggedly to demonstrate his resilience to Ouse and The Father without having to spell it out himself; it feels important.

The first day walking the perimeter of the island he has sacks around his cowboy boots to protect them from the muddy stretches, which cause no end of hilarity for Ouse and The Father. By evening, a pair of sturdy walking boots appears on the doormat of the bothy.

On the second day the spume from the waves climbs up the cliff face and passes through him like a voracious cloud. Despite knowing it to be a cloud made of pearls of water vapour, he is still astounded to be left soaked through.

Feeding off the brio of the morning's long stretching sun, Firth sets off early for a third day running. To his surprise, he has already been super productive on the bird-spotting front – again, inspired more by proving himself a man of prodigious ambition to his hosts than achieving his own goals. And he's sleeping like a sloth, despite the all-hours stridency of sea-thrash, bizarre tintinnabulations in the wind and the scariness of The Father's looming presence – in the main, the thought of him appearing in the dead of night at the foot of the bed. Despite all that, Firth's been going down deep and with dedication, his throbbing body making up for lost time.

He's sighted not one but thirty-six puffins, having managed to sketch a terrible globular mutant version of all of them combined – a creature, possessed, like a fat raven that's been feasting on the eggs of rainbows.

Puffins he would have imagined arduous, almost mythical, spots. But it seems they're little show-offs, congregating on steep ledges for conspiratorial meetings. He spies one puffin brutishly evicting a rabbit from its burrow before claiming the space for its own. They appear tame, too: one evening a pair of them follow him along a clifftop walk, mimicking his steps with comedic plodding. The pair disappeared from his sight when he turned his back and then re-appeared less than a minute later with huge eels hanging out their mouths like elephant trunks. Wee goofy posers, how he loves them.

When the birds return from filling their bellies they appear drunk. He witnesses several puffins crash-landing, almost cartoon-ish in their gracelessness. And there's been some puzzling beak clatter – clapping their bills together percussively in a ceremony that concludes with nuzzling up. Firth suspects nookie might have ensued, but he left them to it – he's no puffin pervert.

He alas also stumbled upon a dead puffin – all the colours washed out of it and its amber eyeballs missing, leaving a putrid-looking black hole of a socket. There was a line, drawn in daisies, around where its body lay. More curious still, there were dandelions laid like a yellow blanket across the corpse, which was well on its way to decomposing. Firth began counting the number of insects picnick-ing on its flesh, then got upset and moved on. Besides, the whole scene looked somewhat pagan, like there could be something spooky loitering nearby – not that Firth stomached such notions, but he thought it best not to chance it at this stage in the game.

His suspicions lie with Ouse as the ceremonial undertaker, but he's also noted Figgie to be overtly lovely and clocked the regularity with which she comes over to Muckle Flugga. He has bumped into her twice already, and seen her from afar twice more. There's such a thing as a right to roam here, although scarcely exercised by anyone but Figgie. Firth speculates that The Father serves as a human scarecrow for the island, smirking about how much trouble he'd get into if he ever actually voiced that opinion to the irascible beast.

Adding to his collection, he uses the guidebook to tick off a golden plover, a whimbrel and whooper swan. An unusual-looking creature that visited his windowsill one morning he identified as a thick-billed warbler, then dismissed the notion (as the guidebook suggests this would be far too rare a spot for someone of his rotten luck). The pièce de resistance is a swaggering little bluethroat, which looks like a robin in fancy dress. There were also several birds he didn't recognise, doubting their reality, including one that had a fencing sword for a beak and appeared to be wearing a bat mask.

To his shame, Firth rather figured the birds that stopped on Muckle Flugga would be lost souls, exhausted, emaciated and unsure about how far they'd flown. Creatures from Siberia or Canada wondering if they'd ever get where they were headed – Scandinavia or France perhaps. It wasn't this way at all; there are many splendiferous natives here he'd greatly overlooked. By way of an apology to the indigenous species, he finds himself reciting nonsense verse to any bird willing to listen.

As for the gannets, they've been plentiful, even more gannetly than he dared dream. Carousing cowboys, pinballing around like drunken goons – fishing, frolicking, jostling, flinging themselves

103

into all manner of wind-sweeps; plunging down gloops and kamikaze piloting into even the most tempestuous of waves. Except, somehow, they never get swept under, remerging victorious with mad eyes marbling. Firth suspects some of them have gone insane.

Then there's the big bully birds, black-backed gulls and wild bonxies that attack the smaller, cuter ones for food, or just for fun. Only yesterday, Firth had to peg it as one of the more dastardly pirates among them started dive-bombing him – first it saw off a pack of puffins and then him when he tried to shoo it away. No warning blows either: the bird was going for blood.

Weirdly, The Father came to his rescue by tossing him a chunky stick. Although freaked out by The Father appearing like an apparition, he was thankful for the back-up. His flailing and flapping of the stick warded off the bonxie long enough to run for cover. Reading up on bonxies in the bird guide left in the bothy (apparently by the book hater), it seems these dive-bombings are prosaic encounters. And in fact hillwalkers, cliff-walkers and moor-walkers often wield thick sticks above their head whilst ambling in their territory. He keeps hold of the wooden shield and shouts insults at the bonkers birds whenever they fly past.

To his amazement, The Father has proven himself to be almost amenable to encounter during the day, informing Firth that the local name for a puffin is Tammy Norrie. And that their white bellies are to camouflage them from predators below the water, who'll mistake them for sky, whilst their black bodies and crowns protect them from the predators above, for the dark colours blend in with the slate hues of the sea when rowdy. Firth did wonder what happened to puffins in tropical climates where the water turned turquoise and violet but thought asking something so whimsical might be pushing his luck.

Thinking on The Father, Firth concludes that perhaps their soup, so to speak, is not as spoiled as he may have thought. Whilst working The Father is purposeful, less terrifying, even admirable in the tirelessness of his graft.

He's constantly spitting though, hawking up rancid creatures from the haunted parts inside of him. Firth had the displeasure of standing on a particularly slimy one, dark as a dead wart, and nearly slipped on his arse from the shock of it.

And, of course, all The Father's gestures of welcome come with a ribbing. He takes pleasure in pointing out Firth's unsuitability to the extremity of the land. And he is more than willing to ravage any of the romantic natural-world notions he sees smouldering in Firth's eyes. He also takes great pride in reminding Firth that it wasn't long back when puffins were a veritable food source here, and that hungry sailors are still known to fish them out the ocean for scran if they're unfortunate enough to get tangled in the nets. *Could fetch you a couple for your pot, if you like?* The Father jests, as he clomps off. At least Firth hopes he's joking.

From his observations, Firth has decided The Father has grave difficulty in admitting better ideas exist than those he practises himself, unable to shift allegiance even when the case for change is crystal clear. Obstinate fearfulness – it is a trait Firth sympathises with in private and criticises in public.

Within this territory, he learns from Figgie, during their encounters, that The Father won't abide jam donuts on the island – he has an aversion to their sneaky grenade-like ability to explode when bitten. The Father is, however, a passionate advocate of the honest shortbread. Figgie later reveals to him that this aversion stems from having made a right mess of himself when eating a donut for the first time in front of The Mother's mother – not a million

105

miles from his own first meal on the island (the Cullen Skink fiasco). Mulling over these interactions, Firth has noticed how Figgie always manages to highlight The Father's redeeming features, however incongruous to their brief discussions.

Firth has also been watching Ouse. He has dedicated several pages to him in his diary, which he feels obliged to keep to fulfil the stereotype of the reclusive, non-intrusive ornithologist The Father expects Firth to be. These secret pages are recorded at the rear and entitled *Encounters with an Ousling*.

One afternoon, whilst Ouse is on all fours weeding through a rockpool, Firth sees something truly shocking. Ouse gently lays a starfish down on a slab of rock, kisses it, pulls out his penknife and severs one of its legs off. What happens next, Firth is not sure, as he heard The Father rustling around in the distance and hid behind a bramble bush.

Later that same day, Ouse is back on the island's most abrupt headland pretending to conduct the wind with his invisible baton all over again, the very same spot Firth saw him head to that first morning. Except this time, Ouse is balancing on one leg with the other arm bolt upright, insectile by silhouette. On this occasion he is also carrying a book under his arm, which he dips in and out of, speaking some of the passages out loud, although indecipherable from Firth's vantage. Reckless, he thinks, given the build-up Ouse gave about books being destroyed if left unattended. Firth later berates himself for being so spineless and servile.

Ouse spends a lot of time in the room Firth was not allowed in, the messy place with all the tools and wool. Firth calculates at least six hours in every twenty-four, normally in short stretches. He has, of course, deduced this is where Ouse makes the knitwear The Father derided as 'pocket money' and 'time wasting', but that Firth suspects would fetch a pretty penny in any city's craft markets – especially given the backstory of Ouse held captive on an island in the middle of the bloody ocean, just an obdurate lighthouse keeper for company. He knows how he'd pitch it – shades of the Rapunzel story. Regardless, he deems it best not to meddle.

On no less than three occasions – assorted times – Ouse sinks into the long grasses like a lioness after a successful hunt. He closes his eyes and travels to parts of his body that most people commonly overlook. Firth records that Ouse is more mindfully in touch with the simple joy of having toes than the average human is with their heart's poetry. At least this is Firth's considered take on the matter as someone who has previously partaken in yoga nidra.

Early on another morning, the earliest Firth's been up, he sees Ouse on all fours gazing at a single raindrop hanging off a gorse bush. When Ouse leaves, Firth rushes over to grab a glimpse of the same bead that held him in such thrall. He beholds the whole island, the sky, and the sun above, reflected back inside it; a tiny wonderland packed into nature's snow globe. Staring into the miniaturised world feels mystical. Ouse *is* mystical, Firth concludes and then flicks the raindrop off the gorse to prove it isn't an illusion. He immediately feels god-awful, like the deity who accidentally invented hell after a squabble with an angel who snubbed his advances.

On at least three occasions he observes Ouse shadow boxing, making *oosh-oosh* noises and then taunting his invisible opponent by yelling, with surprising ferocity, into the wide-open space of the place.

The Ousling is interesting in the way other people pretend to be interesting, Firth writes on the page and then underlines it several times – making a note in his diary to tell him this before the end. Ouse is a goblin angel clacking at the typewriter in Firth's chest.

After several days on the hoof, Firth has surveyed the buildings and the landscape of Muckle Flugga with tenacity. The scale of it has been astonishing; it seems to just keep growing beyond possibility or reason. From what he can gauge, the living quarters consist of: a robust kitchen with adjoining dining table; a capacious feasting chamber with a cobwebbed chandelier; a worship-worthy library; five, perhaps six, bedrooms; a quartet of odd-shaped studies; a workspace-come-studio; a telescope room; a room deemed entirely off-limits to everyone but The Father; a map, globe and compass room; a washhouse; several unlisted spaces; a tool shed; and his expansive bothy, full of all sorts of hipster amenities. The lighthouse itself is composed of a vast assortment of complex parts, but as Firth's not been allowed in it, these remain more elusive to him – except the lantern room, the gallery deck and widow's walk, all of which he can spot through side-eye glances when pretending to look elsewhere.

The most disturbing thing he's seen over these three days of casual observing, however, was not any of the dead birds nor nature's slaughter, but a sight he stumbled upon when, having consumed one of the bottles of wine he'd couriered here, he went for a night walk and nearly fell down a gulch. Muddy-kneed, on the way back to the bothy he came round the flank of the lighthouse, passing down an overgrown path, and chanced upon another of its several outhouses. Peering through a little portal of a window, to a place he'd not be permitted to go, he saw The Father: umpteen whiskies in and bawling like a child – what looked like journals and old photograph albums splayed out in front him. At one point, The Father rose from his seat like a blizzard and came right up to the window Firth was snooping through. He began shooting out expletives and caressing his own face. Paralysed with fear, and sluggish from drunkenness, Firth just stood there. Eventually, he realised The Father wasn't seeing him through the mucky window; the chiding was not aimed his way. The Father was, in fact, haranguing his own reflection, his own broken being. It was then Firth realised The Father, underneath all the stubbornness and bluster, was overflowing with self-hate. Firth took twelve steps back until engulfed in darkness. Although sure some wicked manifestation of this perturbing encounter was going to re-form in a nightmare, it didn't.

This troubling experience aside, what Firth can say with absolute authority is that after a few days on Muckle Flugga, the crisis of his city life and its inexorable posturing and machinations have faded further from mind than ever before. Once epitomised by a bin on fire, Firth is considering a new sigil for his house, something with duende. With this in mind, he retitles his annals: *Muckle Flugga: notes from a shipwrecked heart.*

FIFTEEN

On the way over to the bothy, Ouse counts the number of different types of flowers he passes, including several flowering weeds that the more pedantic growers he knows would snobbily exclude. Ouse believes that if it has petals and it brightens up the day, then it's a flower. More times than he can count, he has dreamed about running through a never-ending meadow of towering wildflowers until dissolving into seeds and giving himself to the soil.

Approaching the path to the bothy, Ouse can see Firth pacing around the room pulling all sorts of dramatic facial expressions, as if playing several characters in the same play. In the process of mixing paints on his mirrored palette, he occasionally daubs the brush on his arm, testing the way the colours seep into the skin. Ouse teeters to a stop and watches for longer than he knows he rightly should – the narrative Firth's acting out becoming increasingly physical, and increasingly troubling. Firth appears swordfighterly, painting sweeping strokes across his chest and lambasting the canvas that hovers in front of him. After casting a final violent blow with the brush, Firth kicks over the canvas and falls to the floor as if badly wounded.

Ouse tiptoes closer to the bothy, until at once the door swings open and he can see Firth flat-backed on the floor, his legs kicking the air and a look of glee swept across his face.

In a panic, and for fear of being caught, Ouse leaps beyond the welcome mat and announces himself with an invitation. *Would you like to see a tombolo?*

JESUS FUCK! Firth screams from the ground. *You scared the living shit out me!* Echoes of The Father in the son, he muses to himself – bloody tiptoe twins appearing like shadows from beneath the muck.

I should have knocked, but there simply wasn't time, and the door swung open, Ouse responds defensively.

The doors are always open, there's no locks here, remember! Firth jibes.

Exactly. And aren't you thankful for it?

A tombola? Isn't that those demonic toy horses you whack with a stick as sweeties fall out?

I always thought those cruel. A beautiful creature beaten for its treasure. But that⊠s a piñata.

I suppose it is sort of cruel, Firth agrees. *Candy guts spilling everywhere – and it turns the kids into little psychopaths, as if they weren't already. It's a tombola I'm confusing it with, the one with the tickets and wheel.*

Yeah, Ouse confirms softly. *This is neither.*

As he doesn't elucidate further, Firth nudges him along, getting to his feet in the process: *You'll have to remind me of the characteristics of a tombolo?*

In this case, it's a stretch of golden sand with turquoise ocean on either side. Often it's swallowed up by the sea, but mostly it's there, shrinking and stretching. Like a catwalk to another planet, or.

Firth, realising Ouse simply isn't going to finish that sentence, takes the reins again. *I'm actually quite busy at the moment, the calendar's brimful – balls, luncheons, book launches, you get the gist. Besides, this drawing of a gannet picking eel guts out of seal shite isn't going to finish itself.*

Okay, perhaps another day then, Ouse remarks gingerly, then turns to walk away.

That was a joke, Firth bleats. *As if I'd turn down an invitation to traverse a golden walkway to another planet just to bugger up my mediocre doodle.*

I know, Ouse responds again, to Firth's bewilderment. *Meet me by the cove when you're ready.*

I'm ready now!

You're not dressed for open water, Ouse utters as leaving, gesturing to the huge slipper socks and silk kimono dressing gown Firth is still sporting – not to mention the paint caking half his body.

Who says I'm not?! Firth shouts wryly, then realising Ouse has already evaporated from sight.

SIXTEEN

Sunlight quivers the air, the moon as bright by day as night, as Figgie heads off on her rounds. She travels from the northern tip of Shetland's mainland to six of its surrounding islands – it's half a day every day out on the water, but she revels in it: drifting between stops, daydreaming without the sound of anyone's voice to puncture her imagined worlds. Besides, she's a tonic to the remote and lonely and a lodestone for gossip, and she'd not be without any of that. Plus, she's Clyde for company, for fun, for protection – although Figgie's dad argues the dog's more likely to drown a villain in drool than growl them into submission.

In her boat is the usual run of food and groceries, special delivery mail and notes of a professional, private, and strictly secret capacity. Figgie can be trusted with them all; discreet, shrewd, savvy. The boat leaves packed to the gunnels and returns with just her and Clyde and whatever trinkets or gifts she's handed along the way. If there was to be a keeper of shibboleths up here, it would be Figgie. Meek as she can be, she is also everybody's go-to for advice, and in possession of more 'off-the-books' information than anyone on the islands, perhaps even the mainland. Because of this, the family business is prospering once more. For a while there it was on the ropes, but now it's winning again (as their bank manager in Lerwick puts it) and Figgie's the one to thank for that. Everyone is glad she came back.

After school, she'd left for Aberdeen to work in administration at the University. They were accepting women by then, and no doubt she was smart enough, but knowing how to apply wasn't in her family's ken, and the tuition fees were higher than was worth talking about. She was smart, but not full scholarship smart, or so she'd ruled retrospectively – having not known such programmes existed before entering the University's employ. What she did know is that she wanted to be around an ancient university, able to stroll the grassy grounds and eavesdrop on the clever conversations in the courtyards, to access books, and maybe fall in love with someone who was top of their class, whilst down to earth with it. After all, they'd be studying geography or biology, not medicine or law.

She got the job only weeks after voicing her interest in a role there. Men were drawn to Figgie, women too, but it was men showing off that delivered her opportunities quicker than she asked for them. In this case, a local teacher with an older brother who taught Latin at the University and dined out with the Dean.

Figgie began a part-time post in the law school's admissions and exams department, working for a Welsh orphan named Ogwen, who excelled in academic management and sent nearly all his money back home to his mother in Barry Island. Ogwen was a real provocateur, she would find out, who could come across as pompous when he needed to, but underneath the façade was sweet and venerable, championing workers' rights via his trojan-horse policies and undermining of the Dean.

In her free time, she attended many lectures open to the wider university staff and even joined a few of the University's more liberal societies. She also went on numerous dates to dancehalls, picture-houses, pubs and taverns, none of which were incredibly successful. She very quickly went from being in awe of the gentlemen of the University to developing a disdain for them. The most odious among them mocked her accent and threw coins her way, gesturing that she should make for the bar and return with their drinks. Even the kind ones tended to talk down to her, expecting her to be interested in the most banal of things, adopting silly voices and then enquiring how quickly she wanted to have children. Figgie was, of her own volition, highly sensitive, but could be ferocious when something she loved was at stake. In this case, her own heart. Despite her best efforts to blame herself, she really did loathe these dating days full of bush-bearded Bernards and clever Vincents.

Her perception of college men was exacerbated further by the buffoonery she had to deal with whilst working at the law school. Entitled toffs with lawyers for fathers – or worse still, judges – remonstrating against the low marking of their essays or exams. Regardless of the paucity of their claim or the fecklessness of their reasoning, Figgie would have to type it up. From claims of jealous or vindicative marking by the tutors, to conspiracy theories of other students interfering with their papers, Figgie had to hear them through and write it up. These situations were made all the more abominable when accompanied by indecent propositions, non-consensual touching or blatant bribery – the latter being the least innocuous, and occasionally tempting, of the bunch.

Back in Shetland, Figgie had been popular with peers throughout the schooling years, and with neighbours and family alike, but in Aberdeen she really struggled to make any female friends. Her talent for trying to see everyone's point of view was labelled as 'sympathising' at the women's rights meetings, and her dissatisfaction with the gentlemen of Aberdeen was seen as stuck up, or frigid, by women who subsequently copped off with those she rejected.

Figgie's inability to make friends was hindered further by the frequency of visits from her mother. Her mother, it turned out, was less than immune to the charms of Aberdeen's University men

115

– she would go on to leave Figgie's dad for an ambitious young lecturer in economics who had approached them drunk at an inter-departmental social.

Unbeknown to Figgie, over a period of six months of visitations, her mum had been spending the takings of their family business on travel, fancy frocks and other luxury items to impress her suitor and had left the store in dire straits.

Wracked with guilt, Figgie left her Aberdeen University job and came home to Shetland to help her father out and get the business back on track. Her mother, on the other hand, stayed in The Granite City and married the young lecturer, who was quickly making a name for himself in local politics – although not on the good side of it, as Ogwen saw it.

Her dad moped for a while, heartbroken but mostly humiliated, and then met someone himself – taking solace in the business acumen of his daughter: Figgie worked hard for years, getting the family business back to where it had been, and then beyond. Whilst her father constantly apologised for the life she had sacrificed to offer him aid.

The Figgie of today, on a bigger and better boat than any lighthouse keeper could afford, lets her eyes drift in the direction of Muckle Flugga far too often. She would offer what support she could to its current residents, in as subtle a manner as she could bear, for as long as they'd let her. Alms for her own, these island dwellers, a special breed. It felt like something she was supposed to do, the least she could do, given what they'd been through.

SEVENTEEN

Firth has managed to scour most of the paint off his body and dressed himself in outdoor clothes – not ideal garb for an oceanic expedition, but as outdoorsy as his wardrobe affords. His efforts have not escaped Ouse's notice, who has, in fact, donned a few of his more flamboyant wares in order to mark the occasion.

On approaching Ouse, who's busy tightening ropes, Firth first catches sight of the slender size of their vessel, certainly in comparison to Figgie's, then it's peculiar name.

Covenant? Your boat is called The Covenant, Firth queries, curious. *I'm guessing a compact between you and whatever god you pray to in the hope they keep you safe out there?*

No, Ouse shakes his head.

So, what is it? Firth prods, realising he's going to have to push the boy for the details on near everything.

It's a homage to the boat in Kidnapped. *The Robert Louis Stevenson . . .*

Of course it is, Firth interrupts. *Actually, isn't that bad luck? I mean wasn't* The Covenant *described as 'little better than a hell upon the seas'?*

It'll get us there, Ouse confirms, patting the vessel like a pet pony.

Is it a sailboat or a rowing boat? Only it looks sort of puny. It's not as big as Figgie's boat, is it?

It'll get us there, Ouse repeats, almost under his breath.

Wait a minute, didn't the bloody Covenant *sink?* Firth yells in a eureka moment that he feels is bound to win some points.

There's only wavelets out there and I've made this crossing a thousand times. You are safe with us.

I suppose we'll see! Firth chortles.

Besides, we'll lash ourselves to the mast if the sea gets going, Ouse states, steady yet teasing in tone.

Oh you needn't bother with that, replies Firth, scrambling onto the boat then scurrying on his hands and knees to the front. *Your cabin boy cares not if we end up at the bottom of the deep blue sea.*

Firth, on his feet now, clocks the colourful handkerchief looped around Ouse's neck and the stunning jumper he's changed into. This one features a sleeping ostrich as the sea hangs off the branch of a bony tree like a wet rug; the stars, not in the sky, are littered across the seabed filling in for the absence of ocean. Firth can't take his eyes off it.

Ouse notices him admiring the jumper, which would have been fine if he wasn't the one wearing it. To divert Firth's attention off his body, he makes an enquiry. *Did you know people used to think ostriches could eat iron and hatch their own eggs just by staring at them?*

No, I didn't because nobody knows that, Firth counters cheekily. *In fact, where did you even learn that madness?*

Instead of answering, Ouse shakes out the sail of *The Covenant* and the boat thrusts forwards, sending Firth tumbling backwards – he keeps upright only by clutching on to Ouse's arm. A tight grip for someone who doesn't care whether he floats or sinks, Ouse thinks to himself.

After a few minutes of staring off into the distance, Firth – who has noticeably been counting how long he can hold his tongue for whilst Ouse focusses on cutting through the wavelets – buckles and begins.

118

Okay, I have a question for you, Firth proposes. *What do you think of when you think of rivers?*

Drowning, Ouse retorts as if anticipating the question.

Firth's eyebrows shoot up, but he tries to hide his surprise. *I think of light dancing off the water,* he says, beaming holy as a seraph. *Salmon leaping on a long migration home. Campers on the riverbank as the dusk sets in.*

No you don't, Ouse refutes.

YES, I do. At least I have done.

A little dull then.

Now, I don't believe you mean that, Firth protests. *Those are some of the most life-giving and beautiful uses a river has!*

Exactly. A river shouldn't have to be useful or beautiful. It just is.

You're right. I am dull, Firth says flumping to the floor. *They're not even my thoughts. I have thought about drowning though, my own. Seriously. Except that's a story for another time.*

After a few seconds in concentrated silence, Firth's lips begin to twitch with irritation. *What's wrong with you?!*

Ouse barely registers the comment and simply continues steering the ship, mindful of their course.

Why wouldn't you ask me about it? Firth demands.

About what?

My wanting to drown!

Oh I'm sorry, Ouse says softly, but with a distance in him. *It seems rude talking about ourselves when there's so much ocean out there.*

Firth is both incredulous and flustered at this response – how Ouse could seemingly be so cold in his remarks yet utterly naïve, almost sweet, with it. Firth silences himself in protest, this time lasting a little over thirty-six seconds, then decrees it's his right to speak on the matter and, in fact, Ouse is being insensitive. *I didn't want to live anymore and found myself on a bridge.*

I'm fascinated by bridges, Ouse responds.

Firth almost yowls in shock, equal parts disbelief and hilarity, but instead parleys with the ocean.

For a while, Firth keeps to himself at the rear of the boat, trying to give the appearance of a cad in a strop. Catching Ouse glance back to check on him is enough to lure Firth back – he lunges forwards as if bitten by an electric current.

The problem with drowning is that I can breathe underwater, he explains. *At least for longer than a human rightly should be able to. The first time I noticed was on a childhood holiday, collecting oysters. I was more than two minutes under before I needed to come up for air – Mum was in a tizzy the rest of the day.*

Perhaps you're a selkie, Ouse ponders. *Have you ever removed your skin?*

Ignoring him, Firth ploughs on, determined.

Then there was when I saw someone throw a cat in a bag in the Figgate Burn, so I jumped in. It was four minutes before I found it the muddy waters – the cat had died, but I cleaned the silt off its fur and buried it on the banks. I mourned that cat for months.

What Firth doesn't get into is years of dreaming about how long he'd have to sink before he knew it was over.

Anyway, I'm babbling again, Firth recants. *I'll be quiet. Really, I mean it. The silence in me begins now.*

Listening to Firth talk pleases Ouse immensely, though he has no desire to tell him that. He feels the need to keep his cards close to his chest; Firth's conversation thrills him and in that is the temptation to reveal more than he's ready to, more than he should.

• • •

120

Bopping and bouncing most assuredly, *The Covenant* soars up and down the wavelets, and even a couple of their bigger siblings. Ouse doesn't take the calmest route, but avoids some of the more bolshie waves that pass their way. The wind serves them well, romancing their sails and playfully slapping at their cheeks.

He spies a small whirlpool forming due west but doesn't risk mentioning it for fear of causing panic. He never forgets what The Father taught him: the sea, for all its playfulness, will never stop being a murderer – what *The Covenant* gambols across are battle-grounds and killing fields, beautiful as they are in their azure robes with turquoise sequins. Underneath this serene surface is an immensity that could wipe out an army in a micro-second. Skilfully steering a ship, on a day that's generous in both light and breeze, never fails to thrill Ouse.

All its terror aside, Ouse still loves the sea: it is easier to sniff out people's secrets at sea. He puts it down to them being so distant from the corruptions and contradictions that hold them hostage back on land – a life they can neither touch nor destroy from the middle of the ocean.

Firth, feeling liberated, farts into the wind, realising it's impossible to detect the smell out here. He doesn't care if Ouse hears him, in fact he hopes he does.

After several blissful nautical miles, the tombolo appears like a bar of gold that's fallen from the sky. Firth is utterly gobsmacked, having expected to be underwhelmed by its significance. The colour of an elderly bee, a light once bright enough to blanch the landscape now accentuates the tombolo's majesty. *It's magnificent*, Firth remarks, then hushes into reverent silence.

Reaching the shore, Ouse thrusts the ship's anchor into Firth's cradling arms and then leaps out of the boat. Cheetah-quick, he lashes a second rope around a boulder on land and looks to Firth expectantly. Firth, anchor in hand, stares back at Ouse bewildered, clueless as to what to do with the thing. Ouse indicates for Firth to slip it over the side of the boat into the water. Rather than just drop the anchor, Firth flings it with such moxie it jolts the whole boat forwards and causes him to lose his footing for a second time. Though smiling through his embarrassment, he issues himself a severe scolding.

Firth notices that when he makes a fool of himself, Ouse doesn't jibe or mock; in fact he hardly blinks – nothing like the jackals back in the city. He ponders whether it's because Ouse doesn't find his buffoonery funny or if he's simply more kind-hearted than most. A more dismal prospect, Firth considers, is that perhaps laughing at everyday blunders when living with The Father carries too great a risk.

Ouse proceeds to lead Firth across the sandy spit, regaling him with his range of tombolo knowledge – information retained from school then added to by eavesdropping on local experts conducting tourist walks. He explains that a tombolo is essentially a huge wash of sediment spat out due to wave refractions. That each time it appears it's a miracle, as each time it disappears it might be gone for good. He ends by noting: *It flares and thins like something healing then splitting back open again. Sometimes here, other times gone.*

Firth is impressed by the volume of words unspooling from Ouse's mouth, and listens intently, keen for it not to end. The sand itself is a princely spread of marmalade, the stodgy stuff – it looks as if it should still be sticky, but thankfully isn't. Ouse takes off his shoes and lies down, gesturing Firth to do the same. He does so, with pleasure. They're positioned in the narrowest squeeze of the sand, where the ocean on either side comes all but ten feet from touching and their bodies become the distance that separates a never-ending force. And so they lie, spines to the sand, penned in, watching the clouds ribboning. *Shipping lanes of the sky*, Ouse mumbles, closing his eyes.

Seizing the opportunity, Firth takes a stealthy, close-quarters look at Ouse. He draws the conclusion that Ouse's face is deceptively simple in its anatomy, increasing in complexity with each new viewing. Whereas he once thought he could summarise Ouse's features in thirty words, or less, he now knows this to be apocryphal: he had the headlines but none of the fine print.

Ouse has never lain here with anyone else, and it feels so intimate. Even more intimate than the time a classmate put their hands down his trousers behind the town hall after the ceilidh when they all tried alcohol for the first time. But not so intimate as when he touches himself on his own terms, in the long grass as a soft breeze laps at his skin and he dissolves into the shapes that make him: circles and triangles; a thousand tiny stars; a twist of miracle toffee and a spark-spitting wire – the current of which Firth has already felt.

Ouse recalls his first erotic touch, terrified he couldn't put it back in, that a part of him would be forever missing, lost, and his body would pine for it like a ghost searching for its killer. If only he'd known there was more cum in him than he'd ever dare dream. More than he could wreck, raze or pay tribute to, more than any ode could hold. Except that one time, when he feared he'd emptied himself, and he wept into a stupor. It returning to him the next day, after a bowl of porridge and a long stroll, was such sweet relief. But from then on, he slowed down, discovered the twin beauties of less becoming more and savouring sensuality. How little he had learned, but how much he relished in each lesson – to be deep within the body's unwritten passages.

123

Hearing the two tides roll in and out provokes something altogether different for Firth. Though the song in the waves starts off melodic, chiming triangles and clarinets, its music soon becomes hectic – maracas and cymbals, discordant clatter, then a shrill static. Not tranquil, but clangorous, not waves but the screech of a train breaking hard like all the life on board depended on it; blood on the tracks, the roaring waters below a high bridge, the call of the drop, his dead mother weeping by his graveside. Of recent, Firth's mind, in peaceful moments, has been subject to violent eruptions; he's given up on hoping it'll ever correct itself.

Abruptly, Firth leaps to his feet and begins pacing about, attempting to temporarily contain the darkness invading his head. Ouse opens his eyes to see fireballs where Firth's soft pupils once were, limbs flailing in the sun as sounds flee from his stretched lips. His words are mostly indecipherable, a means of talking himself down from the hypothetical ledge, a method of ebbing the din of the disturbing visions thundering around inside.

Feeling a pressure valve burst, Firth begins leaking from the eyes. In order not to blow his cover and expose the doomed human he's lugging around inside of him, he charges into the water and hauls out the first thing he sees – in this case, a huge branch covered in barnacles. Firth holds it above his head like a title belt and grins so hard and wide he feels something rip within his mouth. Then comes the blood.

Thumping down onto the sand, the branch sinks with the weight of its cargo. Firth feels instantly better, and ostensibly shifts his attention to the kooky little creatures sucking on to the branch for dear life – focussing on another species in the hope of not having to mention his outburst.

Ouse, reading the room, and also not wanting to interrogate

Firth, chooses instead to join him in hunching over the branch. *It's like we're pharaoh gods gazing down upon the ruins of temples*, Ouse remarks. *I hope that's not silly to say?*

You're brilliant, Firth speaks steadfastly, tears still in his eyes.

Ouse, deliberating whether to now share a sentiment on Firth's upset, is sidetracked when a gang of seagulls begins ransacking the branch for its juicy barnacles. Amongst the gory onslaught, the boys have to run for cover.

Once the spectacle is over the pair piously return the barnacle-plucked branch to the water and set off on a stroll along the tombolo. During the walk, Ouse makes it crystal clear he's not going to mention Firth's freak-out by talking exclusively about several strange sea-dwelling beasts he's seen only once then never again. He's gracious to such an extent Firth debates whether his lapse of behaviour actually happened. When they return to their starting point, Firth approaches Ouse fully intent on hugging him for the tenderness he's shown him until Ouse's arm puts a halt to any such embrace – open-palmed he stops him and signals to the sand below.

At their feet, by the rope-tied boulder, a crab has come up the rear of another crab and begins to mount it. First come claws around the shell's frontage and then the dart-like legs begin twisting in – a mishmash of intertwined brittleness. Transfixed, the boys watch the slow amorous dance of the sand-shifting crustaceans: claws clip the air and eye-flowers flutter in perfect prosody. Firth squats down, bringing his face so close to the carnal scene that his eyeball must have appeared to the crabs like a great Saharan sun. Ouse tugs him back up and away from the crescendo-ing creatures and begins untying the boat.

The weather will soon be turning – it's time to get back, Ouse whispers. *We'll see snow tonight.*

Codswallop, Firth clacks back, *it's sweltering!*

Ouse smirks knowingly and responds, *You'll have to be ready for things to change faster here than where you're from. We're up higher and much smaller – time spins faster.*

Firth laughs this off, boards the boat and begins heaving up the anchor. The wind is picking up and back on Muckle Flugga The Father begins readying the great light for any battles the night may bring.

One thing I want to ask you before we leave, confesses Firth. His intention is to ask how The Mother died but he chickens out and instead asks something he decides is perhaps even more perplexing. *Why did you cut the arm off that starfish?*

Without pausing in his unfurling of the sail, Ouse warmly explains: *Their numbers have been falling, and that arm will grow a whole new starfish. I take my stewardship of the island seriously.*

Firth nods, aware his own response would have been something natty and defensive about having been spied upon.

By the time their boat reaches Muckle Flugga, Firth has irrefutability decided that he needs Ouse to like him. Firth, who has a tendency to fling himself at new people with such force it can knock them off their feet, has always found himself at odds with the slow pace at which people familiarise themselves with each other. Whereas things are quickening in this new age of bohemian ideals and outré social antics, for Firth it's never quite fast enough. Though his time here might be short, he wants to spend it in Ouse's favour.

EIGHTEEN

The Father enters the lighthouse like a panther boards a boat. He has cleaned the bulbs, polished the brass, tied his boot laces tight enough to mark his feet with skin snakes, and tested his grip on the wet bars of the terrace. Crossing the threshold, he mumbles the keeper's prayer out of habit and superstition, then locks the door.

Every time he ascends the lighthouse's hundreds of stairs he reminds himself he is the only one who can make the light flash fast and swivel fierce enough to dig tunnels through the dark. The glut of portraits he passes on the way up, nailed to the wall and hung crooked, remind him of the enormous crew that has served this same mission. These are the mugshots of the bravest keepers Scotland has seen, very few of whom lived until their beards greyed. Alongside them, the faces of the engineers who designed these illustrious watchtowers of the sky – the Lighthouse Stevensons – take pride of place on the first and final furlong of the climb. Also featured is a mixture of stone-heavers, glass-blowers, ships' captains, religious clergy, and a few rogues no-one has been able to identify (though thought to be cooks, gardeners and carpenters that performed their posts with such élan they merited a spot amongst the heralded).

The Father has already put a nail in position where his picture will hang, a humble spot by the organ room, and has left instruction regarding who should paint him. When selecting his bit of wall, his final resting place, he made sure there was enough room for Ouse's portrait to sit beside him. He wishes he could put a picture of The Mother up amongst these greats, but kens that as much as it would strengthen him on good days, it would weaken him on the bad. Both The Father and Ouse have noticed some of the pictures shifting places, each presuming the other is to blame, playing some secret game that goes ignored.

By the time The Father reaches the top stair, he knows he's as alone as he can be on Muckle Flugga. He has completed a meditative process of disowning his faults and become the most efficient version of himself – all muscle and instinct, lessons hard-learned and repurposed wrath. Up here The Father is more than the sum of his parts – pilot, farmer, voyager, healer, mystic, meddler, megalith, a tireless soldier; devotee of the light; martyr to God's mayhem.

He must forget he is a man with a weakness for jam and figs, often covered in crumbs. Must forget his tickly bits, where he comes from, a citizen of nowhere but here and now. Must forget the ceilidh in his mind, and the dances he had, never had or nearly had with The Mother. Must forget grief, longing, soppiness. He must extinguish any fear concerning where he's heading, come hell or highwater. Must be baited by the present – hook, line and sinker – living in the impossible moment between the dropped glass and its collision with the floor. He must forget he is father to a broken-hearted boy; a child who, wearing the face of The Mother, has (against the odds) bounced back, brio-filled, full of love.

He must be not a father but The Father – life-saver, miracle-worker – first in line for the slaughter.

Whereas some hands land like wings glancing – a ladybird's, a butterfly's – and other hands have only unrest in them – hyena jaws, tusks mauling – The Father's hands must be both at once.

As a great watcher, his eyes have always been sharper than most, almost superhuman, even to many of his keeper comrades. What were smudges, blurs and silhouettes to them, were clear as reflections on still water to him – he could see tiny buds emerging on tree branches when others could barely decipher the thick trunk. He deems his vision God-given, yet only so he could fulfil his duties; he tries never to be showy with it, though doesn't always manage.

Before finishing any shift, The Father takes a full-circle compass view of the land. Only then, after this ritual, will he have attended to the lighthouse with full diligence. He looks to the north where most of the treachery comes from. There are rain clouds tiger-striping the coast, none with any growl in them, shot to pieces by a rising sun only getting stronger in its will.

He looks to the east, to Out Stack, its rocky fangs marking the air like the opened mouth of a dracula fish. It takes all he has not to get lost in a pastiche of memories of him and Ouse romping over it. How they'd pretend to The Mother they'd been searching its stony jaws for flotsam rather than playing explorers, though she knew the truth; not easily fooled, The Mother. More recently, he caught sight of – happenchanced upon – his son's sketches of Out Stack, and nearly wept at the warmth he cast over such a cold and jagged rumble of rocks. It was drawn exactly how The Father saw it: garishly alive.

He looks to the south: the mainland. He needn't fret much about the south. By the time the storms have passed over Muckle Flugga the island has shred them to splinters. It's the people on the mainland that cause him worry. The ones he'd rather avoid, the ones snooping in his business, the ones who know too much and lord it over him. He could take any man on that island in a fist fight, even half-cut, and has done; sometimes for honour, other times for sport. They all owe him, though most of them resent that and see his worth only as a mascot for their safety.

He looks to the west, to Muckle Flugga's cove, the way everything comes in – fish, food, whisky, Figgie, his boy, that arrogant lodger. Not the KLAMS, they'd come up the south passage, ascend on ropes, sneaky like. He makes sure there's always eyes on that vertiginous gateway, and often loosens the rocks so they offer no grip and would come away if used as a foothold. Beyond the cove, the Faroes, the tip of Greenland and, eventually, North America – with all its chintzy thrills and New World promise. How glad he was of the distance between them and this circus of bravado, this land of braggadocio. The Mother read book after book about the great American dream, twaddle by frowzy authors making a mint off peddling false hopes and quick fixes. He'd pulp the lot of them, and their books, but not the way The Mother laughed, sobbed or glowed after reading their stories.

With the compass complete, The Father marks his shift over, a clock driven by uneven skies. It's then and only then he affords himself some rest and reflection. He sleeps on the floor of the lantern room, out on widow's walk, hunched over on the gallery deck, or the top landing of the great staircase by a portrait of David Stevenson. He sleeps where he can with an exhaustion that makes bones dissolve to dust and eyelids pull down like anchors.

On the other side of a fierce kip, The Father shakes the rain out his hair, reinhabits his skin and descends the stairs – letting the life he's lived seep back into him, the memories return. At this point, he notices he's picked up a cold, curses it, then tries to be grateful for the snot.

NINETEEN

Tonight's the night, Firth decides: after such a rejuvenating expedition there's no other way to sleep but in the hammock. He fills the giant bath beneath it full to its bubbling brim. If he tumbles out of this sky-swing at a fortuitous angle, it'll be a wet water mattress for a landing. Nightshirt ready, he clambers up the rungs of the ladder and deposits his bag of bones into the embrace of the hammock above.

Ouse. Ouse. Ouse, he scats to himself, rolling the name around his mouth like a gobstopper until it crumbles into popping candy. And for a moment, he's flying there, under a massive bevy of stars, miles away from the consequences of any of his former actions, feeling elastic and fresh.

Swinging in this netted bed, Firth concludes that there is a magic to Muckle Flugga, yet, in his case, it is a dangerous type that makes life feel more liveable. And so his mind, ruined as it is, returns to the nastiness that keeps him leashed to his sorrows.

If only Ouse knew how shitty and petulant he could be behind this veil of kindness. It is not so much a façade – for he *does* feel most himself when being kind – but is worked for harder than is natural for someone who is truly good.

He recalls that one time when friends invited him round for dinner to cheer him up after a rush of rejections on his new manuscript, and he cycled over on what started as a crisp, cool autumn night but ended up being a gelid ride in unforgiving rain. How he cussed them on the way over; calling them repugnant name after repugnant name, digging up personal traumas to smite them most grossly. Drenched to the bone, he decided upon arrival he would demand they apologise for this shoddy situation, them being the reason he was out in the first place. After all, they never come round to his gaff because they've the new baby now and everything revolves around their 'saintly' existence as life-givers. Any cretin can have a baby, he thought, it's hardly a miracle, it happens by accident all the time, to fuckwits and scuzzbuckets alike – what an absurd and selfish desire to want to multiply in an already over-populated city. As if their little sprog would amount to anything more than sandwich-filler in the grand scheme of things. They were never this puritanical before they had this 'darling' infant, and he slandered them for it. Worse than that, he wished their child away – lost, stolen or condemned to a life in the workhouses, he couldn't have cared less.

By the time he did actually arrive, the rain had eased up and he was thankful for the feast they'd prepared, which smelled scrumptious even from the street below. He acknowledged that he hadn't ever actually invited them to his home for a meal, nor could he have hosted a dinner-crowd in his cramped little attic apartment. Most of all, he really did love these humans who cared for him more than he deserved. Not only that, he was proud to be godfather to their thoroughly lovely little human who had gorgeousness glimmering in her eye as soft as fresh snow.

The audacity of it came when they opened the door with a warm towel for him, remarking how they presumed he'd be sheltering from the storm, in a pub perhaps, and might not make it over. Instead of admitting he nearly did just that, Firth made a big show of how refreshing the journey had been and derided the inclemency of the weather. In return, the couple complimented his adventurous spirit and sangfroid. Christ on a bike, what a toxic wretch he had become.

This same friend, Cam, struggled as a writer, despite having double the talent of Firth – they never knew how to play the game and were too besotted by lovely Tay, their beau, to truly participate. Little did Cam know, Firth on more than one occasion had downplayed their friendship, pooh-poohing and even ridiculing his friend's work to people in the publishing world – truly baleful behaviour. An injustice done not just to this friend but to several young writers Firth had become close with – all of whom were clearly much more remarkable than he was. Firth is a true galvaniser of talent in humans, that is until they become competition. He's so lavishly championing of artists outside of the literary world that nobody would ever suspect foul play; not of him.

With eyes narrowing, from *bon vivant* to bestial, Firth had acted out of fear. Fear that the arrival of fresh voices of a high calibre might well put him out of business. Fear that the finite number of opportunities within Edinburgh's literary scene were already fought over as furiously as spam scraps amongst the starving. He was sickeningly ashamed of his ruthless actions when things were going well. Yet when his livelihood was hanging by a thread, and he'd just had to shirk out of another high-society shindig for lack of funds, he felt entirely vindicated.

Worse than his scheming was his hubris – Ouse would soon see the full extent of such ulcerated vanity. Firth remembers corrupting a perfectly good morning upon hearing the results of a writing competition he'd not bothered to enter, nor was even aware of. A morning that was not without its pleasantries, because the bread was warm, the milk cool, the juice freshly squeezed, and it had all been paid for with money earned by whisking up words. Plus there was the afternoon still to come, glorious and full of promise. But now suddenly he was not a winner – a not-winner, the unwinner of a writing competition that wouldn't have changed his life even if he had bothered to enter and won the bastard. How ill he must be never to see a smile, only the teeth behind it.

Then there was that time the guy in the coffee house watching him write said, *Best of luck to you, laddie, maybe one day it'll be you in all them shops*, with a big thumbs-up of encouragement. Firth retorted bombastically that this was the fourth of his books, for which the advances were getting higher and the readerships larger. The old man looked deflated, as if swindled out of the chance to cheer on his outside bet to win the race. Firth knew what the man wanted, to give a boost to the underdog, yet he couldn't restrain himself from gloating. And everyone lost.

He's so tired of falling short of his own prophecies, hoary tales he'd lied into existence in the first place. Tired of acting smug and invincible when inside he's begging for mercy. This body – an ungrateful, itchy, little boy's body – unworthy of the heat beneath, he had laid it to waste.

How many other writers out there had been spat on? he wonders. Really spat on – where spit is propelled from the mouth like a snake casts venom from its fangs. Firth has been spat on, many times, everything from light demonstrative sprays to huge gelatinous gobs; saliva loaded up with half-chewed food or creamy with blood. He'd deserved each assault. And worse – in some cases, much worse.

In an attempt to steer away from this black hole of cognitive chaos, at least for now, Firth begins listing qualities that might well suggest he's on the side of the good guys. Although he believes such clear-cut divisiveness between good and evil to be a form of religious fearmongering that warps the minds of those looking to live productive, contented lives in the middle ground, he puts that to one side for now – as the desperate often do.

Wriggling in the hammock now, attempting to sleep, he starts reeling off his meagre saving graces.

He's always rooting for the passenger running for a train about to pull off. He feels happier when they catch it, carries its warmth, and never derives any pleasure from someone narrowly missing their chance to leave.

His heart melts for the soppy songs the busker on the High Street plays – even when out of tune, slurry and raspy with hunger. Even though he knows, now, that many of the original tunes were written ironically by wealthy writing collectives pretending to care more than they do about the plight of the working classes.

He could be brought to tears by the sight of an abandoned mitten mulching in the gutter.

He adores the way people's eyes shift when they enter a frightening room only to be surprised by the warm glance of someone they love – the appearance of dry land, coated in heather, over the bow of a lost boat.

When witnessing a kid being bullied – wearing the signs of anguish on their face – he experiences an ache wash through his body until a drum beats in his chest.

He misses his mum an awful lot, and she was a really, truly good person – at times, maudlin and sentimental, but unswervingly lovely. He hates how easily she was overlooked, and how much more he could have done for her. Fuck, he misses her so much.

The main reason he wishes he was dead is to alleviate the burden on those he cares about and to prevent himself from further hurting people he loves.

That'll do for now, he gasps, beginning to well up. Seven is plenty, his best friend at primary school's favourite number, a lucky number. Enough to stay the heart from frosting over for another night or two. Sufficient to cast the darkness out his headspace for just long enough to let exhaustion take hold and slumber creep in.

Even the moon sometimes feels tied to the tracks, Firth muses, drifting, desperate to go somewhere no-one knows its name. He feels his body lighten as he moves beyond the lead weight of sore bones. Eyes flicker open, then closed, then open – he swears he sees a ship on the horizon – then closed.

TWENTY

Firth wakes harshly to a *rat-a-tat-tat . . . rat-a-tat-tat* at the old stained-glass window, forceful enough for him to worry about the immediate future of the glass. Outside, dark encases dark. A silhouette smears its print onto the glass, all but invisible until a flash of light in the hinterland exposes something terrible.

He leaps out of bed and rushes to the window, where he strains to hear what is happening outside. First, there's a shrill cry then a huddle of low, sonorous voices. A song, it seems, a song amongst cries of terror. Pressing his face against the glass he deciphers amber on the clifftop above the cove, flames on spears thrust up into the air – a cluster of humans of assorted shapes and sizes armed with fire. It's more of a ruckus than could possibly be made by The Father, Ouse and Figgie alone. Something is gravely wrong.

Wrenching the door open and clambering out the bothy in his bare feet, he's soon immersed in mud and running through the long grass. Sharp reeds snap at his legs like striking scorpions. To his right, the bright of the lighthouse is muted, faded, lower in the sky than the usual. It's less a beam, more a wisping gauze. Must be the queen of all fogs, Firth thinks; a pea souper. The guts of slain ghosts are raining down.

The wind howling and the rain razoring, he sinks deeper into the mud, shin-deep now – the boggy ground near claiming his feet for its own as he squelches onwards, ungainly but moving, still moving. Firth burns all the fuel in his body, empties his reserves.

Reaching the pinnacle of the cliff, before the dip, before the fall, he stumbles to a stop. The people, the light-bearers, are no longer there but down below. There must be ten of them, no, more than ten, many more. Still they huddle, still they sing. The only way down is by a steep and treacherous path, rocky and inches thin – a difficult descent by day, with guidance. He had only seen The Father take this path. Firth panics. *Where are they?! Ouse and The Father . . .*

As the fog begins to ebb, the collective torchlight of the mob scratches a partial vista in the sky. Firth sees a huge ship out at sea that's crashed onto the rocks. Yes, so clear now, how could he have missed it before? It's in peril, it's sinking. The flotsam of the vessel crashing to shore, a deathly disgrace of what had once been magnificent.

And the shrill calls, the desperate animal howls. Men and women on the ship, screaming for their lives; bodies already in the water trying not to drown in the vicious, hurling sea. A man collapsed on the sand, could he be dead already? Firth tries not to look.

That's a dangerous cove on a clear day, a gauntlet of hazards and tricks, never mind in this merciless dark with a net of mist laid over it. Firth feels it calling him: the black, dismal rocks full of malignant intent – when the swell empties the waters around them, their villainous crowns open into crocodile jaws. Those perfect chiselled hunters of unbeatable death.

Why aren't you helping? Firth screams at the light-bearers. *There are people dying.* But the phalanx of bodies large and small simply knots together, singing, resolute. A few more people he hadn't seen before line the fringes of the shore, while others sit on rocks staring, still as spectres: it's like they're an audience in an amphitheatre watching gladiators fight to their death. Watching and waiting for the show to finish, for the sea to drown them.

This is insanity, Firth whimpers through trembling breaths.

Suddenly the ship breaks in two with a thwacking sound akin to wood splitting in a hungry fire. At once, it begins to sink more rapidly. The boom of men's hopeless voices bleeds upon the air as they're thrown into the warring waves, sucked into a whorl of death. The sight of a father hugging his child and calmly pointing to the catastrophe fills Firth's bones with fear. A spiritedness inside of him bellows out, *Ouse? Where are you? Where's The Father?*

He looks to the horizon and sees the befogged glimmer of the lighthouse. He rushes towards it, passing huts, fishermen's huts, which surely can't have been there before – two, three, four more of them. All apparently empty, all their dwellers down on the shore participating in this circus of despair. It's a race now, he thinks, a race for survival.

Firth arrives on the doorstep of the lighthouse only for the thick fog to unveil something terrifying. Not the lighthouse, not buttressing bricks, but a great collapsing bonfire with at least three, no four, bodies crowded around it. They're wearing dark earthy tunics with scowling faces and hissing voices. Where are the bricks? Where are the hundreds of feet of watchtower? The great life-saving giant, that emblem of hope marking the horizon. For all The Father's faults he is committed to that, committed to hope. The Father is no doomsayer, he said so himself. Torn down in the night? Can't be, Firth concludes, he must have gotten lost in the confusion, deceived by the fog's obfuscation and come upon a fresh side of the island he's not yet travelled to. This land is ever growing.

HELP! he screams. *Help!* Deaf to his calls, the tunicked figures are busy wrestling with the wood and hurling dirt. Aghast, Firth sees now that they're not building up the fire, not providing light, but tearing it down. The rabble are clubbing at the stumpy iron structure that once supported the flames, mangling its frame. The bludgeoned fire crumbles in on itself – a beggar on its knees. Already castrated, buckets of water, mud and wet blankets are tossed onto what fight the flames have left in them. As the amber glow diminuendos, a darker still comes upon them, as if to signal the end of days.

Why won't you save them? Firth pleads. *Cowards! Fucking cowards!* this time catching everyone's attention.

To save those men would be a sin, the leader declaims, incensed. *This is God's will. God has sent these winds to provide us succour. It is God's storm. God's judgement. How dare you question God, you wretch!*

With this Firth drops to his knees, violently sobbing – the rain falls ferociously, the soil turning black.

He's rewarding us for our fealty, a softer voice hisses in his ear; the figure's coarse lips touching his neck send knives down Firth's neck. A brute of man approaches from the rear and yanks Firth's arms behind his back; he gives no fight. Joined by a third body, they bind his wrists with rope and bear down upon him.

The wood from that ship is for our houses, to expand our church. Them crates washed ashore will feed our children. Yes, God is good. God is benevolent to his loyal servants.

Down in the cove, a flare is sent into the air, illuminating the true depth of the devastation. It's becoming a graveyard out there. This is not a rescue mission, this is sport; these people are gathering the spoils of tragedy.

And then he sees the worst of it: an exhausted sailor paddling into the shallows is seized upon by the gaggle, kicked then thumped with rocks until the last embers of life in him wheeze out and die.

With bloodshot eyes, Firth appeals to his imprisoners, hoping this sickening act will be one step too far for them, hoping it'll have pushed them to the brink and summoned their sanity. But no such sympathy lives here. One of them is praying now, in thanks for the deliverance of the wreck and the cargo. Others join in, creating a haunting choir of voices. The leader smiles, smugly nodding as if a grave injustice has been rectified. There is a wickedness in the way they jeer the waves on that spooks Firth to his core.

The mob, Firth's imprisoners, take forth their staffs and torches and beat them upon the ground, injecting poison into the heartbeat of the earth and cheering emphatically to their saviour. *Where were the witches to save them?* someone calls facetiously from above, the crowd cackling with laughter.

Upon catching the disgust, the bitterness, the brokenness in Firth's eyes, the leader of the group has seen enough. *It's lights out for you*, he snarls with rancour, clubbing Firth across the head until everything descends into a deep, pitiless dark.

TWENTY-ONE

Firth wakes, wet and panicked, in the bathtub; submerged in water, gasping for breath. The hammock swings like a pendulum above him. It is morning now. He is alive and pleased about it.

He leaps out the bath, through the door and into the fresh chirruping day. The sun has risen, as it always does, the lighthouse stands sentry on the summit, and there is Ouse, also alive, which relieves and delights Firth no end. He calls to Ouse, but is an inaudible distance away, so must instead rush back into the bothy to dress and join him, whipping off his soaked kimono and bundling into chunky cords, woolly jumper and clomping boots. What a classic country bumpkin he's become in such a short time! Firth laces up his boots proudly, with fidelity, watching Ouse as he does so.

Ouse is loading rocks into his coat pockets and down the slip of his wellies. Stocked up, he makes towards the sea. It's suspicious enough to send Firth running after him – though he's not fearing for Ouse's life, he is keen to make sure nothing's gone awry. Still being tethered to a horrid dream undoubtedly has Firth thinking more drastically than is rational. The sickening images are still pinballing around inside of him, distorting his vision and bullwhipping his other senses.

Firth reaches the summit: chest-thumping, breath-heaving and dribbling. And there is Ouse, in the shallows of the water, long coat and rubber boots, with a bucket, collecting seaweed. Catching sight of him, Ouse waves in Firth's direction and summons him down towards him. With the gift of daylight and determination, Firth powers down the treacherous path, which is smaller and much more manageable in the waking world.

Firth attempts to speak, only to discover his voice missing, frazzled, so instead flings his arms around Ouse like he'd intended to back on the tombolo. For his efforts he finds himself on the receiving end of another almighty electric shock. But this time he pushes through it, into it, not letting go nor recoiling as the voltage snaps at his skin.

Surprised by Firth's frantic state, Ouse pats him reassuringly and narrates the situation in an attempt to mollify the frenzy in him. He explains the seaweed is for the soil, fish-feed and cooking. That the stones in his boots are to make sure he's not blown off his feet, because on severe wind days up here humans too need anchors.

Firth scrambles between attempting to splurge the details of the dream he's just plummeted out of and refuting the logic of stone-weighted shoes. The result being a raggedy description of fire and huts and a huge crash and terrible people with clubs comingled with the assertion that there's barely even a breeze out today and the sun is swooped all over them.

Focussing on the weather, Ouse reluctantly concurs. That said, he strains to point out there was no birdsong this morning and that this tends to be a harbinger for a windstorm, so he was merely exercising caution in the rock gathering. With that settled, Ouse slips off his wellies and turns them upside down, letting their cargo plop into the tide. Firth paces around, a sprung coil – his mind clearly still spinning, so Ouse recounts stories of wild storms past, of gales of such a magnitude it felt the world was ending; such gusty force they couldn't go outside, and The Father had them holed up inside the lighthouse for days on end.

During these enforced periods indoors, The Mother was a true blessing; she would do impressions of everyone in the community and read out loud, theatrically. The Father was not quite so averse to books when The Mother was reading them. In fact, when The Mother was alive, he wasn't averse to many things he seemed to reject so fully today. It is, however, Ouse's description of himself playing the organ until his fingers seized up that causes Firth to rattle back to life.

An organ? Firth mumbles, beginning to gather himself.

Ouse confirms that, yes, there is an old church organ in the lighthouse. He recounts how The Father rescued it from becoming kindling and now has Ouse play it during the meanest stretches of any storm. He speaks of how The Father believes filling the air with music betters their chances of distracting the tempest long enough for ships in trouble to flee its grasp. *Every monster has a song that soothes the smite of their swell*, Ouse concludes.

Though the crueller part of his brain thinks that Ouse is the song and he the monster, Firth finds the sentiment beautiful, and starts to smile as he separates last night's dreams from Muckle Flugga's reality. Just a nightmare, he settles with adamance, removing his boots, slipping out of his cords and beginning to dutifully help collect the seaweed. Ouse indicates the colour, shape and size they're looking for, then takes a ceremonial chomp out of a chunky bit to demonstrate the zest locked within. Soft waves lick their legs like a hundred cheeky tongues, and Firth mellows further. He finds a strength in being useful: the slimy tails in his hands, the cool water lapping at his skin, the weird gurgling sound Ouse makes when either of them unroots a piece of seaweed that's of the cooking-pot calibre.

Continuing the same conversation that Firth presumed had been laid to rest ten minutes previously, Ouse picks up where he had left off.

One time the winds ran so bad Figgie couldn't make deliveries for

144

weeks. Living off stale bread and soft biscuits really makes you appreciate potatoes and cheese. The Father hardly ate a mouthful, making sure me and The Mother were fed first.

Without thinking, Firth blurts out, *When did The Mother die?* Having been building up to asking this question, he hates himself for unpacking it so utterly tactlessly.

After a few seconds deliberating, Ouse answers, softly casting out the words as if sending dandelion seeds into a wind.

She left here two years ago, two years to the day.

Firth, getting the feeling Ouse has more to say on this, bites his tongue in reverence. His wait is rewarded.

She was special, Ouse furthers. *Her leaving changed everything. There were more people on Muckle Flugga, an extended family, but the heaviness of her absence, and the ferocity of our grief, scared them all away. She was . . .*

After a few seconds thinking on it, Ouse simply squats back down and returns to picking seaweed, defeated by the impossibility of translating the haecceity of The Mother into language.

Firth has trouble with the notion that the collective grief of father and son scared away any previous denizens. He ratifies to himself that no doubt it was The Father's grief alone that was responsible for all such ructions. Firth would fear the repercussions of presenting The Father with an overboiled egg; the size of the chasm the man could carve from true tragedy is petrifying to consider. Firth literally quakes at the thought.

Ouse puts down the bucket and picks himself up again, ready to speak now, as if suddenly granted safe passage across an impossible crossing. He senses Firth's judgement of The Father and feels compelled, both viscerally and morally, to add some virtue to his reckoning.

The change in The Father has been heart-breaking, Ouse explains, *but we all understand it. I'm just hoping the ire in him will burn out. All pain must have an end point, right?*

How did The Mother die? Firth asks, more careful this time, pushing into Ouse's reticence.

To Firth's surprise Ouse's arm comes down in front of him and, with a finger to his own lip, he squeezes out a *shhhhhhhh* to hush them into silence. Ouse's finger draws back from his mouth and out towards the water. Firth follows the direction he's pointing in. Just a stone's throw away is a pair of sea otters, floating on their backs, bellies in the air and holding hands. He didn't see them at first because they're festooned in kelp, cocooned in it like pigs in blankets.

Ouse and Firth look at each other in tacit agreement that it's time to stop talking and begin marvelling. For a minute, could have been an hour, they watch the two otters bobbing around in the shallows as if old friends on a once-in-a-lifetime trip. Ouse has picked which otter he would be, and with neither knowing, Firth has picked the same one.

After a short run of wordlessness, Firth can't help but insert some sort of commentary, as much as he tries to restrain himself. *Fabulous, aren't they?* Firth muses, finding his voice back with brio. *You know, a Canadian friend of mine once saw an otter having sex with a dead seal. Funny thing was . . .*

Ouse curtails this sentence by raising his finger once more. However, this time it's towards Firth's lips – not touching them but offering a glimpse of what it would be like if they did touch, finger and lips.

The otters, upon noticing this exchange, begin frolicking all the more. One twirls a few times, showing off, while the other starts scraping around for molluscs, returning successful, with a bounty for both.

Firth, at first eyeing up the otter's oysters, soon finds himself distracted by a disturbance further out at sea – something has the waves cresting white and the water groaning in despair. Something he can't see or fathom but feels in his gut. With a lurch, Firth is pulled back into the tumult of his terrible dream. Shrapnel flashes of the drowning figures and the pulverised fire scattergun through his mind, hammering his head like rivets into a ship.

Hey, have you hit your head? Ouse questions concerned, looking directly in Firth's eyes for perhaps only the second time since they met. Tracing his forehead with his fingertips, Firth finds there is indeed a lump – a bulge with a gash through it in the exact place that murderous bastard had clubbed him out cold. *It can't be!* Firth wonders in disbelief, pushing at the lump until a surge of pain shoots between his eyes, the gash beginning to weep.

K-A-B-O-O-M

A loud bang erupts into the air at such a volume both the boys rush to cover their ears. Firth notices the echoes cause such a reverberation in the cliff face that a few rocks dismount, landsliding down, kicking up dust as they ride.

Above them is The Father, contrapposto on the precipice of the hill: a raised gun in one arm, the other pointing in the direction of the cove. Casting his eyes back out to the shallows, Firth sees nothing more than a couple of ripples in the otter-emptied ocean. He's glad there's no blood spilling from below, fearing for his own. *That fucking man*, he winces, equally terrified about what comes next.

Firth turns to console Ouse, but the tide is already filling the prints his wellies have left in the sand. At this point Firth notices

147

he's only partially dressed, his cords now floating in the shallows. The Father, like a devil on brandy, howls wolfish into the ether then sinks into the long grass, vanishing from sight.

TWENTY-TWO

Firth contents himself through the day drawing and walking and doesn't see Ouse again. He does, however, come across Ouse's bucket tossed into the pond, all the seaweed they collected together cast across the gravel, spoiling in the sun. All day, he stealthily patrols the island in case Ouse needs him, or simply needs to know he's there and not afraid. He catches in the wind a sound akin to horse hooves clacking in an empty alleyway, attempts to track it but can't source where it's coming from.

Later, he hears shouting, not necessarily at Ouse but certainly about him. Whether Ouse was directly within The Father's firing line or not is by the by; such cantankerousness will always have repercussions for someone so gentle. The thought of Ouse being tormented wounds Firth in a most immense and oddly refreshing way.

All these uproarious sounds make Firth recall the time he saw a drunken man beat his dog in the local pub, putting cigarettes out on the poor creature's snout and kicking it when it whimpered. That was until a tougher, and more caring, man confronted him on his nefarious behaviour; seeing the canine torturer off with the challenge of a 'square-go round the back'. Later that night, old pusillanimous Firth chanced upon that same odious man in a graveyard punishing the creature all the more for the humiliation it had caused him. Firth turned the other way, only braving to shout out in the animal's defence once over the other side of the wall and hidden from sight.

Plagued by these thoughts, and determined to do better, Firth passes Ouse's studio as the dark draws in and notices a light still on.

He makes to knock but finds himself too trepidatious to enter and so sneaks around to the back window to take a sly swatch at what's happening inside. Ouse is not knitting but sketching. He had presumed the patterns on Ouse's extraordinary knitwear were copied from books or other seamstresses. If those were his own designs, taken from his own sketches, Ouse is not just a supremely talented needler but a real bloody artist.

The focus in Ouse's eyes as he scratches pencil lead across sketchpad is transcendental – testament to a conviction in a future beyond their beginnings on the page. Firth stays only long enough to satisfy his concern for Ouse's safety is unfounded and feels venerable on leaving, knowing he could have snooped further, and wanted to, but didn't.

Instead, Firth goes to bed – in the bed this time, as opposed to the hammock – with the skylight sheeted over and a fuse lit inside his heart. A self-proclaimed, stiffened heart he currently feels thawing, for good reason: talent is Firth's obsession. Being near it, propagating it, recognising when it needs protection to flourish, separating it from the bloodsuckers, feeding the mettle in it, growing the myth of it. He has an acute ability to identify talent embryonically, before even the beholder knows its full scope. Firth is not creeping around the trunk of talent, not throttling it, but extracting its sap in order to bottle it, and, in time, enhance its power. He has a nose for this. He sees himself as talent's perfumer. Its impresario. More clandestinely, he's also accessing the threat of it, determining when and how to play his hand when the moment comes.

Firth cherishes talent for its incandescence in a grey and murky world. Keeping so close to it also means that eventually, by osmosis, he absorbs a little bit of it. More than anything, he adores how talent can redeem the irredeemable life – how in its presence people

150

forgive the unforgivable and excuse the inexcusable.

How enthralled Firth would be to put Ouse in this esteemed category of human, to collect, care for and service him. Firth's eyes marble and glint at the thought of protecting Ouse – he could use his wit, his badness, his doggedness and garrulous grit to keep him safe, and thriving. He'd be most capable of that, best placed for it, in fact. Rattling around Firth's mind are bold thoughts and bolder propositions. As he drifts, he feels his tongue throb with purpose and words fortify. Sliding into a dream he wriggles in the sheets like a hunted eel.

TWENTY-THREE

Firth stirs to the sound of desultory clatter, like billiard balls *click-clacking*. It's not light out, not dark, the half-dark of dusk. Then the sharp sound of bleating bursts into the room. He snaps opens his eyes and comes face to face with the mad grimace of a goat; its wet coal of a nose, slabs of tongue for ears, and sharp devil horns just inches away. The sound of its bleating enters his body as it lurches forth and bites at his hooter. Firth howls as it removes flesh from his face, blood gushing from the wound; the cloven-hoofed lucifer scuttles out the door with its corporeal prize.

He wakes suddenly, this time for real, to the bothy's door rattling at its hinges, the goat-faced assailant nowhere to be seen and his own nose stone-cold but fully intact. Surprisingly, he feels cosy as a wet cat brought in from the storm and plonked down by the fire.

This fucking place! Firth yells, rankled, then laughing at the absurdity of it all. *Perhaps this is a purgatory?* he muses before remembering he doesn't believe in such things. He's quick dressed and out into the fine florals of the day – it's calm and clear with the toatiest wee breeze. As he passes the main living quarters, where he collects his supplies, he spies a note tacked to the kitchen door: *The Father & I are off to the mainland for food and things. Help yourself to breakfast (big as you like). O.*

Firth, suspicious of the notion of being left alone on the island, does some further checks. *The Covenant* is gone, there's no smoke coming from the pits, the lighthouse looks to be sound asleep. Astounding to think The Father would down tools for a day and take

152

a trip to the mainland, even for practical reasons. It's the most serene, sun-speckler of a weather-yard they've had to date, but still, The Father guards that lighthouse like Cerberus at the gates of Hades. Firth does a quicksilver lap around the main section of house and then confirms it: the coast is clear.

He enters the kitchen like cock of the north, smooshes a banana into a bread baguette and makes himself a strong coffee. Spotting a dish of salmon flakes marked for his attention, and feeling louche, he smacks the fish into the sandwich and takes a voracious bite.

King of the castle: he validates himself, flumps down on The Father's seat and begins parodying the way he drinks his whisky with vociferous slurps. Once he's scoffed and quaffed the lot, he rises to his feet, feeling gutsy and purposeful, and heads back out for a bit of overdue snooping.

In honour of Ouse, he stops to make himself a dandelion crown, a far more intricate and sturdy construction than the daisy chain, which he immediately dons. Content with this new weedy headpiece, he marches to the library, looking over his shoulder with every second step, then pounding through the door with such force he ends up on his knees. Having convinced himself that his mission here is to survey the special shelves – the ones where Ouse houses some of The Mother's books (really, all but her most treasured few) and a flock of his own favourite reads – Firth plays the role as if being watched. Of course, he knows, heck even the puffins know, it's a nosy in Ouse's studio he's really after gawking at.

Fingering his way through Ouse's favourite books makes Firth's heart butterfly-flutter – it's such a pure and exultant feeling. Amongst Ouse's choice cuts are those writers he expected: Robert Louis Stevenson (the whole oeuvre as far as he can recall), Mary Shelley, J. M. Barrie, Oscar Wilde, Charles Dickens; and then some more surprising one-offs: *The Poetry of Rumi, The Tibetan Book of the Dead, A Guide to Scotland's Topiary: from palaces to parks.*

Yet when he makes towards Ouse's studio to look round, he can't do it. It feels like burglary and he doesn't want to cheapen whatever is awakening between them. If he is eventually invited in, he won't risk defiling the experience by having to lie his way through it, pretending to see things for the first time. No, the studio shall remain unsoiled by his trespassing eyes. However, The Father's forbidden gang-hut, which he had stumbled on the other night, feels ripe for the raiding.

Firth isn't so cavalier that he doesn't do another swift check of the perimeter before entering this forbidden realm, but with the boat still gone and no-one in sight he slinks on in.

The smell is the first thing that hits him – he would like to say it is an unprovoked attack on the senses, but he's the one trespassing. Noisome whisky wafts, then the smoke of a fire that's chewed through all manner of precious things; their mangled outlines protruding beyond the ash. A juicy tobacco pouch lies half open, spilling its stringy guts. The ashtray is overflowing with butts puffed right to the arsehole, yet he's never seen The Father smoking.

A gun soon jostles for Firth's attention – a violent creature slumped pitiably against the wall; death masquerading as a crutch; a harmless thing. Even homicidal maniacs look innocent when dreaming, he reminds himself. Firth doesn't know the first thing about guns, yet he has witnessed the power they wield over men. After a few ales, he's seen dear creatures, both old and young, crumble at the thought of the harm they've caused when armed by the state. Worse still are those who boast about the lives they've taken, having lost all compassion to the battle of balancing their lethal acts.

An old bird's nest sits in the corner of the room like a thorn of crowns, a couple of small unfertilised eggs inside (pale blue and freckled with faces drawn on them), alongside a much larger goliath of an egg that shimmers golden and looks to have been glued back together. A huge toy toad is sitting in there with them like a roosting mammy. Nope, on closer inspection, very much the real deal, a dead and wizened monster toad. Getting close up to the nest to inspect this bizarre nativity confirms to Firth it's, at least in part, culpable for the odour. Firth confirms to himself that this is likely the single weirdest thing he's seen on Muckle Flugga, perhaps anywhere.

Apart from the untidiness, the malignant device, the pungent aromas and whatever abnormality that nest is, the remainder of the room is pretty much an arcade of sentiment. Hundreds of photos are strewn across the walls. Their frames a little decrepit, sitting crooked or hung squinty. Each marks a memory The Father must savour, too many to count.

One photo features The Father and a woman that Firth presumes is The Mother – with shock-black wavy hair, her beauty immediately recognisable. Alongside them are two other couples, hanging off each other's shoulders or looping arms. He assumes these people are the other keepers Ouse mentioned, his extended family. Two babies on a picnic blanket loll in front of them – one eating grass, the other cheering them on. Baby Ouse is the grass eater, he reckons. Cats eat grass to be sick, Firth recalls. Then thinking with pathos – this place was once teeming with happiness, love, and comradery. How quiet it must seem now in comparison, how eerie, bare and still.

Another photo is of Ouse, definitely toddler Ouse, being pushed on a rope swing, holding on for dear life, yet with a smile as wide as church music.

The biggest photo is of a scrappy little dog. In fact, it's not a photograph but a portrait, amateur but not far short of a photographic likeness. The name Lomond is laced in fine calligraphy on the bottom of the frame.

An unframed map is on the wall, partly torn, but with the intact section of it focussing on Scotland's westerly side. The top of the Isle of Lewis and all of Scotland's left shoulder, right up to the tip of its crow beak – that's Ullapool to Durness and just beyond is Tongue. The coastline of Durness has been scribbled over, its lines reinforced, in what looks to be blood. Garlanding that, the word *RESURGAM* is poorly written, as if traced but not understood. Firth recalls this to mean 'I shall rise again' in Latin (he'd heard this used as part of a play to devastating effect; Latin not having been part of his poor boy's education, which he commonly has to muddy over).

Is this where The Father is from? Firth questions aloud, squishing his pointing finger onto the map as if to leak some oil upon it. He's never thought of The Father as being from anywhere, nor of having a childhood, just cast from nettles and bracken, skelped on the arse and sent forth to battle with a bottle in hand and a bush-fire in the belly.

This map, its morose bloodlines, make a muddle of the monster in The Father. Nostalgia and longing are at odds with the lost crusade of his fury. A mucky shard of glass on the floor below confirms Firth's suspicion that The Father has been using blood as ink.

The site of this combat zone of a room provides Firth with another confirmation – The Father's heart is not just nicked but lacerated. An ailment to which it might eventually succumb, if pawed at and fed enough booze. He knows only too well the difference between things that prey on the mind and those that fatally wound it.

An armchair sits side positioned to the fire, the creases in it

156

connoting this is The Father's seat alone, his spot of choice for captaining this messy affair; its horse-hair stuffing spilling out where the seams have ruptured. An old-fashioned dressing cabinet crushed into the corner of the room appears to be the vessel feeding everything. The mirror on it is smashed, perhaps punched. Its half-opened drawers are bulging with crumpled papers, more photographs, a smorgasbord of mishandled trinkets and well-thumbed objects. So much life stuffed in there, Firth doesn't know where to start.

A worn little model of Jesus crucified on the cross sits atop the dressing cabinet's mantel. He's looking savage with paint peeling off his dish, a black eye and a missing shin – though both bleeding feet remain.

Firth opens one of the upper side-cabinets to find a jewellery box within it. It's olive wood, finely polished, coffin-like in appearance. He can feel its wobbliness as he clasps it in his hands. There's a wee key sticking out of its lock, a blue tassel tied around it – it looks like a bluebird's bahookie hanging out a nest. Gripping the fragile box, he slowly winds open the lock. It's stiff and gives some pushback before flipping open. Firth gets an almighty fright as the box begins playing its loud and discordant music. In the commotion, the box fumbles out his hands and begins to plummet. Somewhat miraculously he manages to catch it from his own clumsy drop. *What a save*, he chuffs – the silenced box, snapped shut in the process, raised into the air victoriously.

Even with it back in his grasp the feeling comes over Firth that he's about to drop it all over again – a foreboding notion deriving from the petrifying consequences of destroying the irreplaceable. The tyrant inside him whispers that he might as well smash it and be done with it, destruction on his own terms. Foremost, he feels this way when holding babies.

Carefully re-opening the box reveals the top of a protruding screw rotating in circles to the clunky music. Likely there was once a dancer, a dove or a dog on top of it, Firth decrees, a little statuette of a pretty thing – perhaps it now lies scorched, twitching below the ashes.

Inside the box is rather barren, but what *is* in there shocks him: a lock of hair, plaited and tied with a silver ribbon. It's a clump; thick and dark. *Christ! It's The Mother's*, he winces, must be. The plaiting is tousled now, he suspects from being used by The Father to lightly brush his stubbled cheeks. There's a ring in there too, silver with the face of an owl on it – a purple stone in its right eye, the left eye's stone missing. Both objects sit on top of a thick sheet of folded paper, thick yet the inky writing on the other side is still visible through the folds.

He slips the paper from under the objects, reticent to touch the hair in case it unfankles or bites him. Unfolding the paper, he reads the words: Statutory Register of Death. It's a death certificate. The Mother's death certificate! He draws breath for courage, goose-pimpling as he does.

The Mother's name, not what he expected.

She was born in Edinburgh, that's a revelation. She died young. She must have been younger than The Father.

There's dear Ouse, his name and age at the moment she died, what a stilling thought, the world crumbling off axis into a murkiness that may never pass. A bit of Ouse will live forever in that day, he's no doubt.

She died here on Muckle Flugga, of course she did!

Where's the damn cause of death? he begs an imaginary administrator, parsing the page for the only answer he now seeks, until disturbed by the thud of someone trying to hoof open the door. His heart misses a beat and the blood rushes from his face at the noise,

158

which carries consequences so grave he's struggling to fathom the full extent. Thankfully, the doorstopper stymies their entry for a second or two longer, affording Firth some time to scramble and flail.

Abominably, in the process of jumping out of his skin, the jewellery box slips from his hand and clatters onto the stone floor, splitting open in the process.

Fuck! Fuck! FUCKING FUCK! Firths yelps, dropping to his knees to scoop the plait back into the box and shoving the death certificate back on top.

The Father might kill me, he thinks, *he might actually kill me*. Firth begins looking around for something to hit him with, calculating how ably he could arm himself with a dead toad and fistful of ash. Turning around to face his executioner, he sees not The Father but Figgie! It's Figgie! To his rapture, it's Figgie. Only Figgie. He may yet live to see another night.

I can explain, he squeals.

Figgie's face is at first a stopped clock, paused in place and time. She stills the world within the room and then decisively closes the door behind her. *No need*, Figgie responds calmy, taking the jewellery box from him and slotting its fallen wall back into place using the wooden peg she's scooped up from the edge of the fire's powdery loch – a peg Firth knows he'd have certainly missed in the cover-up. The box looks even wonkier than before, and there's a definite crack around the lid's hinge, but he may just get away with it. The thing's on its last legs any which way, and The Father only comes here pulverised, from what Firth's seen – he'll likely think he heavy-handed it himself. Yes, that'll do, Firth settles.

She drowned, in case you were wondering. In case Ouse hasn't told you. Figgie looks Firth dead in the eye as she delivers this news and he feels his skin wrinkle upon receipt of the words.

Firth's blindsided by this candour but doesn't dare question it – he's still caught in the utter relief that she is not The Father. Plus, he's getting the answers he's been desperately seeking, whether he deserves them or not.

Did she . . . was it . . . how come . . . ? Firth scraps around for the right diction but is thankfully put out his misery.

Nobody knows. Everything was fine, Figgie begins. *They'd been celebrating on the mainland that night: The Mother, The Father and the other keepers. It was The Father's birthday, which is the day before Ouse's. I was helping cover the light and keeping an eye on Ouse and Talla – she's the other keeper's bairn in that photo there, though she's aw grown up noo.*

They all came hame drunk and singing, you could hear them coming across the water – lairy, but laughing. I had a drink with them when they were back too. We stayed up late, everyone reminiscing and talking gibberish, they aw seemed pleased to see me. The Father and The Mother had a bit of a tiff about where they'd live in ten years' time. It all started as a stupid game. The Mother wanted to live in Paris and London before settling back into Edinburgh. The Father only wanted to be here, this was perfection to him. Not for The Mother though, she always wanted more, we were never enough for her. The only quarrels The Father ever lost were with The Mother.

Figgie stops and stares into the distance, attempting to temper her emotions. She picks up the thread again just as Firth itches to begin prodding. She's more factual in this tranche of the story, as if giving evidence. Notes how she stayed in the bothy that night on account of the lateness of the hour and booze having being taken – highlighting, again, it was just a little for her not being much of a drinker. A few hours later Figgie, being first up to check on Ouse and Talla, headed for her boat and her exit. And that's when she saw her, The Mother, floating in the shallows, drowned. Figgie ran back to get The Father, who rose wordlessly, pushed past her with a force that knocked her flat and raced to where The Mother's body bobbed. Though it was too late; The Mother's spirit had left her skin, which was spoiled, sodden and blue.

Why did I have to be the one to find her?! Figgie laments, sobbing. *He's never forgiven me.*

Firth, dumbstruck by the lugubriousness of the tale, embraces Figgie. In his arms she bawls like a child: a full fit of doleful sobbing. And then it's over, Figgie composes herself, comes up for air and begins again. She recounts how the rumours flew – the Father being who he is – that he drove her to it, that he killed her. It didn't matter what was done or said, from then on he would never be forgiven, and the gossip would only pustulate and grow more heinous as time passed. Just by looking at Figgie in that moment, Firth could sense the work she must have put in to protect The Father's reputation, the sacrifices she must have made.

Figgie, sensing Firth's confusion, jumps to the defensive. *He wasn't always so broken. He had a temper, aye, but that's his cross to bear, a toll paid for battling all that destruction – those malevolent forces that sink ships and snatch lives. He's always been fighting them. It doesn't matter how many he saves, it's those that died that stick wie him. And now, The Mother. The one thing he loved above aw else – above Ouse, and the light, above duty even, above . . . us all. Taken by the same force. It's just too cruel, his burden wiz heavy enough.* Figgie hides her face in her hands, sobbing from somewhere deep inside: a haunted pit within her lungs emptying its wet gravel.

You love him, Firth mutters, stunned, whispering near inaudibly: *And he barely even sees you.*

161

I did, she says after a deep breath – her voice cracking. *Perhaps I still do, but that love belongs to a version of The Father that lives in the past.*

Dumbfounded, Firth simply utters back, *But how?*

Why do we love any broken thing? Figgie shrugs.

Guilt? Pity? Firth guesses meanly, a little too eager to take a bite out of her feelings.

No, it's not that, Figgie rebuts. *It's knowing they deserve love more than most. Because they once weren't so broken, because they once had love and it was taken from them. Because I'm the happier of the two of us and that's not fair.*

He's a dragon, Firth rasps, *one wrong foot and he's breathing fire.*

You don't know him like I do, Figgie lambasts, *who he* used *to be. For someone who never felt love as a child, never had a Christmas dinner or a comforting hug, he's not doing badly; it's a miracle really. The reason you're safe here is him! He's protected these islands for years. I met him the first day he came here. A teenager, fresh to the service, me just a few years younger. And the life he's lived, what he was running from, what he escaped . . . He confided in me then.*

What *did he escape?* Firth interrupts, intrigued.

He was the most precocious teenager to ever enter the keeper's service. He got a medal from the Royal Humane Society after just two weeks on the job. Everyone always took him for ten years older than he was because of the troubles he carried. Those eyes. Terribly old eyes in such a strong young man, but still sparkly, never dimming, same as the light. And then came The Mother. The Mother was . . . So much. It wasn't until he became an assistant keeper that he met The Mother. I knew him first, she used to forget that. The Mother was holidaying on the mainland and The Father had a few days' leave. And, well, they met and that was that. I loved him first, though they married six weeks later.

Firth notices Figgie is spiralling, her caring countenance has splintered and her nerves are stretched.

I believe you, Firth says, raising his palms as a gesture of appeasement. It seems to work, as Figgie stops, draws breath like she's back from the brink of drowning. A few gulps of the moment and her face returns to itself.

Firth, sensing Figgie is at her most vulnerable, sits her down and opens a window to let in the fresh air and birdsong. Figgie finds relief in this; it is her type of music. He offers up a nip from The Father's nearby stash and then takes her hand as she sips it. Firth is also sensing Figgie's likely to now be at her most receptive to his machinations, so he seizes the opportunity to discuss the small matter of the future.

Ouse could do well with his work, you know. With his designs and drawings. If he studied, if he dedicated to the craft. He could make a life of it. I swear it to you, I know people who could help. I could help.

Intimidated, Figgie stands up and turns to the sea, knowing fine well how dangerous a suggestion that would be in The Father's presence. Yet something in her also longs for Ouse's freedom from the tough, solitary life of Muckle Flugga.

He was in the paper, you know, she says, quietly. *The Father keeps it hidden, but keeps it all the same.* Figgie quickly finds the exact tear of newspaper she's looking for amongst the mammoth jumble of detritus with a swiftness that serves, to Firth, as an admission that she, too, has been snooping in here. Firth is handed the paper and thumbs around it, not seeing the story at first for some sort of exposé on local twins who claim to have seen a crew of female pirates rescuing a beached basking shark. But once he does, that lit fuse in him turns into a flare.

Local lad wins Scotland-wide design competition, it reads. And

163

there's a picture of Ouse in the market on the mainland, the one the knitting women on the ferry had spoken about. He's holding up his sketchpad with an illustration of the giant rug that graces the floor of the library inked across it. Firth is awestruck, wondering how long it took Ouse to make this intricate, complex creation, how he could have conceived of such a thing at such an age.

That should be hanging in a gallery, Firth declares, verklempt. *What a feat. He's amazing, you know that, right? Ouse is amazing.*

The way Firth says this puts Figgie on alert, and her inspecting eyes in the moments that follow cause him to wince and confirm her suspicions.

You love him, Figgie says with appreciation.

I do.

Me inawl, she confirms softly, as if admitting to the same sin.

Figgie . . . ? Firth ventures, soft and solemn as all summons rightly should be. *I may need your help with something, but it'll require me to settle another matter first. Something big.*

Figgie stiffens, sensing something of portent is about to happen.

Will you help me? Can you help me? he pleads. *For Ouse.*

Figgie remains silent, stalk-still, and then she nods – meekly, mousily, but a nod all the same.

Come on! she says sombrely. *We need to get out of here. They'll be back soon, I can sense in my bones that they're setting off.*

TWENTY-FOUR

The Father seethed yesterday, Ouse concludes. He seethed the day away. Ouse hates such wastefulness when it comes to time; he doubts he has ever really seethed. Sobbed, snapped, whimpered and smouldered, sure, but really seethed – teeth-grating, face-reddening, blood-capillary bursting, seethed? No, it's unlikely he has it in him. An abundance of compassion and curiosity would soon put a stop to such an impertinent act.

In the boat today, however, on the way to the mainland, The Father is no longer seething, but trying to catch Ouse's eye after having a stern word with himself.

Ouse, di you remember that day when you were wee, and a butterfly came n'landed on the boat? We'd picked up a catch o'cuttlefish fae the mainland, great ugly monsters, and were doing this same crossing. Must've been aboot here inawl. Near enough.

Yes, you said you'd never seen a butterfly in the middle of the ocean, not even on Muckle Flugga, not once, Ouse confirms, the moment still vivid in his memory.

The Father, who's been rowing rather than sailing, for the winds are low and his arms are strong, pulls the oars back into *The Covenant* and turns to face Ouse. He awkwardly puts a hand on Ouse's knee, gives his hair a feisty ruffle then pulls back. The Father spans out his arms so as touching either side of the boat – an eagle exhibiting its wingspan.

Landed on the cool box, then fluttered right onto yer chest fur the heat. Was a huge 'hing – thought it was a wee bird at first. With this

165

detail The Father cracks a smile. *Flattened oot its wings like it wiz showing off, busking fur compliments.*

It was glorious, Ouse concedes, finding it hard to hold his anger towards The Father in the face of this rare intimacy. *Orange-marmalade with black tigering stripes and a violet trim around the wings.*

That purple was something, looked like a fancy skirt, The Father suggests.

A tasselled cape! Ouse corrects.

Aye, anyway, just as it flew off, it wiz joined by a heap of others. A pure raft o'them, cruising aboot as if they owned the ocean. And maybe they did. I've not a scooby where they were going, but they were going in style. Afterwards, we never said a word aboot it, just rowed hame and kept it. It was our wee secret. Something special between us.

Ouse is enamoured by The Father's sudden attention, but tries to hold himself back. Having been humiliated by The Father's wrath, he's still wearing his melancholy like a sash. He was embarrassed in front of Firth and wept to think of all that sumptuous seaweed spoiling in the sun. He would have went back out to fetch it, to salvage it, but The Father warned him not to and it was gone in the morning. His guess is that The Father kicked it into the pond. At least that'll have given the fish a rare feeding, Ouse admits.

Ouse, ma laddie, I think about that day aw the time. It gives me courage when I'm up there. Keeps me battling when the energy's doon. The Father stands up in this moment and looks up to the lighthouse like a servant to its master. He slicks back his curling locks of hair, flicks sweat from his brow, and lets the sun beat off his chest. In the middle of the ocean, The Father can let his boyishness loose and give Ouse a glance at what's inside. For the first time in a while, he looks like Ouse.

166

I didn't think you'd remember that day, Ouse says abandoning the huff in him and raising his eyes to meet The Father's.

Magic, The Father states excitedly, *it wiz fucking magic. Aw my life I've never been able to tell anyone things like that. Even wi The Mother I held back, she wiz relentless when I softened up. So I kept it tae myself, though I wish uh hadnae. Point is, you get it. And I love that you get it. I jist wish there was more of that in me. And a little less of that in you.* With this The Father smiles, just a sliver, and Ouse does too.

I am trying, The Father mutters, verging on pleading.

I know, Ouse responds, about to tell him how living on pins and needles takes its toll on the soul, but choosing instead to honour the leap The Father has taken in this confession. He gestures to offer The Father some consoling sentiment but is interrupted before the words hatch.

Death and the sea go hand in hand, The Father begins, shifting into his less fatherly more preacherly voice. *I've seen men made zombies of fishing fur its treasure, baying it takes a brother instead o'them so as they might fill their pockets. Our lighthouse is there to address that balance – it is a beacon o'hope, but it's only as good as its keeper.*

I know, Ouse responds again.

I know you know. That you carry it tae, The Father solaces. *U'm, u'm . . . Och, we'll be alright, eh? Now grab them oars, laddie, you've been working me tae the bloody bone.*

Ouse suspects The Father at his worst is very much splashing in the kiddy pool of men at their most truculent. He continues to keep this to mind when The Father's ears begin steaming and his words are spat rather than spoken. However, while forgiveness could always be mustered, his reasons for haloing The Father are

167

waning. To thole such treatment and then gift The Father yet more years of his quickening youth is a different ask altogether. Ouse is changing. He must speak to RLS, RLS will know what to say; he's seen it all before.

Ouse grabs the oars and stomachs his disappointments. As he does so, a peacock butterfly takes flight from the boat's lip and stitches itself into the sky. In the time it takes to decide whether to share this sighting or keep it for himself, the butterfly vanishes into the horizon's twinkling tapestry. As they approach the shore, an outstanding sunset spills its last for the day – swirls of cherry red and tangerine sink below the indigo sheet of an oncoming dark. It's so damn juicy Ouse begins to salivate. The Father, too, wipes his mouth.

TWENTY-FIVE

A few days trundle past with congruence, a sort of attunement, between the residents of Muckle Flugga.

Ouse, having mended some bridges with The Father, gets to work on his extracurriculars – the designs, sewing and knitting. In between those, some curriculars – lighthouse keeper's apprenticeship duties, the gardening and cooking pots. The most time-consuming task is cleaning the lighthouse's myriad windows – the gallery deck and lantern room requiring umpteen hours' work and leaving his elbows aching.

The Father does as The Father does: he grafts. When the deep is tranquil, he spruces up the lighthouse, builds dry-stone walls and lays slabs – creating walking paths and stepping stones, scraping the seaweed off them for steady footing. The Father's drive and stamina are his most admirable qualities. He's up late and rises early, all creatures alert to his presence.

Firth powers forth with his portfolio of birdlife and makes remarkable progress. What he misses in nature he touches up by referencing the birdlife guidebook. He employs a creative understanding of the meaning behind their songs – that's to say, he allows the reason he believes they're singing to influence the way he captures their aesthetic. If there's magic in these birds, it's as much a product of the notes in their lungs as their patterned feathers. He had heard from some know-it-all in Edinburgh that all birdsong was about mating, staking claim or fighting talk. Whereas he feels that could be true in the capital, up here on Muckle Flugga he refuses to believe some of these birds aren't telling stories or making jokes.

Both days, Firth bumps into Figgie, who's become omnipresent on the island since their last fateful encounter. Both times she makes the excuse of having to drop off eggs, or letters, which Firth is sure she splits over the days in order to find extra reason to come. Between them bubbles the intimacy and absurdity of coagulating secrets. Firth feels they are somehow linked in fate, albeit a little out of sync in purpose and pull.

Although Figgie tends to tentatively walk the edges of Muckle Flugga, rarely penetrating the living spaces, she sees a lot more than she lets on. Firth finds her remarkably odd and, as such, very pleasant company – each time they see each other something new is uncovered: fresh gossip about people he doesn't know, details from The Father's tumultuous young life, a funny story from Ouse's childhood. Ouse never fails to light up in her presence, which brings everyone joy.

One afternoon, there is a semi-civil lunch, to which Figgie too is invited, during which The Father regales them all with stories of great storms and the shipwrecked survivors who have had to temporarily bide on Muckle Flugga until their health recovered or someone came to collect them. Firth is particularly enthralled by the story of a Ukrainian circus ship forced to shelter with them for a couple of nights, waiting out a whirlpool that was prowling around the island. As a result, Muckle Flugga was full of performers, props and exotic animals. Of course, all but the circus master spoke only Ukrainian, so it was more of a physical vocabulary that existed between them. Yet, as Ouse points out, when dealing with acrobats, sword swallowers, fire jugglers and contortionists, that's as much of a first language as the wielding of words.

Punctuating these stories, Ouse cooks up one of his best ever stews and The Father doesn't scrimp on the portions or the amber nectar. Figgie stays relatively quiet, but her affectionate gazing at all involved doesn't go unnoticed, and her deftness at amplifying everyone's best bits is a real boon.

The Father even gives Firth his own bottle of whisky; it appears in his room one afternoon when he returns home early, having been chased the whole way back by a brotherhood of bonxies. The whisky's nose of aromatic smoky peat and syrupy fruit cake are as tantalising a funfair of fragrances as any he's ever smelled. With his olfactory senses fully charged, he thinks it only prudent to make a dent in the bottle that same evening, taking it out roving and having nips in the bath, in which he has been growing accustomed to having two soaks a day.

Unspoken between Ouse and Firth is the fact they've been giving each other some space. The reason for doing so is a mutual awareness that it would be wise to let The Father settle some, in the hope his paranoia surrounding their fast-fire closeness might abate. It seems to have worked, and the harmony on Muckle Flugga keeps the weather fair. Firth continues to take furtive glances at Ouse in the workshop, and Ouse lets him believe he's doing so unnoticed. RLS is distinctly absent during this period, though The Father's more affable presence manages to bridge the gap.

Firth, as is his way, begins to dread the next mistake he's going to make to spoil things, and fights the temptation to simply do something crappy to get it over and done with. So when Ouse comes to him proposing another trip, he's at first delighted and then nervous. Firth can tell it's a trip of some import, that Ouse is even more invested in it than their tombolo adventure. Ouse, too, is not immune to vulnerabilities when it comes to conjuring and then captaining these quests, and has the added anxiety of having to ease in the notion of the trip with The Father. Although he's not sanctioned it, he's not raised the red flag either, so Ouse gives Firth a time and a place and ensures it'll happen when The Father's at his busiest, after their breakfasting together – the food cooked with extra oomph to placate the risks of the day.

TWENTY-SIX

Where to, Captain? Firth calls gaily, loading into *The Covenant* with considerably more aplomb than last time.

The boat is stacked, there's wind whispering in the sails, the oars are polished to a glint, and Ouse appears to have upped his slender brawniness for the occasion – his wiry limbs appearing more sinuous than before, then perhaps it's the way that seaman's vest hugs his svelte frame.

Ouse offers a secretive smile before announcing: *Only my joint favourite place, our closest neighbour, northest of the northest – and don't they lord it over us.*

We're going to Out Stack?! Firth cries, as if promised safe passage to the afterlife.

Yes, Ootsa, Da Shuggi, our dearly beloved, Ouse happily confirms.

I've been waiting for this, Firth beams. And it's true: he has eyeballed Out Stack every day since his arrival. Most of the birds he's startled by prowling too close have fled there, and it's the uncontested favourite spot of the seals he watches. He loves how some people have referred to Out Stack as the full stop of the country. It has an even greater falling-off-the-edge-of-the-world feeling than Muckle Flugga, on account of being too rocky and treacherous for anyone to live there.

Ouse, having finished loading the fishing rods and a big fat tackle box onto the boat, pushes off. He's rowing today rather than sailing. And bewilderingly, The Father comes traipsing over the summit to wave them off – not an ardent wave, a sort of crooked armed thrash, but a wave nonetheless. This unusual congeniality unnerves Firth.

As they cross the water, conversation between the boys flies so fast and flurried that it's hard to tell where one sentence begins and the other ends.

Do you ever consider how you'd fare as a cut-throat? Ouse enquires. *I've been reading about pirates and bounty hunters.*

I'd be terrible. I'd crumble under the pressure, couldn't detach myself from the crime. I'm weak, impulsive and sporadic, all the things a good cut-throat is not. You'd be just as bad.

Feigning outrage, Ouse protests: *I'll have you know I'd be a perfectly sufficient cut-throat. I could lock my morality in a cage if needs be. Just you watch! I'd never be able to hurt animals though. Couldn't do it.*

No, me neither. But hold on. You could make a pin-cushion of a pirate but not his parrot?

They both burst out laughing at the notion.

Ouse comes back a bit more serious. *It's not being scared of death that's key.*

I'm not scared of dying, but I'd be scared of taking a life, Firth confesses. *Wasting your own life is one thing, wasting someone else's, someone capable of living, now that plagues me.*

Ouse – conflicted between calling Firth a wimp and expressing that although he's not scared of dying himself he is terrified about the way death damages the left-over living – steeps in his thoughts.

Firth instinctively launches into a raft of abstract comments about humanity and the universe. Instinctively, Ouse reroutes the conversation, not quite ready for Firth to begin wrangling with the emotional multitudes of life and death. *You know we're closer to the Arctic Circle here than we are to London?*

That's good to know, Firth states soberly. *I love London but it takes you for a fool and leaves you broke, blistered and forever vying for its fancy.*

Ouse has a gaggle of queries about London, curiosities piqued from so many books set in the southern neighbour's capital.

Is it true you can't walk down a street without seeing a fox or encountering someone trying to sell you a newspaper?

The naivety of this notion causes Firth to experience a rush of sensations – from joy to pity, admiration to protectiveness. Somewhere along that emotional journey he wells up, but thankfully Ouse misses this whilst drawing the boat to a stop around a hundred metres from Out Stack. Instead, Firth merely replies that they'll have to go there together and find out.

Ouse catches Firth's eye and points with intent to the right of the boat.

Scanning the water, Firth spots a pair of jellyfish. Beyond that another pair and beyond that an uncountable number of them. A hundred, it could be a couple of hundred, a thousand even – they all sort of meld into one another, becoming a huge amorphous blob of squiggling jelly.

Isn't it beautiful? It's called a bloom, Ouse furthers. *Like the surface of the moon has fallen to earth.* A mareel mists up from the water.

Dangerous though, aren't they? Firth warns, then whisks the closest of the creatures away with a thrust of the oar. Overzealous in doing so, he propels *The Covenant* right into the centre of the swarm. To Firth's surprise, Ouse tears off his vest and dives into the water, swimming right in amongst them.

What are you doing? Firth yells at him, as Ouse turns belly-up like the otters they were fawning over just the other day. The jellyfish look more endearing with Ouse in about them, Firth concedes. There's even more than he first thought, a whole colony just floating there like a jelly blanket over a giant's blue bedsheet.

These aren't the stinging type. They're chasing plankton is all, Ouse assures him. *Old as time, jellyfish, much older than us and all our nuisance and trouble.*

Oh fuckety-fuck. Fine! Firth squawks, disrobing and jumping into the sea after a few anxious dips of his toes. *Fuuuuuuuck, it's freezing,* he yells on impact, using yoga techniques to steady his breathing.

And there Firth and Ouse float, flippers flapping, engulfed in jellies, with salt water washing over them. The waves push them together, and though Firth thinks to clasp Ouse's hand, he doesn't, for fear of becoming as clichéd as the otters. He does, however, feel their flesh connecting through a pulse in the water – Celtish, Pictish, pagan, soul-mates. The purest of moments, but it's no longer than a couple of minutes before Firth's body can't take the cold and he scrambles back onto the boat. Ouse springs aboard more lithely, offering a teeth-chattering Firth the towel for drying before taking a turn himself. Even after the towelling, both their nipples remain as sharp as letter openers.

Ouse grabs the oars and aims the boat at Out Stack. He deftly steers it into what he claims to be the only landing spot the island proffers, ties it to a man-made hole in the rockface and then flings the fishing rods up onto a plateau. He affects their mooring with such prowess it appears choreographed, which in a way it is.

It's a fair old scramble to where they're headed. On seeing the vertiginous ridge above them, Firth quickly labels the climb impossible. Ouse, on the other hand, leaps into action, scaling the cliff face by uncovering footholds that were fully camouflaged to Firth's eyes – or else they appear only for Ouse: a secret password uttered.

He does all this with the muckle tackle box roped around him.

Ouse, having made the initial ascent, begins preparing a rope to sling down to Firth for extra support. Just as he finishes his knots, Firth emerges, having marked Ouse's path in his mind and followed it to a tee. *Okay, so what now?* Firth wheezes, catching his breath, mettled by pride. Ouse gives him a nod of approval, which means more to Firth than he'd care to admit.

A fire, then we fish. There's a place I'm meant to take you.

From what Firth can see, Out Stack is composed of sudden steep gradients and dramatic drops with shards of rocks jutting up everywhere. The thought of having to traverse it any further makes him nauseous, in spite of his desire to spend more precious time with Ouse. *It looks like the back of a sleeping stegosaurus*, Firth utters, beginning to warm up in the shelter of the rocks. He walks around their little landing spot, trying to make himself useful, as Ouse unpacks a couple of wrist-thick cuts of driftwood from the tackle box, which is turning out to be a bit of a magician's chest in terms of the abundance of kit he can draw out of it.

A lit match and the fire's off. Although podgy and humble, it's a hungry little beast and burns through the wood in no time. It feels odd to Firth to be huddled around a bonfire on a sunny day, but it does wonders for drying his breeks and the heat comes upon his palms as if summoned by an oracle.

By the time Firth's back in the warmth of his body, Ouse has attached the reels to the rods and is busy tying hooks to the end of their lines. His flair in doing so does not go unnoticed by Firth, nor unadmired. He casts his rod off the edge – the hook sails through the air then lands upon the water elegantly as a swan. Underneath his insouciance is a sassy look held back from breaking out – Firth can feel it though it's hidden from sight.

Firth's fished a few times in Edinburgh, at Duddingston Loch by his favourite pub, The Sheep Heid. But that's more wasting time on a weekend before the bar opens rather than proper fishing. He picks up the rod, immediately feeling the pull of the wind as the hook begins zapping around like a carnaptious wasp. Ouse, seemingly playful today, leaps behind the tackle box pretending to duck for cover as Firth makes an ungainly cast.

This first attempt leaves Firth wrapped in his own line and scrunching his eyes closed in case the cruising hook plunges its fangs into him. It doesn't, but does bite at the laces on his boots. With a little tuition from Ouse, Firth casts the line again, this time reaching the water, but barely, the waves spitting the hook back out upon the rocks like a baby rejecting its dummy. However, before Firth can reel it back in and have another go, Ouse is up on his feet and uncharacteristically abrupt.

That'll do. Leave those there. We can check them later, Ouse commands, wedging the handle-ends of the rods in tight between the gaps in the rocks.

Wait! We've not even baited the . . . But Ouse is already out of earshot, pushing up the rockface, steady-footed as a mountain goat and gesturing Firth forth with a flush sweep of his arm.

The climb to the other side of Out Stack is steep, and Ouse leads the charge like he's chasing a gold rush. The geography of this land has a talent for derailing even the most tried and tested ambler. Like its sibling island, it's rumoured that these rocks, too, are shape-shifters, able to roll and rotate as if they were alive. Ouse, however, works their contours and crevices as if born from them. Firth – who sees Out Stack's impossibly jagged surface as proof of asteroids hitting the earth – is in awe of Ouse's dexterity. He falls behind repeatedly, but Ouse stops in wait for him, though never letting him get quite close enough that they're in alignment.

Firth stops for a rest after a particularly tricky tranche of the climb, during which he almost loses his footing, twice. Rendered speechless by the view, he fixedly appreciates it for longer than he otherwise might have done in order to catch his breath. He also guzzles back a good dose of whisky, which he's carrying in his mum's old hip-flask. Raising the vessel to the heavens then sipping with wetted eyes. She'd have loved it here, Firth thinks; loved Ouse, and loved her own son with all this fresh air and good fortune in his lungs. *This place*, Firth utters, *this magical place*. There are rare moments when Firth feels like the type of person songs are sung about.

It's a strange thing being on an uninhabited island, especially this Out Stack; a feeling unlike any Firth has ever felt. Being the sole passengers on this ancient uprising, Scotland's last landing bay before the Arctic. Yet it's not a place of respite; it repels visitors – guarded by rocks that hover below the surface ready to strike, a tectonic experiment gone wrong. Any intrepid traveller that makes it past those thrashing teeth does so only to land on an untrustworthy terrain. The rock is blackened and dank, old and angry about it. Its mud becomes a quagmire, its crevices lethal. Nothing much can grow here. The waves, too, are protesting the outcrop's very existence – blasting them, causing them a constant headache. And there's no chance of calling for help, of SOS-ing – if things go wrong here, there's little to be done.

Despite all that, perhaps because of all that, Firth feels instantly at home on Out Stack. Happier than at his recent birthday party when dozens of singing friends encircled him; where he took so little joy in blowing out the candles he tried to suck the flames inside of him just to feel something salient. More than Out Stack though,

Firth credits Ouse as the antidote: thank science, luck and longing for Ouse, he praises.

Just as Firth is about to start bemoaning how much longer they have to go, he rounds a corner and sees they've reached their destination: the other side of Out Stack. After so much unrelenting rock, jumping down upon the spongy sand feels divine underfoot. Ouse is already busy making friends with a starfish, checking if it's one of his gang. They've landed on a circular cove of sand, walled in at either side by sheer cliff face. Although it nearing sea level, there's still a decent drop beyond the rim, making this as much a plateau as a cove. More pertinently, it marks the entrance to a vast sea cave.

Though the water must creep in when the sea is at its most fantastic, Firth surmises the steep path that snakes up its side would provide safety against all manner of rises in water level. He surmises, rather than asserts, because about ten stomps up ahead the path becomes engulfed by darkness, after which again is light. The sea cave is partially roofless – cast in and out of shadows and blackness – and so all its lights and darks appear skew-whiff.

Thankfully, Ouse has considered everything, and pulls out a huge torchlight with *Property of the KLAMS* scored across it.

Welcome to the hidden world of Da Shuggi, he announces. *This has been my hideout these last couple of years, I bring all manner of worries here and always leave lighter.*

It's miraculous, Firth swoons.

Ouse examines Firth as he says this, his lively eyes and batting lashes, curious as to whether he's given anything away unwittingly. It is not uncommon that the voice in his head begins manipulating his lips and before he knows it a secret has been spoken. In this instance, he's safe. Firth is the first stranger to be welcomed here, at least by Ouse, and the excitement in that should be matched by a healthy dose of trepidation. But Ouse isn't feeling nervous at all, which is worrying in itself. He's been many things of recent days, but never clumsy.

Firth, eager to elaborate, cuts himself short because Ouse is already off, leading them into the cave and up the path's steepest side. Following suit, the burn of the incline immediately begins gnawing at Firth's calves after such an enduring hike. He's tempted to ask Ouse if it's safe in here but doesn't want to appear cowardly in the face of adventure.

As they pass through the darkest part of the path, Firth clasps Ouse's hand to steady himself – there's a spark, but it's minimal, or else Firth's body is just becoming better equipped at absorbing the shock. They step slowly together, Firth with one hand on the wall and the other palm to palm with Ouse. Ouse steers the way with his torch outstretched.

As the gradient settles, the daylight returns, a glowing disc shining down from a hole in the cave above like a portal to another universe. *The upper balcony*, Ouse whispers.

The cheap seats, Firth jokes, a snobbish response, particularly given those are the only seats he's ever able to afford (unless mooching off a plush chum or a patron). Just as shame starts to seep in, a scuffing, scuttling noise fills the arena of the room, then the heavy plod of feet. Firth instinctively jumps to clasp at Ouse again, but he's disappeared. Alongside the staunch plodding comes a chirruping sound like a baby bird but much louder in volume. Before he's picked up his stomach from the floor, Ouse reappears and begins making introductions to someone (something?) that remains hidden in the shadows.

This is Nile. Nile, this is Firth.

181

Out the dark and into the centre of the room steps a huge creature with fireballs for eyes and roll upon roll of dark feathery fur. Its raw pink shins catch the light as its gigantic clawed feet disturb the dusty ground.

What the fuck?? Firth rattles, higher pitched than usual. *It's the last of the dinosaurs.*

Nile is an ostrich, Ouse corrects.

But how in the love of God?! . . . I mean, an actual ostrich?

You're not the only weird thing to wash up on our shores. Far from it.

Is that thing really real? Firth's usual loquaciousness is hampered by the shock of the beast in front of him.

Do you remember the Ukrainian circus ship The Father told you about? Ouse queries. *Well, they left us a large egg as thanks. We thought it was a good-luck charm, that whatever was inside it was likely dead, but kept it warm regardless. The Father put it in a nest by the fire and swaddled it in straw, and love. Then one day it hatched. The Father thought it might be the goose that lays the golden egg, I guessed a python. It was better. It was a chick, a Nile. Isn't she glorious?*

With this, Ouse claps Nile on her back, who bends her knees, jiggles her wings, and then proceeds to gallop around the cave demonstrating her speed, agility and brawn.

They're African, Ouse continues. *Although I'm pretty sure Nile wasn't made in Africa. She's the first and only of her kind. A Celtic seafarer with the circus in her blood.*

In a moment of eureka, Firth realises that's what the bizarre egg he spied in The Father's lair was, but bites his tongue just in the nick of time to avoid divulging his snooping.

In all the books I've never seen one as big or hairy as that. It's like a bloody Yeti . . . he ogles.

I've been thinking on that. It's got to be evolution, eh? In the desert ostriches moult, sweating under a punishing sun. But here, where our hot isn't half that, there's no need to moult. So she simply keeps hold of all her feathers. And, of course, the salt in the air has made her grow twice as fast.

She wouldn't attack us, would she? Firth asks.

Shaking his head in response, Ouse dismisses Firth's concerns with a flick of his wrist. *It's her lashes I can't get enough of, who would even dare dream that big. You're gorgeous, Nile,* he mouths, so softly only Nile can hear it.

Feeling the need to make it up to Nile, Firth switches to flattery. *I love the flightless birds, always have. They're such a sub-species.*

Ouse furrows his brow at this, upset and surprised by the barb in it.

No, no, Firth pardons himself, realising he's been misconstrued. *What I mean is they're birds that can't do the one thing people idolise birds for being able to do – fly. They're renegades. Shouldn't be alive in that sense, but look at them, extraordinary creatures, they just keep on living. It's pure defiance.*

This pleases Ouse in all manner of ways, and seems to please Nile too; or being an emotionally intelligent creature she senses Ouse's glee and is soothed by it.

Nile has done her laps of the cave and so returns to Ouse for attention. Ouse pads around the perimeter, Firth trailing behind him, and Nile running rings around them both. In its rocky splendour, the cave feels akin to the keep of a great castle, rather than a marine hideaway – it's cylindrical, conical and grandiose, but with razoring edges. Ouse draws Firth's attention to the gargling below their feet, and the tremor in the ground from the force with which the ocean beats against the outer walls. The wet stone catching the

183

light appears at times like marble, glitter-flecked; Firth's eyes deceive him into finding shapes in the more curiously sculpted rock surfaces – a fireplace, a throne, a locked door.

But why do you keep her here? Firth probes. *Why not on Muckle Flugga?*

KLAMS rules, Ouse explains. *No pets.*

What about your fish – are they not pets?

That's a sea pond, we can return them to the ocean if we see someone coming. One of the previous keepers kept a wolf as a pet. A pregnant wolf swam to Muckle Flugga to have her pups, likely fleeing fur poachers. The mother wolf died in childbirth, so did the first two pups, but the third one, the runt, survived. And the keeper brought it up as his own. That was until a visiting inspector from the KLAMS heard it crying for the keeper from the cellar he'd hidden it in. By order of the KLAMS, the wolf was drowned the next day.

That's terrible . . . Firth is stunned by the brutality. *But is it true? I mean, were there really wolves here?*

Who's to say? Ouse shrugs. *A great bear-eagle once landed on the lightning rod of the lighthouse. The Father named it Zeus. It stayed for a fortnight feasting on fish and keeping The Father company. Then one morning it was gone. The Father still keeps the bones from Zeus's kills in the lantern room for luck. Zeus was a fearless hunter; he admired that.*

Bet he did! Firth snarls, then regrets his splenetic tone.

Defensive, Ouse states, *The Father feeds Nile just as much as me, maybe more. He can be very caring when people aren't watching. Especially when it comes to birds.*

Firth reprimands himself for showing his dislike of The Father so flagrantly, risking the magic of this moment in a cave with Ouse, and an ostrich, which is now scraping around in the dirt with its great bulbous beak. An ostrich called Nile.

What do ostriches eat, by the way?

Nosy artists, Ouse snaps jokingly and then throws Firth a carrot from his satchel, continuing to dig out a couple more, and a juicy orange. *We feed her fruit and vegetables, orange ones mainly, but she hunts insects, too. The Father swears she steals eels from the puffins, but I'm not so sure. The Father favours animals that eat other animals.*

Ouse pulls out a mirror and begins using it to bounce light around the room. Nile chases the reflective beam like a dog would a rubber ball. *We leave these buckets here to fill with rain water, but I always bring a fresh flask from the tap in case she kicks the buckets over in a protest.*

Ouse, having fed Nile his supply of orange edibles, begins decanting the flask into the bucket. Nile on the other hand is now all up in Firth's business, because she knows him to be in possession of the last carrot. Her investigative beak has him on the run, a quick hiss has him cowering. Horrified, Firth thrusts out his arm wielding the carrot like a knife. Nile makes swift work of the crunchy vegetable and takes a celebratory lap around the boundary. Needing to slake her thirst she rushes off and begins guzzling back the bucket's liquid.

Ouse gives Nile a big scratchy shoogle, getting in amongst her deluge of feathers. He tosses a final hidden orange to the rear of the room so that she chases it down. As soon as this is done he's clicked on the torch and leads Firth back towards the dark downward twirl of the path out, gesturing for him to remain silent.

It's best to leave her eating, Ouse whispers. *She's terribly clingy.*

Delivering this sentiment, Ouse turns around to face Firth. Although the torch is still beaming forwards, and the darkness around them is blinding, they can feel the heat in each other. Turning back to face his direction of travel, Ouse loses his footing, his left leg

185

slipping off the crumbly rock and into the drop. Not missing a beat, Firth grabs his waist and hauls him back to his feet; he's no idea how deep the fall below is but clasps Ouse's body like both their lives depended on it. It is the closest they've been and it is thrilling. As if to mark the moment, the torchlight slips from Ouse's clutch, blinks, plops, fades to nothing.

They traverse the final few metres in a silent, slow procession, pressed against the wall, and emerge again onto the sand, which has become a little boggy for the waves flinging water up and over the cove's fringe. As they find their footings in the gaps in the rocks, ready to start the ascent to the other side of the island, a chirruping song comes echoing out the cave. Nile is calling for company.

I told you. A right old sulk.

Hearing himself in the cries, Firth probes, *Doesn't that break your heart?*

Now don't you start, Ouse cautions, *she'd have you here all night playing games.*

With Nile's trilling fading out of earshot, and a lavender hue oozing across the sky, the boys draw to a natural stop. They're out of their rocky emporium and back in the light, their eyes adjusting to the unfathomable distance all around them; both sky and sea feel even vaster than before. They watch each other's chests beat and their breathing steady with a level of comfort that outshines all their previous wordless moments. As Ouse signals to move out, Firth announces that he has something important to say. Surprised by the outburst, Ouse silently waits for him to speak.

I want to say, that you, this, everything that happened here today . . . I'd never in my wildest dreams have imagined a day like this a month back. What I mean is, I've felt stuck, worse than stuck, empty and useless. Bloody condemned even. Whatever you want to call it. But

186

now . . . What I'm trying to say is, today I felt unstuck – free from the shackles of the sickness inside of me. And that's completely and utterly because of you. You make things feel possible I'd long given up on, and I can't thank you enough. Thank you, Ouse. Thank you so much.

Firth wants to go beyond this and say that today felt like Ouse and the world saying to him, *Don't die,* but he doesn't dare put words into Ouse's mouth that he hasn't yet earned.

Ouse looks to his feet as Firth delivers this speech, listening all the more intently for not having the distraction of a face to focus on. The words touch him deeply. He's never had anyone express such gratitude to him and he feels powerful in this moment. He feels an atavistic energy rise up within him – electrons charged, fingers becoming wands full of spells. Not wanting to rush the words, he opts for a laconic, yet heartfelt, *I appreciate you saying that.*

Although the trek back is mostly silent, the glances the pair exchange have a synergy in them. And, yes, Firth fears he's spilled too much and freaked Ouse out, but he doesn't regret his outpouring. As they blithely pack up the gear, Firth twigs that Ouse had no intention of catching any fish and smiles to himself at the deception.

As if the day couldn't get any more golden, on the way back over, they spot a family of seals going somewhere in a hurry, a club of younger-looking adults and a chunky titan leading the way. In his wildlife guidebook, Firth has read about seals that weigh over a ton, with a mating call louder than dynamite exploding. It occurs to him that Ouse, despite being a wisp of a thing, need only let his soft sigh fold into a smile in order to melt the hardest of hearts.

TWENTY-SEVEN

The exuberant seals are the calm before the storm. The Father is waiting for their boat to moor with the temperament of a pot boiling over. There is a whole gang of angry men inside of him joining forces to revolt. The Father feels foolish now, having given that soft, silly part of himself to Ouse, having succumbed to his fickle fatherly impulses. And how did Ouse repay him? Trespass, burglary. Entering his private space while he was sleeping, or working the light, doesn't fucking matter which, deception aw the same. Naw, worse, it's betrayal.

Bet they did it together, The Father intuits. Yes, Ouse wouldn't have come creeping without Firth's encouragement, he must have been asking questions. *That arrogant shitehawk's been making him cocky*, The Father yowls. Having settled the matter of Firth's contributory guilt, The Father bursts into his room and snatches back the whisky he gifted him, tearing one of his drawings in a rage and spitting on his sheets. Further infuriated by the sight of his things, echoes of Firth living on The Father's generosity, he comes up with a better plan. He plops the top off the whisky, thankfully a wide-girthed bottle, then he pisses, just a dribble, in what remains in the vessel. This helps to temper him, but since then he's been broiling by the cove, watching for their return.

As soon as *The Covenant* lands, The Father tears Ouse, one-armed, from the boat, then slaps him across the face mid-air with the other hand.

You think you're so fucking clever, don't you?! Snooping around in there. Bet yiz had a right good fucking laugh aboot it together. The Father unleashes these words from behind the cage of his teeth.

Ouse, dazed and confused by the aggressive onslaught, closes his eyes and tries to drift into another realm: somewhere he's not losing the battle for The Father's humanity; somewhere Firth hasn't snagged a front-row seat to his humiliation; somewhere where the air is not wet with spite, spiked by shock and heartache.

You're not that fucking clever that you didn't cover your tracks! The Father roars. *The Mother's ring had rolled into the ash. I nearly burnt it. Nearly fucking lost it. Then I saw the crack in the jewellery box. Little fucking vandals. Poking around for yer entertainment, eh! Snooping bastards!*

Fuck! Fuck! The ring! How could he have missed the ring! Firth's mind implodes with the guilt of it. He should own up, confess it was him, that Ouse had nothing to do with this. But The Father will kill him. He might actually murder him and that's not the way he wants to go, not now, not after all these discoveries. Besides, he'd likely not believe him either way. Would he?

I . . . I . . . Firth begins.

You shut the fuck up! The Father growls to Firth, pushing Ouse back into the water in the process, as if to demonstrate their combined powerlessness. *You'll be fucking leaving is what you'll be doing, early. You just lost a week. Three days you've got until I can get rid of you on that ferry,* he says, stabbing his finger in Firth's direction. *Three days and you better keep out of my fucking way, you pretentious little cunt.*

The Father, having said his piece and flexed his terror, storms away, leaving Ouse in the shallows and Firth trembling with self-hatred. Both boys are now crying. Firth tries to help Ouse up but he shakes him off, turning his back to Firth and unloading the boat with a conviction he hopes will mask his humiliation.

189

I'm sorry, Firth manages to mutter as Ouse leaves up the path, carrying all the weight of their belongings and all the wrath of a crime he's not committed. *I'm so sorry*, Firth repeats feebly.

Unable to temper the rampage in him, The Father jumps in *The Covenant* himself and heads out to clear his head and distract his fists. A necessary measure to prevent his violent mood becoming more physical. At least he's mustered that modicum of restraint, though a fat lot of good it'll do, he thinks. *Why must Ouse do this to him?* The Father leaves lamenting. It's the embarrassment that really stokes his fire, the idea of a stranger and his own son laughing at these objects of sentimentality, mocking the last embers of his vulnerability. The Father thought better of his own laddie – they're family, family first – but professes he always kent Firth was a snide cunt. The Father will be drinking today, that much he knows, drinking to forget.

TWENTY-EIGHT

Slumped over the desk, Firth attempts to make amendments to his drawings; to return to the task for which he came to the island. The promise he must fulfil for his dead granddad, which had lured him down from the bridge that night. Once again, every inch of his being is attempting to fight the gnawing, cloying feeling that he's ruined everything, that the comfort he vowed to bring to Ouse has ended in catastrophe.

Of course he wasn't going to better Ouse's life, Firth relents – this is him, after all, contagious in his wretchedness. Of course he was going to worsen matters – he makes life less bearable for all good humans he comes into close contact with. He wanted to be an avuncular guardian angel with nothing to lose; instead he's a human ulcer, putrid, harmful, a stinking mess of a thing, overdue for a big shift in the soil below. Why couldn't he just leave Ouse alone?! He's no doubt inadvertently encouraged him to squander his talent and submit to The Father's martyrdom; sealing his fate. Why should Ouse trust *him* after all – why run from an ape into the arms of a circus monkey?

Frustrated, Firth violently scribbles over the bird he's been fiddling at drawing, extincting it. Baffled by the ripped drawing of his mutant puffin on the floor, he emits a long sullen sigh, takes a swig of the sharp-tasting whisky and then drops his head onto the desk with a thump. With the impact comes a piercing pain and a brain full of static. Trembling in disgust with himself, he makes a last selfish wish to anyone listening:

Please, please, please, let it not be too late to fix this.

• • •

In his studio, Ouse is knitting with conviction. He has all but shaken off the feeling of dismay, parked it and let it dissolve. He'll come back to it when the sting has settled. He channels the intelligent spiritualist, the Zen Buddhist inside of him, a composure composed of Rumi's poetry and the teachings of *The Tibetan Book of the Dead*. He thinks of his favourite moments with The Father: of the butterflies on the boat whose flutter has melded into his heart; of the way he doted after The Mother whenever she was dressed for dancing; the pride on his face when he brought home a Christmas tree from the mainland he'd pilfered from a bigwig's plot. How Ouse, when younger, was allowed to put the star on top, while sitting on The Father's shoulders, feeling like the mahout of a giant; he would often fart out of excitement and The Father would feign death by stink bomb.

Ouse remains thankful. He *is* thankful, thankful for his hands, the way they work the needle without over-thinking it. Visceral, as if the design was knocking from inside him, desperate to come out. As if he were just a cog in its machinery of creation.

And he has dear RLS, who is a wizard when it comes to softening the aftermath of these mêlées. A wizard of succour and distraction. Who else has their favourite writer doling out life advice, appearing every time their life's under threat of fouling? And with that, as if willed into being, RLS appears, busy in the folds of another sermon. He tips his hat, yet doesn't miss a beat; entertaining as ever, what a tonic, what a treasure.

In nature's great chase somebody always goes hungry. It is the way. If the prey escapes, the hunter fails and starves. Or do we reverse the

192

results, and the big cat catches its target and feeds her ravenous pups?
Who are now themselves baby eaters, caked in blood from the day they
were born, but surviving – surviving as the ancient earth instructs them
to do. Just remember, you can't pick sides when you're dealing with a
life-cycle. Or you can, but you'd be a fool to. Speaking of surviving,
young prince, did I tell you about my time in Chicago?

Chicago! Ouse smiles, despite having heard the story twice before. *No. I'd love to hear about that, RLS. I really hope to see such*
things as you have. The way RLS tells the tale, there's always new
accoutrements – details he'd misplaced somewhere in the sphere
of the living, words that come back to him, making each bright-
eyed, bushy-tailed rendition utterly original.

Well it ends on the floor of the train station . . . where it starts, I
don't quite recall. RLS, seemingly fazed by this lacuna in his memory, puts his hat back on and makes towards the door in bit of a
hurry. *Come to think of it, young Ousling, I've somewhere I'm meant*
to be. We'll have to pick this up . . . Before this sentence is complete
RLS has effected his exodus, leaving Ouse chuckling at his sponta-
neity, but not without an afterthought of worry.

• • •

Firth decrees to issue himself a marker of his idiocy with the sharp
end of a knife. Then opts for a more personal approach, heating up
a coin over a flame and pressing it into his skin – burning a small
circular O into his flesh as a reminder of the harm he's caused sweet
Ouse. He lifts his heavy head up, resolving to dull his mind, and the
burning, with the dregs of the whisky, but instead is frozen in disbelief, gazing out of the window. It's snowing. Not just one flake but
thousands of them. The grounds are already coated in powder with

the flowers disappearing under a great white cape. He was risking sunburn an hour ago and now it's fallen thick enough to build a snowman. He slaps himself around the face to check he's not dreaming. Painful, just as it should be, Firth confirms. Scanning the room, he finds the bath empty and the hammock still and unoccupied, so it's on with his jumper and boots and out into the open air.

On the race over to Ouse's studio, for he knows that's where he's recuperating, it feels like the snow has been gifted. A divine offering, the impetus for reconciliation under the auspices of a natural phenomenon. He has to tread carefully when passing the pond as it's nearly fully camouflaged. He thinks of the frogs, only a matter of hours back trying to make sure the sun didn't dry them out. He remembers that some frogs can freeze solid, heart-stopped, then thaw out when the temperature rises. If he were a frog, he'd be one of that species, perish for the saddest seasons then come back with ice on the heart desperately seeking heat. His nose begins to leak; he resents being bullied from the inside by an invading chill that might never leave him. Fuck, he's already that frog.

The snow is even higher than expected by the time he hits the other side of the island, his boots sinking below its surface, the powder compressing with a crunch. As a result, he stumbles into the library head-first and at pace, landing on all fours on the rug (yet again) and crawling into the studio like a randy dog. But Ouse isn't there, though his needles are out, clearly still attached to the work he's doing; a sign the craftsman has left in haste.

Up on his feet, he sees Ouse immediately, not sulking as he expected, not in a ball in the corner full of bleakness and woe, but outside, leaping around catching snowflakes on his tongue in a deerstalker hat. Firth gallops over to the window, watches for a few seconds and then knocks. Ouse, exhilarated, signals he's coming back in.

194

Sudden snowfall means change is coming! Ouse calls from the library, his voice reaching Firth before his body does.

But it's impossible, Firth replies, befuddled. *Impossible. I'm still turning pink from this afternoon. And how is it still light?*

Welcome to Muckle Flugga. I told you the world turns faster up here.

But that's simply not true! It can't be, Firth protests, though he likes the sentiment.

Last time snow fell this quickly was on my final day of high school, Ouse recalls, his gaze drifting off into a different time and place. As his new friend is reminiscing, Firth realises this is his first time in Ouse's studio. He's imagined it so vividly, and pilfered so many peeks inside, that he already feels acquainted with the place; at once at home here.

Noticing Firth scanning the room for treasure, Ouse is inclined to do his customary cordial introductions.

This is my joint favourite room on Muckle Flugga.

Along with the library, yes?

And one other!

Firth thinks to quibble on how having three joint favourite rooms feels a bit non-committal, but takes no risks in causing upset, however jovially intended.

Please, explore! Ouse outstretches his arms, wide as they'll crank, in invitation.

Firth steps forwards, thinking he's being implored into a hug, but realises just in time Ouse meant only for him to have a good poke around the room. Firth both taunts and pities himself for his flagrant neediness. Too much daydreaming for someone with the Sword of Damocles hanging over them is a dangerous thing, Firth rules.

He begins poring over the sketches, which are even more disparate and extraordinary than he imagined. *You're a real artist*, he

195

states – not feeling in the least bit trite ploughing this well-trodden platitude, because in this instance he's never meant it more, and he's damn sure Ouse doesn't hear it nearly enough.

I wouldn't say that, Ouse fumbles, expectedly humble. *It's here I'm most fluent though. The stitches speak for me, then head off into the world to keep someone warm. What a privilege, right?*

In response Firth simply grins, tickled pink by the notion and still gaping in disbelief at the snowfall, pondering what trouble it might augur.

Ouse picks up the needles again and begins working, indicating to Firth that's he's not being observed and there's no real hurry. After some time leafing through the pages of the sketchbook Firth moves on to the small stack of completed jumpers, scarfs, socks and tablecloths; alongside them are works-in-progress (labelled as such). He wants to take it all in quickly, then home in properly on his second tour.

I would love it if you'd do me the honour of letting me purchase one of these? Firth interrupts, thinking he can wear it, admire it, and then send it on to someone who deserves it; preserving a little bit of himself in the process (his skin, starch and pipe dreams coating the fabric).

Ouse raises his eyes from his sewing, not as high as Firth's, and kindly nods. Then Firth sees something that makes him gasp in both excitement and horror.

That drawing! That one of the crashed ship with all those people huddled on the shore. I've seen that before! Firth yelps, spooked.

Ouse's eyes are fully raised now, wiring into Firth.

It's exactly like my . . . my . . . it came to me. Right down to the tunics and the branched torches they're carrying. And there's that dishevelled bonfire on the headland that's not really there! It's uncanny, Firth gasps. *But . . . but . . . how did you know?*

196

Ouse puts down his sewing and beckons Firth over. With a discipline that rarely furnishes Ouse's voice, even in the most serious of situations, he commands Firth to tell him all.

Firth recounts the whole revulsive vision in intricate detail, not forgetting a morsel of it, as customarily happens with dreams in the moments after waking. He acts out what he saw with theatrical zeal, swinging his arms, dropping to his knees and thumping his own head (a little too hard) when knocked out at the end.

Ouse admires the beauty of Firth's portrayal despite the ugliness of the content.

You saw The Wreck Harvesters, Ouse confirms with resolve.

No, these were murderers and thieves . . .

Not everybody welcomed lighthouses when they first arrived, Ouse begins, his voice taking on a deeper resonance than before, as if combined with The Father's. *Whole communities of wreckers all along the Scottish coastlines lived off the misfortune of sunken ships. They sold and traded the goods and built with the wood. Some grew fat off the spoils of wrecks. A better life washed in by the shore. So when the lighthouses came and started saving ships, guiding them to safety, the wreckers were up in arms – it cut into their supply. They saw these lights as an obstruction of God's will and went to war with them.*

Yes! Yes! That's exactly it! Firth feels less crazy for hearing his dream deciphered and articulated. *They were yelling stuff like that. 'God has sent the storm.' 'The ship must sink.' All that horseshit.*

Ouse shrugs, in gentle protest. *Well, it wasn't horseshit to them; they thought they had God on their side. They claimed they were chosen to receive these blessings. Some groups even had their ministers leading the congregation in prayer for a shipwreck to come their way. They willed it in and started tearing down the lights, even attacking some of the keepers.*

197

Poverty and hunger are merciless adversaries, Firth puffs portentously, *add in a religious nutter to sanction the whole shebang and that there's an unshakable conviction in even the crummiest of causes.*

In my dream . . . vision . . . experience, Firth elaborates, rootling for the right word that doesn't make him sound too unhinged, *it got much worse. Some of these, these wreckers, bludgeoned the survivors to death. Men that had made it to shore, they just killed them. Monsters.*

Then it's as bad as we feared.

No survivors, no claim to the goods? Firth guesses.

Not just that, Ouse explains. *The wreckers claimed that God, in sentencing the ship to sink, had also sentenced the men to die. Those men, in the wreckers' eyes, had cheated fate.*

Loonies. Fucking savages, Firth snarls back.

Ouse recounts a locally infamous story whereby a shipment of wine came in so large the community struggled to see it all away before the stuff spoiled. Despite putting it in porridge, using it to soften stale bread and giving it to thirsty strays – dogs, he explains, the dogs were all drunk for a month – the supply barely dwindled. Ouse, finding humour in the crapulent canines, restrains his rising laughter as Firth is still clearly caught in the dreadfulness of revisiting his dream. Channelling Firth's sombreness into his next unveiling, he continues: *It's not uncommon that the wreckers' restless spirits plague people up here. It's The Father, you see, he comes from a long line of wreckers, a notorious wrecker family. Perhaps the last active wreckers before they disappeared – fading to myth.*

Nooooo! Firth cries in disbelief, as if having just turned the page of a novel to find himself hoodwinked by the most unexpected twist. By this point, Firth is hovering directly in front of Ouse who, still sitting in his knitting seat, begins working the needles again.

Yes! Ouse verifies, explaining how The Father ran away from his wrecker family young after witnessing a terrible massacre, not too dissimilar to the one Firth experienced. Furthering that, after years of working as a farm hand, then a milk boy, then a cobbler's apprentice, The Father was finally old enough to apply to the KLAMS to be a keeper. From the age of fourteen, he had dedicated his life to bringing light to those lost at sea.

Accounting for the sins of his ancestors? Firth ventures, completely captivated, as if the words had been given to him. He attempts to sit on all fours below Ouse, but doesn't like the angle, and has too much energy surging through him from the unfurling revelations to stay still, so immediately springs back to his feet. He walks towards the window, where the snow is still coming down thick and fast, and presses his face against the glass in the hope the chill will settle him. Ouse watches Firth work the frissons out of his body, beginning again only when he sees his friend has eased a little.

The torn souls of The Father's wrecker forefathers have followed him here, Ouse whispers as if they were being listened in on. *They call him a traitor and torment anyone who sides with him.*

Pffffffftt, well I'm not sure why they're hounding me, Firth argues. *The Father can't stand me, and I . . .*

He stops himself before saying something hurtful. He was about to suggest that he would happily oblige in letting The Father annihilate himself. In the end, he's glad to curtail the sentence because a semi-sympathy begins to seep through him. The root of The Father's biliousness at least has a bloody good story to it.

It's partly why The Father hates himself, Ouse proffers. *Sometimes life is a bucking horse.*

Firth nods attentively, as if having been given his marching orders. Ouse can see Firth's mind is working up some line of extended enquiry, hoping to delve deeper into what he's just heard. Keen to close the conversation down, Ouse throws out a non sequitur of a question (signalling this particular story, so far as he wants to tell it, has come to an end):

If you could do anything right now, what would it be?

Stopped short by this sudden change of direction, Firth opts for the simplest answer – if perhaps not the most honest.

I'd like to see the third room of your favourite rooms on Muckle Flugga!

TWENTY-NINE

Firth never thought he'd enter the sacred realm of the lighthouse – he's not brave enough to trespass here; and it's rare, so rare, The Father is ever more than a thirty-second dash from his light. And, of course, he'd never permit Firth safe passage, not now anyway. Yet here he is, crossing the threshold, the only gatekeeper in sight his own hang-ups and hesitation.

Ouse welcomes him in like the madame of a burlesque club, spreading his arms out towards a great spiral staircase, which looks like it's been lifted from a luxury hotel or a high-end passenger liner. Except it's filthy, and chipped, and crammed into the light-house's throat. It's carpeted though, a long rolling emerald carpet coated in years of muddy boots. Today, however, it's snow rather than mud falling off the boots; icy powder marking this moment.

Ouse leads the charge, excited to commence the climb and knowing time is of the essence. Pounding up the stairs, he twists out of sight in seconds. Firth trails Ouse, and although the clump of boots initially suggests Ouse is not too far in front, in seconds, the footsteps have faded above Firth.

Ouse can't resist the temptation to have a quick blast on the organ as he passes it, knowing how wonderfully bizarre it is to send music tobogganing down the stairwell. And so he does: ten thunderous seconds of music are set loose like a carnival of dragonflies. The big fat notes smack Firth right in the face, and as he reaches the organ, the sound is still ringing in the air. *An actual church organ*, he says out loud in amazement. No time to spare, he proceeds onwards,

201

not wanting to fall too far behind – Ouse, after all, is travelling at record speed, cutting corners and zigzagging with perfection.

Around two-thirds of the way up, an opened window has resulted in snow being cast across the stairs in the shape of a bear. Firth notices Ouse must have deliberately skipped over it leaving the shape intact, and so he does the same. Through the window, he's shocked to see how fast the night's come in. There was just enough light to have travelled to the lighthouse without torches but now it's veritably dark out there. The clocks are spinning funny as the weather, Firth notes, deciding that, if he is dreaming, then this is a dream he could happily live within; a dream better than the life he'd leave behind.

Gulping at breath, Firth decides it's got to be a couple of hundred steps he's climbed now. He'd read somewhere, or perhaps Ouse had mentioned, that the lighthouse has three hundred and one steps. *Legs don't fail me now*, he chants, sprinting up the next section as if aiming to outrun the arrow of time itself.

Firth notices portraits bedecking the wall as the stairs begin to narrow and slows to a halt to look at them more closely: a bearded, austere man gazes back at him, then another and another until there's a whole fleet of them with varying degrees of death and desire behind the eyes, beards brimming and bristled.

Lost in the miasma of these haunted faces, Firth continues to race upwards, getting dizzy in the process. Just as his vision begins to go dotty, and his lungs appear ready to capsize and he considers keeling over just for the respite, there's Ouse, ravishing and ready.

They've reached the gallery deck and so the spiral staircase has come to an end. *Close your eyes for this bit*, Ouse instructs, covering his own in demonstration, as Firth now notes he tends to do – a real leader by example.

Ouse clasps Firth's hand and this time the spark surges stronger than before. Firth can't help but flinch away from the voltage, but lunges straight back in for Ouse's palm like a kid trying to catch the string of a balloon before it takes off skywards. Ouse leads him across a grated floor – he can feel the gaps in it – then comes the chomp of a chilling air, the crunch of snow, wind that knocks him off axis, only to be supported by an arm around his waist. The next set of stairs has a thin banister he grips on to, tightly – the steps here are steeper, thinner, and the metal handrail is so cold it burns. As they reach the precipice, Ouse behind him supporting his back, the room gets warmer and the wind begins to whisper. An incredible brightness crashes into Firth's scrunched-closed eyes.

Now lie down, Ouse instructs, lowering Firth onto the floor like a child onto a bench. He can feel the metal replaced by wood, can hear the rattle in the windows. He knows he's in the lantern room, sharing space with the heroic beam and its life-saving lens. There is an atmosphere to such presence; a prayer room for lunar light.

After what feels like an aeon, Ouse tells him to open his eyes, which Firth duly does and is at once overcome with the bright of the beam, but then it blinks off and his vision returns to the room. Lying flat on the floor, he's gazing straight into a ceaseless sprawl of planets, stars, moons and whatever else is up there, emitting light or hiding in the never-ending dark. From his vantage, he sees into outer space and nothingness; no clunky human obstructions, no suffocating modernity. This is the closest Firth's ever been to true greatness.

Watching the stars together causes a cosmic glow to spread across the two boys' chests, like butter on hot corn. Both are buoyed by it; it's them who are bulbs now, charged by starlight.

Lying beneath a prism of the light makes Firth feel monastic; the lighthouse's great reflectors are temple-worthy – a pulsing luminosity continues to cast him in and out of blindness, as if an angel stands among them revealing its glistening wings on the heart's half-beat, leaving them eclipsed by darkness the next.

Ouse breaks the silence: *An American freedom fighter that once stopped here told me the holes in the firmament were made by golden bullets in a great gun-fight between God and the devil. She said the exit wounds give us mortals a glimpse of what it costs to fight your way into heaven.*

It's all volcanos and lava explosions up there, isn't it? Firth counters, beginning to draw from the slopstack of facts he can recall from the single space lecture he attended at the University. *And black holes feasting on dead stars.*

I wonder what it's like to be amongst them, Ouse says dreamily.

Firth shivers: *I'll admire the galaxy from down here, thank you! Safely out the reach of all those flaming asteroids and slingshot fireballs.*

There's explosions in us, too, Ouse retorts, *all the time, just on a smaller scale. We're nothing but a bunch of colliding particles after all.*

Lost, insignificant and likely already dead? Firth counters.

At this Ouse laughs, not at all voluminously, and just for a second, but audibly enough for it to be a verifiable chuckle. Firth considers this might well be his life's crowning achievement.

Worm moon, wolf moon, flower moon, hunter's moon, portal moon, harvest moon. That's just some of the moons we get up here, Ouse states plainly.

That moon's five times bigger than I've ever seen it. The glass is surely magnifying it. Is it magnifying it? Firth queries, rapt.

No, we're just closer to the craters, or your eyes have grown, Ouse responds in a tone that suggests that should have been obvious.

Firth chooses to accept this as fact – for the fun in it, for the magic in it, and because Ouse seems more content with their meagre lot in life than Firth has ever managed.

What do you want beyond what you've got? I mean in terms of your art, Firth qualifies, sensing Ouse might go deliberately elsewhere with this change in tone. *Those wonderful things you create that come rushing out your big, beautiful brain – where do you want* those *stars to go?*

Ouse is careful with his answer, and deliberate, but chooses not to hold back. *I want to turn my sketches into more than socks, rugs and jumpers, beyond cardigans even. I've read books that talk of tapestries of such a size you'd need a castle's great hall to hang them in. I like the sound of that.*

Firth looks invigorated by this, his body feels stronger for it and he sidles in even closer to Ouse, so their hips and shoulders are touching, so their voices vibrate in each other's throats.

I don't suppose you've seen the stars so clearly in Edinburgh? Ouse queries, steering the conversation towards his own form of elsewhere.

Coming from anyone else that might have been a jibe, a my-stars-are-better-than-your-stars brag, but Firth knows that from Ouse's mouth it's a genuine form of enquiry. He shakes his awestruck head in response. What this also proffers to Firth is the perfect opportunity to bring the conversation he's been trying to finagle into being to the fore. A conversation which, up until a few hours ago, he had assumed was likely dead in the water.

Quite formally given their intimate circumstances, Firth seeks Ouse's permission to tell him a bit more about life in Edinburgh; a life he's relished and hated; a life that's brought him adoration and agony; a life that went from being dreamy and accomplished to a hollow he hoped to never return to. He knows Ouse will accept

205

his invitation into this story, and has fastidiously curated how he'll tell it; the things he'll focus on and those he'll muddy over or miss out, in order to make it best thrum for him. Firth can be despicable, egoic, pathetic and self-centred, but when it comes to storytelling – to dream-selling – he's both engaging and quick-witted.

Firth draws on all his reserves to deliver the tale that follows, a treatise on his life at Edinburgh's Academy of Art & Thinking. He explains, in his own inimitable style, the inner workings, machinations and movements of this great Academy. How it's very much a school within a school – the University having hoovered up the city's art colleges and an independent writing centre in a bid to absorb, or run out of business, all competing learning institutions within its orbit. However, the avaricious monolith of a University bit off more than it could chew, and thus regurgitated the writers and artists into an off-shoot institution that became the Academy – a body it was keen to profit from whilst essentially wiping its hands of at the same time. The result was an artistically liberated, hedonistic, collective of chaotic free-thinkers; not entirely autonomous, but not far from it. Provided fees were paid, a certain degree of prestige was upheld, and the building remained standing; the University overlords rarely cast their eyes in the direction of the infamous Academy.

Ouse is struggling to keep up as Firth describes, at pace, faction after faction of the student cohorts – the painters, poets and dramatists, the sculptors, illustrators and textilists – but doesn't dare interrupt in case Firth is tempted to start again. From what Ouse does catch, some of the students seem to consider themselves primarily agitators, committed to criticising the commercialisation and commodification of art, whilst others have taken vows of silence, ridding themselves of the distraction of having to communicate by mere words when superior forms of expressions exist. Some refuse to label their work at all, deeming genres a form of effete classification, essentially rendering themselves unmarkable. The poets appear a particularly prickly bunch, believing themselves capable of writing satire so potent it can cause insomnia, disfigurement or even death in the subject of their ridicule. Within each section there's anarchists, who produce political pamphlets and spend most of their time setting other people's work on fire and encouraging everyone to revolt. As for the staff, they seem to mainly be based off-campus in underground bunkers, reminding students of overdue fees and appearing at the end of the semester to solicit bribes in return for favourable grades and honeyed references. Which Firth explains is just as well, as it appears to be more fashionable to fail than pass these days; because at least that's an honest grade.

Though Firth apologises for talking over the stars, the apology appears to be no more than a device to permit him to keep talking, even further, guilt free. That said, the conclusory statement Firth wheedles Ouse's way comes both abruptly and as a total surprise.

But put all that to one side, Firth insists, *it's completely bananas, violent at times, but also extremely inspiring, in its own bonkers way. And the work you'd create while you were there – the studio and supplies at your disposal are second to none; and the time, time to really focus. That's the stuff that changes things, forever. Ouse, it'll set you off like a firework. What I mean to say is, you'd be brilliant there, you'd soar, and I can help make it happen.* Firth stops to catch his breath at this point, but not for long. *So, what do you think?*

Ouse, basking in the splendour of Firth holding court, and not having to bother with eye contact, is trailing astral lights in the galaxy above. He's lolling too deeply to fully register the question at the end of the story, and when it does register, he can't quite

207

fathom what it means. Thankfully, the holy grail of distractions arrives, and with infallible timing.

Look, cries Ouse, *it's greening over. Aurora borealis: the electric seaweed glacier.*

Up above them a green hue sweeps across the sky like a dragon – a big snaky body of glowing emeralds, scales of pure light, a tail turning of tessellated smoke.

Few things could have stopped Firth from pressing for an answer, from doubling down and relaying his reasons for Ouse to enrol in the Academy, but this is one of them. If the earth's history is a book of scripture written in starlight, then that tome has just been pulled out it's hiding spot and cracked open right in front of them. All manner of colours unspool from the sky's galactic reel.

The pair remain within the throes of aerial wonderment for an amount of time that can't be measured in seconds on a clock – roughly equivalent to the miles between Jupiter and its furthest moon when travelling twice the speed of a bolide. As the green dazzle-merchant begins to leave for its next dance, Firth notices Ouse twitch and waltzes back into his eardrums.

Ouse, you're interesting in the way people I know pretend to be, Firth blurts, delighted he got it out. *Going to the Academy will be the making of you! I can put a scholarship recommendation in. They listen to me. It'll all be taken care of.* Firth doesn't exactly know how yet, but he can beg patrons, blackmail graduates, and bribe corrupt lectures. Whatever it takes, he'll bring the grist to this mill.

If you stay here, you'll be utterly miserable, Ouse. Peripheral. Parochial. The Father is killing you – death by oppression, death by lovelessness, it's no way to go. Firth immediately regrets the vigour of this plea, but instead of back-tracking he chooses to level up. *Stay here and you'll forever only be skimming the surface of life.*

Ouse looks at first puckish, then crestfallen, until he's staring off in a thought so deep and palpable Firth reaches out to touch it.

That didn't sound right. I'm sorry, he stammers. *What I mean is, you've so much to offer. Your joy could be more, could be bigger.*

There is *love here!* Ouse retorts, brusquer in tone than Firth has ever heard him, than he thought him capable of. *My joy is not small. There's joy in the way the light turns the rocks opalescent every day of the summer. It sustains me. It brings me out of the silence. It's plenty big. I could never feel lonely under such infinite starlight.*

I'm sorry . . . Firth stutters.

This is no half-life, Ouse presses, getting to his feet and leaving Firth sitting down. *It's full-on sensory living. Most of the dreams in cities are swallowed by smog, and I'll bet most of your lot don't even notice, too addled on ale or bloated by the hubris.*

Firth thinks this might be the fiercest thing he's ever heard exit Ouse's mouth and secretly he loves the fact that he's to blame. It's passion from the pip.

We're shaped as much by the landscape as the people who rove over it. And have you not changed from being here? Journeyed for miles to come here?

You can't blame me for wanting more for you, Firth disputes. *Oh, have some heart.*

The heart's a silly, fragile thing, Ouse snaps, *foolishly doted over.*

In this moment, Firth sees a flash of The Father in Ouse and is overcome by the dread that he's overestimated Ouse's ambition for his work to become something that transports him beyond this sequestered spot. After all, who is he to recommend anything to anyone? He is not revered, nor wealthy, nor seriously acclaimed; he's not in love, not anything of real value to this world; not even happy enough to want to stay alive. Certainly not as happy in

Edinburgh as he's been on Muckle Flugga, galvanised by the notion of furthering Ouse's life. Perhaps this whole scenario has been contrived for his own benefit, to give him purpose, Firth concedes. And Ouse, Ouse has simply been a prop, a plaything. Ouse had not asked for his help, had not asked anything of him. Who is he to expect Ouse to toss his life here aside as if spare change, as if old pennies down a dank well?

But I do admit, Ouse begins, softer, warmer, walking towards the glass, *at times, I desire things beyond Muckle Flugga, something just for me, though I know how selfish that sounds.*

Firth's drowning love resurfaces for air. It feels as if he's just waited out a lethal fog and found a comely cottage hiding behind it. He wills Ouse to speak on, his lips quivering, gimlet-eyed.

But where do you draw the line? Ouse compels. *I'm not sure that matters to you, which worries me.*

Of course it matters, Firth protests, offended yet impressed by the gravity of the insinuation. *Let me prove that to you. You're amazing, Ouse, you deserve an amazing life.*

With this, Firth rises to his feet and joins Ouse at the edge of the lantern's glass, as far as they can go without stepping out into the night. A silence creeps in, and not one either would dare disturb, for now what needed to be said has been said. They hear each other's lips moisten, they see each other's breath, the luminescence above casts green masks upon their faces so as they might hide together in plain sight.

Time passes slowly talking under a natural phenomenon, but not slowly enough that The Father hasn't finished his drink, shovelled the snow out *The Covenant*, hoisted off, traversed the crossing and arrived back at Muckle Flugga. That's to say, The Father is home.

We have to go! Ouse announces, panicked, spotting *The Covenant* back in the cove and hauling Firth towards the exit with a sturdy yank. *Say goodbye to the stars.*

By the time Firth manages his goodbye, Ouse has him hurtling down the stairs – this time keeping just a few steps ahead of him, whilst never disappearing out of sight.

Firth feels the closeness between them fracture, yet something is stirring. He'll think it over in the bath, come up with a verdict. Ouse is flustered, it's a lot, but there's skin in the game yet.

Ouse knows how fast The Father can ascend those stairs, even quicker than him, knows how his eyes are drawn to the lighthouse as soon as it's in sight; they are connected: the lighthouse can't keep a secret from The Father and he's powerless to its gossip.

The Father has been listening, this Ouse knows for sure by the time they hit the snow bear spilled across the spiral staircase, which now has The Father's footprints planted in it, and not by accident. The Father has never failed to cover his tracks when he wants to, if he needs to. Instead, he's left his stamp.

THIRTY

Do you think I should go to Edinburgh? Ouse asks tenderly, turning to his favoured source of advice and wisdom.

To Auld Reekie? Of course! RLS responds, crooning. *Lay down upon her lap and present thy soft belly to her fingers for a good old ruffle. If not now, then sometime. And if sometime, then why not now? Your life poses a brilliant question, Ouse, one that doesn't yet have an answer.*

My favourite questions are those without answers, Ouse retorts cheerily.

Questions for questioning's sake. Crucial cutter, right enough.

Just this once, I wish you'd tell me what to do! Ouse appeals. *Straight between the eyes.*

It's not for me to conjure the answer, but coax it out. Any clergyman worth their salt will attest to that. I'm an old cajoler is all. Should I issue the wrong advice you'll have me up in court for professional negligence.

With this RLS leaps onto the crumbly end of a dry-stone wall at the most southerly tip of the island. In order to reach this headland, Ouse had to scurry down a scree-slide then meander up a rocky corkscrew of paths that thin to the size of a belt. It's a tightrope walk to travail the final few metres, but once on the summit the views to Unst are spectacular – a tawny smudge encased in cerulean. The dry-stone wall is cut off at either end like a disconnected pipe; it's sheltering a small, unkempt garden, that despite obvious signs of neglect remains defiantly fecund, harbouring an opulence of wildflowers.

Ouse is squatting down on his back haunches and cupping the soil in his hands; thinning it out, removing stones and increasing its growing power. He lets the soil spill from his closed palms like a river of grains flowing from a sand-timer. The wind, however, makes a mockery of his contemplativeness and, sneaking through a hole in the wall, blows the dirt all over the place, his face included.

RLS, watching on, holds back a laugh, holds strong to his hat, then begins to lose his balance, sliding off the wall and nearly colliding with Ouse.

Edinburgh is where The Mother was born, you know? Ouse says quietly and factually, dusting himself down.

Oh I know, we've taken parley in the past. She's awffie proud of her brave wee laddie! RLS utters sweetly, as Ouse crumples into tears.

Oh my boy, my boy, RLS consoles, taking the young Ouse into his chest like a marsupial coddles its cub.

They're tears of joy, RLS. I wish you'd said something sooner.

Couldn't, I'm afraid. There's a surprising amount of bureaucracy about what the dead can say to the living.

Then tell me about Edinburgh! Its wellsprings and warts, Ouse compels, wiping away his drippings.

Well then, it's best you take a seat. That's to say, buckle up.

Ouse is already sitting down in the dirt, garlanded by flowers, readying himself to be tended to. It is RLS's Edinburgh, not Firth's, that he is most ardent to unravel.

• • •

Having spotted Figgie tarrying by her boat, Firth abandons the paintbrushes and winds his way down to her via the treacherous path. When he reaches her, she's rifling through rockpools, plucking out

213

what look to be small crustaceans, presumably for the cooking pot. Figgie's wearing an ornate dress with floral cuffs, alongside thick working trousers and a hefty pair of boots. The lower hem of the dress is mawkit, a melange of green and black smears from her comings and goings. Although she doesn't make eye contact with Firth, she gestures him to sit down on a rock-like seat next to her flank.

Firth seats himself, as instructed, the tide licking the toes of his boots then retreating back to its salty master. Figgie begins ruffling Firth's hair, pinning it between her fingers and examining the length.

I cut his hair, you know, Ouse's. I've cut it these last couple of years since The Mother passed. I'd cut The Father's too if he let me. The Father just sort of hacks at his, I wish he'd let me see tae it. I could cut yours if you like? Figgie makes to her pocket, rummaging for scissors.

Thank you, Figgie, but no, Firth asserts firmly, getting back to his feet, the tide now rising up to his ankles. *I didn't come down here for a haircut.*

It'd be nae trouble.

That's kind, you're kind. But no, it's your help I need.

I've been thinking on that, I just don't think I can. She pauses, swivelling her body away from Firth and back towards the boat. *It's The Father.*

But you love Ouse, too, Firth appeals, trying to inhabit the feeling in the words and taking Figgie by the arm to draw her in to him. *The Father keeps him hostage here, not physically but emotionally. He's hit him, you know, slapped him and pushed him, and I'll bet that's not the half of it.*

Figgie begins to shudder in upset. Firth leans in to swaddle her but she shakes him off.

214

I do everything I can. It's just. The Father. I mean . . . and . . . Figgie stops herself there, on the cusp of telling Firth how she supplements their food deliveries from her own purse, but feeling it too much a betrayal, and not wanting to fully admit to herself the true tally of it. *I'm always thinking of them. And I've never married, not for lack of people asking either. It's just.*

You promised me you'd help! Firth pleads.

I just didn't think what you'd ask me to do would be so . . . so . . . Figgie sniffles.

It's for Ouse. Only for Ouse. The Father . . . He'll survive. He has the lighthouse. And he'll have you, Figgie. And Ouse can come back and visit . . . We have to act now, otherwise he might as well choose which room to die in!

With this Figgie throws Firth a sharp look, then begins scraping circles in the sand with the tip of her boot; two circles which overlap in the middle. There is a lot of sadness on this beautiful, mystical place, Firth observes. In talking about Ouse's survival, he has disturbed the notion of his own mortality: he was the one who was not supposed to leave this island. He shakes these maudlin, selfish thoughts out of his head and focusses again on what he needs from Figgie, appealing to the softness in her eyes.

And he'd really be okay, there? Figgie presses, scouring in the undergrowth of her mind for the gallantry this requires.

I'd make sure he had a full scholarship, and somewhere to live, and I've friends who'd check in on him. Good people, much better than me.

But you. Would you be there to look after him? Figgie questions, clutching both of Firth's hands in her own and coming in close to his face.

I would. I will. At least at first. As long as he needs me. Firth delivers this sincerely, not knowing if it's deception or newfound duty.

Then that's good enough for me, Figgie replies sharply before dropping Firth's hands and boarding her boat, not looking back, nor flinching neither.

• • •

RLS explains to Ouse that the trick to succeeding in the capital is to find his version of Edinburgh within an infinite number of Edinburghs. He explains that in settling on his own version he gave up on God, absconded from the study of engineering, then the study of law. Explains that the rumour was, in doing so, he also gave up the acquaintance of religious types and sought out the company of vagabonds, prostitutes and lowlifes; roistering carousers, who glugged straight from the bottle. RLS does not deny any of these allegations and, in fact, deems this a felicitous period of his life, suggesting the city's 'mutton shunters and pearl gurglers' were the real snakes in the grass.

He talks about the conflict in the city, its bifurcation, its Old Town and its New, its castle and its Cowgate, its fine-dining societies and seedy underbelly, its art and literature alongside its dark drinks and mucky powders. As RLS describes the peevish duplicity of the capital, his voice and features, too, seem to split. He appears to revel in the nefarious secrets the streets are lined with, and the vulgarity of what happens below ground clearly thrills him.

Ouse has always thought RLS moves as if made of water, akin to himself, but in these moments, he appears like a wrought-iron gate swinging off its hinges. Whilst listening, Ouse draws shapes in the soil, taking notes from RLS's sermon in earthy hieroglyphics, symbols he can come back to at a later date. Either way, it all sounds muddy to Ouse, too tumultuous and fast-paced. It puts

216

him on the side of resistance in terms of Firth's great Edinburgh offer.

RLS, with a dutiful nod, takes encouragement from Ouse's lack of enchantment in the more rambunctious side of his young life. Contrarily, it's also an impetus to play the other hand. In a shift of tone, RLS explains that Edinburgh is where he first read the great poets, Whitman included. Not only that, it's where he truly found his tribe – a core collective of comrades and companions, a selection of whom became the founding members of the L. J. R. (Liberty, Justice, Reverence) League, a key tenet of which was to disregard everything their parents taught them. A smaller selection still became his compañeros for life, in both love and letters. Whereas Ouse's ears prick up for the poetry and fierce friendships, his allegiance wavers on the relinquishment of any lessons he's been taught by The Mother and The Father.

RLS reminds Ouse he was born to Edinburgh, whereas Ouse would be travelling, and neither party needs reminding of the heralded place in which RLS holds the pursuit of travelling.

This leaves Ouse more torn than ever, and he makes a show of it, thrashing his fingers over his doodles in the dirt in a rare moment of frustration. A few panicked earthworms surface to see what all the fuss is about. And then a resounding sound of birdcall beats down upon them, serving as nature's reminder that their problems, no matter how personally important, are just tiny specs of noise in the grand chorus of this world.

Please, could you just boil it down for me, you're so brilliant at that when you want to be? Ouse begs.

RLS affects an offended look and then switches to a kindly disposition. *Beyond all the blood and brimstone, I met myself in Edinburgh, Ouse, and I rather suspect you would too.*

And of The Father? Ouse questions, hugging his own body like a stranger might.

Leave The Father to The Father, RLS snaps. *Your fealty here must be to yourself. Or, let me put it this way, there is no duty we so much underrate as the duty of being happy. To be what we are, and to become what we are capable of becoming, is the only end of life.*

I understand, Ouse says solemnly, then lightens as the next sentiment hatches in his mouth. *You're going soft on me after all!*

RLS flings him his best 'how dare you' look and in (jovial) protest disappears from sight, leaving a mucky-pawed Ouse to reset the compost and dig deeper into his thoughts.

• • •

The last person Firth wanted to bump into was The Father, but fate is a prankster, and so after another secret rendezvous with Figgie, it is inevitably The Father he stumbles upon. The Father, who, like clockwork, is in the lighthouse this time every other day, whom you can set a watch by, is today sat at the table polishing his gun when Firth brings in the deliveries given to him by Figgie to mask their ulterior motives.

Firth bids The Father good morning with a nervous smile and then holds up the bags of shopping he's straining to carry. If he wasn't so craven, he'd give him a piece of his mind for his outburst at Ouse, for the misplaced aggression and the vitriol; instead he's proffering groceries.

The Father sits like a sultan waiting to address his people – expectant, haughty, brooding. He thinks to himself, *you've been drinking my piss in your whisky, wee boy,* and smirks crooked for it. Whilst Firth obsequiously unpacks the groceries, The Father

218

silently lifts the gun off the table so it's pointing at the back of Firth's head. He shocks himself as the vision of a hole in Firth's skull starts to appear – the grotesque mess his brain would make spattered over the kitchen cupboards. He begins to consider what items from the shopping would be salvageable and what would be spoiled. Firth turns around to see The Father and the weapon now pointing towards Firth's balls.

Don't suppose you want me to teach you to shoot? The Father enquires coolly, a little sportive even.

Firth, staring down upon the barrel, considers his options. He abhors guns, always has, but perhaps The Father might respect him if he accepts. No, he couldn't do that, it's one of the few principles he's not compromised on – he's picked up the pieces of friends lost to the perniciousness of its vile allure. Besides, The Father would have the opportunity to kill him, to say it was an accident; lots of noble and ignoble people have died in shooting accidents that were far from accidents if you ask someone in the know. It would be Firth's word against The Father's, but he would be dead. It's surely not a genuine offer anyhow, more a tactic of intimidation. It's a mad offer, he decides; The Father is a psychopath, a psychopath pointing a gun at him! In the circumstances, Firth surprises himself with his relative calm. This is not a situation in which he'd normally be unflappable, far from it. Likely he's just numb with life and stiff with fear. Regardless, it wouldn't be fair on Ouse, the messiness of a murder, and he's not yet finished his portfolio of bird drawings, which really are much better than he anticipated – not art for market, but they'd make a poignant gift; a flawless swansong.

I've got work to finish, I'm afraid, Firth offers in response, as if turning down an invitation for luncheon.

Your loss, The Father retorts. *A man should know how to shoot. Ouse can shoot, a damn good shot he is, too.*

Firth is thrown by the steadiness of the statement, a discombobulating tone to The Father's voice – insulting yet not without some warmth in it, as if he actually wanted him to accept the invitation, and not merely to kill him. He fathoms The Father may have even been impressed by his calm under pressure – joke's on him, it's not machoism but a flagrant disregard for his own life. Firth continues putting away the messages and does so at record speed. The Father's eyes burning a hole in the back of his head. *Right, I'm off*, Firth announces skittishly, not realising The Father, whilst his back has been turned, had left his seat and crept all but a foot away from him.

Wait, The Father snaps, grabbing Firth by the forearm. Of course, The Father's grip is strong, as strong as Firth expects it would be, vice-like and commanding, bone-crushing brawn, and so he winces with the pain as any weakling would.

I want you to give this to Ouse. Looking down at the hand thrust towards him, Firth sees an envelope. *It's a letter. No the day like, but soon, soon enough. It's . . . it's important. I need to ken you cin do that fur me? Cin you do that fur me?* The Father's voice growing more gravelly, even a little desperate sounding, in this final sentiment.

A whole gallimaufry of things Firth should have said come to his mind later that day. *Why not give it to him yourself? What's in it for me? Why would I help you? I never knew you could write? Away and take yer face for a shite! I'll not be a puppet in your sordid scheme! After all the harm you've caused, not a chance in hell I'm helping you! Now let go of my arm, you fucking ogre!*

Wanting to get out of The Father's grapple as quickly as possible, and being somewhat blindsided by his tiger-like approach and the bewildering nature of the request, Firth replies none of these things, but instead whimpers: *Fine* – then takes the letter and attempts to scuttle out the door.

As Firth is fading out of earshot, back amongst the weather, he hears The Father once again. *I heard yiz talking in the lighthouse!* The Father growls, churning like a belly chewing rotten meat. Firth gasps, pretends to miss this, then continues on his way.

As soon as he's escaped The Father's presence, Firth admits to himself that the main reason he so readily took the letter was out of nosiness for what it might contain. And that what he is really thinking is, keep your friends close, but your enemies closer.

THIRTY-ONE

The following day the letter sits upon Firth's desk like a ticking bomb. He puts it in a drawer, under his pillow, in the wardrobe, inside a book, up on the hammock, beneath the mattress, in a fishing wader, in a kilt sock, in a pillowcase, under a loose floorboard.

Firth labels it a Pandora's box, a bête noire, a curse, a lifeline, his arch nemesis, his fairy godmother, a clusterfuck, a gift from the gods. He ruminates The Father's psychology, his reverse psychology, reconsiders it all under the haze of entrapment. It is not the only stowaway in Firth's room at this point, not the only curio belonging to another; this too weighs heavily upon him – the hypocrisy, the gall.

Foremost, Firth believes The Father expects him to open the letter. Pondering that in fact it could be stuffed to the gills with an airborne poison that would kill him as soon as he snoops inside. But would The Father take that risk? Firth debates. The risk that he, Firth, might not burgle his way inside and instead would hand it straight to Ouse, as instructed, who would perish in his place. The Father needs Ouse, he wants him under his and the lighthouse's servitude: Firth has no doubt he's willing to play dirty to get what he wants, but he covets 'his laddie' strong, not stricken down. There's a legacy at stake in The Father's eyes and not one he'd risk cutting short. Could it just be a veritable letter? Firth puffs. And, if so, of what intent – confessional, defamatory, scandalous? No, not The Father's style – Firth puts that one to bed. Perhaps it is admin, a keeper's contract for Ouse's lifelong service, a pay rise, or a simple shopping list? Oh, fuck knows.

No matter what the nomenclature, Firth has spent the majority of an afternoon trying to draw his latest bird, making the type of progress that might take a more focussed artist twenty minutes or less. He did, however, collect several types of guano and mix them into paint pigment for an authentic touch; a technique he'd read about at the Academy. This being his greatest feat of the day – harvesting bird poo. And a full day *has* passed, during which Ouse has been busy with The Father in the lighthouse. So why didn't he deliver the missive to his son himself? Or leave it in his room to find on his return.

Using the binoculars he found in the cupboard, whilst searching for further places to hide the letter, Firth spends a few minutes stalking the silhouettes of The Father and Ouse in the lantern room. They appear close together, The Father pointing a lot, Ouse circling around him like a duck – up and down to the level below, then disappearing for a while until Firth thinks he can hear music, suggesting they must be expecting mischief from the waves as the weather takes on an edge.

Firth admits that if he were a sailor out in that choppy ocean, The Father would be an invaluable ally. Both Figgie and Ouse have lionised The Father's knowledge of the way gales behave, breakers break and storms prowl the coast. Not the science of it, not *their* science anyway, but his own school of thought. Firth had attempted to suppress how enrapt he was to hear The Father had made a playbook in which he turned hours and hours of observation into lessons and etchings, a book he would gift to Ouse (no-one else) before 'tapping out'. The Father thinks himself akin to the coach of a prize-fighter working out his opponent's weaknesses (glass jaw, clumsy footing, unsteady jab, cocky with their guard). Firth reluctantly concedes, any fighter would have a better chance at a title shot with The Father by their side. And with that admission, he launches the binoculars onto the bed and takes another slurp of the whisky.

Firth notices that the light has now submitted to the dark and that he, having worked himself into a stuporous exhaustion, is shaking. He slugs back the dregs of the bottle and puts the letter back under his pillow. Once in bed, he continues to debate his seemingly endless spool of options, whilst watching a candle strip itself to a charred wick and collapse into a blob on the brass below. Firth gives the goo a comforting poke, before melting into a hot mess of dreams.

THIRTY-TWO

A thick spout of light splinters into a thousand fragments over Firth's sleeping body; he stirs to find Ouse at the end of his bed.

Good. You're up, Ouse announces, revealing he'd been standing there for some time. It's late morning and Firth has slept through a chunk of the day. *I'm off to the mainland today to catch the mid-morning market closing. It's the last of the month, so I check in on my knitwear sales and I thought . . .* Before he can finish, Firth has intuited the invitation and is scrabbling to his feet, trying to shake the sleep from his voice as he declares, *I'd love to.*

Be by the boat in ten minutes then, Ouse smiles, running off as if he'd left a pot on the boil.

Firth slaps his face with cold water, then dresses fast enough that he has extra time to take the long way round to *The Covenant's* mooring, which also lessens his chances of stumbling upon The Father. The walk is interspersed by birdsong, including a throaty sound he hasn't heard before wrapped up in a melody he's sure he has. Ouse, by the boat, is awaiting his arrival, bolt upright and radiant, having clearly readied everything the night before. Firth is delighted to know Ouse has been anticipating the trip, that he went to bed with the morning's invite bubbling in his belly. Ouse wastes no time in summoning Firth into the boat and pushing off: it's a wordless ceremony but there's fondness in every gesture.

On the boat ride over, Ouse spies a ripple in the waves, then shadowy strokes below the surface, suspecting the shapes to be a pod of dolphins. He pulls the vessel to a stop and recounts a fable from his youth, that The Father had told him, in the hope it draws the dolphins out of hiding. Firth is a little perplexed by the story, unaware of the true purpose behind their tarrying, but listens attentively all the same. This is the third boat trip Firth has been on with Ouse, a new direction every time, yet despite his constant observations, every sight on the horizon, every rock sculpture and distant island pimple, still feels brand new. Firth stretches out his limbs and comforts in the cracking of his bones, letting Ouse's storytelling flow through him as the sun showers their bodies in light. Either way, the nebulous sightings below the water are not so easily summoned back.

Suddenly, Figgie's boat comes tumbling into sight, having snuck up on them whilst they stopped to investigate the ripples. She's travelling at pace and doesn't notice them until she comes careering over a wave and nearly crashes straight into the bow of *The Covenant*.

Careful! Ouse calls to her. *Were you dreaming of something fabulous and forgot where you were heading?*

Figgie smiles briefly but is too busy righting the boat's direction to respond. Firth starts to fidget anxiously at Figgie's presence.

What news from the mainland? Ouse enquiries theatrically, leaning over and helping her by pulling the boat around.

Well, market's on, Figgie says, catching her breath, *but you'll ken that. Oh and there's a big passenger-liner in the port, biggest I've seen for years. They nearly emptied our shelves, I had to wrestle back some bread and eggs for youse lot. Cabbage too. I'll drop it in noo. Aye, best be going.*

We're off for the whole day. A proper outing, Firth declares with a lack to joy in his voice unbefitting of the sentiment.

Figgie nods only at Firth as she sails off, with barely a glance in Ouse's direction. Ouse registers this anomaly but thinks nothing more of it. Firth swears for a second Figgie's face morphs into

226

that of a fox, her eyes glowing amber and ears beginning to bristle. But she's too quick to leave to confirm the strange sighting and his companion is vying for his attention.

Oh ya beauty! The markets will be mobbed, Ouse muses, secretly hopeful that his cache of woolly creations might find good homes and bring in some extra money for provisions.

Firth fills the remainder of the boat journey with his own anecdote – a long, rambling, at times incohesive, yarn about an artist friend who built an illegal absinthe shebeen in the centre of Edinburgh, calling it an interactive exhibition. Ouse has never met someone that talks so much as Firth – such winding narratives that take off on huge, often barely relevant, tangents. None of the boys he went to school with would be capable of such sustained periods of word churning. It's not the way up here, he attests to himself. It is a little exhausting, but mostly he finds it refreshing: all those letters manufactured in the mouth and sent fluming from the lips without a care in the world.

Firth's tale takes them all the way to the harbour, overseeing the boat's anchoring, and only comes to a close when the music of the market canters into earshot. It is catching sight of the central square heaving with activity that causes Firth to leap from the endtrails of his story back into the present; exactly as Ouse knew he would, just a little later than expected. Only now can Firth reflect on the dexterity of Ouse's mooring, the cluttered cobbled walkways they've just traversed, the colourful bunting, the tall gothic buildings, and the flamboyance of the flowers bedecking every windowsill. There is a great pride here – expressed in cheerful décor – and it causes both their gaits to loosen. Ouse is walking more springy than ever and Firth veritably skips.

A mix of local folk doing proper household shops and tourists collecting souvenirs of every sort inundates the stalls. The Shet-landers tut at the pussyfooting visitors finding everything so exciting and quaint, whilst the smug stall owners count their tak-ings. There's local prices and then taller tariffs for out-of-towners. Sales have been tallying up since 6 a.m. and countless bargains have already been had; some swindlings too.

Ouse leads Firth through the bustling market, meandering, with their arms chain-linked. They pass chocolatiers, mead-mak-ers, wild-oat sellers, miniature train set displays, rows of soap made from goats' milk, jams, jellies and local cheeses; knitted bonnets, antiquated books and hand-drawn maps of the islands, including Muckle Flugga and Treasure Island; shortbread and the sugar chief-tain itself, tablet. That and everything in between.

Firth's salivating by the time they've done a lap of the place: Ouse's cooking has been exemplary but outside of a few hot meals, he's been living off carrots, cabbage, porridge and toast, the odd egg or scrap of chicken skin. A little whisky helps fill the holes, mind, Firth acknowledges that – it's an act of generosity he, annoyingly, can't take away from The Father.

Nectar aside, Firth doesn't miss the opportunity to draw their explorations to a swift halt when he spies The Oyster Witch (as her stall is boldly labelled). Firth orders three molluscs a piece for him and Ouse, buying another couple for onlookers who join the huddle. These are shucked so majestically that Firth claps loud-ly and shouts 'Bravo!', which to Ouse's surprise goes down well with the gathering group. They clack the shells, toast to eternity, and slurp back the pearlescent slabs with hot disco on their lips. Laced in sharp lemon and salt-kissed, Firth can't help but make a zapping sound in celebration of the zest injection his body's just been gifted.

I'm ready for anything now, Firth declares. And Ouse, The Oyster Witch and a couple of passers-by cackle at his exuberance. The Oyster Witch stalls them a minute to clean and polish their shells as mementos. *Those will bring you luck*, she sniggers, then scoops up an oyster for herself: a racy wink as she sloops it back all dribbly spills.

What with Firth being late out of bed, the crowd is already beginning to thin at the mid-morning market. Upon witnessing a couple of eager stallholders commencing their pack-away, Ouse jolts into action, remembering the point of their trip. Firth counts the money in his pocket to make sure he's flush enough to buy one of Ouse's jumpers. Ouse weaves out of the main swell of the market and into a chapel where the textile sellers are assembled. All the tables are compacted together in the cosy space, laid out in a holy cross formation below the dome above. The dome's stained glass is luscious and animated, turning the already colourful wares technicolour in the gathering light.

Ouse, despite being a veteran of these market pick-ups, always stops to swoon upon entering this temple; he worships not at the sight of a crucified Christ but at the altar of each cross-stitched woolly creation. Firth follows in Ouse's shadow, thrilled by his sense of purpose within the space. Ouse explains that the knitwear is normally stacked six feet high, casting shadows over the room and constantly toppling over. The fact that the stock has diminished to such humble piles, he notes, is a fabulous thing.

A gaggle of ebullient woman barter with customers at the fast pace of a trading floor or an auction house. Firth immediately recognises the knitting woman from the ferry, plus a couple of her cabal, and it makes him feel like part of the clique. It transpires her name is Nith and it appears, even here, she's the matriarch. Finishing a couple of big sales, she turns her attention to the boys

– greeting Ouse with the warmest of affection and Firth with a chipper ribbing; then more sternly revealing she's glad he's still with them, a sincerity to her manner that makes Firth tense.

Nith catches Firth clocking the cross-like layout of the knitwear stalls and rolls her eyes towards the religious busybodies hawking their miracle-inspired doilies and tea cosies in the corner – clearly below par but understood to be a condition of using the space. That said, the bobble hat featuring Jesus turning water to wine does appeal to Firth, in a tokenistic way, but he can quickly tell it would be a traitorous purchase and so he abstains.

After pointing to the empty table where Ouse's knits once were, Nith pulls him aside to deliver the good news. Firth, examining the celestial light slung over the colourful patterns, feels surprisingly moved; he also manages to coorie in close enough to eavesdrop on what's being said to Ouse.

Not only did you sell oot – AGAIN – but you sold oot first, and some toff from Edinburgh even left a muckle tip fir you, and his postal address . . . in case you fancy making them some special commissions.

Should have heard the names that jealous wench next door wiz calling ye when he wouldnae take ony of her stock, Nith's pal chips in, chortling. *Her face turned to fish guts, did it know?!*

Pus like a bag of rusty spanners! another of the team barks.

Nith hands Ouse a fat punnet of takings and encourages him to follow up on the offer of special commissions, and also to get busy knitting for the End of Summer Market happening on the mainland's mainland in just a few weeks' time. Ouse mulls it over with serious intent. Meanwhile, Firth is trying to hold his own against a blitz of teasing banter from Nith's best pals. He's failing ridiculously but it's smiles and spirit galore all the same.

With sparks in his eyes, an elated Ouse extracts Firth from the ribbing and ribaldry of the knitting squad and walks them back out into an all but disappeared market. Firth can't believe how quickly the market has dissipated, aligning it with the fast algebra of the weather and the kooky turn of time that seems to haunt these parts. Firth wastes not a second in congratulating Ouse with a wordless hug and a look of deep pride; the moment only slightly dampened in Firth's mind by recalling how he had hoped to pick up a genuine Ouse knit for himself.

We have to celebrate, Firth declares.

Heading back into the main hall of the market, they jump over a crimson river of water – offal and intestines from the butcher's counter colouring the torrent – and arrive just in time to snag the final few chocolates from the chocolatier, who's affected French accent has now switched back to the local brogue.

Clutching a pouch of chocolates, the clatter of coins in his pocket and a surge of self-respect in his chest, Ouse takes Firth down to the harbour. They sit with their feet dangling over the edge and their bums wettening on the planked jetty. Whilst watching their legs swing like pendulums above the sea, Firth confirms to himself that Ouse must not simply be wooed by his Edinburgh pitch but steered towards it by any means necessary; less a charm offensive more a crusade. And so he volleys back on in.

Come to Edinburgh, Ouse, please, let me help you apply to the Academy! You wouldn't have to worry about money or upkeep or anything – your needlework will do the work for you. Think of what you just achieved. And that's here; great as it is, it's a million miles from anywhere.

I'll not be anybody's burden, Ouse responds shaking his head. *I would need to stand on my own two feet.*

Firth launches into an impassioned spiel about the different artists he knows who make sufficient, plentiful and, at times, lavish incomes out of their mostly mediocre practices, stressing that what Ouse does will blow them all out the water. He gives it some emotional welly, attempting to reassure Ouse that his knitwear business would prosper all the more in Edinburgh and that he, Firth, would aid him in taking it to the next level.

Ouse cocks his face in an attempt to downplay the superlatives Firth is casting his way.

Are you worried you'll be unhappy in Edinburgh? Firth prods.

No, Ouse counters coolly, lying a little. *I'd keep busy: a busy person never has time to be unhappy.*

Firth goes on to explain how the flat he lives in on Candlemaker Row has a space below it, his mum's old candle-making shop. And that, with the talented ghost merchant currently occupying it soon to be upping ship to York, it would be imminently vacant.

Firth senses Ouse letting himself entertain this prospect, slapping the top of the water with his now exposed toes, having furtively slipped off his footwear whilst Firth was full throttle talking. With Ouse's appetite whetted, Firth doubles down and begins narrating the space with exaggerated brio – a veritable cave hidden in the bowels of an old tenement featuring low-slung ceilings and a secret cellar; on one of Edinburgh's most iconic streets, flanking the infamous Greyfriars Kirk Graveyard.

It sounds a lot, Ouse sighs – his interest piqued but daunted by the prospect of the Academy plus the shop space, both of which individually dwarf any of his endeavours to date, never mind the two combined.

It is a lot, and at the same time not nearly enough, Firth says with the resolve of a king, taking Ouse's hand in his and squeezing it for effect.

Thank you. Truly. For everything you're offering, Ouse says, with a soft, singing sincerity. Letting his hand rest in Firth's whilst continuing to stare off towards the ocean.

Before Firth has a chance to bring the conversation home, having been readying himself to go for the emotional jugular, spurred on by the sugar rush, Ouse draws it to a premature close, removing his hand and remarking, *I'd like to leave this conversation here for now.* As if to ritualistically mark out a full stop, Ouse throws the peanut from the centre of his chocolate thimble into the sea as proof of intent.

After a palpable silence, Firth enquires, *Did you make a wish?*, aiming to prove that he's cool and capable of leaving such a crucial conversation on the stove parboiled. In actual fact, he's finding it excruciating not being able to play his next, better, hand; whilst deliberating ways to resurrect the subject as quickly as possible.

Yes, for the fish. I wish for them to enjoy a peanut, Ouse proclaims.

Ouse leans forwards to see if any fish have risen to the occasion. Firth follows suit, leaning in and focussing his eyes to tune into whatever's below. Firth remains wrestling with the notion of giving Ouse his requested thinking space. He is on the cusp of adding one final chapter to the great Edinburgh pitch before managing to restrain himself. In the end, it is a voice booming from behind that crumples through their thoughtfulness: *Ouse, you little tit-wank! I've no seen you in pure ages! We all thought you'd been sold to sailors for a spunk-rag!*

Behind them is the most ginger-haired, near translucent, teenage girl Firth has ever seen – egg white and its yolk.

Who's the weirdo? she snaps, pointing at Firth. *Actually, I dinnae care, I'm late. Nice to see ye. Not!* And off she hops, before drawing up short and twirling back towards them. *In fact . . . hold on . . . you*

233

two can walk me over! With this the freckly girl hauls the pair of them up off the jetty with bravura, grabbing each of their arms in tandem and propelling them forth.

Ouse makes a half-hearted introduction between Firth and the girl, who it turns out was in the year below Ouse at school and now works various stalls at the market alongside seasonal shifts on the ferries. Firth can't gauge whether Ouse is mortified by the intrusion of a figure from his past or simply knows her well enough to let her do the talking. This comes with an afterthought of worrying whether Ouse is, instead, embarrassed to be seen with him in front of a peer. A recondite range of theories flap around Firth's brain as they collectively kick up dirt on the uphill track she's jostling them towards. Thankfully, events take a turn for the better when the girl begins unpacking her plan for them and the day ahead.

There's a ceilidh oan at the town hall, for the tourists like, she explains. *Their boat takes off at five so we're giving them a big ol' send-off . . . making sure they spend the last of their holiday cash before they go. There's a band and a bar and aw that. Might be a few rides worth dancing with inawl.* At this she licks her lips, her tongue twirling in such a determined manner that Firth chokes on the air in his lungs.

Dinnae 'hink so, fanbelt, she sneers at Firth, *yer no that lucky.* Despite the girl's rude greeting, Firth can now tell she's genuinely pleased to see Ouse, and he's warming up to her. On the way over, she talks non-stop about friends from schooldays and makes paper-thin excuses as to why her chums went on to the ceilidh without her. It's apparent to both Ouse and Firth that arriving with two 'weirdo-losers' is preferable to arriving on your own when your friends have done the dirty ditch. Apparent, in the main, because she states this in no uncertain terms, whilst warning them they will be cut loose as soon as she finds better company, which she notes *winnae be hard*.

By the time they arrive at the grandiose doors of the town hall, the music is already spilling out onto the street, as are a few of the early starters. One of whom, about Firth's height, is heaving up the contents of lunch as another rubs circles on their back. A jealous onlooker gurns away, shooting eye daggers from the sidelines. Firth clocks a chalked-up noticeboard advertising the band – The Howling Hearts – and what appears to be a pumpkin-punching competition, though he convinces himself he must have misread that latter bit.

In through the great doors and a rush of music, laughter and sweat drenches their skin. On the stage an eight-piece band of accordions, pipes, fiddles and guitars fills the space. A couple of hangers-on crowd around them, adding a whistle and a tambourine into the mix – uninvited and to adverse effect for anyone with ears. A set of hands on every table thumps along to the beat, mostly out of time, drink spilling out of glasses with each excited wallop on the wood. The dance floor in the centre of the room is rammed, sticky and damp with a mix of disparate bodies – some obey the rhythm, attuned to the moves, whilst others are completely wayward, swaying to their own mad, sporadic beat.

One man in the middle of the room, his head upon his own chest and shirt flapping open like a victory flag, repeatedly fist-pumps the air with a stoater of a grin slapped across his bumfuzzled coupon. Another couple slow-dance to a fast song, engorging each other's mouths as their jaws crank wider and wider and their tongues lap up all the sugar to be had.

The girl who brought Ouse and Firth there catches sight of her friends, who've looked over, curious, as she arrives with company. True to her word, she pegs it, ditching them in a nanosecond without so much as a cheerio. Ouse, despite being the local, looks to Firth, wild-eyed, to take lead. Firth can tell Ouse is out of his comfort zone, that he never would have come here unless strong-armed into it by the girl. Firth, on the other hand, is delighted by their current standing and so gingerly asserts himself. Only one thing for it, thinks Firth, and javelins them both to the back of the hall where the bulge of the bar summons him.

The queue is hefty, but with as many people serving as waiting it moves fast. To the left of them some straggler stalls have claimed their canny patch – a final slew of sozzled tourists buy up the discount whisky, confectionery and all the other tat that didn't sell earlier. Ouse points Firth to the sign above the bar which reads: *The Twice Drowned Rat.*

Once is never enough, Ouse explains, deadly serious. Firth notices that vast swathes of this section of the room have already regressed to little more than farting mouthpieces, drinking themselves into a collective boozy goulash.

Sitting at the table beside the bar is a huge tree of a man in naval uniform, highly decorated, who seems to be talking in Russian. Though it could be any number of languages, neither of the boys being experts on the phonology of an Eastern European tongue. Beside him, yoked to him in fact, is a monkey – its right wrist rope-tied to the man's left. Both the monkey and the human goliath have a beefy stein of beer in front of them, their glasses shaped like boots. The monkey is leading the race to drain the sauce on account of the man's incessant chitchat.

Whiiiilll it beeeee, the lassie behind the bar slurs whilst taking a dribbly swig from her own cup.

To Firth's surprise, Ouse winds in front of him and orders rum. *Rum*, Firth repeats delighted with the outcome, having anticipated some serious inveigling was going to be necessary to convince Ouse to partake in a daytime drinking session.

Firth slops his money across the counter, enough to pique the pourer's addlepated attention. It has the desired effect and she free-pours them half-pints of the stuff. Firth, already fretting Ouse might only be in it for a single swallie, isn't accepting any half measures. She thrusts the money into the front pocket of her apron, takes a swig straight from the bottle and then hands Firth the remainder to enjoy at their leisure. His soul's seeping wound for the sauce bursts from its stitches with this relishable gift.

Naturally, the only free table in the room is neighbouring the monkey and the military-medalled jarhead, but they take it, nonetheless.

Yo-ho-ho, and a bottle of rum, Firth toasts, taking a monster gulp. Ouse sips to the glee of it, watching agog as happy bodies on the dance floor birl and grind. He nudges Firth and gestures towards the dance floor.

I don't dance in public, Firth shouts back over the music, gawking at the clammy horde who've just had their tempos upped by the fiddle ensemble.

Bullshit, roars a plangent voice behind them. *Everyone dance. Even the fucking monkey, he dance.*

Firth and Ouse turn around, mouths agape as the Russian stands up and offers his hand to the monkey. The monkey lets out a disgusting ripper of a belch, and then sympathetically takes his hand in return. The Russian puts him up upon his shoulders, the long rope now scarved around them as they gallop off into the throng as if charging into battle.

Firth drinks to that and this time Ouse takes a good guzzle too. The pair quaff their glasses over a few songs whilst watching the dancing and pointing when they catch glimpses of the monkey above and within the crowd (with assorted partners by the end, having chewed through the rope that leashed him to the Russian). Firth wastes no time in topping them up. This keeps them busy for another few songs, their glasses chinking, Firth leaning in to make witty comments and Ouse highlighting locally famous faces and their assorted talents, quirks and backstories. It becomes clear to Firth that Ouse is a precocious and unassuming observer and he begins to worry what's been seen of him that was intended to stay hidden. Ouse is visibly pleased to be out and has relaxed into the raucous vibe, tapping his beer mat on the table and occasionally kicking out his foot in time with the drum. He watches tourists begin to leave for their boat as more well-kent faces start to arrive. Firth notices the intricate carvings on the upholstery, gesturing to point them out until his attention is tugged elsewhere. *What the hell is going on there?* he shouts above the racket, gesturing to a row of pumpkins lined up against the rear wall.

That's the pumpkin-punching competition, Ouse explains casually.
Hold on, what the fuckety fuck – that's a real thing!?

Oh yes! A prize goes to whoever punches through the biggest pumpkin. People train all year for it. Ouse seems enthralled by the notion.

And right enough, Firth sees a brigade of humans of all shapes and sizes limbering up to punch lumps out a row of pumpkins: six men, two women and another monkey in various stages of drunkenness and costumes, psyching themselves up to hit vegetables really, really hard.

One of the former champions was caught masturbating in the pumpkin field, sweet talking them into his favour! Ouse whispers this scandal below the volume of the hullabaloo, looking over his shoulder as he does so. *The judges say it brought shame on his entire family, but I'm not so sure.*

You're not so sure?! Firth asks incredulous.

I know the family and I reckon they'd approve. It's thinking outside the box, Ouse commends. *That's him there in the string vest and velvet kilt.*

He's not disqualified?! cries Firth, even more incredulous now.

Why would he be? Ouse shrugs. *It's not been proven he's gained any advantage. If anything, he carries more weight now. It's such a lot of pressure.*

From their table they watch the first few contenders ramming their fists into the pumpkins, which crumple or explode if the blow's a good 'un – pips, goo and innards spattering over the walls, tables and the other contestants. Firth's flummoxed to see the dancing continue and the party proceeding as normal whilst a group of grown adults beat at orange fruit until it detonates. It's taken as by the by by most, eventful but not unorthodox, seemingly akin to a game of high-stake cards perhaps.

To Firth's shock, Ouse enjoys it immensely, cheering, biting his lip and clenching his fists in anticipation. He reveals he'd like to learn martial arts, having read about the origins of Shaolin kung fu, but thankfully not with the sole objective of pounding edibles.

One contestant appears to break his hand, thumping all the way through a pumpkin, which must have spoiled, and pranging a hole in the wall behind it. This stirs as healthy a dose of sympathy as it does hilarity, calls of *sair yin* and *eejit* puff up from the crowd. One lewd onlooker suggests it's the former champion and his masturbation malarkey to blame, like he cursed it, or softened it up with his body's juice.

The music abruptly stops as all but one of the band vacate the stage to take a break, immediately lighting up pipes and cigarettes as a fresh-faced bar steward appears with a tray of drinks – the table soon overflowing with receptacles full of wine, beer, whisky and other concoctions. The lone accordion, left upon the stage, begins a gentle melancholic drone that consequently causes everyone, even the glassware, to hush down a few notches. The pumpkin-punchers, too, have taken a recess as the scores are tallied up and a winner waits to be crowned. Ouse, a little tipsy now, is feeling more garrulous; he notices it alongside with the shift in sound, yet leaves his defences down.

I want to toast to you, Firth. You have been a tonic to me. I've never met anyone like you.

Firth, at first, suspects these words of tribute are a drunken mirage dreamed into being, but as he focuses his eyes on Ouse's beaming face, it seems they are legit. As delighted as he is to hear these plaudits, Firth is also hit with a thwack of guilt. His manipulations, his intentions, have not been so pure as Ouse assumes and he's keen to put a stop to any undue praise.

If you drilled a hole in my head and looked inside it, you'd not like what you saw! I'm like that foosty pumpkin, held together by a shiny pelt but underneath it's gone to mush because I'm rotting away.

Ouse senses the liquor talking through Firth now and is keen to move on to more pertinent matters – Firth's sulking is of no use to where he wants to take things conversationally.

What I've not told you is that KLAMS rules state there should be at least three keepers at the lighthouse at any one time. They say it's necessary to prevent murder and adjudicate disputes. We lived as one big family before, cheek by jowl, Ouse reminisces. Glancing over at Firth to check he hasn't lost him, he continues. *Nowadays, The Father works the lighthouse like a sleepless spectre. He's listed me and Figgie as the other two keepers. He says it's just paperwork, that they know it to be apocryphal and couldn't care less provided the light keeps shining.*

He says if they were going to dispute it they would have by now. But if they did come and we weren't around to at least pretend to be his assistants, they could take the lighthouse away from him.

I don't think that will happen if it hasn't happened yet, Firth consoles, attempting to hide his ulterior motives, even from himself. *The Father's probably right. He knows about these things. Besides, is it not more likely they'll automate the lighthouse first? That's what Nith said.*

Funny thing, Ouse responds after some thought, totally ignoring this suggestion, *it was The Father who insisted I invite you today. He said it's something you'd not want to miss. He even permitted me to spend more of the takings than usual – 'provided there are any takings', he always qualifies, though there never hasn't been.*

It occurs to Firth that The Father must have intended this trip to be the occasion for him to reveal the letter to Ouse. There's no other reason The Father would will them together for the day. But seeing as Firth didn't bring the letter, that's not a possibility.

I'm thinking on it, Ouse says coyly. *Edinburgh. But the odds are stacked against us. I just don't see how my leaving wouldn't ruin things for The Father. And I'm not willing to carry a pain that size. Curious as I am.*

You are? Firth simpers.

I am, Ouse settles.

Hauling them away from their important thoughts, the ceilidh band – having cleared the table of the complimentary refreshments – roars back into action. As if in competition, a cheer louder than all the instruments combined erupts up from the pumpkin-punchers, indicating a winner has been crowned. Ouse leaves this conversation lingering and leaps upon the dance floor like there are snapping turtles in his pants.

241

Firth takes a champion's slurp and watches Ouse complete the second half of a complicated sequence that involves having to do some sort of improvised tap dance as the rest of the group spin circles around him until everyone collides like comets chasing a new planet out of their already too full solar system.

A trollop-faced church elder spinning too rigorously ends up on Firth's lap. Before bucking herself back up onto the dance floor she whispers something into his ear, the sloppy words lost to the volume of the room. Either way, Firth's attention is elsewhere, his blood rushing upon seeing Ouse do-si-do faster than the lot of them.

The band changes tempo, again, and on comes 'Strip the Willow'. As the song blasts into action Ouse shimmies over and pulls on Firth's sleeves.

I don't dance! I told you! Firth protests flirtatiously.

Nonsense, Ouse chides. *Besides, there's dancing and then there's 'Strip the Willow'.*

Okay okay, Firth responds, quickly abandoning his resolve. *With you, I dance!*

Firth readies his feet as Ouse offers a reassuring second tug. To settle the matter the passing Russian, his monkey nowhere to be seen, jerks on Firth's other arm, which propels both him and Ouse onto the dance floor like they've been launched from a catapult.

The next few minutes bring with it an adoring clamour – a haze of hot palms, rogue figures-of-eight and fast-paced, two-handed birls (a few wobbly-legged participants ending up on the floor). Amongst the action Firth yells into Ouse's ear, *I'm so excited for you. All I need to do is show them your sketchbooks and you're in.*

Do you think I'm a kite about to hit the wind? Ouse responds with fizz in him.

242

Oh absolutely, a kite-running colossus with a propellor on top.

Seconds after the song crescendos, the pair collapse into their seat – the band uncaging a slower, soppier melody that has the dance floor fast-filling all over again. Both the boys are left glistening with sweat, their chests panting. Though desperate to talk, Firth is equally happy to sit side by side with Ouse, watching couples begin to link up and dance romantically – some gyrating, all hip and thrust, others with more old-school swaying moves.

By the time the soppy song ends, and umpteen snogs and body wraps reach their own grand or small finishes, Firth has caught his breath. *Ouse, I want to tell you something. And I want you to listen.* He notices himself slurring at his point, attempting to pour more rum from the empty bottle for a second time. *You, Ouse, are interesting in the way the people I know pretend to be interesting. I've wanted to tell you that for a while.*

You've already told me that! And I am thankful, even if I don't believe you.

Fuck, have I? Firth gripes, bamboozled. *I must be steaming! Forgive . . .*

I'm worried in a big city I'd be just another coward lost in the crowd, Ouse confesses.

NO! Firth yells in protest. *Courage comes to you every day, so frequently and effortlessly you don't even recognise it.*

Firth then draws a deep breath working himself up to what follows.

Since meeting you, Ouse, I've decided not to die. That's what you've done for me. I'm not going to die and it's all because of you and how fucking extraordinary you are.

That's fantastic, Firth, really it is, but we all die, Ouse lilts chipper. *It's one of the best things about us.*

243

Soused as he is, Firth decides that this one's probably best left there – lost in translation and less morbid than it otherwise might become. *Ouse, you're amazing, a supernova locked in a storage container,* Firth rallies on. *And no-one's been applauding you, and that's criminal. But now I am. We have this awful habit of not applauding people until they die, but it's time to start celebrating them for still being alive. For surviving, when it's easier not to. So here I am applauding you.*

Seeing Ouse look bemused, Firth seizes the moment and clambers up on top of the table and begins clapping above his head, coltish but really giving it laldy. *Let's hear it for Ouse. The best fucking person I know,* he roars, clapping more and cheering in praise. A few tables around him begin joining in, most of them with no idea what they're applauding for but absolutely game for it. Even Ouse joins in, wolf-whistling and stamping his feet. *Let's hear it for me,* he howls, *let's hear it for Cat and Rabbit. Let's hear it for joy! Back by popular demand.*

Firth begins twirling around in rapture and lunges down to grab Ouse's hand with the intention of yanking him up on the table's platform to greet his loyal subjects. In doing so he tumbles off the table and hits the deck with a hefty thud, the room immediately spinning into darkness.

Next thing Firth knows, he and Ouse are outside and he's throwing up as Ouse rubs circles on his back – the exact position those maulers were in when they first entered this place. So redolent is the scene of this image that Firth suspects it was them from the very beginning, a premonition of indulgence and pleasure.

Hey! Hey – have you seen the monkey? the Russian booms. *They throw him out. Something about rude gestures to the band. But what they expect? They didn't play his favourite song and he asked three fucking times – real nice too, like a princess.*

A miscarriage of justice, Ouse bellows back, *we'll keep an eye out and sign the petition.* The Russian dashes off at extraordinary pace, seemingly satisfied with the gesture of moral support.

Firth intends to make a joke but all he can manage is, *Here comes an oyster*, and right enough an oyster comes flippering out of him – a little alien drowned in the stomach's stinky soup. He's chuffed to know the other two oysters made it through his system, that it was only one that reappeared. He'll be zinc-pumped as a result, and so reassures himself, with the pluck of someone that's just thrown a record-breaking shot put, that everything is going to be okay.

With the regurgitated oyster greying in the gutter and the dark seeping through the sky, Ouse announces perfunctorily, *Right then, back to base-camp. An absolute cracker of a day.*

Ouse, Firth bumbles, slurring extravagantly, *I wish I could reach into my chest, pull out my heart and pickle it. It's never been so full and I want it to be found this way a hundred years from now.*

Ouse grins for this declaration as he directs them back to the boat, swaying as they go, Firth's arm swung loosely around his shoulders. In his head, Ouse is replaying scenes of epic pumpkin punches and kung fu kicking at the starlight, whereas Firth is smirking wider and more wistfully than even his own face thought possible.

THIRTY-THREE

Behind them, a razzmatazz of fireworks streaks across the sheet of night: whistling and singing and exploding with filthy colour. The pumpkin-punching champion is crooning *glory-be* on the dance floor whilst drumming her chest to a gonzo beat, a fleet of suitors fawning by her flank. The runner-up, donning a seeded sash, enjoys a well-earned kip under the emptied buffet table where the Russian's monkey cuddles in. The stewards of the big cruise liner are desperately herding the last stragglers back on board – passengers and even a few crew – the vessel now twice the weight for all the souvenirs they're couriering.

Firth has the savvy to pick up a cone of chips and a tanker of water before boarding the boat. This is the sapience of a reveller who knows how to mitigate a hangover when the next unmissable party is only ever a day away, soirées at which the visible bite of a hangover – or worse still, someone whinging on about one – is seen as horrid and tacky, despite the constant expectations of extreme indulgence at all such occasions.

Ouse has the savvy to let down the sail and have the wind carry them out the harbour and towards Muckle Flugga. A perfect angled gust affording them the pace of a Viking longship manned by a crew of twenty. The lighthouse has blinked awake as twilight will soon follow.

Firth demolishes the chips, guzzles back the water and starts drawing pictures in the stars with his pistol-finger, connecting dots to fashion a fresh constellation. In no time at all he's drifted off.

Ouse, alerted to the situation by a guttural snoring, keeps them fleeing smooth and fast over the waves, adding occasional bursts of rowing to the propulsion of the wind.

Seaward, ho! Hang the treasure! It's the glory of the sea that has turned my head.

Ouse's heart skips a beat and he nearly drops the oars at hearing RLS's voice thunder forth in the company of another. He's only appeared once before with others present – the first time he ever appeared, in fact: the day The Mother died. Ouse dare not speak, for Firth's not stirred.

Fifteen men on the Dead Man's Chest / Yo-ho-ho, and a bottle of rum!

With this second vocalisation RLS appears behind Ouse, one leg lunged up on the boat's starboard beam and the other straight as the mast pole on the deck. A feather in his felt hat and his shirt open with the moonlight reflecting off his bare chest – it's a louche, raffish look in comparison to RLS's usual sartorial tidiness, and Ouse loves it.

The rain is falling all around / It falls on field and tree / It rains on the umbrellas here / And on the ships at sea.

RLS, what are you doing here? Ouse whispers, exulted and panicked by his unexpected appearance.

Do you know the prison slang for someone who confesses is 'a novelist'? RLS responds quite unhelpfully and a little slurry himself.

Ouse gazes at him, astonished. *Hold on . . . RLS, are you drunk? And keep it down or you'll wake . . .*

Pfffft, how dare you. See . . . we are all travellers in the wilderness of this world, and the best we can find in our travels is an honest friend. Let us pray you have one here, RLS sermonises, cannily ignoring the question.

I do hope so. I mean, I think so, I just don't know *so.* Saying this, he casts an anxious look at his sleeping friend.

Do you know what my Softy Softy said of me when I passed? He said, To me it is as if a bit of myself had died, the romantic part, which was forever running after him.

I wonder if he's chasing it still, Ouse ponders, *that empty part of him. Did he ever catch you?*

I'll tell you that in Edinburgh, RLS quips knowingly.

The surety with which RLS asserts this both elates and startles Ouse, goosebumps and a chest-flutter to boot. It's by no means a done deal in his mind, but alcohol-laced, with the moonlight sloshing its majesty all over their skin, Edinburgh makes for a romantic notion. Ouse gives the oars some extra oomph and gazes skywards for any anomalies in the firmament that might want to pass on an auspicious message. He lets his mind drift into what he'd look like in a capital city, sauntering down a busy street, having changed his dress sense and found a new place for his dreams. Perhaps he'll wear a waistcoat there, a pocket watch, a moustache; perhaps he'll get a dog; perhaps he'll find a new way of walking altogether – chin higher, strides longer.

Do you know they still teach celestial navigation to sailors? RLS announces with intrigue. *Despite all the advances in technology, despite machines and engines and clever compasses, the stars are a seafarer's fail-safe. The only thing that'll never break down. And why is that, Ouse?*

Because they're not of our making? Ouse utters, smug knowing he's bang on the bell with this one.

Exactly, trust the bigger players. Because when it comes it'll come sudden as a flock of sparrows chased from a tree by someone trying to get a better view of their city on fire.

We've watched so many murmurations together, RLS.

I'm never far from where you need me to be, RLS replies soothing-ly. *But remember, once you raise the pirate's black you can't go back.*

This is the way! Ouse shouts, breaking out of his whisper.

Firth, stirred awake by this surge in volume, leaps to his feet as if he's just been caught napping on the night-shift. He quickly piv-ots round to investigate. *What's aw this commotion?* he says, groggy from drink.

Can you see him? Ouse asks nervously.

Firth gazes past Ouse, and a look of alarm creeps into his eyes. *I see smoke*, he thunders, *Ouse! LOOK!*

The Covenant may well have raced them home, gently and in record time, but the ruinous sight that awaits them offers no such sanctuary. There's smoke streaming from the island, billowing, blis-tering plumes of it. Ouse can tell straight away it's from a hungry fire extinguished before it's done burning, but one that ate its fill all the same.

Que sera, sera, Ouse utters sullenly, in a voice Firth barely rec-ognises.

THIRTY-FOUR

The Covenant clunks up against the shore – Ouse is off it like his feet are ablaze, heart in his throat and racing up the path for home. Firth follows close behind, all whimper and dribble and looks of despair.

The Father waits atop the summit, puffed up with trouble on his face. He explains there's been a savage fire, that he got it under control, but not before it ravaged through half the library and a hunk of Ouse's studio. The building's structure was not damaged, he reports, but it stripped the surrounding timber down to its sphincter.

The Father pleads that he doesn't know how it started, swears to it that he never goes in there, why would he, none of his business what Ouse gets up to in there, they'd agreed to that and he'd honoured it. Ouse knows that if The Father's pleading, rather than simply telling him to brace himself and take it on the chin, it's bad.

The Father holds Ouse back in a grapple when he tries to rush to see the aftermath, shakes him by the shoulders, assures him the flames are out but that he has to give the beast time to finish smouldering. *Let the last o'it choke itself oot*, he compels him, before urging him to prepare himself. Proudly, he informs him that it's not a complete ruin in there, that many of the books were saved, and that he brought them all – the singed, charred and chewed through – into the washhouse for Ouse to take the measure of.

The Father reckons that they're lucky really, that the studio took the brunt of it. Gorged and feasted upon, all that wool and paper fluffed up and gave itself to the flames like the perfect tinder it

250

is. *Couldn't gift a fire better feed than paper and fabric,* The Father stresses, meaning it harmlessly, whilst causing real harm.

Ouse – having heard enough – contorts then dashes from The Father's grasp towards the wreckage. The Father puts his voice on a hook and casts into the wind, shouting at the fleeing silhouette of his laddie: *You huv to believe me boy, this wisnae ma doing.*

Firth makes to follow Ouse, but The Father obstructs the way, telling him to leave the boy, to give him a moment's peace with the damage, to return to his room and let Ouse come to him; if he wants to, if he needs that.

The Father now needs Firth to know that it wasn't his fault. That he was in the lighthouse until spying the flames from the gallery deck. In Ouse's absence, he desperately wants Firth to believe him, then, seeing the doubt in Firth's eyes, snarls waspily that it doesn't matter if he does or not.

With the shock of breaking the news over, The Father begins to fortify himself for what comes next: defending his position; rebuilding; keeping an eye on that swine bastard Firth in the days that follow. He must not let chagrin take hold of him again, it's too late for that, too integral a moment.

• • •

Ouse runs first to the studio – just to it, not in it. It is still standing but slashed with huge tongues of charcoal and soot; steaming like a teabag fresh out the cup. One window is smeared with a smoky fetid paste, the other window has shattered; ashes hang in the air, obfuscating the way in. Ouse feels like a martyr staring into the grave of his fallen faith. He screams into the wreckage, first for the witches and next for his mum.

• • •

Within the bothy, Firth paces the boards of his room like a bird trapped in a cage, ready to beat itself bloody. He scratches at his forearm until it bleeds, then picks up a brush and paints over the gash with thick black daubs. He doesn't smoke but wished he did. He's ill from the drink but vying for more, wondering if it's all wrong, every twisted bit of it.

• • •

Within the washhouse bides an even dimmer view: Ouse gazing upon what the fire has left of years of careful work – it's not much, not decent. The shock of it sends a current coursing through his veins; the voltage in it knocks him to the floor.

Shedding tears into the ashes of his reason for being floods him with a loneliness that exceeds all expectation. He feels all goodness ebb out of him: body withering, mind somersaulting; like a fish harpooned and tossed into a bucket of sand, gasping and bleeding from the gills – it would be a mercy to dagger it to death. Too beaten to rage, he hugs his shadowed sorrow.

RLS places a hand upon the shaking, bawling, broken Ouse. *What a guttery rut! my dearest dear, my little prince. What a sodding guttery rut! Don't forget I love you.*

I love you too, RLS, Ouse quivers back through staggered gasps, now writhing on the floor like a suffocating eel. Slowly yet sternly, he pulls himself together and barks: *Enough. ENOUGH! You are healthy and alive.* Three deep breaths and he quells his tears. Three more and he is on his feet, wiping at the waterworks and thumbing through the useless fragments of his once cherished oeuvre.

I will wake up tomorrow and smile, RLS. I swear on a stack of bibles, that's what I'll do. I will wake up tomorrow and smile.

Everyday courage has few witnesses, RLS mutters doughy-eyed whilst disappearing, *but yours is no less noble because no drum beats for you and no crowds shout your name.*

Ouse sleeps that night in the washhouse; The Father sneaking in to spark up the fire only after he's heard him submit to exhaustion. Witnessing the body of his boy sleeping after crying himself empty tolls between The Father's eyes – listening to someone dear suffer through a wall is just as painful to him as any actual wounding, perhaps even more so. With this, The Father convinces himself he's done all he can and heads for the lighthouse.

THIRTY-FIVE

Ouse wakes gently in the middle of the night, and then the remembering comes at him like a bull elephant in musth It takes a few moments to reprocess the pain. A bit of focussed concentration on some of his favourite things still alive in this world helps to keep the balance of his mind. He assures himself: this night is a vigil; that when day breaks he'll let the hurt pass beyond him like a slow rain that he's eventually outrun. The old stone of the washhouse holds the heat well: funny, to be kept warm by the same thing that destroyed what you love, he thinks, glass-eyed at the dying embers of the fire.

In the fresh light of the day, Ouse counts his blessings; it's forced and fought for, but it's also real:

One—he is grateful so many of the books appear to still be intact: smokier and mankier than he left them, but life-givingly readable.

Two—he is grateful The Mother's small stash of favourite reads (five books) are in a locked chest in the organ room of the lighthouse, hidden under sheet music, where no harm has come to them.

Three—he is grateful for the money in his pocket to buy new wool, needles and art supplies; the opportunity to conjure new designs lives on in fresh supplies.

Four—he is grateful that the amount of needlework destroyed was minimal, with market day having just passed.

Five—he is grateful to The Father for what he rescued and the burden he bears for battling the flames.

Six—he is grateful to Firth, for the encouragement, the protection, for making chimerical ambitions seem possible.

Seven—he is grateful he doesn't want to stop creating after such a bruising blow, that nothing is more appealingly restorative than what comes next. He has read of brilliant artists that gave up after such blootering losses. Instead, his will has become as powerful as the blaze that took from him. Channelling its force, he will use such redemptive thirst for good. The kindling within is already smoking.

Ouse stops himself there: eight doesn't come unstuck the way he wants it. He can't quite square the lost sketchbooks just yet, the blueprints of hundreds of designs to come, years of squiggles representing his most precious thoughts denied their glamorous futures. No, he will tackle that leviathan when his mettle has returned, when he has restocked the heart's pantry.

• • •

Firth wakes up having paced until his feet fumed from it, having slept in the hammock and nearly fallen out into the empty bath. In a moment of even greater weakness, the thought of Ouse so vulnerable draws the image of a sweet pink carnation into Firth's mind. He reprimands himself for this smutty fantasy. He is sorry that the real cure for Ouse's pain is not yet invented. Despite the traumatic nature of the night, Firth is galvanised by the pain and decides the future is looking hopeful.

Firth is up before the sun is, focussed and not wanting to die, ready as he'll ever be.

• • •

The Father does not sleep, restoring what was lost and applying himself to improvements –mopping and scouring, chopping and sanding. He applies fresh wood to the structure of the studio, buttresses, embulks, rebuilds the bookcase, boards up the window, wipes away the stinky scrim, paints as if his honour depended on it. For the dead bird he finds choked by the fumes, he says a few peaceful words and then watches it fly from the cliff into the sea one last time, propelled by the solidity of his arms. He does not glimpse it sink but hears a body hit the water, its wings failing to open in spite of the prayer. Just before the sun comes up, he burns peat and warms his coarse hands by the flaming pit. Slowly clenching his fingers into fists, feeling them smack with the tension of how hard he works them, feeling the salt crack in his skin. He half expects his fists to turn to stone and crumble away. They don't, so he sips a little spirits, dashes the rest into the fire and continues his labour.

• • •

Firth is determined that today will be the day he scrambles up onto the seaweed-thatched roof of the bothy, via the window ledge, and watches the sunrise finish its morning symphony. He'll feel the eel grass underneath his feet like a mermaid's wig, and curl his toes around its flesh like talons gripping carrion. This will provide the music he needs to soundtrack such a formidable occasion – dawn's orchestra of grasshoppers stridulating, birds chirruping, sea gurgling and wind combing the beard of the long grasses. Yes, he won't beat that for an alarm clock, Firth confirms, readying himself for the day's great games ahead.

Half-dressed, in a goonie and barefooted, he swings open the door with intent and gets the shock of his life; at least, one of them, given the ubiquity of shit-scary assaults this island has unleashed upon him. The Father – wearing a cloak of the fire's soot, covered in grime and paint – is standing exactly where a vista of this beautiful world (far too taken for granted) should be.

Yer up. Good, The Father craws, *I've checked twice already.*

It's not even . . . I mean, it's early. The sun's still rising, Firth protests, pointing to the light flares streaking the sky. *What do you want? I mean . . . Sorry, why are you here?* The Father's presence, even when embattled, is enough to disturb him.

The letter, The Father snuffs.

I've not had a chance, I mean, it's still . . . Wait, how is Ouse?

You've no gieing him yet then, that's right, The Father resolves. *Aye, that's right. Hold fire. You'll ken when soon enough.*

How's Ouse? Is he okay? Did anything survive? Do you have any idea what caused it?

You can read it yourself if you like. After though, no first. NOT first, The Father repeats with brass and flex. *He's lifted by you, I wouldnae choose that, fuck no, but it is whit it is.*

Firth, cowed, simply says, *Thanks.* Feeling blessed that even his most resistant foe has recognised that he, Firth – an inexorable squanderer of everything gracious life has given him – is of value to Ouse, a far better human than either of them could ever fathom how to become. This is a reinforcement of the plan he has put in action, yet leaves the niggling feeling he has perhaps lambasted The Father beyond what he truly deserves. Firth forces this from his mind and reminds himself of The Father's most abhorrent qualities; he will need this resilience to slay such a giant. As Firth watches him thump off like a lonely dragon, something The Father said during that animated lunch they all had together comes back to him – the totem words ringing in Firth's ears. *Our lighthouses*

were always free. The southern neighbour's charged a toll for passing
the light; chasing profit fae the start. Imagine that, you're alive but it'll
cost you, maybe more than you can afford.

• • •

Firth waits all day, takes three walks, makes two superfluous trips
to the larder, keeps the candle in his window lit, his face visible to
anyone that's passing. Although he catches glimpses of his friend,
Ouse spends most of the day in the washhouse, the door closed,
with two trips to the lighthouse. He does not appear to stop for
brunch, lunch or supper.

With The Father busy illuminating rock traps and pelagic
potholes to a convoy of passing cargo-ships, and Ouse having returned to his living quarters after a couple of hours on the organ,
Firth submits to temptation and makes his move. He climbs in the
window of the globe room, sets a few of them off spinning, and
scurries upstairs to Ouse's bedroom – somewhere he's never been,
it being in the precarious position of neighbouring The Father's
cesspool of pit.

The gap in the door reveals Ouse is in, sitting in a stylish pyja-
ma suit, reading by torchlight. Firth knocks and enters, taking in
as much of the room as he can in as short a time as possible so as
not to appear nosy at such a tender moment. He makes a bevy of
garbled comments to announce his presence, apologising for the intrusion, apologising for not coming sooner, apologising for coming
so late, apologising for his apologising, apologising for not asking
how he's doing first and foremost.

It's a terrible thing that happened, Ouse, I'm so so sorry.

Ouse shows no visible signs of movement, but words quietly

force their way out of him. *I'm not ready to talk about that yet, but thank you. I'm cleaning the wound.*

I just can't think how it could have started? Firth probes. *You put all the candles out, right?*

Double, treble, quadruple checked. I've went over it a thousand times.

And The Father was the only one on the island, right? Firth carries on leadingly.

The only living human, yes, Ouse confirms.

He heard us talking the other night, you know – in the lighthouse, he heard us! Firth pushes pathetically into these words, painting blame as he does.

I know, Ouse verifies. His mind casting back to The Father's prints in the lighthouse's snow patch, and the way his voice undressed Ouse's every extra attempt to please him. The Father is not one for grovelling – he'll not do it, won't abide it and will commonly call it out or deride it in public, much to Ouse's embarrassment. Despite all this, Ouse grovelled from his body through his lips.

You don't think . . . No, he wouldn't. I shouldn't even think it. Forget I mentioned it, Firth spits, juggling the words.

There's no love to be gained from hunting a desperate heart, Ouse rules firmly. *It's only . . . how would I start afresh some place new without any of my drawings?*

Firth feels the sickly bark of his sins ready to rise up and sabotage his life again, but instead manages to change tack, petitioning his surety that good things lie ahead if he remains committed to this cause.

Ouse, I've something to tell you, and I hope you'll understand. The other day, when you were working in the lighthouse with The Father, I went to the library to return my book when I happenchanced on the studio's open door and one of your sketchpads – the fat one. Having

259

kindly inducted me into the space, I didn't think you'd mind if I leafed through it a bit more – I had seen it already, remember. And, well, I borrowed it, to look at again when I had more time. I was going to tell you, it just slipped my mind in all the drama that followed.

Ouse carefully closes the book he's not reading. He looks to Firth's face with the nearest he's come to urgency. *Are you saying you still have it?*

Yes, I've still got it. I've brought it for you. It's why I came.

There's two years of work in there, Ouse utters liltingly. *These last two years. My best.*

Firth produces from behind his back the bulging sketchpad. Ouse approaches the book as if it were a manger hosting a sleeping infant, takes it two-handed and suspiciously, suspecting it might disappear into a puff of smoke once touched. Back on his bed he clasps the pad into his chest, connecting it to his body and breathing it in. He thinks of jumping for joy and kissing Firth a hundred times over; instead he sits deadly still and basks in a blaze of deep relief.

I'll leave you be for the night, Firth chimes piously. *But perhaps we could take a walk tomorrow, or the next day? Maybe those otters will come back to see me off. I've only got a couple of nights left after all, my days are numbered, and I'd love to see them again.*

All their closeness, yet Firth can't ask Ouse to simply go for a walk with him without using otter-spotting as an excuse. To move to Edinburgh and leave life as he knows it behind, sure, he can ask that of him, but not a bucolic saunter along the coastline – that needs the lure of a water sausage.

Firth, cringing at himself whilst trying to remain serene, steps slowly out the room, backwards and reverent as a servant would leave their master. Just as he swivels to leave, he's stopped in his tracks by the words he's been craving.

I'll come. To Edinburgh. The day you leave, I'll leave.

Ouse prevents any response from Firth with a firm hand in the air.

We mustn't speak of this again until we've left, Ouse orders, commanding in tone. *I need to make my peace, alone.*

Firth, flabbergasted, can't stop himself asking, *And The Father?*

That's between me and him, Ouse resolves, and Firth worries again he's pushed him too far.

Whatever you need, I'll be there – wheels oiling, springs stepping, my coat in a puddle, my . . .

Go now, please. And thanks. Ouse's tone leaves no room for manoeuvre, no room for follow-ups, fandom or cross-examination. Firth, seeing no other course of action, makes an obedient exodus – rhapsodic in his success whilst feeling somewhat told off, like a kid who's been given the toy they were begging for but warned never to ask for anything else again, at least not until Christmas.

THIRTY-SIX

On his walk back to the bothy, Firth is pulled by the moon's magnets into taking a longer, more circuitous route. This gives him time to concede there is a lot he won't tell Ouse about Edinburgh. He confirms to himself that delivering a total verbal account of Auld Reekie – the Athens of the North – would be unachievable and that, in fact, some editing is not only advisable but essential. The Volcanic Viscount of the Central Belt is too mammoth a being to be fully translated into words; it is algebra and architecture, ineffable, something to be witnessed and beheld. Of course, what this ruling primarily offers Firth is the opportunity to validate the tailor-made version of Edinburgh he is selling to Ouse, one that best serves his aims.

For example, he has failed to mention: how Edina's stars prickle palely until given a good enough reason to frisk for gold; how even on a sunny day its people stream through each other, passing without notice, a gauze of dreams and hurry. How, come the night, greedy with desire, these same bags of skin collide like the whopping great sacks of feeling they truly are. How he had sold his poetry on street corners like punnets of plums and felt nourished; how he had once fallen in love in a public toilet with someone he'll never see again – he wouldn't say illicit, not here, not in the same sentence as love, but it did carry its risk like a set of iron shackles. How Edina is built on the backs of brave mongrels so that light-footed fawns might glide through life brightly suited; how his dad had lost himself to the city's booze bazaars, conspiracy obsessed, a self-proclaimed hunter of monsters – any but his own. How it felt like a fresh start after he died, his dad, a gulp of air in a gas leak: they moved away from Leith, took new names and started over. How shame – even in a city of hidden streets, dark alleys and secret fissures – always wins the chase.

Firth labels Edinburgh a terrible wonderful place, then a wonderfully terrible place. Settles that if he's not leading Ouse to his death, he's almost certainly leading him to greatness, and for such splendour it's worth a tussle with any old fool of a god. He comes to the conclusion that much of the world's best work comes from simply trying not to fuck up a good thing – confirming that Ouse is good, so he can be too: for him, Firth can be better than he's ever been.

Firth bays at the moon then falls forwards into the damp grass, stretching out into a star shape. How he loves the smells dampness brings on, especially in moss and heather; it plugs up the holes in him. He grabs handfuls of dirt and squeezes them in his fists like his life depends on it, the blood hot in his hands. On the ground, and totally mawkit, he feels as if his skin finally fits his body's awkward frame and weeps with joy and fear in response.

THIRTY-SEVEN

On a familiar corner of Out Stack, RLS and Ouse sit side by side with fishing rods in hand. Their legs hang off the front of a sheer cliff face and swing like pendulums. From this vantage, Muckle Flugga is all but hidden from sight, meaning even the lighthouse can't listen in on their chatter, despite its questing nosiness.

Oh RLS, it's such a lot. Ouse squeezes out the words like the last drops of juice from an old lemon.

And isn't that what we're all after – our such a lot? *Lot enough to make the earth tremble.* RLS speaks this like a riddle then stills himself with a thought. *I've just suffered a potent rush of déjà vu. You there, mimicking fishing, and me by your flank, issuing sage advice. Bizarre, don't you think?*

We come to Out Stack to chat four times a week, RLS. Have done for the last two years.

Yes yes, alright, that does increase the odds, RLS concedes.

At this point the sun sweeps across their laps and illuminates the jagged landscape behind them, momentarily shooing away every trace of shadow, including their own. RLS looks perplexed at this occurrence, his eyes moving from Ouse's bare toes to his own tasselled loafers. He gets up and outstretches his leg to try and cast his shape in shadow on the uneven rocks. Nothing appears and he flumps back down, looking baffled.

The sun has something to say about us, Ouse announces pointedly.

A squad of inky squiggles in the distant sky makes a beeline for them, soon revealing themselves to be a flock of cormorants. One

264

by one the noisy birds land on the rocks below and begin their own, much more efficient, form of fishing. The sun increases its sheen and turns the ocean into a great bouncing mirror of light.

In such weather one has the bird's need to whistle; and I, who am specially incompetent in this art, must content myself by chattering away to you.

Cheek of you! Ouse jokes.

Ouse, your rudder is showing. You can't hide that twitching compass needle from me: my explorer's heart thumps to the same rhythm. I think you're getting ready to leave.

I know it's selfish, potentially disastrous, but my body's telling me it's right.

Then take the sea to the city, young Ouse, and come back only if you must.

But I don't know Edinburgh at all, Ouse groans. *It's an imagined city, flossed up from second-hand stories.*

Imagining places is much harder than going places. I tip this excellent hat to your years of jink. Fling yourself at the world, Ouse. If it kicks back, it's working, you're living right.

Bloody Firth! He could be everything to someone, Ouse edges in to say, *just the way he wants, if only he slowed down and breathed better. He's someone's something either way.*

It's not a bad consolation prize, RLS consoles, *but don't forget about yourself, who you are in spite of us all.*

I just don't want to let anyone down. The Father . . . Ouse trails off. With this, he disregards the fishing rod he's failed to tie a hook to and walks to the edge of the rockface, letting his toes curl over the cliff and grapple with its firmness. Staring down into the briny commotion below, he lets his thoughts dissolve into the breaking waves. He always tries to imagine the shapes the waves will shatter

265

into as they smash to shore – whips of water, corkscrews of froth – but never gets it right. Before long, he senses RLS close behind him; a hat placed upon his head confirms this fraternal presence.

My father once told me I'd rendered his whole life a failure for not following him into the family profession – he'd have had me unhappily locked in a lighthouse too. I did three long and desultory summers of a Stevensonian apprenticeship in a grey, grim, sea-beaten hole. The unbearable meanness of the stone, starved and ragged, brought out the worst in me.

And you survived. What a joyous miracle you are, Ouse swoons.

To miss the joy is to miss all. I never once regretted not succumbing to my father's duress, yet despite all this conviction it never stops throbbing. RLS cushions into Ouse and throws an arm around him like a scarf. At the same moment an otter pup emerges from the shallows and flops onto the rocks, sunning its plump, fluffy belly. This causes the cormorant elders to sound the alarm and take the flock off again in a curious direction; blinded by light, Ouse loses sight of them.

Do you have any final advice? Ouse asks, dogged in tone, realising it's time to be less whimsical and more pragmatic. Knowing RLS to have a penchant for undulations, he qualifies this further: *I mean, advice that might aid someone Edinburgh-bound and hopeless at it.*

RLS, despite his best intentions, delivers a vast monologue of tips for canny city living, everything from keeping cogent notes in diaries for future biographers to the best place to pick herbs in the city's public gardens; from alleyways to avoid when its dark out and the streets reek of beer to the best oyster shuckers on the promenade; from watching his pockets in Leith to words of reverence he need utter on the spot where they hung the last Scottish pirate. Ouse takes it all in whilst fretting over whether he really wants to

266

live somewhere where people think tactically about handshakes and cutlery and everyone locks their doors, even in the daytime.

What about all the beauty I leave behind?

It'll be just fine without you, RLS giggles. *Most of it hasn't moved much in the last hundred years.*

I'm starting to see it, Ouse confirms with some music back in him. *I just wish we could leave together, RLS.*

Of course I'll be coming with you! RLS proclaims.

But . . . you're . . . you're . . .

You think I'd be stuck here in your absence, idling? Absolutely not. I can go anywhere my body went in life, and trust me this body has bloomed aplenty over Edinburgh.

Why didn't you say so? Ouse yells in pure elation.

On at least two occasions I insinuated just this very thing, RLS claims, his chin in the air as triangular as he can make it. Then suddenly a little sheepish: *Oh I say, young Ouse, one small matter – to my shame, there might be a few side-streets and cellar-bars it's best we avoid. Unfinished skirmishes with men with faces you could bounce a penny off, that sort of tricksy business.*

Ouse taps his nose conspiratorially, then leaps head-first from the clifftop into the sea, emerging frocked in seaweed and resplendent as the sun itself.

THIRTY-EIGHT

The Father's letter is sealed sloppily, gum spilling from its lips, with easy views inside if held horizontal and pressed from above. Firth wax seals all his important letters (the gossipy ones, records of his fragile financials, book pitches, belles-lettres to his childhood friends), deeming it remiss not to. The Muckle Flugga living quarters are absolutely infested with candles, wax gets everywhere, it's under his fingernails now, it's easier to have wax than avoid it here. It would have taken seconds to slop wax across the envelope and demonstrate its chastity; he considers the lack of it deliberate.

Sure, The Father had said Firth shouldn't read the letter first, before Ouse for whom it was intended, but that can be creatively interpreted. A text, of which a letter is one, is not read, in Firth's mind, not fully comprehensibly read, until it's been read in its totality, wholly absorbed. Before then it is only part-read, it is being read, undergoing investigation. It is not read.

For example, if he were to loosen the gum with steam from a pot heated by a candle, and then slip out the paper and skim through the epistle before placing it back inside the envelope, he would not necessarily have 'read' the letter, he would have merely glanced upon it. He would be the letter-reading equivalent of a royal food-taster, ensuring it's not dusted with poison, that there's no rotten apples infecting the pack. It could be seen as a conscientious act, due diligence, considered, sacrificial even.

Of course, Firth knows he's bullshitting himself, a practice he is most skilled at. But on account of feeling all holier-than-thou by means of positively influencing Ouse's future – for he honestly, consummately, emphatically, perhaps deliriously, believes this plot to be a rescue mission – he affords himself a generous margin of discretion. That's to say, he is opening the damn letter.

The Father has terrible handwriting, poor grammar, no grasp of syntax and a limited vocabulary. Firth expected as much: he suspected The Father had grown up illiterate, whilst being able to recite vast swathes of the holy book, badly and peppered with mishaps, though in some cases Firth has heard improvements in these blunders. He knew, however, The Father must have learned a little bit of mathematics and remedial reading, the rudimentary level required to pass the keeper's training. He wonders who the steering hand had been that made this possible, what human had been patient and invested enough to push The Father through an examination.

Despite all of these considerations, Firth's ego causes him to purse his lips priggishly upon witnessing how much smarter he is on paper than The Father. He allows a gloater's glint to furnish his eyes; this grin a spiral of smugness. He does his utmost to ignore all the physical prowess and practical knowledge The Father possesses that he, Firth, can't even fathom; all the lives The Father's been busy saving whilst Firth indulged, imbibed and extolled his cadre and their mordant takes on art and society. Information like this is best put aside at this juncture when trying to dress someone down.

The letter states that The Father had to be true to something and so was true to himself. Yes, Firth remonstrates, sounds about right, The Father first and Ouse miles down the line, bottom of the pecking order – so far so good, he roosters.

The letter states that The Father did not take Ouse out of school vindictively. It's because he couldn't afford to have people asking questions about who was helping man the light after The Mother died, and he didn't have the courage to admit how much he needed him. *Well too little, too late!* Firth grumbles – Ouse had said as much, no revelations here.

The letter then drops a proverbial grenade down the tank-hole right onto the major's lap. From what Firth can decipher of the hodgepodge of a scrawl, The Father would not prevent Ouse from leaving the island should he feel the need to – should he choose to seek work in Edinburgh, or any of the mainland cities. The Father all but confirms it's Ouse's choice, his alone, to make. The Father's not promoting it, not imploring it, not at all in favour of it even, but he is giving Ouse permission to choose. *Cunning old crocodile*, Firth gripes aloud, he's taking all the thrill out their fast getaway, butchering its covert appeal. Yes, Firth snipes, that's exactly what The Father's doing. Ouse would now not be fleeing an oppressive captor but leaving behind (no, deserting!) an emotionally repressed old warrior who's long suffered for his service and merely wants to pass along the baton.

The next tranche of the letter – from the affected swift skim he's giving it in a meagre attempt to mitigate his robbery of the news – is of even greater risk. It implies The Father blames himself for much of the upset Ouse has suffered since The Mother died, that he knows he's held him hostage (this word being the most surprising lexical appearance in the letter, albeit misspelt) from living his own life. The Father concedes he's been cold and harsh and angry and has been trying to cast Ouse in his own image.

It's not a full-on admission of guilt – it doesn't mention his violence, the bilious bullying, emotional blackmail or undermining, doesn't mention his bullishness towards strangers or acute selfishness in denying Ouse the opportunity to truly mourn The Mother – but it is contrite, even remorseful, in parts. *Too little, too late*, Firth assures himself again, repeating this a few times with increasing certitude.

Thankfully, it also comes with a, totally unironic, warning that the grass isn't always greener on the other side and an aggressive comment about not becoming a ponce. This then allows The Father opportunity to air some petty grievances about city dwellers, their infatuation with politicising everything and their incurable obsessions with money, neckties and drinking tea.

Firth, recognising the threat of a bad review with truth in it, reminds himself to keep his opinions of Edinburgh almost utopic. He will remain unflappable in his touting of the prosperous life that lies ahead for Ouse, reasserting the power he has to propel such prosperity. It is not a fabrication, just an edited version of Edinburgh life – Edinburgh with all his friends, champions and allies brought to the fore, and all his foes, doubters and haters eviscerated. It is those perfect days where Firth might only bump into three people that love him and receive unexpected good news. Not a day where his skin burns from shame and he has to walk out of coffee shops or hide in bar toilets until a certain somebody leaves or passes out drunk. He will not talk about the people lost and idling on street corners, vacant-eyed, gurning for more of something that's already rifling their insides. He will talk only of the halcyon days where even the poorest had claret and crab for supper.

The worst of the letter is saved for the end. A reminder that wherever he goes he'll always have the sea in him, that there's salt water in his blood, and never to worry about the well-being of Nile or any of the animals here, that The Father will continue to protect them like the prince and princesses they are.

He calls Firth something that he can't quite unfankle, which may be a flâneur, but more likely it's a fuckwit. Despite this, The

Father admits Firth might not be all bad and at the very least will be useful in helping get him set up. Then suggesting, more tersely, the friendship will have fulfilled its purpose once he's found his feet and should be gotten rid of. Christ, it's not too scathing at all, Firth admits, feeling almost sanctified to be deemed of use, albeit ephemerally – a premise he is not inclined to refute.

The confessional splurges and apologetic nature of the letter blindsides him. It's not at all what he expected and, although he remains suspicious of its intentions and sincerity, he can't deny there's authentic pain within it. The rickety-hearted ones of bulleted insides have a radar for true sadness in all its mucky man- ifestations. Firth had expected the letter to increase his conviction to this cause, validate his choices and gift him agency, not to loosen his grip or shake the mind's certainty.

What to do with this correspondence was the pressing ques- tion. He'll not make any drastic choices, he'll put it back, reseal the glue, push it far from his mind. There's another day ahead, anoth- er night, a final meal, a crunch time. Perhaps the conundrum will resolve itself; the riddle unriddle itself. He is under no compact to deliver the letter with any great hurry, he'll not have The Father make of him a cursed messenger. Not when everything is so close to coming to fruition. For all Ouse knows, The Father started that fire maliciously as a means of keeping him imprisoned on Muckle Flugga, enslaving his free will and cowing him into taking a path thrust upon him; with no consideration for the harm it will cause, the dreams it will throttle.

The Father's life – at least the version of it scribbled onto these paper sheets – feels like an ice cube melting between Firth's pressed palms: a structure once thought solid will vanish into a nothingness if only Firth pushes hot and hard enough.

THIRTY-NINE

When he set off from Edinburgh to die upon this island, Firth knew there would be a last supper. Knew he'd have a ceremonial meal, before which he would have to consider the permanency of his actions, the repercussions this inalterable move would have on others. He anticipated his suitcase being packed, but this was more as a matter of courtesy so as to not cause the keepers of this island any further bother. He would have left money enough for them to send his drawings to their intended location and compensation for all the inconvenience – the spilt paint on the floor, the disposal of his perishables, the potential of his body washing up in their cove, and all the nuisance and gossip that might cause.

He did not anticipate his suitcase would be packed for a homeward voyage, that he would be leaving in the morning by cover of dawn. Leaving with another who took all the drudgery out of travel and made him feel like he was starting something, not ending it. He did not imagine spotting two seals on the way to the meal, their wiry whiskers and robust bodies slathered in the sky's gloss, and shouting chipper: *Best of luck with it, lovelies*, as the pair plop off to see about their own scran.

He truly was the slug that climbed back out of the beer trap, vitalised, with a taste for the hops.

• • •

The Father brings a handful of Shetland bere up to the gallery deck of the lighthouse. It's still fair enough out to be deemed day, though the moon's in early, attempting to steal the show. By the time they've finished dinner, that big milky dish won't look so gawky and out of place just hanging there. He swoons at the sky with puckered lips, then strikes his own face to keep him spirited.

The light's primed for whatever the eventide brings in. And just as well, for The Father senses something stark raving mad out there; the unrest picking at his bones. Whatever it is, it's unlikely to come too close to a structure as strong, bright and warm as the light-house, The Father decides – it knows there's no place for it here. It would rather travel undetected, but you never know, *you just never know*, he mutters to himself – mercurial forces have derailed many a sleepless hunter and sent them screaming into their orbit.

The Father will be ready: he needs to be kinetically charged and strong-jawed, though Ouse's current anguish bores into his chest, rattling his breath. He makes a pact with God as he extends his arm out into the flickering wind, feeling it slap at his wrist. His hand solid and steady, he slowly uncoils his fingers, offering the bere into a passing zephyr. It's whipped away in a nanosecond, the grain taking the shape of a sledge as it's carried off. The Father hears what could be whispers, or perhaps the flutter of bat wings; the sound intensifying becomes a drum in the distance then suddenly stops, as if a heart torn from its chest. Portentous enough to nettle him, portentous enough to keep a piece of him harnessed to the wheels up here as he descends the stairwell for supper.

• • •

Ouse is content with his work in the kitchen this afternoon. Content to have made tomorrow's vat of bean stew and the day after's

Hairst Bree, vast and hearty enough to see any hunter through a few meals. He's stuffed the pantry to the gills and knows Figgie will be coming with another food load in two days – he suspects she'll stay and cook, suspects she'll be the key to keeping The Father afloat over the next couple of weeks, months even. He hopes the island runs out of whisky, that the grain moulds and the yeast spoils, any sort of force majeure to dry the island out. Ouse has toiled and struggled with not saying farewell to Figgie, but he has left a letter for her, as he has for The Father. With The Father, he knows an unannounced departure is the only way. He hopes his epistles are read and not burned, ripped to shreds or tossed into the deep. He hopes they can both forgive him, that they will understand. Regardless, the tasty offerings he's leaving in his stead go some way towards assuaging such formidable guilt – knowing there's foody succour to bung the upset is a stupendous relief.

RLS has been nothing if not a saviour, talking himself silly as a means of steadying Ouse's nerve, keeping him company as he cooks towards a better future. Anything that needed assuring of, RLS has assured him of. He assured him: The Father would take him back if it all went fish-belly up; that Figgie will understand the necessity of keeping his exodus under wraps, that she'd be cheering him on if she knew; that the ancient and abstruse wonderland of Muckle Flugga will be here long after he's turned to dust. Finally, he resolves that it's not boring to dish up Cullen Skink again and that, in fact, it's a sweet end to their marathon of feasting to serve up the same meal with which this particular chapter began.

RLS makes a melodrama out of the way the onions sting his eyes until remembering that he's a ghost and beyond the acerbic bite of sliced onion. His parody of Jesus's Last Supper with his disciples, although hilarious, is perhaps ill-advised, Ouse thinks. After all, it

275

has a heavy shadow of betrayal hanging over it and starts the journey towards a kindly man's crucifixion.

• • •

The Father arrives first and Firth second. They take the seats they had previously co-opted, the seats they've filled every group meal this last wee while; meals framed by The Father's flare-ups and subsequent pandering.

Firth welcomes the smell of the fishy soup, recognising within it a chance to rectify the debacle of his previous attempt at chowing down like a local.

The Father stirs to the chapter-ending significance of the menu, but keeps it to himself, fearing to acknowledge it would make Firth feel special. He's here for Ouse, he's keeping his eye on Firth: he's not going to fuck up, not tonight. The Father reckons Ouse is wavering on his future and that the season ahead will either quell the restlessness in him or fuel it. Once Firth has gone, they'll do some talking, they'll settle some scores, he'll take him away for the night, when it's quiet, get Figgie over to cover the light. Firth will write to Ouse, The Father's sure of it, he will make arrangements in the capital, provide encouragement, allurements, false hopes. Whether the letters get through or not is an altogether different matter, The Father rules – he'll be vetting them, he kens that for sure.

Ouse serves up the steaming boules, lidless, for Firth's benefit. Firth notices this and a smile is split between them. From a quick glance into the bread cauldron he can tell there's a heartier serving of fish in this one, a crustier clunk of bread.

The Father pours everyone a whisky and begins proceedings by toasting to the lighthouse, to the great watchers, to the

276

heaven-taught craftsmen, and the ingenuity of the lighthouse Stevensons. Firth susses that The Father, as well as being on his best behaviour to gladden Ouse, is on a mission to glorify the keeper's profession – to push the piety of the role by aligning it with the goodwill of a Godly world.

Firth tries to find a way in, an opening to shift the subject matter, but fails, his stuttering intrusions at one point brought to a halt by The Father, whose hand is raised as if informing a beggar to save their breath. The Father recounts how those that built these structures are part granite themselves; he tells heroic tales of keepers who went above and beyond the call of duty and had their names scraped into the stone they captained. He speaks of engineers rewarding their loyal troops with nips of whisky exactly as old as those they lost – often tragically younger than both the boys. He drinks to the lost as a matter of precaution, as a matter of superstition, as a matter of faith. Of course, his intake might appear indulgent to an outsider, but even the KLAMS couldn't quibble with his work ethic, The Father points out – that was part of their dilemma: he is invaluable; nobody could hold this station like he could.

The Father reminds Ouse, ignoring Firth, that the health of any lighthouse must be constantly toasted to, no matter where he is or who he's with. Firth is riled by Ouse's obvious affection for the man's blather.

When a silence finally offers up an opportunity to speak, Firth compliments the Cullen Skink and toasts to all the extraordinary meals Ouse has prepared for them during his stay. The Father competitively follows suit, praising the Cullen Skink, remarking it to be one of his best but not his very best, which The Father assures him was when they caught the fish themselves and smoked it together. This prompts the story of how it happened, when they sailed halfway to Norway in a fishing trawler that took them out for an expedition, and they slept in the cabin of the ship and witnessed a pod of orcas heading towards the Arctic on a hunt – relieved they saw them when they did, having been just about to dive in for a paddle, harpoons to hand.

Ouse can tell The Father is nervous, overcompensating, and that makes Ouse ponderous; quieter than everyone at the table would like him to be. He's only too aware his contributions to the conversation are vital in terms of keeping the tempo and, more importantly, the peace.

Firth steers the conversation away from nostalgia by offering an unsolicited update on his progress in painting Muckle Flugga's birdlife. He begins listing all the stunning specimens he's seen and captured in pencil, paint and ink. Firth knows well that birdlife might just be the only other thing, besides lighthouse business, that The Father will talk about freely and fervently.

It turns out The Father can identify a raven, a jackdaw, a rook or a crow just from the shadow it casts on the sand. Firth has to hide how impressed he is. They talk about birds until the soup in their bread bowls has been drained and Ouse offers each of them another ladleful, which everyone gratefully accepts, not knowing how to end the evening, who should leave first.

By the time the second serving arrives The Father has glugged back a fair few snifters of whisky, topping up Firth's glass each time, resenting doing so then remembering the boy is full of his piss. The Father picks up what remains of the boule and slurps the soup back as if quaffing water after a hot night of fevered dreams.

Ouse, drawn to the theatrics, does the same, making similarly disgusting vociferous noises in the process. Firth suspects this might be some sort of final initiation and, feeling childishly competitive with

The Father, follows suit. His attempt, however, is shockingly disastrous. Just as the creamy fish water burns upon his lips he peers over the top of the edible bowl to ensure they're both watching. Instead of catching two impressed onlookers he clocks the face of Figgie, pressed against the glass outside, directly behind The Father!

The fright of her appearing, like the shipwrecked spirit of herself, combined with the scalding kiss of the liquid causes Firth to jolt back, spilling the soup all over his lap. A whole run of expletives shoots from his mouth of the *fuck-fuck-FUCK* variety as he begins cupping the overspill back into the hollowed-out bread, burning his hands in the process – once again!

And once again The Father's patronising laughter comes torpedoing his way. *He's done it again,* The Father roars, *old painter-chops has soppy bollocksed it all over again! What a buggering arse.*

Firth, too, tries to smile, grimacing through his gaucheness. Ouse tosses the damp cloth from the sink to make light of it, which Firth at least catches. The mess is minimal this time, but his beetrooting is maximal.

I'm fine, I'm fine, just keep on eating, please just keep eating, Firth begs, so desperate in timbre it unnerves The Father. Ouse and The Father, having finished their food, are at a loss what to do.

Shortbread! The Father announces like the name of a newborn. He rises up and begins to rake around in the tins and drawers behind him.

Don't worry, Ouse whispers, leaning towards Firth. *Think nothing of it. Unless you're still hungry and then I'll fetch some more?*

To Firth's astonishment Figgie is still there, her eyes turning amber and her face pressed so tight to the window it's steaming up the glass. The Father in his poozling is nearing exactly the window she's haunting and it's ringing Firth's chest like a rusty bell.

Firth can only assume she's having a crisis of confidence, fearing she might have come here to confess her sins, or worse. Unsure what worse is, but damn sure he doesn't want to find out, Firth realises he has to do something drastic to stop this unfolding.

How did The Mother die? he cries out just as The Father discovers the biscuit box he's been searching for.

Ouse knows this one's not for him. He is uncomfortable letting the question hang in the air but equally intrigued to see how The Father will answer. He decides to give The Father until the count of ten to say something before grabbing the situation by the horns. At the same time, Ouse is also marking Firth down for his crass timing of such a provocative question.

The Father returns to his seat, opens the tartan tin, retrieves a fat log of sugary shortbread, offers one to Ouse alone, and then bites into the biscuit. After a few committed chomps, his answer comes, cobalt blue in tone, open-mouthed and accompanied by continual chewing.

Drowned. The Mother drowned.

She was swimming, Ouse softly supplements, *she loved to swim. We all do.*

That's awful, Firth consoles, *truly awful* – holding back how revolted he is by the biscuity mush The Father's exhibiting in the process of talking. As Firth moves to take a log of shortbread, The Father flips the lid closed and draws the tin back towards him. A stony stare and a faint flick of his eyes indicate it's time for Firth to go.

Firth would rather leave on his own terms, head held high, ego intact, with a slab of buttery shortbread, but the opportunity to hotfoot it out of there is not to be missed. He'll be seeing Ouse in the drowsy hours of dawn and the less dopey he is the better. It is a risk to leave them together, but he needs to find out what has brought Figgie out to the island, and The Father's surely finished his pitch for the night.

The Father continues to eat his biscuit and doesn't wish Firth so much as a farewell, despite knowing he's leaving tomorrow and that they might never cross paths again. Firth takes solace in knowing that The Father is oblivious to the fact he will actually be departing in the fledgling hours, and not at noon as their schedule dictates. Firth will leave Muckle Flugga on his own terms and will not be departing alone – he will be taking The Father's most prized possession, his laddie, along for the ride.

Firth thanks Ouse for dinner with a mawkish sincerity intended to convey his anticipation of the adventure that awaits them, then scurries for the door feeling like his hinges are about to come undone.

FORTY

Coming out the kitchen Firth feels his legs turn to jelly, knocked sideways by the wind, allowing his body to breathe a great sigh of relief. He knows how close he just came to bungling the future he's fighting for. A weight he is carrying falls from his brow.

Firth sees Figgie hightailing it down the side of the summit, the rain thrashing after her. He's furious, but remains indebted to her, trying to be brave whilst utterly petrified. Slipping all over the shop as he spills down the muddy wynd, he calls out to Figgie, who doesn't hear him for the extravagant racket of the weather but knows to stop, nonetheless. Under the crab apple tree is the first semi-shelter she finds, and Figgie clings to it to like a crutch.

Firth, upon reaching Grandfather Crab, can see Figgie's face is a mess of emotions, within the plaintive wobble of her voice, a sound like someone chipping at ice.

I watched him weeping, Figgie sobs, shouting against the winds, *smearing the ash of what I destroyed all over his face. I was scared his heart might hae givin' up there and then. And we'd be tae blame Firth, WE'D be tae blame.*

Figgie, this is what you signed up for! Firth bellows back. *It was always going to hurt, destroying what he loved, but it WILL save him! And besides, it's ME to blame, not you! My plan! My concoction.*

Aye, but it was me who did it, Figgie trembles, *who set fire to all those beautiful things of his.*

It was the only way he'd leave, Figgie! If we weakened this place's hold on him. *If he suspected The Father had finally done something unforgiveable.*

I don't know. It's jist so wrong. Figgie drops to the ground, her back against the tree and hands over her face. *I saw our names glowing in the embers as I fled,* she bawls. *We're cursed.*

Firth huddles in beside her and makes a tent of himself. *I was already cursed,* he mutters inaudibly, and then, in his most consoling voice, he pleads with Figgie. *When opportunities like this are turned down, the future becomes infected by the disease of what's lost. If Ouse passes this up it will gnaw a hole inside him that he'll never recover from. One way or another, it would have killed him.*

But it's not honest, Figgie bawls.

Not everything that's honest is right, Firth snaps. *It rarely is.*

God will judge us, she cries. *We deserve His wrath.*

He deserves ours! Firth roars with bite in the words. *War, genocide, famine, murder and rape, diseases so nefarious even our most rotten specimens couldn't have cooked them up. What about that? Where was God when my mum died of cancer despite being the best, most selfless person I know? Where was God when they killed my dad, murdered for the change in his pocket and a bag of presents?*

That's awful. I'm so sorry, Figgie whimpers, *but that doesn't change what we did. It still doesn't feel right. It's plaguing my dreams!*

That'll stop. I promise it will, Firth yells, taking her face in his hands with force. *And we saved his biggest sketchpad, the new one, the one he loved most. He was so grateful when I gave him it.*

He was? Figgie asks beggingly, a glimmer of hope breaking beyond her state of desolation.

Yes, he was. It comforted him immensely, Firth soothes. *And it will give him what he needs to start anew. A key to the life he deserves. He'll end up hating himself, Figgie, this life will ruin him if we don't do this.*

283

Despite the slight cover of the beaten tree, the pair couldn't be wetter if they jumped in the sea, their soaked clothes beginning to slip from their skin. Exactly when it should feel darkest, the moon suddenly ups its glow and it settles Figgie's nerves.

Hug him, even when you're scared to, hug him for me, she commands, almost threatening. *Even when yer body's arrow points the other way, hug him. He'll try and hide. Don't let him. You look after him now. You promised me.*

He's surviving this, Figgie. WE . . . are surviving this. I'll give him everything I've got. They're going to love him there. He's going to thrive.

When yer safe, when yer away, I will tell The Father what we did; he deserves the truth.

I wouldn't do that, Figgie, he'll never understand. He'll hate you. He might hurt you. Please don't do that.

I hope it works out for you both, Figgie hymns sombrely. *You'll be in my prayers. Both of you, in my prayers.*

With this, Figgie darts off into the night. Firth calls after her, assuring himself that she wouldn't risk making the crossing to Unst in this weather, whilst knowing she's nowhere else to go. She disappears into a thick haar and Firth traces the wet for her silhouette until finding, not Figgie, but a fox. Sleek, wet-nosed, ginger and auburn, with glowing amber eyes. His corrupted mind's at it again, he fumes, as the creature disappears, leaving a trace of light hanging in the fog and a sweep of tail taunting his eyes.

On the walk back to the bothy, Firth lists his reasons for doing what he has. He convinces himself, again, that had they not burned the sketchbooks, wool and art supplies, The Father one day would have destroyed them. Or worse still, he'd have cajoled Ouse into doing it himself as a rite of passage into the keeper's life. He would have forced Ouse to live forever in shame, a gruesome act that could have manifested into something vile and ugly like self-harm or painful tics or worse. Yes, Firth ascertains, The Father would have been the death of him.

The thought of Ouse being made aware of their deception before reaping the benefits – that's to say, before Firth is proved right in doing what he's doing – causes him to baulk, retch, then boak the Cullen Skink contents of his belly into the pond. As the fish rise to the surface to see what's good for eating, Firth slinks off, fearing that he's just turned them into cannibals.

Lying in his bothy bed that night, Firth thinks about the way his mother always talked about how he'd be the one to succeed beyond the limits of the family name: he was so sorry to have disappointed her. Perhaps this was his chance not to. *Help me in my harvest, holy mother!* Firth puffs into the night, with the pluck of someone who's just jumped a wall they were certain was too high to even climb.

FORTY-ONE

With Firth out the way, The Father gestures Ouse to coorie in, pulling his seat closer with him still on it. He tops up the glass Ouse has barely touched and slooshes the whisky around his mouth to clean the biscuit from his teeth.

It's building up to something out there, Ouse intuits to The Father, *there's heat in it.*

Aye, could be a battle in an hour or two. The haill clanjamfrie might be coming fur us.

Do you want my organ music? Ouse offers with occult undertones.

Nah, yer alright the nicht. I've got this yin.

I could never do what you do, Ouse says reflectively. *I know you've wanted more from me – more commitment, more strength. I'm not like you and I'm sorry for the hurt it's caused you.*

The long pause begins to make Ouse anxious that The Father might be deciphering the wider sentiments at play here, but then he registers his thinking face and a rejoinder forming.

Neabody said this wid be easy, and fuck me it's been any'hing but. But I'm a keeper o'the flame. I chose this, ken, wanted it mare than anything I've ever wanted. And you didnae, didnae choose this, I see that noo. Well, you might say uh heard it.

As The Father sermonises, Ouse glances his eyes back and forth over him, tracing his brawny body and circling his penetrating stare.

This lighthouse will never fall, Ouse, it huz roots of iron wrung around the rocks below – digging deeper than any tree's ever gonnae go. The light's no a feat o'engineering any mare, it's part of this island; part o'me. The only way it goes is if the whole island does.

The Father stands up from his seat to project himself better, facing down what's out there, coming their way. *I'm no its master, nae fortune teller, but I'll man this rock as long as it needs me tae. And I hope you'll want to do the same, but I ken that's no a foregone conclusion. I only pray, and uh do still sometimes pray, you'll no write it off so easily.*

Ouse contemplates all The Father's great contradictions, vacillates on his virtue, as he has done his entire life. The Father courts physical fear, seemingly immune to its terror, yet can be as emotionally vulnerable as a toddler when challenged on his views on very simple things. He can be uncommonly kind to small creatures, and yet speaks the language of violence freely and fluently. He has rebelled against the tyrannical codes of the last wreckers, perhaps even contributing to their extinction, only to become lovingly at war with a new set of codes he calls his own.

The Father is deeply flawed, at times dangerous, whilst martyred to a purpose that will continue to save lives. He saves these lives, at least partially, in the hope of atoning for the wrongdoings of his wrecker ancestors who willed in death and destruction to profit from it. He is repulsed by the way they lived their lives yet cannot shake their judgement. He hates them so much he will not love himself.

The Father's complexities run rife – Ouse once heard him describe his own heart as a jagged husk of a thing. But for all this, because of his deep understanding of all this, Ouse loves him unconditionally.

Ouse loves him more today than ever, because he is leaving him; because The Father might never forgive him; and because, from a

287

distance, Ouse might begin to view him under a more resentful lens. They are, in Ouse's mind, not parting so much as severing.

Anyhoo, ye mad wee pagan. Let's see what the morrow brings. The Father's voice bringing him back into the room. *I best get up top, it's blowin' a hoolie oot there.*

As they trail off into their separate corners of night, Ouse imagines The Father saying comforting words to ease the sting of his desertion. Something like: *Wherever you are, remember, you are one of the guardians of Muckle Flugga, whose memory is enthused within stone and imprinted upon the land. I will make sure your name forever rings out from the high tower of the lighthouse.*

I will carry this place with me always, Ouse would respond raising his arms in the air like he was made to fly and had just found his wings.

Ouse knows of keepers that lived here for decades longer than he has himself, more integral to the island's survival than is fathomable. He knows of keepers that have become the most passionate advocates the lighthouse could have dreamed of, in this world and the next. But Ouse alone is the only one alive whose totality of time on this planet has been spent living here, on this island, with these rocks and this sweep of sea as his home.

Good luck, Dad, Ouse utters almost inaudibly – his heart like a sprig of heather pressed between the pages of a photo album.

Tae you as well, my baby boy, comes waltzing back.

FORTY-TWO

Several thousand tons of water come at Muckle Flugga Lighthouse that night, shattering one of the panes of the lantern room and trying, yet failing, to knock The Father off his feet. The whole tower shakes beneath him, and the reverberations enter his body like a seizure.

Next comes the lightning. The lighthouse takes the brunt of it, its fat conductor rod drawing the fork towards it, expelling the current through its copper spine into the rocks below, though not without some overspill: electric sparks spaghetti everywhere and the brickwork gets a dusting of black. A shock leaps up off the metalwork and into The Father's arm, the runaway train in him lurches forwards. The second one floors him, singes his beard and eyelashes. Brought back to life by the gritty water, he gets to his feet again. His hair smoking, The Father lets out a war-cry, the torment behind his eyes surfaces as pure courage.

As the storm hits its zenith, The Father calls out for help to the spangling moon – begging it to re-emerge from behind its gossamer sheet, where it's ensconced away from the drenching. Reluctantly, out it comes, everybody's hero, the real author, to help him bounce the light around.

There are ships out there lost in the guts of what is spilling out the cloudburst. The Father tunes into the faint chords of distressed sailors leaking through the air; now, with the moon in his corner, he can draw the gale away. After all, it is the devil's gale, Lucifer making the waves malignant, using them for destruction.

Together, as moon and servant of the beam, they fight on, for hours, The Father working his body until it feels as if the marrow in his bones might catch fire. Eventually, the wrestle pays off, and the thundering skies simmer down to a wily rumble.

Melodious cheers of relief erupt from a ship that had been battling the tide, held tight in the lighthouse's beam – now safe, now on the other side of the deluge. The Father dances the light across their deck in celebration, spotlighting the grasping hands of the crew, jumping and high-fiving the ether. A captain, who could be his brother, waves whilst smoking a victory pipe. The Father blinks the light back in full salute.

A small firework is set off in The Father's honour, from the bonfires in their bellies, lit from the embers of still being alive when the odds were stacked against them. The Father listens intently to the wispy gist of their songs and yells in rapture, *Not tonight!* at the sky, pointing directly to the darkest patch of the firmament.

Exhausted, he lets his body fall upon the floor. Just as his eyes close, he swears he sees a crow slaughter a snow-white dove in mid-air, knowing fine well it's too far for both these creatures to have travelled in such a storm. Just in case, he lets a prayer chute off his lips, the words swan-diving off widow's walk into the deep below.

FORTY-THREE

Ouse falls asleep as soon as his head hits the pillow, feeling guilty about the lack of restlessness in him. He sleeps thinking he shouldn't but has no other option; tiredness lays siege to his body and takes control. In his dreams he walks through the centuries – first as Pict, then as a Viking, a Gael, a Celt, a Shetlander and, finally, an Edinburgh bohemian.

He wakes a few hours later, primed, ready and alert. He feels transformed, focussed and esoteric; stronger to the power of ten for a proper rest. He couriers his luggage down to *The Covenant* and scopes around for traces of life, convinced he is seeing better in the dark, owl-eyed with his owl-feather necklace kissed again for luck.

Failing to sleep, Firth remains up, waiting to be summoned. It's still dark and Ouse can tell by the way the light of his candle flails there is movement in the room – fidgeting, fretting, fortifying, all of it caught by the flicker in the flame.

The Father, he assumes, will be passed out in the lighthouse, having washed himself of energy, valiant in his cause. His belly would growl into action a couple of hours from now, by which time Ouse and Firth will be on the ferry to the big mainland, Aberdeen bound, The Granite City. He'll leave *The Covenant* on Unst for Figgie to return. The Father won't be able to catch them unless he swims the crossing, which he's only ever been able to do when The Mother was watching, fuelled by the will of wooing the unwooable woman, as he loved to call her.

Ouse walks around the starboard flank of the island one final time.

Kissing Out Stack with his eyes, imagining nuzzling Nile with his chest, thrusting into the wind in the hope of sending his lustiest atoms off on an Arctic adventure. He's left his trace everywhere: scent, song and slobber. What a place to have found the worth of your own skin, Ouse muses – what a cavalcade of colour. He suspects he'll never see its like again. Even if he comes back, returns home, it won't be this exact cut of home; this incarnation. He'll have missed so much of it, he'll have changed. It'll be hard to talk about who's changed more, delicately bridging the gap and filling in the blanks, without sounding too sentimental or boastful of their differences.

Ouse sidles into the library, which The Father has restocked with survivors and begun rebuilding. The Mother's words whisper in his ear: *We don't call them used books, they're simply long-loved.* He's packed The Mother's three favourite reads, her name and the date written inside each of them, plus that of the Edinburgh bookshop she purchased them in. He should like to visit them all, a bookshop scavenger, to walk in The Mother's shoes. *Clickety-clack.* Alongside her books, three of his own – the gaps they've left on the shelves gape back at him like evacuated graves. He fills their spaces with his hands, slots his cheek into their emptiness and apologises profusely for leaving. Walking out on the rug that was, for years, his everything – his obsession following The Mother's death – takes a fleshy piece of him. Though crispy around the edges and smoke smattered, he's still in awe of what he achieved. No shame in this pride.

Once outside again, he can't think whether to fall to his knees, cry and kiss the ground, or high-kick the darkness and squat beneath the starlight. The result is a scrappy fusion of all these things. With this done, a full stop planted in the soil with his heel, Ouse heads off to collect Firth, who's out the door before he gets the chance to not knock.

They walk together in silence down the long path to the cove, the darkness at its coldest now, the lapping water helping them to keep a beat. Firth, keen to let Ouse enjoy the soundtrack to the movie of his life one last time without his pesky circumlocutions, bites his lip until it bleeds. As their totter becomes a saunter becomes a trot, Firth moves from feeling like he's walking on nails to eggshells to air. On arrival, first light scratches through the purpling patches of night leaving, and Firth near levitates off the ground and up onto the boat.

Connecting to the tide, Ouse slows and steadies his breath, popping seaweed with his toes as he considers the kisses to come in a huge city that lies in wait. A fine thought with which to break away from someone you love, he concedes. With a small knife he slices a little cut on his hand and lets the blood drip into the foamy tip of the sea. Having comingled with the cove, he boards the boat, picks up the oars, clasps them tight as a familiar handshake, and pushes off. One, two, three rows and, in his mind, Ouse is now further than he's ever been from home.

Firth clears his throat, having suffocated in silence long enough. However, his victory speech doesn't get past the first plosive before it's stifled by a high-pitched wolf howl from the summit of the headland above. The silhouette of The Father attaches itself to the sound. His bulk comes careering down the path at a pace neither of the boys thought possible by man nor beast.

By the time The Father reaches the cove he's travelling at such a speed that he skids to a stop like a bicycle on gravel, a veil of dust crowding around him. But *The Covenant* and its crew are far enough out that words, though audible, would not be decipherable.

The Father isn't thrashing around, isn't shouting, no smoke fumes from his ears – he's poised and still. He looks almost godly standing there. He throws his hands up in the air in disbelief, then opening them out as if welcoming Ouse back with the assurance of all being forgiven. The nature of this invitation rips at Firth's skin; he avoids looking in Ouse's direction for fear of seeing his resolve melt. Regardless, Firth is mightily relieved The Father is not plunging in after them. The previous night's dramatics are still causing some swells in the water and dawn is only just breaking out of its shell; both of these factors undoubtedly play to their advantage. This was the plan, the plan is working, but neither boy expected to have to look The Father in the eye as they pulled the trigger. Lucky those eyes are far enough off that the hurt in them is all but invisible.

The Father's stillness placates Ouse – he feels within it the slivers of acceptance. He will miss the noises The Father makes when enjoying the food he cooks him, the half-words half-trills of delight when a new recipe works out. He will not miss the way he lifts his upper lip and grunts when it doesn't, moving the food around the plate like a dead animal he's scraped off an old shoe. He will miss the shape of his shadow in the sun, especially when splayed over the ferns. He will miss The Father's madcap laughter when the storm is full pelt and Ouse's music is making them both feel marvellous – the way he shouts for an encore and gives him all the credit for life's good work. He will miss these things terribly, but not enough to miss this opportunity of living beyond this. You can't own love, he tells himself, but you can trap it – we must set what we love free. The Father did wrong things for a long time, but at least he knew why; at least he had his reasons. Ouse will respect that as long as he lives: he hopes The Father is proud of his own life.

The Father's stillness worries Firth, staring at them like a macabre spectre. He knows The Father has a rough idea where he lives, that he would be able to track them down if he ever came to the capital. But what he's surer of is that the dysfunctional relationship between The Father and the light would prevent him from leaving it for that long. Figgie might watch it for an afternoon, perhaps even overnight, but no longer. He'll make sure to send Figgie some money, if he can, chocolates too, perhaps a snow globe. Firth really hopes The Father doesn't kill anyone, or himself. He thinks duty, again, will prevent him doing anything that severe. Having taken from him, having won, he can now allow himself to admire The Father's loyalty to the light, loyalty of such a strength Firth has never embodied or inspired. He hopes he can feel such life-long passion for Ouse, hopes to match The Father's strength, hopes the thrill of loving Ouse never runs dry, that he doesn't get lazy with it; as he has with every other thing he's loved. Firth stares lovingly at Ouse, trying to will it so. Ouse feels him watching and looks at him like a mountaineer does at the mountain they've always wanted to climb.

To their shock, by the time they return their gaze to the cove, The Father has vanished from sight.

The risk The Father might enter water and swim them down has now extinguished – Ouse acknowledges this, relieved and the tiniest bit disappointed. Firth begins to get antsy as they come back in close to Muckle Flugga; naturally he's constantly fearing Ouse is about to jump ship. Ouse, sensing his trepidation, explains coolly that *The Covenant* must first curl around the side of the island, avoiding sleeping turtles and snapping rocks, before they can continue south. It takes a few minutes and the tension is thick as a winter stew. It's sheer cliff face above them – a huge, tumbling, rocky precipice popular with puffins – so no risk of The Father plunging down it, but they're now close enough to catch his call if he so chooses to cast it. What Firth fears the most is that The Father could scream out his truth, having somehow worked it all out in the last few moments.

At this thought, Firth's taken back into the darkness inside of him; a cunning hunter, it swoops for his happiness at the most inopportune moment. *There's something dreadful you should know*, Firth begins to babble, not believing his own lips to be capable of such treachery.

As if by the devil's intervention, The Father appears on the clifftop above them like a haunted steeple, his giant arms the cross they all will soon bear. Ouse stops rowing and both boys rise to their feet like frightened rabbits; paused in time, gazing up at the bird of prey that hunts them.

If someone's eyes could be described as on, on like oil on fire, it is The Father's in this instant. He pulls a gun from behind his back. Firth sees it first, held high like a spear and then taking aim. Firth pushes Ouse to the floor then flings himself upon him, covering his body like a human shield. The blast from the gun is deafeningly loud, shaking loose rocks from the cliff face. Something in Firth crumbles as his heart races and vision blurs; the ringing in his ear builds into an ear-splitting blindness.

FORTY-FOUR

Firth comes to on the other side of what must have been a fainting, the anchor already in the harbour at Unst. He revisits the shot, the gun-hungry bark of death, then runs his fingers over his skin. No bleeding, no holes. And Ouse, he's okay, yes, he confirms, look at that beautiful face, it's healthy, it's a miracle.

You're okay, we're okay? Firth stutters.

Yes, Ouse confirms. *We're okay.*

The Father, he was . . . I mean, was he trying to kill us? Firth cries, his vision still splintering to sticks.

No, Ouse counters, *he doesn't keep live rounds on the island: it's a noise-maker is all. A racketmonger. He uses it to scare off the otters from getting caught in his nets and oyster traps. That was different though: that was my send-off.*

Firth attempts to get up but fails.

There's still something I've got to tell you, he bewails with tears in his eyes, *something that might make you feel differently about what we've just done.*

Then let's wait until the next boat, Ouse utters softly, *when we're too far gone to turn back.*

Firth nods, elated, *Yes, let's do that.*

Ouse hauls Firth to his feet then picks up both their cases – Firth, feeling weak, lets him.

Firth is a true friend, brave and loyal, Ouse thinks. He threw his body over him when he thought there was a bullet coming their way. He loves Firth, but may never fully trust him. And that's okay.

Firth has shown him the seeds necessary for a new life; it is up to Ouse to grow beyond his sapling self. He knows Firth will let him down, intuits he already has, but what interests him the more is what comes after any anger. The Father will no longer be His Master's Voice, but neither shall Firth. He has seen The Father undone by rage, chasing something loved then lost, something he has never been able to balance. Ouse decrees that this particular form of madness, to which those in pain are most susceptible, will never make a slave of him. He, unlike his father and Firth, is able to look at a gushing waterfall on a rainy day and not see himself in it, just nature, power and a wetter week than most.

Firth, feeling stronger, is not sure if by the time they hit the big ferry he'll show Ouse The Father's letter or come clean about what he and Figgie did. Figgie has forced his hand after all, and he should tell Ouse before she tells The Father, or this all comes crashing down. And then it smacks upon him . . . The letter, the fucking letter. It's under his pillow still! He kept it there until the very last moment, terrified of misplacing it, making sure it would be the final thing he packed. Christ, he winces, The Father will think it deliberate. He could narrate the contents to Ouse, but only if he admits he's read it, pilfered from Ouse the opportunity to be the first one to breathe it all in. Christ, Firth thinks again, had he done that deliberately? Did he leave the letter behind out of spite? He convinces himself not, no, it was a mistake in the heat of a hot, hot moment. In the body of every great lie pumps the blood of truth.

Perhaps Ouse will see the love in his actions, Firth reasons, thinking beyond the letter to the burning of his work. Firth, destroying something beautiful, in a manner that pains him, in order to help Ouse flee, to take the shackles off so as he might chase the happiness he deserves. Yes, that's the way Ouse's marvellous mind works,

Firth settles – he's a lilted-thinker, lullabies and silver linings.

Wracked with guilt, Firth instead renews his vows to Ouse, to protect him in Edinburgh, to give him everything he possibly can – money, friends, opportunities; to work his fingers to the bone so Ouse might live the life he was born for. Firth has bumbled and beetled about for great swathes of his living – no more, he affirms, this beetle's taking flight. He'll be the Ousling's stanchion, his steer, a cheerleader, a patron picket, his human sacrifice. He'll make it easy, make it gentle.

It's not gentleness I'm looking for, Ouse commands from the silence, *it's . . . something else. Something not yet written.*

Despite the ambiguity of this statement, Ouse utters it with a certainty that strikes at Firth's stiffened heart. He's beginning to change, Firth thinks, then labels himself paranoid.

On the ride over to the big ferry, Ouse is quiet, even for Ouse, but it's a smouldering quiet, a steeling, bracing quiet; on the ride over to the mainland, the beating waves become a bucking sea, the ferry's deck sloshed in salty sea-spill. Ouse stands his ground, Firth lies vertical on a shoogly bench suffering from seasickness, chewing on seaweed as instructed. It really does help. He swallows a little and shouts reassuring affirmations Ouse's way to prove his fidelity.

Ouse smiles, like he means it, but not like he needs this, which causes Firth to up the ante.

On the off-chance telepathy is another of Ouse's unspoken talents, Firth begins repeating loops in his head of how he'd burn himself to ashes to see Ouse thrive. He gives this inner monologue such emotional gusto he makes himself teary, soon thinking ahead to what Ouse would say at his imaginary funeral many fulsome years from now. Undoubtably, it'd be a beautifully rousing speech, soft yet stirring, about how Firth before anyone else saw the true scope of Ouse's talent, how he took a spark destined to burn out and raised from it a blazing bonfire. An act for which the whole world would be indebted. Ouse would use phrases like 'force of nature' and 'champion class-climber', expressing an eternal gratitude and stating how he could never fully repay such indefatigable faith. Whilst everyone afterwards would assure him that his accomplishments served as a living testimony, and that Firth was so very proud of the small part he had played in Ouse's remarkable life. Drunk, Ouse would express regret to a nobody on the way home about the estrangement that had stalked their love in later life, to which Firth would be unable to respond despite his best attempts to reach out from the afterlife.

Ouse, still staring out to the ocean, is looking only forwards, never backwards – for that would be counterproductive and painful. He watches birds fly out in a V-shape ahead of him and muses on how he will soon encounter flying creatures that have never visited Muckle Flugga, or any of Shetland. He wonders if an invisible umbilical cord between him and the island is about to snap, what sound that would make; bell-like, but tighter, he confirms. He considers how Firth, at this present moment, is stuck in the middle on many things – the middle of a plan, of a passion, of his own life – and whether that will change for the better when they set foot on Scotland's mainland.

He is supremely grateful to Firth, doesn't underplay the significance of his actions – how he fought for him like no-one else ever had. Yet the cloying notion that Firth is simply trying to collect him, that his life is akin to a big project or the creation of an epic painting, doesn't fully shift. He sees the triumph in Firth but also the tragedian and vows never to be swept under by his modes of moody conflict. It's like having been wronged by someone in a terrible dream and continuing to distrust them the next morn-ing despite the whole scenario being of your own making. At this thoughtful moment, the ferry begins to bob and lurch again, caus-ing Ouse to have to hang on to the wet railing and utilise the full friction of his grips. The ferry careers up a few cojoined waves and then spills down a mother wave, crashing into the basin of the swell with ferocity. The whole ferry vibrates as if nearing collapse, stops as if winded, then courageously climbs the back of another wa-tery ridge to do it all over again. Ouse is committed to this way of thinking.

The turbulence passes and the view ahead, that is the world around them, soon commands Ouse's attention above all these inner musings combined. Aberdeen's granite spires jut out the mottled blur the horizon was once. Ouse scours the landscape for a familiar silhouette taking shape on the jetty. Crossed-legged on the railings perhaps, velveteen jacket, riding boots, lilac fedora and a windswept moustache? The sight of RLS, however, does not ap-pear: in spite of his absence, the city beyond keeps growing; magic and numinous.

Ouse re-joins Firth, who's survived the choppy crossing and is back on his feet, wiping his frothy mouth with a handkerchief he suspects has been slipped into his pocket. They hug in tribute to a safe harbouring, though not as tight as the latter would like. All the same, this gift of cheek-to-cheek softness renews Firth's vigour, yet he can't shake the feeling he's already confessed to all manner of irredeemable crimes, despite not uttering a word. By way of begin-ning to defend everything he's not yet admitted, Firth commences his quest for absolution and lets himself unravel.

Please, please forgive me, Firth begs, *when I tell you what I have to. Remember, I'm building a church and you're the altar.*

301

But what choice did I have in any of that? Ouse asks plainly.

So why did you come? Firth weeps.

Because sometimes it's okay to look the other way when the ugly parts of someone you love are showing.

. . .

The stranger staring up at the approaching ferry has no idea the weight of the drama its passengers carry, how greatly the scale of the risk they're taking outweighs the lightness of their luggage. To the stranger's eyes, they're just two boys stood beside each other, close yet not without some distance. One is taller, sharper-edged, slightly older-looking, all keen darting eyes, twists of hair and wraps of fabric. The other: younger, stiller, more focussed in expression, more harmonised in dress, softer even in the way his shape splits the light.

Ouse, nineteen years old, is now indisputably further from home than he's ever been, gaping at the first city he's ever seen, immediately at peace with its gigantic architecture. He lets his gaze cast nets over the medley of granite stone and then journey onwards to the next stage of their voyage, his body soon to follow.

To his flank is Firth, twenty-six years old, equally brave, equally terrified – juggling his will to live alongside his ambitions for Ouse to succeed in a city that would as easily make grave-filler of him than welcome him in as one of its own. Firth knows he's promised more than he can rightly deliver, whilst hoping against all odds to prove himself wrong, that he will flourish beyond the gestalt of his past selves.

The stranger on the harbour is waiting on a lover – a lover neither boy has noticed on account of being lost in the wilderness of themselves and each other – someone coming home who's been gone far too long. For each passenger alighting the ferry, the walk-way, dropped upon the jetty, feels akin to a bridge between two worlds; as if time itself is signalling it is ready to begin again.

Notes

19 **To travel hopefully is a better thing than to arrive.** *Virginibus Puerisque: An Essay in Four Parts*; Robert Louis Stevenson; 1881.

20 **Youth is the time to go flashing from one end of the world to the other.** *Virginibus Puerisque: An Essay in Four Parts*; Robert Louis Stevenson; 1881.

22 **handsome waxen face like Napoleon's, insane black eyes, boy's hands, tiny bare feet . . . and hellish energy** Taken From: *A Friendship in Letters: Robert Louis Stevenson & J.M. Barrie*; Edited by Michael Shaw; 2020.

104 **In each of us, two natures are at war – the good and the evil. All our lives the fight goes on between them, and one of them must conquer. But in our own hands lies the power to choose – what we want most to be we** *are.* *The Strange Case of Dr Jekyll and Mr Hyde*; Robert Louis Stevenson; 1886.

234 **there is no duty we so much underrate as the duty of being happy.** *Virginibus Puerisque: An Essay in Four Parts*; Robert Louis Stevenson; 1881.

234 **To be what we are, and to become what we are capable of becoming, is the only end of life.** *Familiar Studies of Men and Books*; Henry David Thoreau: His Character and Opinions; Robert Louis Stevenson; 1882.

249 **a busy person never has time to be unhappy** *The Letters of Robert Louis Stevenson*; Yale University Press; 1994.

266 **Seaward, ho! Hang the treasure! It's the glory of the sea that has turned my head.** *Treasure Island*; Robert Louis Stevenson; 1883.

266 **Fifteen men on the Dead Man's Chest / Yo-ho-ho, and a bottle of rum!** *Treasure Island*; Robert Louis Stevenson; 1883.

266 The rain is falling all around / It falls on field and tree / It rains on the umbrellas here / And on the ships at sea. *A Child's Garden of Verses*; Robert Louis Stevenson; 1885.

266 we are all travellers in the wilderness of this world, and the best we can find in our travels is an honest friend. *Travels with a Donkey in the Cévennes*; Dedication; Robert Louis Stevenson; 1879.

267 To me it is as if a bit of myself had died, the romantic part, which was forever running after him. Taken From: *A Friendship in Letters: Robert Louis Stevenson & J.M. Barrie*; Edited by Michael Shaw; 2020.

272 Everyday courage has few witnesses . . . but yours is no less noble because no drum beats for you and no crowds shout your name. *The Letters of Robert Louis Stevenson*; Yale University Press; 1994.

285 In such weather one has the bird's need to whistle; and I, who am specially incompetent in this art, must content myself by chattering away to you. *The Letters of Robert Louis Stevenson*; Yale University Press; 1994.

286 grey, grim, sea-beaten hole Taken from: *The Lighthouse Stevensons*; Bella Bathurst; 1999.

286 To miss the joy is to miss all. 'The Lantern Bearers'; *Scribner's Magazine* 3; Robert Louis Stevenson; 1888.